Nightmare Flower

Tor Books by Elizabeth Engstrom

Black Ambrosia
Lizzie Borden
When Darkness Loves Us

Nightmare Flower

by Elizabeth Engstrom

A Tom Doherty Associates Book

New York

NIGHTMARE FLOWER

Copyright © 1992 by Elizabeth Engstrom

"Nightwind" appeared in *Mauian*, Vol. 3, No. 2 (April, 1986).
"The Final Tale" appeared in *Olelo Hou* (Spring 1986), literary magazine of Maui
Community College, a satellite of the University of Hawaii.
"The Final Tale" appeared in *Eldritch Tales*, Vol. 13 (1987).
"Night of a Hawaiian Sky" appeared in *Mauian*, Vol. 3, No. 4 (August, 1986).
"Nightmare Flower" appeared in *Horror Show*, Spring, 1988.
"Music Ascending" appeared in *American Fantasy Magazine*, Winter, 1988.
"Fogarty & Fogarty" appeared in *The Magazine of Fantasy and Science Fiction*, April,
1988.
"Seasoned Enthusiast" appeared in *Pulphouse*, issue #7 (May, 1990)
"Rivering" appeared in *The Magazine of Fantasy and Science Fiction*, January 1991.
"The Pan Man" appeared in *The Magazine of Fantasy and Science Fiction*, July 1991.

This book is printed on acid-free paper.

A Tor Book
Published by Tom Doherty Associates, Inc.
175 Fifth Avenue
New York, N.Y. 10010

TOR® is a registered trademark of Tom Doherty Associates, Inc.

ISBN 0-312-85404-8

First edition: September 1992

Printed in the United States of America

0 9 8 7 6 5 4 3 2 1

For Maggie

ontents

. . . he folds his arthritic white hands, raises them before him like a nightmare flower . . .

—John Gardner, GRENDEL

Nightmare Flower

The Old Woman Upstairs

My mother came to live with me when they would not renew her driver's license. She tried living in her home after that, but she was too far from the bus line, and there was no cab service in her little town.

She was never one to impose, my mother, and so instead of asking for help, or even accepting it when offered, she did without.

Then the winter came, and I went to visit her, and she cried. And came home with me.

In the spring, we went up to her house, aired it out and shook her rugs, dusted things and readied it for sale. She fussed over each detail as if grooming a Persian for a cat show, never really believing that someone else would actually ever live there.

Someone did buy it, though, and paid a fine price for it and all the furniture too.

Mother cried when we loaded the last of her personal belongings into the U-Haul, and she waved good-bye to the home that had known her since her honeymoon some sixty years before.

I had no comforting words for her. Even though I was mentally and emotionally prepared to let my childhood home go to strangers, I wasn't at all ready to watch my mother resign herself to life's last frontier: old age dependency.

Life with the two of us at my house was fun at first; she helped me sort pictures, can fruit, plant a garden, catch up on chores that had taken me a lifetime of procrastination. We talked of my childhood, and hers, of my marriage, and hers, of our futures. We talked of men and children and people in general. We talked politics and sex and religion and had some heated disagreements, and through it all, we came to know each other better. We played Scrabble and gin rummy and got her affairs in order and then, for no particular reason except that we wanted to, we began to learn Spanish together.

And then one winter morning, she padded down from her bedroom in her little blue slippers, with her matching blue robe zipped up to the neck, her thin, white hair freshly brushed and her face washed, and she poured herself a cup of coffee and sat across the table from me.

"Margaret?" she said, and I lowered the newspaper to look at her. "Margaret, I think I'd like to die today." She sipped her coffee.

Protests clogged my brain, and I dismissed them all as inadequate to our relationship.

I took a deep breath, and finally asked, "Why today?"

"Because I've said everything and done everything that is important. From today on, I shall only be repeating myself. Besides, it's only a matter of time before I'm a complete burden." She picked up the funnies I'd just finished reading and adjusted her glasses. She knew I was about to cry, and didn't want me to be embarrassed by my own tears.

I got up and went to the sink for a glass of cold water, to put a lid on my emotions. The cold water helped, and I was able to take a couple of deep breaths. I wiped the moisture from my eyes and returned to the table.

"We don't have to talk about it now," Mother said without even lifting her head. "You give it a little thought and we'll talk over lunch."

She's right, I thought, as I cleaned my dishes. She could have a stroke any moment and need full-time nursing. I was not prepared for that, neither emotionally nor monetarily, and all those duties would fall to me. I was Mother's only living relative, and she mine.

Don't be so selfish, I thought.

But my thoughts *were* selfish. I didn't want to lose her, I didn't want to nurse her. I didn't want to watch her slowly deteriorate before my eyes, I didn't want to watch her die. I didn't want the burden of killing her, I didn't want her to botch the job of killing herself.

I didn't want. I didn't want. I didn't want.

What *did* I want?

Maybe Mother is old enough to make up her own mind. Maybe this has to be her decision, and what I want or don't want doesn't enter into it. Maybe I want to be silent and supportive, a loving daughter.

I watched the clock until eleven, and then I began to make lunch.

Mother came in from filling the bird feeder, stomping snow off her boots in the utility room. She saw what I was doing, then looked at the kitchen clock, and smiled at me with both eyebrows raised. I put down the knife I was using to open the bologna package, and hugged her frail frame, coat and all.

"Come, Margaret. Let's talk." She unwound the scarf and hung it on a peg.

I found myself a child again, lost in the mystery of the wisdom of parents, and I followed her to the living room. I sat on the sofa while she stoked the fire, then she came to sit next to me, her thin hands taking hold of mine.

"I'm just going to go take a nice, long hot bath, and then I'm going to take some pills I've got saved up. That's all. As far as you know, I just went up to take a bath and a nap, and I slept through dinner. By morning, I'll be with your father."

"What pills? I didn't know you had any pills." That sounded like a stupid question, bordering on hysterical.

She patted my hand and turned to look out the window. "Such a lovely day, Margaret. Let's look at the birds." We watched the birds flock around the feeder, squawking and fighting and spraying seeds on the snow in a wide radius. "I've had a lovely life."

I searched my mind frantically for something to detain her,

something with which to entertain her. Something so good, it would make her want to stay.

"Wait," I said, the tears pushing on my eyes, and I went to the kitchen for the almost-empty peanut butter jar I'd been saving for a winter day. I went outside into the crisp cold and threw it onto the snow-covered lawn, then came back, rubbing my arms to regain some warmth. Mother smiled at me with soft affection. I put another log on the fire and sat next to her, putting my arm around her small shoulders, and we watched the squirrels and laughed together at their antics of getting the peanut butter out of the jar.

Then she kissed my cheek and went upstairs.

The sun went behind a cloud.

I heard the water run in the tub and I sat on the sofa, immobilized, my thoughts thick and rubbery.

To save her or to let her go?

Maybe letting her go *is* saving her.

I heard the silence upstairs and imagined her soaking, a beatific expression on her face, her gray hair piled on top of her head, fixed there with a barrette, relaxing, enjoying. She had something to look forward to.

What did I have to look forward to? Guilt?

I heard the water run out of the tub, and I visualized her briskly drying her skin, then powdering, then combing her hair and brushing her teeth. Settling down.

Getting ready.

I heard the water run in the sink.

She's filling a glass with water. To take the pills.

What pills?

What if her information is wrong? What if those pills just make her violently ill? What if she ends up brain damaged or in a coma or something from those damned pills?

The water ran in the sink again. Rinsing out the glass.

The bathroom door opened. Her bedroom door opened. And closed.

I could see her in her nightie, climbing under the handmade quilt she'd sewn and given me many years ago. Would she read? What? A murder mystery?

No, of course not, she wouldn't read, she wouldn't want to

miss one sensational moment of premeditated death. She would wish the experience to go with her intact. She would spend her final lucid moments thinking about my father—thinking about me.

Would she think of me sitting here, looking out the window, going crazy? Would she understand what she had done to me by giving me this burden?

I could stop her right now. I could lift her right off the bed and haul her into the bathroom and make her vomit. It wouldn't be too late, not if I did it now, right now, right now.

The longer I sit here, the guiltier I will be for her death.

No. I won't be guilty. It's nothing I have done.

I jumped up and put on my coat. I needed fresh air, I needed a little exercise.

What if she needs me while I'm gone? Maybe I should just look in on her and tell her I'm going out. Christ, I didn't even tell her good-bye. I didn't even tell her how much I love her, how much I've enjoyed her company over the years. I didn't tell her how well she raised me, how grateful I was to have her—out of all the possible parents I could have had in the world—I felt specially blessed to have her as a mother.

I never told her those things.

I took off my coat. I have to go tell her.

Let her be, I said to myself. She knows those things. That's why she's trusting you.

I put the coat back on and went outside.

Mother's taking a nap, and I'm taking a walk, I thought. Just as she wants it to be. No big deal.

But doesn't somebody say that suicide is a sin? Maybe she won't see my father Up There, if she checks out of this mortal hotel early. That means she won't be there when I arrive . . . Assuming, of course, that *I'll* get there—me, with my knowledge of her current activity—by allowing her suicide, am I also committing a mortal sin?

I don't believe in sin.

Maybe sin doesn't care whether I believe in it or not. Can I afford not to?

I crunched my way through the snow to the driveway and on down to the main road. I trudged, head down, fists stuffed in pockets, seeing my breath plume out before me. Cars passed, a few honked. Small town; everybody knew everybody else. I didn't dare let any of them see my face, for surely they would take one look and gasp. Oh! Your mother's upstairs dying! Shame on you, you terrible daughter. Go upstairs and save your mother! Did she let *you* down when you were dependent upon her? Do you suppose that if you had come home one day from first grade and said, "I think I'll die today," that she would have let you? Do you for one moment think that?

Of course not! And now she is dependent upon you all the same. Just as you were once upon her. And she is no more competent to make this type of decision than you had been at age six.

I turned around and headed back toward home. It would be too late by the time I reached home; the pills would have dissolved and poisons would be in her blood.

I could call the paramedics; they could administer an antidote.

If we knew what she had taken.

I was running by the time I got to the door. I tore off the coat and stumbled out of my boots, nose running, eyes tearing, saliva thick in the corners of my mouth. I burst through into the kitchen and I heard . . . the silence.

The peace.

She had a *right* to her peace.

I settled into a kitchen chair and gritted my teeth, determined to let her find her reward.

A little brandy would help.

I timed myself. I spent ten minutes and one brandy thinking about my childhood. I spent another ten minutes and another brandy thinking about my mother and myself in our adulthood.

Then I took the bottle and stoked the fire in the living room and spent a half hour being grateful for my home, my land, my health, my memories.

Then I began to wonder what would she would look like when I "found" her, and what the paramedics, and the doctor, and the Medical Examiner would say.

What if they thought I murdered her?

Or they found me to be an accomplice in her suicide. Suicide was a crime, wasn't it?

What if I checked on her in the morning and she wasn't dead?

What if I checked on her in the morning and she fixed me with a horrible, accusatory stare, little eyes glittering in the half-light of early dawn, and she said, "You were really going to let me go through with it, weren't you, you terrible, terrible daughter?"

I swigged straight from the bottle and began to pace.

She could do that. She was capable of such "humor." I'd seen it before, with my father. Once she packed his bags and threw them out into the street, screaming at him that he'd been cheating on her. His denials moved her not one inch. Finally, he came back, begging her forgiveness, and she accepted him back with a smug look.

I had believed then, and I believe now, that he had never cheated on her at all. This was a ruse, an "I still control you" lesson for her husband.

Was this one of the same for me? Was this a test of my faithfulness?

Would I pass? Would she believe that my standing aside and doing nothing was being faithful, or would she expect the mark of the faithful to include ambulances and sirens and hospitals, respirators, tubes and heroic measures?

Ultimately, it didn't matter. I was just doing what she asked me to do. That had to suffice. That *must* suffice.

I collapsed into the easy chair, feeling drunker than I had a right to, and I saw it was snowing outside. I turned on a light in the living room; night had followed dusk and I hadn't even noticed.

What would she look like in the morning, assuming she was dead?

I'd never seen a dead person before. Not even my father.

How would she die?

I looked at the stairs. Suddenly, I was overwhelmed with a compulsion to go sit on the side of her bed and watch her die. "By morning," she had said. "By morning I shall be with your father."

I reached down and grabbed the brandy bottle and hefted it to my lips. Maybe her breathing would just get shallower and shallower until . . . she . . . just . . . stopped . . . breathing.

Or maybe her brain would die first and she would convulse. Or maybe her heart would stop and her body would gag, trying to get air.

Would she turn blue? Would her tongue protrude? Would she wet the bed?

Would she give out with the celebrated death rattle?

I drank another swallow of the brandy and stood, unsteadily. I must see.

I made my way up the dark stairs, hearing my breath loudly in the stairwell.

If this was her idea of a joke, it was a poor one, and we would unmask it right now.

The hallway was pitch black, and I felt along the papered wall with one finger as I walked silently toward her room.

I opened the door and looked in.

Her room was dark, I could see nothing. I continued across the hall into my own bedroom and turned on the nightstand lamp. Then I returned to her. The light cast faint illumination across her pale face, fragile and sunken.

I smoothed her hair. She was warm.

"Mother," I said. There was no response. "Mother!" I shook her shoulder. She was limp and unconscious.

Suddenly, I was angry. I remembered a lot of things she had said and done to me, not only during my childhood but during my adulthood, that had made me feel inferior. She had her little tests of loyalty, and I was always trying to make her understand that she didn't need to test me, that I was loyal to her to death and beyond.

To death. And beyond.

I held the brandy bottle to her nose and the lightest of mists wavered across the glass. She breathed. She was alive.

I pulled the little rocking chair up from the corner and sat down, determined to watch the transformation from life to death. I took a drink from the brandy and watched her.

And watched her.

And watched her.

I finished the brandy, and watched her some more.

Boring work. Aggravating work. Anger-making work.

When had *she* ever spent so much time over *my* bed?

Another bottle of brandy stood in the kitchen cabinet. I could run and get it; a bottle of brandy would keep me company during the death of my mother. The idea, in fact, seemed noble, old-world somehow, and comfortable.

But what if she died while I was gone? I would have wasted all this time of waiting and watching.

I would hurry.

I looked at the bedside clock. It was two-thirty.

By morning, she had said. By morning, I will be with your father.

She could go anytime.

I was terribly thirsty.

I sat back down and rocked slowly. If she wanted me to see her through this, I would. Literally. This, after all, was the last, the final test. I would dutifully see her through it, and then there would be no more. No more tests. No more responsibility, no more guilt, no more aggravation from this old woman.

I would be furious if it didn't work—if she only slept for two days and then woke up. What a terrible waste.

Maybe I should help her along a little bit.

It couldn't take much; just a little pinch of the nostril, a hand over the mouth.

My heart began to pound in excitement.

It couldn't take much, and the waiting, for both of us—for the three of us, Father included—would be over.

And I could go downstairs and pour myself a little brandy, and in the morning, I would call the paramedics.

I looked at her sleeping face again, touched her soft, delicate cheek with my finger, and gently pinched her nostrils shut.

ightwind

I could hear it begin a long way off—a different kind of silence. No noise yet, maybe just a pressure difference. I heard it come from the mountain, rolling down in great turbulent waves, like an avalanche of clear air. I heard it. I felt it.

The darkness of my bedroom cloaked me in familiar comfort. I liked it dark. I liked the night. I pulled the covers up around my neck and lay with my head on the soft pillow, eyes wide open, eager, ready for the wind. I knew it was coming, but it teased me, tantalized me with delicious, wet anticipation of the terror it would soon cause.

I pictured it, hovering over the mountain, looking down upon my little house, my tiny inept gesture at keeping out the elements. It didn't leak, my little house, the rain found no purchase. The dust was kept out for the most part—except when riding the wind.

The wind. I could see it in my mind's eye, gathering its forces, aiming its direction at me, considering my effrontery, my very daring to have an idea that I could beat the wind with my fragile structure. It was insulted. It took a long time for the wind to gather its indignation about it and decide to descend upon my house. I saw it.

When the wind came in great swooping whoops, it found cracks and holes that were not there. It whistled through the house with a piercing scream. It disrupted everything, carrying particles of things which belonged in the ether, not in my house. It swept into my mind and it rearranged my desk. It blew everything out of proportion. The pressure inside the kitchen increased to the exploding point, as did the pressure inside my skull.

And it was coming again. I waited.

Soon I could hear it. I smiled. Sometimes it tried to take me by surprise, creeping up on whispy tendrils, then blasting me awake, but even though it startled me, I was never really taken by surprise. I understood the wind, you see . . . understood its anger, its hurt, its revenge. I understood its egotistical point of view, and I knew it couldn't stand to be jilted.

And that's just what I'd done. Jilted the wind. Stood it up. Suddenly left it for another lover, a different life, a new type of rapture. And the wind couldn't understand.

It tried, but it just couldn't understand.

I heard it curling around the trees, getting closer, gaining downstream momentum. It made the leaves dance, then whip. It bent the grasses one way then another, and all of nature cleaved to its whim.

I listened and I remembered how it tried to seduce me back. It came around as I built the house, whispering in my ear, tickling my thighs. Come back to me, it said. There was no reasoning with it. I continued my efforts.

I knew when realization dawned on it. It became more demanding, more insistent, more of a pest. It grabbed boards out of my hands, it threw dirt into my eyes, but I ignored it and kept on. It would go away, only to return later with another plea for mercy, or attention, or to hear my apology and carry me back.

A cool stream of air spouted through a new opening in the wall, ruffling the bedcovers. I smiled to myself. Flattering, the attention of the wind. It was so persistent. I even thought of surrendering once, but even as the thought entered my mind, the wind was at my side, pushing me, caressing me, eager to lick my hand and take me back. I didn't surrender, though, and this was the final insult.

I knew its capabilities—its rage could destroy me.

I would rather that than go back.

I could never go back now.

I heard it sliding around the house, enveloping it in its soft, powerful grip. The finger in the bedroom ruffled my hair, brushed my cheek.

I'm sorry, I thought.

A crack like a rifle shot split the cherry tree in the front yard.

I'm sorry, I thought. I cannot.

The edge of the roof lifted, nails screeching for their lives, and a paddle of wind swept in, slicing between the nails, and ripped the covers off my bed. The terror was overwhelming, paralyzing, complete. I huddled there, naked, knees drawn to my chest. I closed my eyes.

Do with me what you will—I will never come back.

It understood. It left.

And I will miss it.

 ivering

Margaret pulled the van to a rolling stop on the pebbled beach right at the inside of the river's elbow. She looked through the bug-spattered windshield and felt the weariness creep up the back of her neck.

"Let's get out and see what she looks like, Moose." She unbuckled her seat belt, let it drop to the floor with a clank, then stepped over the dog and slid open the side of the van. The beach crunched underfoot as she stretched.

Moose, an ancient collie, slowly got out of the van after her. He too, stretched, then put his nose to the ground and began to wander.

"Don't go too far, boy," she said. "Dinner in a half hour. We can begin in the morning."

Margaret limbered up after the long drive with ten minutes of calming yoga stretches. Then, before the daylight faded away, she walked down to the river's edge, took off her tennis shoes, and waded in up to her ankles. It was a perfect location. It looked just like the type of place the slivers would congregate. Well, she'd find out in the morning.

She went back to the van, brought out the little cookstove,

dipped water from the river and cooked up some dehydrated stew. It wasn't great, but it was easy and it was protein. She opened a can of food for Moose, and they set to their dinner. Afterward, she didn't even wash the dishes. She set them outside the van, spread her sleeping bag out on the van floor, and fell instantly asleep.

All night long she dreamed of catching slivers. All night long she dreamed of catching the right slivers. *Her* slivers.

She got up before dawn, excitement brewing in her belly as the coffee brewed on the stove. In the early hours, she'd had an important dream, and she knew that this was the place. Here she would find and catch the slivers she'd been rivering for all year. She wouldn't have to scout river after river, state after state, anymore. It was such a peaceful idea, she hoped it wasn't just wishful thinking. But she'd never felt that way before. She'd never had a dream like that before, either.

She let Moose sleep in while she did her morning exercises, facing the color of the sky. Then she breakfasted on a peanut butter and honey sandwich, drank two cups of coffee, did all the dishes and roused the dog. "C'mon, Moose," she said. "It's time to find Dad."

She twirled the combination lock on the little safe she had installed under the driver's seat, opened it and took out the seven little leather bags, each with a long tether wrapped around it. She unwound the tether from her two and put the other five in her pocket. Then she got the net from the front seat and the little cooler with its chunk of dry ice.

Moose walked with her down to the river. She looked at the water, black in the early light. She squinted her eyes and looked downstream.

There! She saw one. The starlight caught the little flash of silver. An untrained eye might think it a minnow. Tingles ran up her spine. She took the cooler and the net upstream of the elbow. She took off her sneakers and rolled up her pant legs.

She waded into the icy water slowly, quietly. The river undercut the bank the tiniest bit, and that's where they would be. She tied the tethers to the rings she'd sewn to the legs in her jeans, then dropped the pouches into the water and watched as they flowed downstream, moving in the gentle current.

Then she stood absolutely still.

Moose, seeming to sense the urgency, also remained motionless.

A little silver glinted in the water. She waited. It seemed to sniff the pouches, and then was off. Not the right one.

She waited until the sun came full up, until her feet were so numb from the cold that her back ached, and nothing had come for the bait. Moose had wandered away in hopes of finding a rabbit.

She brought in her two lines and set the other five out in the same way. No luck.

At noon, she brought them in, and stiffly walked up to the van. It was still a good place, and there were slivers here. It was just that *her* slivers didn't seem to be here.

She heated up some soup and lay down on her sleeping bag. Her bones ached from motionlessness, cold and disappointment. She'd try again after a rest. If she didn't get *something* soon, she'd be out of money.

She opened the pouches so they could dry. In the first one was the tip of Roger's forefinger, the crucifix he always wore, and a dried bud of his favorite rosebush. She lay these things out on a tray to dry. She couldn't let them rot. In her second pouch were her father's little toe, his wedding ring and the waterlogged and no-longer-recognizable picture of her mother he always carried in his wallet. The other pouches held similar pieces of the anatomy and significant memorabilia of the deceased. She didn't know these other people, and had nothing to do with them. She was rivering for hire. Paid to find dead people's souls, slivering about in the elbows of the rivers. And if she didn't have some luck soon . . . there would be no more customers.

She would never forget how she first heard about rivering. She was eavesdropping on her parents' conversation when they had guests over. One of them had just hired a riverer to find his mother, so he could finally, once and for all, have control over her. The discussion heated, and while the adults went into the moral issues, Margaret went deep into her own world, thinking about the life of a riverer. And the concept stayed with her, as if she had heard her calling when she heard that conversation, and she waited patiently for her time to arrive. And a year ago, it had.

When everything was laid out and drying in the back window of the van, Margaret had her soup. Rivering was a lonely business. It took a lot of energy to keep her doubts from taking over. She knew from talking to other riverers that success was infrequent, but she'd feel better if she could just catch *one*. Discouragement was heavy, sometimes. She'd been on the river, just her and Moose for almost a year. With no luck.

When Roger died, leaving so much unfinished business behind him, she knew she would go rivering for him. When he was laid out at the funeral home, she asked for a moment alone with him, and with her penknife, sliced the tip off his forefinger. She put it in her food dehydrator, and saved the little grey, curled slip of leather in her jewelry box.

When her dad died, she paid the mortician's assistant twenty bucks to cut off his little toe. And when Joey started in college on a scholarship up at Colorado State, Margaret began rivering.

It wasn't long before she was out of money. But along the way, she'd talked with others who rivered and it seemed like there was no end to people who wanted to recover other people's souls. So she took out a little ad, and selected five from the hundreds of replies, at one thousand dollars apiece, and now that money was almost gone, too.

That discouragement mixed with the loneliness of a riverer, and Margaret hugged the big, salty-smelling dog who lay next to her and fought back the tears. "You stink," she said to Moose. "Tomorrow I'll give you a bath."

After a short nap, Margaret repacked the tiny pouches and went back to that same spot in the river. The old-timers always told her to listen to the messages in her dreams. She pushed her doubts back and let the truth come over her. She knew she would have success here.

She stood in the shallows with pieces of her father and her husband until she was almost blind from staring at the shining water. Then she changed, tied on the other five, and immediately there was a boiling stir.

One by one, she pulled in the pouches, very carefully, very

gently. She had to know for sure which one had attracted the sliver. When only one pouch was left trailing in the current, and the sliver was still there, swimming wildly around it, she swiped with her net.

And she had it. She'd caught it!

"Look, Moose!" The dog backed away, slowly wagging his tail.

Very carefully, Margaret took the net to the shore, opened the little cooler and turned the net over onto the ice.

The ice sizzled and smoked as the sliver and the water from the net touched it, and for a moment, Margaret worried that she'd lost it. She blew down, and she could see it, a little silver sliver, lying still as death on the block of ice. She put the cover back on. "I got one, Moose," she said gently, her heart pounding. She opened the pouch and emptied its contents onto the cover of the cooler. There was an unidentifiable piece of flesh— it could have been an earlobe—a swatch of black hair, and a foreign coin. Inside the leather was written the name and phone number of the person searching. Seiji Okano. Margaret put the artifacts back into the pouch, opened the cooler, picked up the sliver and studied it. She expected it to look like a fish, but it didn't. It just looked like a little silver slip of something, two or three inches long, maybe a half inch in diameter. No eyes, no mouth, no tail, just a little slip of silver. It was hard to believe that this was the soul of Seiji Okano's wife. She put the sliver into the pouch with the other things and put the pouch on top of the ice.

"We're on a roll now, Moose, buddy," she said, and stepped back into the water.

By dinnertime, she hadn't caught anything else, but she believed wholeheartedly in her dream. This was her spot. Probably every one of the remaining six slivers to be caught were here somewhere. And she would catch them.

That night Roger came to her in another dream.

"Margaret, I'm sorry," he said, over and over again. Her heart ached. He'd come closer, puppy-dog look on his face, hands out, and her heart would pound with fear and she'd back away. Then he would look hurt and turn away, and she would approach him again, *please don't go, don't leave me again,* but as soon as he moved toward her, "Margaret, I'm sorry," she would back away, fear pounding in her chest.

She woke up sweating. She hugged the dog and cried.

In the morning, she remembered what the old-timers told her. "They get frightened when they know somebody is rivering for them. They seem to have no control over themselves. They're irresistibly drawn to those things of the flesh, but they don't want to be. They'll fool with your mind. Pay no attention. It's just trickery, is all it is, it's just trickery. Stay calm and keep rivering."

In the early morning, she caught another one, and she noticed that her little block of dry ice would last two more days at the most. Then she would have to go to town, make her phone calls, ship the slivers to their owners and buy another block of ice.

At noon, she caught Roger.

When his sliver was safely frozen, tied inside the leather pouch, and resting with the other two on the ice inside the cooler, Margaret sat down on the beach, elbows on her knees, face in her hands. She didn't know what to do with him now that she had him.

And who said these things were their souls, anyway?

She knew what the old-timers said. They said the souls were waiting for Release, a periodic occurrence when all the souls went on to their next assignment—whatever that was—all at the same time. In the meanwhile, they were stored inconspicuously and economically as little pieces of solid light in the rivers.

So if Roger was in the cooler, would he go on to his next assignment from wherever he was, or would he miss out?

She picked up the cooler, ran to the van. She threw all her camping gear in, called the dog, slammed the door shut and went in to town.

At the first pay phone, she stopped, got out her address book, and made her calls. First was to Seiji Okano.

"Mr. Okano?"

"Yes?"

"This is Margaret Whittington. The Riverer. I have your sliver."

"You *do*?"

"Yes."

A long sigh on the other end. "That's wonderful."

"I'll ship it to you today. It will be packed in dry ice."

"That's fine."

She verified the address.

"Um, Mr. Okano?"

"Yes?"

"What will you do with it?"

"Stir fry."

"*Eat* it?"

"Yes."

"Tell me, will that keep her from going on, I mean to the next . . ."

Mr. Okano hung up without answering.

She called the next person. A woman.

"I have your sliver."

"Oh." She did not seem pleased.

"Don't you want it?"

"Oh, yes, I guess I do."

"I can release it."

"No! Please don't."

"I'll send it to you today, packed in dry ice."

"Fine."

"Do you mind my asking . . . what will you do with it?"

"I don't know yet. Keep it. Somehow."

"I see. Thank you."

Margaret hung up, then tended to the business of shipping the two and re-icing Roger.

She stopped in a tavern for a hamburger and a beer, but the waitress wouldn't serve her.

"You're that riverer come to town, ain'tcha?"

"Yes."

"Take your business somewhere else, missy," she said, then turned her back.

Margaret felt everyone's eyes on her as she left, and tried to keep her back straight when all she wanted to do was argue with the woman. Either that, or cry.

Rivering for people's souls, it seemed, was a profession not kindly taken to in the high desert country of Oregon.

She got her burger at a McDonald's, and one for Moose, too, and a six-pack of Bud at the grocery store, then headed back to the river. She had four more to catch, and then she would retire.

That evening, she caught another one, but as she tipped the net to put it onto the ice, it fell onto the beach, and before she could think, Moose grabbed it and bit it right in half.

She screamed at him, he dropped it and slinked away, and there, flopping on the ground, were two half-slivers.

She picked them up, panic welling wordlessly within her, and she watched, her horror subsiding, as the two parts grew together again in her hand. Healed. Instantly. Seamlessly. She quickly put it on the ice, then stowed it in the pouch. She took a deep breath and put the cooler out of harm's way.

That night, her father approached her in a dream. She sat by his side, felt his warm hands on hers, she saw the familiar wrinkles on his face. Her heart was filled with love for this man, but when she awoke, she knew it was more trickery.

And then before noon, she caught him. She set his pouch next to Roger's, and then with hard-bitten determination, went back for the others. She had to finish. This was her spot; this was her job.

And she did finish. It took two more days to have them all, get them all shipped off, and then she was left with the two pouches on a shrinking block of dry ice. She sat in her van, hands gripping the steering wheel. Her job wasn't finished until they were taken care of.

What on earth was she going to do with them?

She could donate them to research. She'd heard about some robotics research being done on slivers. She could eat them. She could let them go. She could pickle them and store them on her mantel. A zillion ideas came up, but none of them were right. They had to be totally appropriate to Roger. And her dad.

She drove back to the same elbow of the river, took her beach chair out and sat in it to watch the sunset, Moose on one side of her, the cooler on the other side. She brewed a cup of coffee and reflected on her life.

The pounding, driving force that kept her rivering all these years was gone. Her future spread before her like an open field, and she felt she could build anything there she wished. She needed only step into the picture, but to do that, she had to step over the cooler.

Something must be done with the slivers.

Roger. Roger was a jerk. He drank, he ran around with other women, he gambled and lost money they didn't have, and he paid little attention to Joey when Joey needed it the most. Through it all, Margaret never stopped loving him. She knew that deep within him, he was a good man, and the things he did were somehow beyond his control. When he was straight, he was fabulous. They had such loving times, the three of them. He loved her, he loved Joey, he just had things he needed to do. They caused her endless heartache, and when he died . . . when he died of a cocaine stroke—his body dumped at the emergency entrance of a hospital by a car that sped into the night—he left her in far greater debt than she could ever imagine.

Her father bailed her out.

Her father. Lewis was exactly the opposite of Roger. Lewis was the attentive husband and father, good provider, model of perfection, a true-life "Father Knows Best." From the outside. The truth was, he was cold. He kissed her cheek, but there was no warmth. He bailed her out, but when he wrote the check, there was no sympathy, empathy or anything, and her words of gratitude fell on ears of granite. He sent checks to Joey every Christmas and birthday, but when she spoke with Lewis on the phone, he somehow never asked about Joey.

Lewis hurt Margaret far more deeply than Roger ever could. And now she had control of their immortal souls.

If those slivers were indeed their souls.

And *if* anything she did had any effect on them.

But she believed it did.

She believed that those who rivered altered the course of destiny. That's why it was so hard. That's why hardly anybody did it. And those who did do it were driven. And everybody else hated them.

So what should she do with the slivers?

She opened the chest, took out the pouches. She dumped the frozen little slip from Roger's pouch and looked at it. She lay it on the ice, and took her father's sliver from his pouch. It was smooth and cold and solid.

She knew what to do.

She went into the van and came out with a hammer and her cutting board.

First she smashed Roger's. With just a light tap, it shattered into hundreds of small, crystalline pieces. She dusted them off into a Ziploc bag and set them back on the ice. Then she smashed her father's sliver, and mixed the pieces together with Roger's in the bag.

She divided the pieces as evenly as she could and put half in the palm of each hand. She watched as they defrosted and grew together into two seamless wholes.

"C'mon, Moose," she said, and the dog walked by her side to the edge of the river.

"Maybe they'll average themselves out," she said, and watched as the little sliver slips darted out of sight.

Fifty-five Days of Silence

On the fifty-seventh morning of Arnaud's Silence, Marlima sat across the table from him, staring at the face she had loved all these years. Arnaud was wearing his puppy-dog smile, the "I'm sorry, please don't stop loving me" smile that had begun to sour Marlima's love. The Silence had changed Arnaud, and it was terrible to witness.

Arnaud scratched on the pad of paper and then slid it across the table to her. On it were a crude circle and a wavy line, and Marlima knew he was trying to write that he loved her. "I love you too," she wrote on the same page and passed it back to him, wanting desperately not to watch him try to read it.

She couldn't help herself. He examined the writing, although he couldn't read it, and he touched it, running his fingers across it, then he bent his head down and kissed the words. She could have written anything *anything,* and he still would have kissed the words. He looked at her with that fawning look and her spirits crashed on the rocks.

Fifty-seven mornings.

It would get easier, she had told herself at the beginning. They'd had years to prepare for Arnaud's Silence; he had a randomly scheduled birth defect, and his eventual Silence was inevitable. Their communication spit and crackled from the very day they met, and it had worsened over the years. The last few weeks before Silence, communication had been virtually impossible, except that their souls could still touch in affection, they could still write each other messages, the elaborate language of hand signs they had developed over the years was still an eloquent method of speaking. But now, with Silence, all of that was gone.

All of it was gone. And there was nothing they could have done to prepare for this reality—Silence was absolute.

It will get easier, she had told herself that first morning, but it hadn't. It had gotten worse, until she finally couldn't stand it anymore, and yesterday she had run out in a fit and damaged herself.

It had only taken fifty-five days for Arnaud's Silence to drive her to sin.

And today they would be coming for her.

She pulled the pad of paper back from him, and the pen, and then lay a hand atop his. He looked at her with love in his blank eyes and she began to write.

She wrote how she had felt that first morning when he awakened and discovered he had Silence, how he had run screeching and scritching around the house in a seizure too terrible to describe, how her heart had died when he finally lay empty on the living room floor. She wrote about how she tried to be with him now, tried to maintain a marriage, but without communication, love cannot survive. She tried to be a good woman, and a good wife, she tried, oh God, she tried, but there was much to her life yet, and her husband lived in solitude.

She wrote about her pain.

She turned the page and wrote about the hopes they'd always shared of growing old together, of all the things they had yet to do together, of all the dreams they had spoken of together during their years of love and companionship.

She wrote faster and faster of her obligation to him as a lifelong partner, but also of her obligation to herself.

Tears fell from her eyes and she heard his feet shuffling under the table in discomfort as her pen raced wildly across the pages.

She wrote of her communication needs, and how the need to share had built up and up and up until she could no longer bear it; she could not look at him, or look in the mirror one more time until she had opened her soul and shared with another human being.

Her pen slowed as she drew out her experience of sin, wanting to share it with him the way they had shared every other event in their lives.

And when she was finished, the pen dropped to the table, fingers grasped the pages and crumpled them to her chest, and she sobbed.

Arnaud touched her hair and she brushed his hand away.

They would be coming for her soon. At least she was assured of her penalty; there were no more surprises. Her sentence would be the universal sentence: Silence. At least in that she would again be with her husband.

Slowly, the sadness drained itself. She picked up the phone and called the controller and requested her sentence. Then she washed her face and brushed her teeth and hair. She dressed in the negligee Arnaud had loved most, then sat in his lap and cradled his head against her bosom.

And waited.

Dizziness came first. She felt disoriented, and grasped the table for support, only it felt as though the table were tipping, and she splayed her legs to steady herself. Then a green tidal surge of nausea rolled over her. She leapt up from Arnaud's lap in fear and confusion, as she heard the first circuit close with a snap. Her senses reeled as everything she was tried to compensate for the loss. She steadied herself for a moment by the sofa, when she felt it build again, then another snap, and she thought she would faint—she wished she would faint to be rid of the terrible disorientation. She heard noises, felt strange vibrations from her chest, saw her hands waving about in front of her as if in slow motion, and wondered at the purpose. She saw a man sitting in a chair (help me!) next to the table, and lurched toward him. Another click and she lost interest in her direction. Another and she lost motivation for movement. Another and she just sat down in the middle of the floor, all meanings gone.

She knew only Silence.

* * *

Arnaud looked across the table at Marlima, at that sickening sweet smile that was characteristic of everyone with Silence. It was the only survival mechanism allowed them. That smile preyed on the souls of those who were able to care for them, and it worked.

Arnaud tapped the tip of his pen on the crumpled sheets of paper on the table in front of him. For fifty-five days he'd read them over and over again.

His Silence had been a mistake. A preventive maintenance problem, they had called it, not a scheduled birth defect as he had always assumed. When they came to check on Marlima, they found him and restored his circuits. He had come up through the depths of Silence; as each new, gleaming circuit snapped into place, more was revealed. He regained language, and humor. With the last circuit, he roared to normalcy, howling with laughter, stomping his feet with the joy. Then he'd seen Marlima on the living room floor, a child's smile, an infant's personality with a woman's body, wearing a negligee, yet.

His spirits plummeted to the depths within the space of a moment. He brought her to the table, and covered her partial nudity with a robe. The sheets of crumpled paper were still on the table, tear-stained and personal, and Arnaud pocketed them while they made last inspections of Marlima and tested his new replacement circuits.

Then they left, and he read the papers. His tears of sorrowful anger fell and mixed with hers, still damp on the page.

And he had read them every day since. Every day for fifty-five days.

Marlima had cared for him for fifty-five days of his Silence before she had gone to sin and been sentenced to Silence.

He looked across the table at that face he had loved for all these years, and wondered how long it would be before he was driven to sin—before he brought disgrace and disrespect to this house. He would never. Never. He would never do that to Marlima.

He would never go back to Silence.

He sighed and looked at her idiot face. He ached to share with her. I'm still a young man, he thought, and the yearning to gaze into understanding eyes with intensity and meaning gnawed the hollowness of his bones. Instead, he thought with bitterness, I shall sit here and watch this woman age.

Then a germ of a memory flickered across the screen of his mind, and his pulse quickened.

He took a deep breath and tried to settle the excitement growing in his bowels. Calmly, he wrote on the back of one of the pages, "I love you, Marlima," much as she had done for him, fifty-five days ago. He passed the page across to her and watched as she picked it up and smelled it, touched it, tasted it.

Then he picked up the telephone and called the controller and requested info.

Within fifteen minutes, he had his answer. Only spouses of those with scheduled random birth defects and spouses of accident victims were bound to their mates. As soon as Marlima embraced sin, she was criminal, and Arnaud was free to leave her.

He looked sadly at her childlike smile, so trusting. It was a shame, really. There had never been a pairing such as Arnaud and Marlima before. Never.

He patted her hand with reassurance, then went to the bedroom to pack.

Someone would take care of Marlima. Someone always took care of those with Silence.

· Will Lunch Be Ready on Time?

Sissy stepped aside to let the policemen enter. The hot feeling in her tummy sank down low and rumbled in there like gas. Even though she'd been expecting them, she didn't expect they'd be so—so—powerful, or something.

The big policeman sat down on the edge of the secondhand sofa. His huge belly hung over his wide black belt and he looked uncomfortable and out of place. He set his hat on the threadbare cushion next to him and seemed careful not to touch the sofa arm, which was dirty, and had stuffing pulled out and worried into little balls by children's idle fingers. The thin policeman removed his hat, showing an amazing amount of bright red hair, then he turned a kitchen table chair around and sat on it. Sissy couldn't see them both at the same time, and that made her nervous. She smoothed her dress and buttoned the only two buttons left on her brown cardigan.

"Now," the big policeman said. "Why don't you tell us about the party you had here last night?"

"It was no party," Sissy said. "Those people came and tried to bully us around."

"They said you served them liquor."

"Papa had a jug. They took it."

"Where is your papa, Sissy?" The question came from over at the kitchen table, and it threw Sissy off balance.

"I'm not sure, but he'll be back soon. He always is."

"Your daddy drink a lot, Sissy?" It was the big policeman on the couch again.

"Yeah. He goes off on 'toots,' Ma used to call them."

"Where's your Ma?"

Sissy whipped around to face the redhead. "Ma died during last year's thaw."

"And your papa leaves you kids all alone?" It was the fat one again.

"We're not alone," Sissy said, "we're together. I'm fourteen, and I keep a good house, can't you see? I'm the one sent Jane to call you police when those people came, ain't that bein' responsible? And there's—Meg, she's older . . ." Sissy's voice trailed off as she pointed at Meg, who stood, looking more retarded than ever, leaning against the kitchen wall. "And besides. Papa will come back pretty soon. He's just out hunting."

"His shotgun is leanin' up against the kitchen door, Sissy," the thin policeman said.

The feeling in her stomach was giving way to anger. "He got hisself a new one."

The big policeman stood up. "Okay, Sissy. The house looks—it looks like you're doing a fine job here. We're not here to hassle you. But if you need help, you just give a shout, okay?"

"Long as those people don't come back, we'll be fine."

"You're sure they didn't hurt any of you?"

"Nah. They didn't hurt nobody."

"I don't think they'll be back here. We had a nice long talk with them, if you know what I mean."

Sissy looked at her dirty toes and wished she had some socks or something. She hadn't done a very good job being a grown-up in front of these big policemen and their uniforms. "Okay," she said.

"I'm going to send Miss Ruthie over to check on you, maybe tomorrow, just in case there's anything you need."

"We won't need nothing."

"You got food for all of you?"

The feeling in her bowels gave a lurch. "We got food," she said, and her face grew hot.

"Well, I'll have her come by, just in case, Sissy. And when your pa shows up, have him give us a call, okay? I'd like to talk to him." The policeman bent over and picked up the baby that was crawling over his shoes.

"That's Bucky," Sissy said. "He's always into mischief."

The big policeman held Bucky at arm's length and the baby and the fat man smiled at each other for a minute, then he handed him over to Sissy. "So there's Bucky here, and Meg, and Jane, and you—that's four. Any others?"

"Willie." Sissy looked at her feet again, brushed some dust around with her toes.

"Where's Willie?"

"Out back. Chopping wood for the cookstove."

The policeman put on his hat. "Have your pa come see me, Sissy."

"Yes, sir, I will." Sissy saw them to the door and held the screen so it didn't slam behind them. The baby squirmed in her arms at the blast of frigid air, but all she felt was relief that the intruders were gone and she was back in her home with just her family.

She closed the wood door, giving it an extra shove with her shoulder, then she felt Bucky's full diaper, so she took him over to Meg. "Change him, Meg," she said, "then you better get started on washing them diapers. I'll have Willie bring in some wood for hot water." Sissy waited to make sure her big sister understood, then she pulled on Ma's brown cloth coat, wrapped the plaid scarf around her neck, shoved her feet into Pa's big old gumboots and went out back where Willie was working.

Her little brother, already muscular, shirt off and thrown into the snow, steamed sweat from his skin as he split another chunk of wood and threw the pieces onto the pile. Sissy picked up an armload and smiled at Willie, who looked like a man before he'd seen her and now looked like a little boy about to whine. "Doin' fine, Willie," she said, then went back into the house and dropped the wood into a cardboard box next to the stove. She wrapped the end of her scarf around the handle of the stove and opened it, threw in three pieces of wood, then closed it again, and adjusted the damper. Then she filled two white enamel pots with water from the pump at the sink and set them on the stove to heat. One for washing diapers, one for cooking lunch.

She wet down a rag and folded it, then lay it on the stove between the pots. It sizzled, and she took off the coat and scarf while she waited for it to warm through. Then she turned it over and sizzled it on the other side while she took off Pa's boots and stood them next to the kitchen door. Then she picked up the hot rag, and tossing it lightly between her hands, took it into Ma's bedroom where Jane was in bed with her frostbitten feet wrapped up.

"How ya feelin', Janey?" Sissy asked.

"Fine."

Sissy unwrapped the cool rags and checked the toes. They looked about the same. Bloodless, and pruny from being wrapped up in warm, wet cloths. She rewrapped them, including the fresh, hot rag, then took a look at the picture Jane was drawing on her chunk of chalkboard.

"That was a brave thing you did last night, Janey," Sissy said, smoothing the hair away from Jane's forehead. "It musta hurt like holy hell to run to the Parkers' on them feet."

"Wasn't so bad."

Sissy kissed her little sister's forehead.

"Will lunch be ready on time?" Jane asked.

"Sure will, won't be long. Soon as Willie's finished chopping wood, I'll send him in to tell you a story, okay? Helps to pass the time."

"You're a good mom, Sissy," Jane said, and Sissy felt warm and proud.

"We gotta be a family, Jane," she said. "A family's the most important thing in the world, remember Ma used to say? We gotta stick together, and if we do," she touched her sister's freckled nose, "ain't nothing going to hurt us."

"If those people don't come back."

"They won't. The policeman said—"

"I heard the policemen. I heard you tell them Papa was out hunting."

"I'm going to take care of us, Janey. You've got nothing to worry about."

"What if they come back?"

"You heard—"

"I *mean* the policemen."

Sissy fingered the worn quilt that had been on Ma's bed ever since Sissy was born—before, even.

"You just work on them feet, Janey. You get life back in them feet, and that's all you need to do. Everything else will work out just fine. You just get them feet well."

Sissy patted her little sister on the head, then returned to the kitchen, doubts and worries heavy on her shoulders. People were all the time interfering. Those bad people could come back, Miss Ruthie was coming tomorrow, the police would eventually get nosy . . . With five mouths to feed, now that Meg wouldn't nurse the baby anymore, they'd need a lot of food.

That feeling in her stomach began to burn. Maybe somebody *should* interfere. Maybe somebody *should* come and take over.

No, Sissy said to herself, pushing the feeling away. We can do it on our own. I can shoot a rabbit. I can hunt a pheasant. So can Willie. We can do it. We don't need Pa breathing booze all over us. We don't need no more babies. We can take care of our own.

The kitchen was warming up around the stove. Sissy stood close to it, soaking up the warmth, feeling the tops of her feet warming, even though the bottoms, with their thick crust of callus, were perpetually cold. She tested the diaper water with her finger, and called to Meg to come get it. The frozen pile of dirty diapers out the back door was an eyesore, and Bucky had only a couple of clean ones left. When Meg came into the kitchen, Sissy showed her which pot was for diapers, then took a freshly changed Bucky into the bedroom to entertain Jane. Then she rummaged around in the dusty boxes underneath the sink and came up with a misshapen potato and two runty onions. She fetched the half carrot she'd put on the cold windowsill to keep, and cut them all up into the water.

"See, Ma?" Sissy looked at the ceiling. "You teached us good, and we'll get along just fine. We're a good family, now. A real good one."

She sprinkled salt into the water and threw in a handful of dried beans from the burlap sack Willie had refilled at the church the first of every month.

She stirred the water around with the wooden spoon and looked into the pot. The vegetables and beans floated on top of the water. Children need meat every day, Ma used to say. The hot feeling rose from her stomach and lodged under her heart. We can always afford to eat meat, she said, even if it's just the broth cooked off a chicken leg. Sissy swirled the water around again. Five children can't grow on this—it needs meat.

Sissy put the spoon down and got back into Ma's coat. She wrapped the scarf around her neck and pulled a kitchen chair over to the tall cabinet. She stepped up on the chair and opened the cabinet, then reached way into the back. Ma had taught her good about safety with little children around the house. Sissy took extra care, now that she had taken Ma's place.

Her hand closed on the wood handle and she brought Grandma's heavy cleaver forward, with care and reverence. Carefully, she stepped down from the chair, and without setting the cleaver down again for fear she'd forget it just long enough for Bucky to hurt himself, she put her feet into Pa's gumboots and opened the door.

She stopped for a moment, and listened. Jane was talking to Bucky in the bedroom, and the baby was giggling. Meg was sloshing the diapers in the screened room. Willie brought the axe down and split another piece of wood.

Sissy hid the cleaver inside the big coat and closed the door behind her. The hot feeling wrapped itself around her heart and gave a squeeze.

She stopped to watch Willie for a moment. He'd made quite a pile of firewood.

"Four more pieces, okay, Willie?"

He looked up and she saw he was crying. Tears made streaks in the dirt on his cold-reddened face, and his nose was running.

"Just four more pieces, okay, Willie? Then maybe we'll have enough to last us through tomorrow, too."

Without comment, Willie set another hunk of log on the stump and picked up the axe. He was beginning to move like an old man, Sissy thought, and the feeling eased up its grip.

Sissy hurried beyond him, her feet crunching in the snow. She had to hurry if she was going to beat Willie inside. It wouldn't take him long to finish up.

She unhooked the door in the chicken-wire deer fence that housed the vegetable garden in the summer, slipped inside and closed it behind her. It was a good fence; it kept out the deer in the summer and kept out the dogs in the winter. Sissy shivered, feeling the cold on her bare knees. Her eyes moved to the corner of the garden, next to the shed, where Jane had hidden, huddled in the dark, afraid. The snow in the corner was all stomped down, and Sissy could see the bare footprints with the little toe marks. That snow had frozen those little toes and they might never recover. Poor Janey. Poor, brave little Janey.

Willie's axe came down and split a chunk.

Sissy returned to the task at hand.

The snow covered Pa so thick he looked like a grave mound, which was the right kind of thing for him to look like, Sissy thought. She set the cleaver down and dug through the snow until she found his foot.

She started on it with the cleaver, thinking about Janey, shivering there in the dark. "Get out!" Sissy had yelled as soon as she'd been able to pull Pa off her, and Janey had run out the door, had run here to the garden, barefoot, in just her little nightie, while Pa raged and finally Willie had got the axe and put Pa down.

She chopped on the frozen flesh, and as she did, she thought of how they'd had to deal with Pa ever since Ma died. The feeling in her heart turned to anger. How could he have treated Ma the way he did? It was no wonder Ma died, and after she did, then he started going after Meg, only Meg never put up a fuss, so Sissy and Willie and Janey kind of never minded, but then when Meg got so big with Bucky, he began eyeing Janey, and Sissy wouldn't stand for that.

The foot suddenly came free, and Sissy gasped at what she'd done, then noticed that she, too, was crying. And the hot feeling was gone.

She wiped the tears off her cheeks with her hands, then wiped her nose on the sleeve of Ma's coat. That foot's no good, she thought. They'll all recognize it. She sliced through Pa's trousers with the sharp edged cleaver, then began again, midshin. She worked quickly, without emotion. When it came free, she covered up the rest with snow, then tucked the meat inside her coat with the cleaver and left the garden, wiring the door shut carefully behind her. Willie was on his last piece of wood. She saw that he wasn't crying anymore, either. Sissy ran to the house, letting the screen door slam behind her. She pulled the meat from under her coat, wondered for a second if it should be peeled, then slipped it into the boiling soup.

She smiled to herself. There'll be a nice bone for the hound, too, she thought, then got up on the chair to put the cleaver away.

• Rain

It's only raining now, yet the sky booms with darkness and the leaves on the trees dance with the drops and the little splatters run down the windows, distorting my view.

It's only raining now, quietly, yet it still sounds deep and throaty on the roof.

My excitement began to grow last week, long before the storm showed itself out the attic window. The jittering in my center increased and increased, until at the first sign of dark cloud, at first tang of electrified air, I was flushed with anticipation. I readied myself and went to town for provisions. I vowed to never be caught short at the end of a storm again.

This time, I am well prepared. This time, even if the storm lasts for a week, I will be able to match it stroke for stroke. So far, it has been two glorious days, days so magic that I haven't even slept; I've been spending all my time with the storm. But right now, the storm rests, so I rest as well, and write of my success.

I am well pleased.

*　　*　　*

I had barely enough time to bring everything inside and secure it before the first heavy raindrops smatted against the crazed concrete driveway. The parched weeds perked up, their senses tantalized at the thought of nourishment, while I labored to make everything ready.

Once things were in place, I adopted the slow movement of the storm. I felt its power accumulating—I felt *my* power accumulating—and I found a darkened corner in which to sit and savor my role.

The pressure built, the suspense mounted, darkness gathered about my house and inside my skull. The rain graduated from drumming to pounding, the wind ceased singing and began to howl.

I began to howl.

Lightning flashed and I lit the candles. The first climax of the storm approached, and I worked hard to suppress my enthusiasm. Slow down, I reminded myself. Keep pace. I honed the blade, and when the lightning next split the night and thunder cracked the skies, the cold steel caught the brilliance.

I blew out the candles and fetched the first.

All night the storm thrust and parried. I, in perfect synchronism, ebbed and flowed with the tide that turned my mind. By morning, when the eerie green light that filtered through my clouds lightened the room, the blood that lay dark and jellied at my feet showed green and began to smell. The outside world would stink as well, as things of nature and things long ago buried were uprooted by the fury of the winds, and I sat in the sticky wet and luxuriated.

By noon of the second day the fury had resumed. I strode the wooden floors like the soldier of the storm, the scout, the headmaster, and I brandished my sword with bravado. As lightning slashed, so did I; as black clouds swirled outside, so they did inside; as drops fell on the pane to run and merge on the outside, so they did on the inside.

It is nighttime now. Woodland animals, water-bred creatures, insects, fowl—all cower before the madness of the violence. As others huddle in their homes, afraid of the fury of the storm, four more huddle in mindless terror, afraid of the fury of the attic.

All except me.

I live it, I breathe it, I thrive on it, I AM it. I am the embodiment of the storm, and when the winds blow their black fury into my world, they blow their black fury into my mind—and I obey. I obey.

It is only raining now, but the swelling, the rising, the building has begun again. The rain is light enough to hear the sobs of those who wait their turn. Their emotions throb in accompaniment to the storm too, for we are all connected in our way. Their sobs and pleading will turn to shrieks when the wind begins to shriek, when I begin to shriek, and the slashing of the lightning will begin again and the pounding of the rain and the howling of the storm, and the drops, the lovely drops, will splash on the attic windows and sheet down.

But for now, it is only raining.

I rest.

And wait.

• Grandma's Hobby

I'd forgotten all about Grandma's hobby. But then, it had been years since I'd spent much time with her.

Daniel and I had moved in with her for a couple of weeks while our new house was being finished. Grandma, I was distressed to see, had become quite frail and slightly dotty, so to help earn our keep, we did a few badly-needed odd jobs around the place.

Daniel fixed the gutters, the sprinklers, pruned the apple tree, rehung the shed doors and that kind of thing. I relined the pantry shelves, cleaned the attic, reorganized the linen closet and then tackled the fruit cellar.

The fruit cellar.

My grandpa died in the fruit cellar when I was a little girl, and for years I wouldn't go near it. Grandma said it was a simple heart attack one morning when he was going down for a fresh jar of jelly, but the fruit cellar had always been too dark, too damp, too spooky for me, and knowing that my grandfather, my wonderful grandfather had given up his ghost in there—well, it was still too much for me to take.

So when I asked Grandma what the next job was to be, and

she said, in her adorable, innocent, irresistible way, that the fruit cellar really needed the cobwebs swept, I swallowed, nodded, and mentally scheduled it for a rainy Sunday.

The next Sunday it rained.

I snuggled up to Daniel's back in bed that morning, listening to the water run through the new gutters, and I whispered that he ought to take advantage of this good cuddling, because I was about to descend to no-man's-land. I might not return. He thought I'd probably return, but he took good advantage of the cuddling anyway.

Soon I was up and showered and into my old clothes, ready for anything. Or so I thought.

I had toast and coffee for breakfast, quietly, just the rain on the windows and me in the tiny breakfast nook, while Grandma took her Sunday morning soak with half the Sunday papers and Daniel went back to sleep.

And I thought about the fruit cellar.

And thought about the fruit cellar.

The more I thought about it, the farther away it became, the larger it grew, the deeper it sank, the ranker it smelled, the more *unreal* my chore began to be.

I chugged down the last of my cold coffee, grabbed broom, bucket and mop, basket of rags and bottle of ammonia and opened the cellar door. It was now or never.

No place in the world smelled as wonderful as Grandma's basement. It smelled like coal dust and aging apples. It smelled like little kids playing school. It smelled like old dresses stored in leather boxes and mothballs around Great-great-grandma's precious few things.

I clanked my way down the stairs, took a deep breath of that wonderfully perfumed air of my childhood, and turned to face the fruit cellar door. It was like a barn door, slatted with one crosspiece. It was dark wood, with one knot punched out at five-year-old eye level from the time when Randy, my brother, wanted to see if Grandpa was still in there, dead, and he was too scared to open the door.

I wanted to bend down and look through the knothole first, too, but that was silly, that was silly, that was silly, and I lifted the latch and the door swung out.

What a relief! I almost laughed out loud. You nut, I thought, and stepped into the musty room and viewed it with the critical eye of the cleaner.

It was a mess. Grandma was right. It did need the cobwebs swept.

The one little window-well window was too thickly encrusted with webs and dust and dirt to let in much light, so I turned on the bare bulb overhead. The little room was maybe eight feet square, and ringed by wooden shelves. In the faint light, I could discern rows of canned fruits and vegetables, and then I remembered about Grandma's hobby.

There was a big box on the top shelf of the closet that was filled with hundreds of ribbons, red, white, gold, but mostly blue from the county and state fairs. Grandma took all the prizes for canned fruit, vegetables, relishes, jams and jellies and sauces. Grandma turned food preservation into an art; she grew most of her spices as well as her fruit and vegetables, and her reputation was as widespread as her recipes were secret.

I leaned against the dusty wall and crossed my arms over my chest. When Grandma was my age, she had a house, a husband, three little kids and was winning blue ribbons for food preservation during the depression. She was quite a woman in her youth. It was hard for me to imagine her in her thirties—vibrant, sharp, energetic, witty.

Look what time does to a person, I thought. All that energy, all that ambition, gone out into the atmosphere, leaving Grandma old, frail, and not quite all there.

But at least she's had three children to hold her memory, and a lot of people that she's touched and helped, and secret recipes that must be around somewhere . . . What am *I* doing besides chasing the almighty dollar? What am I doing that's worthwhile?

Cleaning the fruit cellar, I thought, and grabbed the mop.

I looked again at the half-empty shelves of bottled fruit and vegetables and saw the rings of where the used ones had been, their rings in descending order of dustiness, according to when they were taken upstairs. Boxes of empty mason jars and wide-mouth lids were lined up along the bottom row of shelves.

Grandma hadn't canned anything in a long time. The most

recent red-bordered gummed label read three years ago in Grandma's fine hand. And she still had a lot left to eat.

I put my hands on my hips and looked around, pleased with myself for once. I had faced a mindless fear and won. Not only that, but the fruit cellar was so terribly filthy, I'd be able to see real progress.

I wrapped a rag around the broom and began to dust away at the window.

Daniel brought me a sandwich and cold beer at noon. We sat together on the damp floor and ate. I began telling him about Grandma's fame, and while I did, a memory floated up, of Grandma holding two beautiful peaches, ripe to perfection. "These are wonderful," she said. "God meant for peaches this nice to be preserved." My throat filled with sadness for Grandma, and it crowded out my sandwich. Time caught up with a person, and I needed some silence to ponder that. I pushed away the tears of fear about my own aging, chugged the beer, wrapped the rest of the sandwich, and even though Daniel still had half a sandwich left, I stood up and brushed him gently out of my way. I had to get back to work.

Late in the afternoon, the rain clouds parted and shafts of light came in through the newly cleaned little window. I was wiping down the last of the shelves, had only the bottom shelf and the floor left to do, when a little jar caught the sunlight, caught my attention. It looked out of place, being smaller than the other jars on the shelf, and of a different color, and stashed way in the back, in the corner, next to the wall.

I dusted my way over to it, reached behind the jars of apricots and picked it up. It was small, maybe a half pint or so, of fancy cut glass, with a miniature rubber seal and a wire-snap top. Those wire-snap tops were so old that not even Grandma used them anymore. I held it up to the light, but as I did, the sun went behind a cloud. The bare light bulb in the ceiling showed through a clear, golden-green substance. It looked like jelly. I was intrigued—almost enough to open it, but not quite. It wasn't mine to open, and besides, maybe it was special to Grandma. I set it on the floor next to the door to remind myself to take it upstairs and ask.

But by the time I was finished, my muscles were howling. I

was not used to this kind of labor, and when I emptied the final load from the dustpan into the garbage, I barely had enough energy to look around the little room in satisfaction before hobbling up the stairs to the bath. I left the little jar next to the bucket of filthy water, the broom, the dustpan and the pile of rags. I'd fetch them all the next morning.

But the next morning, it wasn't there. I moved the mop around and the bucket, but that jar wasn't there. Then I looked on the shelf where I'd first found it, and there it was. Tucked back in the corner behind the apricots. Next to the wall.

A little chill ran through me.

I reached in and brought it out, wondering again at the strangely rich color.

By the time I'd finished cleaning up the cleaning tools, Grandma was having her toast and marmalade in the sunny breakfast nook.

"You did a beautiful job on the fruit cellar, Jan," she said.

So she'd been down to see. *She'd* put the jar back on the shelf. "Thanks, Grandma. It was a real challenge." I sat down next to her, thinking that I noticed something a little different in her manner, and I wished I'd left the jar on the shelf where she was telling me it belonged. Suddenly I felt a little shy, but I knew if I didn't ask her now, that curiosity would certainly torture me. I pulled the jar from my pocket. "Grandma. What's this?"

She looked at it without surprise, but with an indefinable look that seemed to be a little melancholy, a little misty. Then that passed, and she returned her look to the newspaper. "Jelly," she said.

"It looks so . . . so old."

Grandma smiled to herself.

"Can we try some? Or were you saving it for some special occasion?"

Grandma looked at me, looked at the jar, looked back at me. "Well, no," she said hesitantly, "not really. Sure. Let's have some."

I opened it and the fragrance was deep, pungent and spicy. It didn't smell like any kind of jelly or jam I'd ever smelled before, but it did smell sweet, and quite irresistible. I spooned out a gentle amount and put it on my toast, then passed the jar to

Grandma. She smelled it first, too, then without comment she scooped a dollop out onto her toast.

She spread it around carefully, then lifted it up. A toast of toast, you might say, and she said, "To Grandpa."

And we both took a big bite.

It was delicious.

"He loved my homemade jelly so much," Grandma said around a mouthful. "I always said he'd someday turn into a jar of it."

The toast caught in my throat.

There was a glazed, slightly hysterical look in Grandma's eyes. She wiped a few toast crumbs with jelly from the corner of her mouth and then looked at her napkin. "And now look at him," she said.

The Final Tale

When the dark man walked into the room, he brought with him a chill from the frozen shores of obscurity, that place which haunts every artist. He was otherwise nondescript, yet each person noted him, his aura was that unclean.

He joined our group late, sat unobtrusively in the corner, just as we were beginning our tales. There was no opportunity to have him introduced, or discern even the most basic information about the man. Even though he was an outsider, his presence was soon pushed to the backs of our minds as we became involved in the tales.

The fire crackled and sputtered, flaming up and dying to a glow; the candles flickered wanton shadows on the walls and ceilings. Those of us on the floor found life in the handwoven rug, as the shadows and shapes danced upon it, our imaginations fired by the skills of the storyteller.

This was the final evening of the workshop. The twelve of us had each written a ghost story during the week, and this was the night for telling. Not reading, mind you, but telling, with all the drama and nuance we could muster.

The setting was perfect. It was a cool October night, the sky clear, the moon full. A breeze creaked the monstrous old trees surrounding our lodge, and the little round of firelight seemed the safest place to be. Danger to the body seemed to lie everywhere, but danger to the psyche lay only in that lighted circle. But the danger was of our own making, and that took away its power. Or so we thought.

John spoke first. His story was of a grave robber, a legitimate insurance salesman by day, who would dress in skintight black clothes at night and dig up the graves of the recently deceased rich. He stripped them of their jewels, their dignity, and occasionally a portion of their anatomy, and put it all on display in his little museum in the attic of his home.

John told the story with a calm assurance, little or no dramatic effort, and it was clear that the aspect which was the most horrifying to the author was the concept of the grave worms. When he spoke of the worms, his voice changed, his body quivered, the audience felt something.

His story lasted for probably ten minutes, then we applauded, laughed at our insecurities and took a break.

The dark man was the first out the door and didn't return until we had reconvened.

Everyone noticed this.

When the same thing happened after the second story—we planned the session to go until the wee hours—the talk at the break was that he had been planted by one of us to scare the bejesus out of the rest of us. A real live ghost, so to speak. Well, we would unmask him in due time, but for now, we would let the joke go and maybe even derive some sort of pleasure from the plan, especially if there were some good surprises to come.

This was a fun house of our creation; we cared not to turn on the lights.

Janet was the third to speak, with a tale of vampirism so loaded with sexual undertones that it made all of us physically uncomfortable. She is a master storyteller, even putting on the countenance of the characters whose roles she plays. The tension in the room built to the snapping point, with only the sounds of the fire crackling in the background, the moaning of the trees, and the squirming of the members of the audience, as her well-modulated voice carried us through a tale of perverse horror.

The vampires in Janet's story did not merely drink their victim's blood in order to live; drinking blood was their very life. They wooed, they caressed, they seduced their prey with promises of whatever was necessary, and then in explicitly detailed sexual play, drove themselves and their victims to feverish pitch. The bite was the orgasm; the sucking of the blood ebbed into the slowing, weakening aftermath.

When she was finished, no one applauded. We were beginning to infect ourselves with fear—the very fear we had come here to foster, we had found, and it was not pleasant. After a moment, while brows were mopped and clothes rearranged, someone began to clap, and others followed. It was a shallow acknowledgement for a powerful tale, which is what I told Janet as we broke and watched the dark man go out the door.

And we had nine tales yet to tell.

I began to wonder what on earth we were doing—

And I wondered: Can a group of twelve powerful personalities really evoke that which they seek? The old witch covens were based on exactly that premise.

I used that idea as preface for the next story. I noticed that everyone sat a little closer together this time.

All but the dark man.

It was Rodney's turn. A strangler-on-campus story. Rodney is not one of our star students, but the effect of his amateurish story was rather frightening in and of itself. At the end, in the apparent comic relief that all people need after too much tension, I saw at least three people playfully throttling others.

I shivered, as if I were witnessing an omen. The dark man, I noticed, stayed to watch this.

The next three stories added their gruesome touch to the fire which began to burn within us, and the group elected not to break. The intensity of emotion leapt with each tale. There was a story of a bus driver whose regular route took his passengers to hell; a story of an ancient voodoo rite recently discovered and performed without understanding the ramifications of the evil it unleashed; and the story of the devil coming to dinner at the home of a pious family who was always told to accept strangers into their home—just in case one of them happened to be Jesus.

Long ago we had stopped applauding the genius of the story-tellers. The effect was judged, instead, by the shivers, goose bumps, moans of terror and touching that went on in the group. By the end of this last tale, by the end of the story of that ill-fated family, each person in our group was touching another person in some way. We all needed the comfort of the fellow-ship.

All, of course, except the dark man. He sat quietly in the shadows, out of the circle of brotherhood, out of the warmth, but occasionally I looked for him, to gauge his reaction, and he had an eagerness about him that was similar to ours during the telling of a tale, but when the tale was done, his expression was of unearthly satisfaction, rather than the creepy-crawly fear the rest of us evidenced. He seemed—sated, almost.

I also noticed that no one else looked at him.

We took a break at the end of these three stories, and as usual, the dark man headed for the door. No one else went outside. Everyone remained huddled together by the firelight, stretching, yawning, refilling coffee cups.

I approached Michael, the teller of the last tale we heard, the story of the family who embraced Satan and thus paved their way to hell with their good intentions, and asked him if he had looked at the dark man while telling.

He took a long time in answering, and as he paused, shadows danced across his face. During that brief moment, in those shadows, I knew the history of evil within the dregs of man-kind's collective soul.

Then he turned away, and for a split second I had a feeling that I was—that we were—feeding this evil. I felt as though we had provoked it, and this first taste was the event that would awaken a perpetuating hunger, an ancient hunger, a ravenous hunger that would, eventually, begin to devour my very being. And more.

It was my answer.

I sank to the floor and stared into the fire.

Everyone returned, as if my seating was the signal. I was

ready to stop this. We were beginning to dip into the realm of the untouchable, I knew it. And someone else knew it, too.

And there he sat, right on schedule, looking—oh God—hungry?

The stories continued. The situation was taken out of my control. This was no longer my group, it belonged to someone, some*thing* else. The tellers of the tales raved on with a peculiar light in their eyes, the tales were grislier and more despicable than any I've ever even imagined. It occurred to me that some of the tellers were surprised at what came from their tongues. All this added to my own discomfort, my own terror, until I felt a band tighten about my chest. It was difficult to take a breath, but I suffered in silence and listened to the insanity about me.

I cannot actually say how the evening ended. We all huddled together like twelve kittens sleeping in a pile. Each shadow, corner and crevice of the large lodge around us filled up with harmful spirits, and we kept in close touch with each other throughout the remainder of the telling, helpless to stop ourselves from reciting the horrors. We cringed, we cried, we moaned, we squirmed, and still we told of the unspeakable.

And the dark man leaned forward and licked his lips.

I awakened with the dawn. I heard birds singing. I rubbed my face and removed those bodies which had rested atop my own for the night. It was morning. There were twelve of us; the dark man was gone. I didn't remember going to sleep.

But morning it was, and I threw open the door and made a big pot of coffee, and one by one the sleeping authors awoke and arose, smiling sheepishly as the morning sun illuminated the corners of the lodge and the nooks and crannies of our minds.

The night before was a vague blur, and whenever I tried to focus in on just exactly what had happened, my body twitched with discomfort and told my mind to leave well enough alone.

No mention of the previous night was made by any of the participants. They discussed the foregoing week with enthusiasm, and reiterated much of what they had learned in our workshop, and after breakfast, they all drove away.

I've not heard from any one of them since. I have, however, heard *of* them.

Janet was found dead with no blood left in her veins. Rodney was found strangled next to the student union building at his school. Michael disappeared one day from his bedroom, never to be seen again, John was arrested when they discovered the collection of human parts in his attic. They were, he said in his defense, food for his worms.

Everyone in the group found the fear which they sought to purge—even me.

I have slipped into irreversible insignificancy as a writer and a personality. This has always been my fear, and the fear has found me.

And the dark man? A friend of one of the workshoppers, as it turns out. An actor, hired to play a part.

His acting that night was impeccable, and if he is who I think he is, his writing is just as good. A volume of horrendously familiar short stories has found the best-seller list.

No author's photo graces the dust jacket.

•Quiet Meditation

Nessie hummed to herself as she steeped a cup of tea in the kitchen of her small apartment. A quiet evening. She'd been looking forward to this evening all week. Not that she went out much anymore, but there were always people coming by to see how she was doing, the bridge club met twice a week, there were the ladies from the auxiliary she had to call, and then of course, the shut-ins she talked to on the phone every day . . . the list went on and on. But not this night. This night was for her alone.

She stirred a bit of milk into her tea and carried it into the living room, setting it gently on the table next to her overstuffed chair. She turned the knob on her old round-headed radio and found the classical station. She loved classical music. It could take her places, show her things, keep her mind occupied in ways the television never could.

She eased carefully into the chair, then settled down hard. Her weight had become a burden lately. She knew that was why her knees gave her such trouble. And the doctor, kindly Dr. Miller, had told her very gently that some of the weight had to come off if the old heart was to go on much longer. He was right, of course.

The music drifted into the room, violins lifting her spirits. Eyes closed, she could muse through the music for hours. She sipped her tea and picked up the pieces of cloth on the arm of the chair. Blank shapes of muslin, soon to be a beautiful doll for some little girl to squeeze and love and talk to and play with and confide in. This would be a very special doll, Nessie thought. She would take particular care with this one. The stitches would be even and neat and strong. The face would return the love its little girl would give it, and this doll would be the first one sold at the church bazaar next weekend.

She threaded the needle with a needle threader and made a knot in the end. Before she sewed her first stitch, she closed her eyes and listened to the music for a moment longer. Then she sent thanks and praise to the Lord above who had given her so much in her life, and especially this one night of quiet meditation, with just her, the wonderful music and these little scraps of fabric that her talents would soon turn into a thing of love and beauty.

She began to sew. Tiny, rhythmic stitches—her fingers knew the way. They began at the neck, sewing the front to the back, needle poking up and down through the fabric, the music relaxing her, and her mind strayed to the old days, when she was young and gay, and not fettered by the bonds of age and weight and bad knees. She remembered Will, so handsome, so tall and straight. They had loved each other in the way of young love . . .

"Nessie?" The voice whispered in the clear night. She was in bed, nightgown warm and cozy around her body. She awakened instantly and lay there, hoping she heard him, hoping she didn't hear him. The voice came again. "Nessie?" She slipped out of bed, long red hair done up in rags that caught on her pillow. She quickly jerked them all out, to let her hair hang long and loose, and she went to the window and opened it. Will stood in the moonlight on the back lawn. She giggled behind her hand.

"Nessie," he said. "Come out."

She whispered back to him, projecting her voice so he could

hear her, but not loud enough to wake her parents, asleep in the next room. "I can't. I'm in bed." She grinned down at him. "Come on. It's a beautiful night. Let's go for a walk." She sat on the windowseat, looking into her darkened room. The temptation was powerful. She felt naughty. She looked again out the window and saw him standing there, looking up for her, waiting for her answer. He wanted her with him. Flattered beyond control, she giggled to herself. She put her face to the window screen again. "Okay. Wait." He sat down in the middle of the lawn.

She bunched her pillows up and pulled the covers over them, in case her mother checked on her. She dressed quickly and quietly, then slipped out the door and down the stairs. The house was so quiet, she could hear her own heartbeat. She carried her shoes and put them on in the kitchen. Then, ever so slowly, she opened the kitchen door and tiptoed down the back steps.

Once out, she felt exhilarated. She was free! It was a feeling like she'd never known before. The whole world slept, and she and Will were defying all of that. She ran toward him, then slowed as she approached. He stood up, hands in pockets, and silently they walked around the house together and down to the sidewalk.

"This is crazy."

"It's fun," he said.

"My parents will kill me if I get caught."

"You won't get caught."

"Just a short walk, though, okay?"

"Okay. I just wanted to be with you."

She blushed in the darkness. Her heart thumped. How could someone like Will court her? He was three years older, that made him nineteen, and the girls at Garfield High almost swooned whenever he boxed their mothers' groceries at Thompson's.

They walked along in silence, the elm trees keeping their secret. The night was so quiet.

"Where are we going?" she whispered. She didn't want anything to spoil the quiet effect, but she couldn't quite stand the silence.

"I know a place where we can go to talk."

The temptation to stay out all night was overwhelming. This was the most daring thing she'd ever done. She wanted to turn and run back to the house and snuggle down in her bed, before she was gone too long, before her parents missed her, before— before she liked this too much. Before she liked Will too much.

They got to the corner. No cars. They crossed the street quickly, he taking her hand and giving it a gentle squeeze. The streetlights looked down on them, making long shadows in front of them as they continued, casting the whole neighbor- hood into shades of gray. They passed house after house, all silently standing guard over the sleeping, trusting, defenseless people inside. She felt a surge of power and squeezed his hand in return.

Two blocks south, they turned down an old pickle road between houses. In the back was an alley with garages on either side. At the third garage on the left, Will opened the side door and they went inside, into darkness thick with the smell of gasoline and oil. Nessie clung tightly to his hand. He led her gently, letting her take as much time as she needed. She stepped softly, blind, sensing large shapes around her but seeing noth- ing, until Will put her hand on a ladder, and she climbed up quickly, with him right behind her. At the top was a loft, and bedding, and she crawled on hands and knees to the corner by the wall to make room for him to join her.

He fumbled in his pants pockets, then struck a match on the floor of the loft and the bright light illuminated his clean, hand- some face. He held the match close to her, looking into her eyes. She blushed and looked at her hands. He touched the match to an old piece of candle in a tin tray and they had light.

"Is this where you sleep?" Nessie whispered.

"Yes." Will stretched out on his back, his hands behind his head, staring at the beams. She lay on her side next to him, her head propped up on her hand.

"Why?"

"Because it's a place of my own." He turned toward her, and the candlelight flickered patterns of shadow and light across his face. "It's a private place." She watched the shadow patterns. "You're the most beautiful woman I've ever seen, Nessie."

Woman. She'd never been called a woman before. She'd always thought of herself as a girl. She looked at his shirt collar to avoid his eyes, but then she saw his arm move and then she felt his hand in her hair, and she lifted her gaze to meet his. This was absolutely the most romantic thing she had ever experienced. In fact, it was more romantic than anything she had ever imagined. Here she was, in Will Nelson's loft. In his . . . his . . . bed!

She sat up and bonked her head on a rafter. "Will, I think I better go home now."

His hand followed the hair to the back of her neck, to her shoulder. "Please don't. Please, Nessie, just stay a few more minutes. Unless you really *want* to go. Do you want to go?"

"No, but I should."

"Why?"

"It isn't a good place for me to be, Will, in your bed like this."

"Do you like it?"

She closed her eyes and took a deep breath. Mustn't lie to him. "Yes," she said softly.

"Then please stay. Just for a little while. I get so lonely up here sometimes, Ness. I lie here at night and I think about you, and think about what it would be like if you were here." He touched her sleeve. "And now that you're here, I'd hate for you to go . . . so soon."

Her resolve melted in a rush of emotion. She lay back down next to him. Once again, he fingered her hair, twisting it, feeling it, and her skin thrilled each place he touched her.

"Can I kiss you?"

A tingle went through her, raising goose bumps on her arms. Men weren't supposed to ask things like that. They were just supposed to do it. What was she supposed to say? Yes? No? She wanted him to, wanted him to kiss her, but she didn't want to say it.

He pulled gently on her hair and brought her face to his. His lips touched hers, ever so gently. She thought she would cry, he was so tender. She kissed him back and felt a warmth in her stomach. She broke the kiss and started to move toward him, to feel his arms around her, to have him hold her, just to lie together in the dark, in the quiet. Then she thought of her parents and sat up again.

"Really, Will. I have to go."

"Okay," he said, then he touched her nose and smiled. He sat up and made his way down the ladder. She blew out the candle then followed him down—sad, sorry and mad at herself. She wished she could take it all back, just climb back up to the loft and kiss again, but the moment was gone. She had broken it.

They walked back in silence, hiding behind hedges as car headlights came toward them. Soon they were back in her yard. He caught her by the waist as they were about to go around to the kitchen door, and in the shadows he held her close and kissed her deeply, lovingly, tenderly. She leaned against him, feeling his warmth, his power, his masculinity. Holding Will was far different than hugging her soft, tiny mother, different from the occasional squeeze from her tall, thin father. Will was broad, and muscle-hard and . . .

He held up his hand, and in it was a tiny red rosebud. She hadn't seen him pick it—it was like magic. She took it, smelled it, kissed him one more time, then he let her go and she ran around the house and tiptoed up the steps.

Safely in her room again, she stripped off her dress and put on her nightgown. She lay the rosebud on her pillow, then walked across to the open window. She looked down, and he was standing there, in the center of her back yard, where he had stood earlier. He was looking up at her. They looked at each other for a while, then she turned and got into bed. Holding the flower in both hands, she snuggled down under the covers and anticipated wonderful dreams. Dreams of warmth and love and Will.

Nessie took a sip of tea and regarded her handiwork. Not too bad. Her tiny stitches were perfect and made with far more love than any Singer could manage. She reached into the basket beside her chair and took out her half-glasses. Sewing the hands was the difficult part. She bit off a fresh length of thread and began again under the arm.

* * *

Will had actually gotten down on one knee on her front porch to propose. Nessie was sitting in the swing, and before she could ask him what he was doing, he had pulled a diamond ring from his pocket and slipped it on her finger. Surprise, shock even, left her speechless for the first time she could remember. And then, she couldn't say yes fast enough. Nessie Nelson. She'd been dreaming about it for months.

She leaned over and kissed him. "You'll have to ask Papa," she teased.

He pretended to scowl, but couldn't suppress his joy.

"I already have." Delight spread across her face.

"And?"

"And he gives us his blessings." He stood up, pulled her to him and hugged her, then swung her around in a circle. Her feet left the ground and she was flying. He stopped and kissed her slowly. She didn't know if it was the swinging or the kiss that made her dizzy, she only knew that her whole being was happy.

"C'mon," he said. "Let's go for a walk."

"Okay. I'll go tell Mother." She walked through the door, careful not to let the screen bang shut behind her. She looked back and saw Will watching her, waiting for her. She giggled. Life was so wonderful.

She went into the kitchen where her mother was drying the dishes. "Will and I are going for a little walk."

Her mother smiled a knowing smile. "Okay, dear. Don't keep him up too late."

Nessie held out her hand and flashed the diamond at her mother, whose mouth fell open. "Oh, Nessie, I'm so pleased!" Her mother hugged her and put wet finger marks on the back of her blouse and wet tear marks on her shoulder. Both her parents loved Will—the son they never had.

Her best friend, Mary Jane Hampton, gave her a wedding shower. All her good friends were there, and they gave her wonderful things. Grown up things. Household things, and naughty lace nightgowns that made her blush. They played silly games and giggled. Dorothy was the rascal in the bunch, and when Nessie's mother had gone to bed, she brought forth a pint of whiskey from her purse. They passed it around, all of them choking on it, except for Dorothy, of course. The second round went down easier.

Nessie got tipsy and said some things about Will that were a little too personal to be made public, but drunk on happiness and friendship as well as the whiskey, she told them anyway, and the girls laughed until they cried.

There were over a hundred guests at the wedding and piles of gifts wrapped in beautiful white and silver. Her wedding dress was handmade by a friend of her mother's, with a long white train and lace up to the neck. She carried a bouquet of yellow roses and white orchids. Mary Jane wore a yellow lace dress, and all the men wore white tuxedos. She'd never seen Will look so handsome.

There was a little nervousness in her when she was up there in front of the minister, her knees shook a little, but she was so sure that Will was right for her, and she for him, that she looked deeply into his eyes when she said her vows and she really meant them.

The reception turned into a fabulous party. Too much champagne flowed, and her papa got a little drunk, but so did Will's father, and that made them friends.

They spent their wedding night in the bridal suite of the Palmer House Hotel. They decided against a honeymoon; they would take that money and buy things they needed for their little apartment instead. But the wedding night was special. Will had put a cold bottle of champagne in the getaway car, and there was another in the room, compliments of the management.

Since that first night in the loft, Nessie and Will had spent many nights there together, sometimes talking, sometimes drifting into sleep, only to wake up with that awful jolt, afraid of being too late and found out by her parents. Always had he been a perfect gentleman. They held each other, touched and kissed, but never anything more. Even when she'd wanted more, and she'd known Will did too, Will's good sense and concern for her prevailed.

They looked at each other across the room, in their bridal suite as Mr. and Mrs. William Nelson. Nessie nervously unpinned her little traveling hat and put it on the nightstand. Will loosened his tie and sat on the edge of the bed, looking at his hands. Suddenly they felt like strangers to each other. Married, their wedding night, and now they were to share that which only husbands and wives shared. Nessie knew nothing of what to expect, except the cryptic little phrases her mother mentioned with a blush.

Eventually, Will stood and came to her, put his arms around her, held her close, kissed her. He gently unpinned her hair and ran his fingers through it as it fell to below her shoulders. Little chills rippled through her, chills of expectation, of fear, of love. They slowly undressed each other, then when almost naked, modesty overcame them both and they turned out the light and climbed underneath the covers. They finished undressing there, and in the safety and comfort of their wedding bed, self-conscious, unsure and halting, they made love to the tune of the universal music that had played for thousands of wedding-night couples before them. Softly, slowly, lovingly, they rocked together with the rhythm of young love.

Afterward, they lay entwined, looking at the darkened ceiling, seeing a motion picture of their future unfolding before them as they talked. Nessie was filled with wonder at the act they had just completed, and hoped she would be a good wife in bed for Will. Finally they slept, worried but trusting.

Nessie looked at the doll in her lap. The dreams tonight (They're not dreams! They're memories!) were nice ones. She was happy. She turned the right side of the doll out and examined it for sewing flaws. None. She reached into the bag of stuffing, and with a knitting needle, began poking the stuffing through the opening in the doll's head, into its feet.

It's been a good life, she thought. I've lived a long time. I've been useful to many people, many people have used me. ("You're hurting me, Will!") I've had many joys, many sorrows, many loves, many hurts. (Hiding in the bathroom, "Oh, God, don't come near me again!") I've been on the peak of happiness, the valley of despair. ("Lies!")

Here they come again, she thought. Those creeping feelings, those thoughts that come unbidden from God knows where.

Stop those filthy thoughts, Lord, she prayed. The calm once again soothed her mind. She relaxed in her chair. Taking up needle and thread one more time, she closed the gap in the head with expert stitches. The doll was now ready for hair and face.

She looked at the doll, turning it back and forth, eyeing its contours. Most people put the faces on first, but Nessie needed to see how a doll measured up before the face went on. Long, dark red hair, she thought. Clear, ice-blue eyes. Like me when I was a young girl. That's where the stories are tonight, that's what I'll do with this very special doll. She looked at it again. Yes. Perfect. She hugged it to her breast.

Their first child was born at home, with Will and her mother attending. Dr. Olson didn't have time to get there, he arrived as their newborn son nursed. It was an easy birth, her mother had said. Nessie wasn't so sure about that, it had seemed pretty hard to her.

Will was the model father. He doted on his son, changing him, washing diapers, buying toys and playing with him for hours on end. They named him Silas, after Will's grandfather. He was a good baby; he had his father's quiet smile and dark hair. He had Nessie's eyes—blue, with snowflakes in them. He was such a joy.

With Silas in his carriage, Will and Nessie would take him for walks on Sunday mornings through the park, feeding the pigeons, talking about what a handsome gentleman he would be someday. "Like you," Nessie would say to Will, and Will would look at his son and say, "I hope you grow up and find a woman as good as your mother."

Then the terrible thing happened. When Silas was still a toddler, bright, inquisitive, happy and fearless, he pulled the cutting board from the kitchen table, and the big chopping knife fell down . . .

Nessie rubbed her face with her hands. Only happy thoughts tonight. God, please remove the thoughts of sadness and despair tonight. This is a night of quiet meditation ("I'll kill you, too, if you don't stop that screaming!") and nothing would interfere with it. ("Oh, God, my baby! My baby!") Feeling dizzy, she put the doll down on the arm of her chair. She stood up carefully, picked up the cup from her delicate end table and went to the kitchen to refresh her tea.

Hot tea in hand, she returned to the living room and felt the first pain. Her hands clutched her chest, the teacup went flying to smash against the wall. The band tightened around her chest, cutting off the air, her left arm fell woodenly to her side, liquid fire coursing through it. She fell to her knees, heavily, hearing the bones crack like a handful of toothpicks. ("Not my knees, Will! Oh God, Will, I'm sorry! I won't scream anymore, please, Will! Not my knees!") Her face flushed as she fell on her side, right hand grasping her chest, as if to tear away the binding.

Memories filtered through the years to show themselves on the inside of her eyelids. She blinked quickly. "Take them away from me, Father, I wish to die in peace," but this time the prayers didn't work. She saw the truth of it, in its brutal black and white reality. She saw the real Will, forcing himself on her in his loft, and her parents, not understanding, exiling her from home. The baby had been born wrong—maybe it had been her fault, because she'd been alone when it came. She saw Will desperately working—trying for years to get her attention, but she was too busy; she was secure in her fantasy world—until he finally fixed the baby in the only way he knew how, and then followed in escape, leaving her a mess to clean and a life alone in which to grow old.

It's finally over, Nessie thought, and she lay on the floor and listened for the last time to the classical music. At the final climax of the program, her perfect doll, with its one ice-blue eye, fell forward at the waist, bowing in grotesque acknowledgement of its creator.

"At last," Nessie whispered, and her life leaked away.

The Night of a Hawaiian Sky

On any other night, I believe, I would have just hefted the heavy, wet sheets into the laundry basket and taken them outside. I would have untwisted, matched up ends, folded and hung the sheets on the line, knowing that they'd be dry and not yet stiff if I harvested them right after breakfast.

On this night, though, when I heard the washer finish its spin cycle, I left the television news of famine in the East, drought right here in Hawaii, economic terrorism and spiritual bankruptcy in most of the world. I left the cozy family scene in the front room, loaded the laundry basket and hauled it out back. The clotheslines, empty but for a dozen weathered clothespins, gleamed their bizarre skeletal formations in the starlight. I felt the night on my skin, and it felt cool and soothing. I set the basket down on the grass and slowly turned around.

The sky lightened over Haleakala.

The moon rose.

The grass, damp from a sparse evening sprinkling, sparkled at me and I could not resist kicking off my slippers and prancing a bit. I felt a little silly, but soon my body grew lithe and spry as I danced, and I began to luxuriate in the sleek movements of my muscles, no longer weighted by ripples of fat. I cast off my shorts, and then shirt, and then confining and uncomfortable underwear, and my body seemed long and smooth, gentle and waiflike in the bold light of the Maui moon, and I scampered about the yard feeling young and shameless.

I danced into the neighbor's yard, and then the yard after that, drawn to the source of my power by the music in my head. It became louder and louder, pulling more from me, my dancing became more intense, more pleasurable, more meaningful. I danced and twirled, jumped and twisted as I made my way toward that which made me feel so *alive.*

The music slowed, calmed, and reverence flowed through my tingling body.

Restraint felt as voluptuous as abandon. I slowed to a walk, felt my stride long and proud, my carriage straight and tall, and I walked toward the drums, the chants, and I felt the night in my hair, on my lashes, along my thighs. The night cloaked me in richness and I felt worthy, privileged, special, chosen.

The neighborhood fell away as I approached the torches on silent feet. The drumbeats echoed in the damp heat, the close tropical vegetation catching the notes and making them almost visible. The music rose to a crescendo, and I saw the red-yellow gleam of sweat-slick flesh in the firelight as those who worshipped me danced homage.

I had come in answer to their prayers. They had called, with their music and their dance, and from somewhere far away, ancestral memories were awakened, my purpose unfolded.

I stepped into the firelit circle and felt a shudder surge through those gathered. The drums ceased. The chanters fell silent. The dancers, proud in their own integrity, turned, saw me, and their arms fell to their sides, their chests heaving from their efforts. I walked through them, pleased, and touched each on the head as I passed.

"It is a moon of plenty," I said to the musicians. "Let us give thanks."

Tentatively, one bold drummer began a beat, and my body showed him the rhythm. Within moments, the others had joined in; the dancers watched me with heated eyes until I beckoned them, then they eagerly joined me in the ecstasy of Plenty.

Our dance spoke with the moon and the tides. We enriched the earth and nourished the crops. We bid the fish thrive closer to the nets, we let wisdom to the children. We sought the rain. We grasped the gift of plenty and shook it, squeezing it dry, and basking in the worship of its greatness.

The moon waned, and one by one, the dancers fell and slept where they lay.

I felt the night recede, and began to walk home, feeling as I walked that I became shorter, heavier, my posture not so tall nor so straight. I found myself naked and ashamed in the yard of my neighbor, and I dodged behind the hedge, my heart pounding, my mouth dry.

Weeds choked the back yard of my house, dry and brittle as insect carcasses. The house was empty, open, vandalized, abandoned. The clothesline still stretched across the back yard, weedy vines growing up the poles and across the lines. Hanging from one end was a plastic bag, sun-scorched and brittle. I touched it and it broke open.

Out fell my clothes and the sun-bleached remnants of a plastic clothes basket. I dressed and walked through the vacant house, my soul filled with sadness and confusion.

I knocked on the neighbor's door and a stranger opened it. What happened to the people next door, I asked.

The old man finally died, she said. The children grew up and moved away years ago.

And the wife?

Never met her, the woman said. Some say she ran off with her boyfriend, others say she was a victim of some crime. Her husband always said she'd fallen in love with the night and it had spirited her away, but who knows? He always said she'd return, and he left her clothes on the line for when she came back. I don't suppose they're still there after all these years.

Years of plenty? I asked.

Oh yes, she replied.

No, I said. I don't suppose the clothes are still there.

• The Pan Man

When Constance awoke to the crowing of the rooster, the sun was already flooding through the windows. She stretched luxuriously, feeling guilty for sleeping so late, especially since it looked to be a wonderfully unseasonable springlike day.

She got up, wrapped her robe around her, slid her feet into the lambskin slippers and padded into the kitchen. She stoked the fire and set the kettle on, then made her morning trek to the outhouse.

It was a beautiful day, she noticed. A glorious day.

The three sheep looked up, expecting their due of hay, the chickens scurried around, and the cat walked with her. It was so different with Jim gone.

When Jim was home, which was all the time except when he went hunting twice a year, he did most of the chores. He got up well before dawn, fed the livestock, started the fire, and usually had breakfast cooking by the time she got out of bed.

It was a luxury, really, to sleep in so late and feed the animals at a leisurely pace.

There was much to do yet. While Jim dealt with the firewood, Constance was in charge of splitting kindling. And she had the week's bread to bake, and it was a perfect day to do laundry and hang it out in the sun.

But the beauty of the day after a cold and stormy winter made her a little dreamy, and a little lazy, and by the time she had finished in the outhouse and was making her way back to the cabin, she had decided to set aside at least an hour to sit in the sun and spin.

Spinning the fleeces from the sheep was the winter job. All winter long, she dealt with those fleeces, washing, dyeing, carding and then spinning and knitting. This winter she'd made each of them bulky sweaters and long johns, and that was necessary work, but the spinning was such a wonderful pastime, she would relish a little sunshine and a little spinning, where the contented dreams of her imagination could wind on and on, just like the yarn she made. She'd never be able to afford such a luxury when Jim was home, and even though getting in the meat was a lot of work for him, she knew he enjoyed his three-day trips away with his friends.

Having decided to spend a little time in solitary pleasure with her spinning wheel, Constance went about her chores with a purpose in mind. She opened all the windows to let the fresh air in, fed the animals, mixed the bread, then swept the cabin and beat the rugs as it raised. She washed clothes while it raised for the second time, and chopped wood to heat up the oven.

Then, when it was finally in for the baking, she took her spinning wheel and a kitchen chair out onto the old wooden porch. The sun was warm, and even though the air up in the Cascade Mountains was always cold, and chilly now in February, she took off her sweater, leaving only a thin cotton dress, so her pale white arms could see the sun. Jim would never approve. He would want her dressed in woolens anyway, just because the calendar still read February. But Jim wasn't home.

She chose wool she'd dyed with Queen Anne's lace, a weed, really, that was abundant around the cabin. The wool was a lovely yellow-green, and she set to treadling the wheel and spinning the yarn. This would be knit into a little coat for their baby, she thought, whenever the Good Lord found fit to bless them with one.

The spinning wheel ran smoothly, and the sun beat down

warmly, and Constance thought back to their first arrival in the woods. They lived in a tent while Jim cleared the land, loving every moment of it. And in the two years they'd been here, many things had changed, but her love for her husband and their love for this land hadn't. And probably never would.

Birds twittered and darted in front of the cabin, picking up little pieces of straw to build nests, and Constance spun on.

She saw the grass turn green in front of her, and little wildflowers and the bulbs she'd planted in the fall grew. She felt the wool slide through her fingers in an even, fine thread and she dreamed of the family they would someday have.

And then she heard the bells.

Her father was a minister down in California, and some proud rich man who'd come to love the Lord had given him a set of three beautiful bells to ring of a Sunday morning. And the reverend rang them with glee, summoning everyone within earshot to the House of Worship for Sunday services. They were huge bells, each hanging from its own tripod of lodgepole pine. They weren't only beautiful, they were glorious-sounding bells, with a rich, deep tone. Her papa's ministry increased about sevenfold after that, and he grew wealthy off the goodness of the Lord and their congregation.

Constance heard the bells as she sat on her front porch and spun.

Papa was a good man, she thought, and she remembered her daily Bible lessons, and she remembered her mama before she died, her mama was a soft, loving woman who was always putting the coffeepot on in the middle of the night to help some neighbor in distress. There were always neighbors in distress, it seemed. Too bad Constance and Jim didn't have any neighbors. She'd like to help them the way her mama had.

Constance heard the bells, they seemed to be getting louder. The bells. The glorious bells.

Daddy would ring those bells early on Sunday morning, while he was still in his nightshirt. Mama would open the window and say, "Hush that, now, it isn't proper. You'll wake the dead." And Daddy would say, "Good. Then maybe they'll come to church, too."

So once awake, the townspeople had nothing better to do

than to come to church. Mama stopped complaining after a couple of weeks of heavy collection trays.

And all of Constance's friends would come. They'd have their ribbons and bows and lace and new shoes. They'd sit in the third pew and since she was the minister's daughter, she always had to wear her gloves, but she took them off as soon as the service got under way. The girls would sit and giggle and look around at the boys while the sound of her father's powerful voice went on and on.

One by one, those girls found boyfriends and got married, but Constance didn't find anyone she liked for a long, long time. And then, of course, her mama died and she had to help her daddy and she had to play the piano in church and wash his clothes and bake his bread, wondering day by day if spinsterhood was to be her lot in life.

And then Big Jim O'Connor came to church one day. Constance took one look and lost her heart. And she married him the next Sunday after church and he moved her to this land he'd staked in the Cascade Mountains high in the Oregon Territory.

Her girlfriends rang those bells for her as she and Jim rode off on horseback to their new home that Sunday afternoon. They rang those bells and rang those bells and Constance cried because it might be the last time she'd ever hear those bells . . . Until now, that is. Constance could hear those bells now as she sat and spun the yarn for her mama's grandchild, in fact the bells kept getting louder and louder. Tears she never had time for began to pour out of her heart. Tears for her mama, tears for her papa, alone down in California, just him and his Bible and his bells. Tears for the womb that had remained empty for two years, tears for love of the land, love of her man, yet with the sadness that her wonderful childhood of giggles and play had gone forever. In its place was the work of a woman, the load of responsibility.

Constance cried and spun and listened to the bells. They were nearer now, yet softer. She cried and heard the bees and felt the hot sun and watched the wheel spin around and around, and the grass was green and the wind whooshed in the pines, and she laughed and she cried and she spun and those bells, those bells, those glorious bells.

She looked up and a man stood in front of her.

"Daddy?" Her hand whipped out and stopped her wheel.

But it wasn't her daddy, it was a stranger, come up the path and she was so busy with laughing and crying and spinning that she'd let danger enter her world.

"No, ma'am," he said with a soft voice and Constance turned her chair over in a scramble to get up and get away from him. Jim had left his loaded shotgun next to the door in the kitchen. Constance backed toward it, wiping the tears from her vision. The man certainly seemed to be no threat, and yet . . .

"Pardon me for giving you a start. Usually people hear me coming from a mile or so away."

The man was wearing a leather harness fitted with hooks, and hanging from those hooks were cast-iron pots. He was covered with cast-iron pots and pans and lids. He lifted his arms and they touched, bonging softly. He turned around and Constance heard the bells of her father's church.

"Name's C. Cricket Wilson, ma'am. I make the finest cookware in the territory."

Constance knew she should continue to back toward the kitchen door, reach inside, grab that gun and run this peddler off their land. How dare he come sneaking around!

Yet he didn't exactly sneak up on her, he couldn't really, not with all those cast-iron pots hanging on him. And he looked gentle, he was certainly soft-spoken. She leaned against the house.

"Is your husband at home?"

"He's out cutting wood. He should be back anytime," Constance said, hoping he couldn't read the lie in her face.

"Well, then, may I take a moment of your time to show you my fine wares?" C. Cricket Wilson was perspiring. "And may I have a drink from your well, please?"

"You stay right there," Constance said, and it sounded like a halfhearted attempt at a threat, and somehow she was ashamed. She went inside, leaving the door open, and she looked at that shotgun and touched it, and decided she didn't need it. She dipped a cup of water, slipped into her sweater, and returned to the front porch. Mr. Wilson stayed put, just as she told him.

"Much obliged," he said as he drank the water down. He smacked his lips and handed back the cup with a smile. Then he took off his hat and wiped his forehead with his handkerchief. The pots rang. He cleared his voice. "Now, then." He removed a Dutch oven from its hook on his right shoulder. "A right stewpot. Ain't she a beauty?" He held it out to her.

Constance knew she shouldn't be talking to this Mr. Wilson while Jim was away, but he was such a nice gent, and he had walked all the way up here just to see her, she couldn't just turn him away without giving his wares a complete looking over, now, could she? She stepped forward.

"Maybe you better have a seat, ma'am."

Constance looked at him, but she sensed that he knew what he was saying, so she righted her chair, and sat down. She was still looking down on him from the porch as he stood in the dirt. She still felt like she had the advantage. C. Cricket Wilson handed the pot up to her. She held out her hands.

And when she touched it, the world turned dark, discordant, threatening. The pot fell from her hands as Constance gasped and recoiled.

The pan man's eyes were green, she noticed. Green and deep set. They were squinting at her.

"No good, huh? Well, not everybody matches up with every pan."

Constance looked at the Dutch oven that had landed upside down on her porch. She moved her foot away from it as if it would bite.

Mr. Wilson began removing his pans one at a time, polishing them with a chamois he pulled from his pocket, and then stacking them on the porch. Each time he took a pan from its hook, he squinted up at Constance.

"We don't want anything too heavy now, do we?" He kept up a comforting banter as he went through these practiced motions, but Constance had missed most of his words. Her heart was still pounding from the very strange experience she'd just had. She wondered if she was sick. She felt her forehead. Perspiring, but not feverish. What on earth could have made her feel that odd way? She ought to tell this peddler to be on his way. They weren't in the market for cookware; they had no money.

Constance felt that her shaky knees would support her and started to stand, holding to the back of her chair. She should lie down, just in case it was something serious.

"Please, please, just a moment more," he said. "I know I've got something here for you."

Constance sat down again, knowing she would be rid of him in a moment. If she ever felt that dizzy again, experienced that horrible nosedive into swirling black poisonousness . . .

"This." Mr. Wilson held up a small, flat pan. "My omelette pan. Do you have chickens?" He squinted up at her.

Constance nodded.

"Make your husband an omelette he'd never forget with this one." He gave it a final wipe with his cloth, then handed it up to her, squinting.

The pan had an energy of its own; Constance could feel it before she touched it. Then she took the round griddle from him and began to giggle. It tickled. She looked at the pan and wondered how in the world someone could make an omelette on such a silly pan and giggled and giggled, and then the pan man tried to take it away from her, and his face was so serious that she just had to laugh. He had these absurd little eyebrows that kind of tented up over his eyes and he'd missed a place when he'd shaved this morning and she held her sides and laughed, the pan banging on her chair, and she felt weak all over again from the giggles.

He wrested the pan from her grasp, though, and she was left to wipe her eyes and her nose and wonder at the mirth that came and went so fast.

Such an odd morning, Constance thought.

". . . pride myself on suiting the pan to the customer," Wilson was saying, "but not even a lid would tone down that terrible giddiness . . . Here." And he thrust a little long-handled cup at her.

It felt warm and comfortable. "It's lovely," Constance said. She wanted to just sit and hold it. The cup was so finely crafted, it gave her such a sense of peace . . .

Mr. Wilson peered at her. "You like it?"

"Oh, yes. It has . . ." She felt a loss of words.

"Balance."

"Yes. Balance." Constance looked around. It seemed as if the day just became a little bit nicer, the colors a little brighter, hope a little higher.

"Do you like it?"

Mr. Wilson's question brought her back to earth. She held it out to him. "Yes, of course, I'd love to have such a ladle, but I'm afraid I have no money."

"I don't trade in money, my dear. If you like the cup and it suits you, then it is yours. Let me just look it over . . ."

He took the ladle from her, produced a flannel cloth from somewhere under all his pans and began to rub it.

I could never take this from a strange man, she thought. What on earth would Jim have to say about that? He never even wanted her speaking to strangers.

"Uh-oh," Mr. Wilson said. "This cup has a crack in it." He smiled at her. "Can't have flawed merchandise, nosir. It's unpredictable, that's the problem. Can't never tell . . ." He set it on the step and began bonging around his wares, looking for something.

"That's fine, Mr. Wilson," Constance said, as she stood up slowly and backed toward the door. "We're not interested in any cookware now, really we're not."

"Oh? Did I tell you? It's not a matter of money?"

"Yes you did, and I thank you for coming all the way up here, but I really must insist you go now. My husband will be home at any moment."

"Aha." Mr. Wilson unhooked a loaf pan and held it out to her. "Here's a beauty," he said.

Constance looked at the little man. He certainly seemed harmless. And her loaf pans were almost beyond salvage. She had planned to get a new one the next time Jim took her to town. This one was cast iron; it would last forever. How she missed her mother's cast-iron cookware! In spite of herself, she stepped closer again to Mr. Wilson and held out her hands.

The loaf pan, when she looked at it, was ordinary. Black,

loaf-shaped, with a lip at one end where it could be hung on a nail. But it was anything but ordinary in her hands. It felt fluid. It felt strong and utilitarian. She thought she could bake the best bread in the world with this pan. She thought she could provide hearty nutrition for Jim and their family-to-be with no other tool, no other implement, nothing else, nothing else but this loaf pan. This marvelous, marvelous loaf pan.

"I must have it," she said.

"Good. Good. Well, then, for another drink of water from your well, it is yours. And I'll be on my way."

"I must pay you."

"The pleasure on your face is pay enough for me."

"We don't take charity in this house."

"My dear, my dear, what I am offering you is not charity, not at all. It's a gift. It would please me if you took this pan as a gift from me. I make these pans myself. Each one is personal. Each one is individual, just like my customers. And I seek out the people who need them, and I match them up with one of my creations."

Constance just stared at him.

"Don't you see? This is what I *do.*"

"Then I must give you something in return," she said, but he halted her with an upraised palm.

"The pan will exact its own price, missy," he said. "The better the pan, the higher the price. This one here," he pointed to the loaf pan she held, "is a fine pan, but it won't be too expensive. You'll lose a lamb, perhaps, or maybe your husband won't get that deer he's hunting. I have some that are more expensive, but that one you've got there . . . it's a good choice."

Constance looked over at the sheep, peacefully grazing, and she felt a chill. She pulled the sweater tighter around her shoulders. She wasn't sure she understood the man at all. What an odd little man.

She dipped him another cup of water and watched while he drank it.

"Good luck to you, missy," he said, and started off down the way he'd come up, his pans bonging in a musical rhythm that was very pleasant to the ear.

She took the pan into the house, feeling its energy, feeling the wonderful, comforting weight of it, and she wanted to bake more bread. Immediately.

But she hung the pan on the wall, and vowed that she wouldn't touch it again until it was paid for. She wasn't sure she quite believed the odd little vendor, but then again . . . she wasn't so sure she should have taken the pan without knowing its exact price, either. She'd keep the whole thing from Jim, that was for sure.

The sky clouded over, and a cold wind blew through the cracks of the cabin. Constance donned a heavy sweater and went outside to bring in her wool and spinning wheel, and that's when she saw it, the ladle. The cracked ladle. The pan man had left it on the step. She grabbed it on her way into the house, and after storing the wool and stashing the wheel, she lit a lantern in the sudden dusk and inspected it.

It still made her feel wonderful when she held it. It was like holding something precious, yet invincible. She felt safe with it in the house. The fears of being alone fled.

And there was a crack. A tiny hairline crack from the handle down the cup.

Constance dipped it into the water. It held. It dripped a little bit, maybe, but it was a serviceable utensil.

And the price could not be high at all. Something very, very small. A stubbed toe, perhaps, if there even was a price. Maybe he had thrown it away, and there would be no price.

At any rate, she was happy to have it, and hung it on the wall next to the loaf pan.

She stood back. She had begun a collection of cast-iron cookware. Somehow, the cabin finally felt like home.

Jim came home without a deer. Constance tried to be glum about it in front of him, but baked a loaf of nutty wheat bread in her new pan to celebrate. The bread was cooked to perfection, evenly browned and wonderful. Constance thought it tasted better than her other bread, and even Jim commented on it.

And being a busy man, he never asked her about the new loaf pan or the ladle.

But the ladle bothered Constance. It just hung on the wall,

she swore she would not use it until it had been paid for. She tried to believe that it was free, but her father had always taught her that nothing in life was free; everything must be paid for, so on its nail it hung, until she was certain that it was hers to keep.

A thousand times she looked at it, and a thousand times she resisted the impulse to touch it, to hold it, to run her hands over it. It was so *gentle,* it was somehow comforting. She wanted to ladle a hearty stew with it, stew made with her own garden vegetables, and the meat they either raised or hunted themselves. But she left it hanging on the nail.

Spring brought its own set of chores, and with summer came other problems. But the nights were mild and romantic, and as summer waned, Constance knew a growing in her belly.

The cabin felt different after that. Jim was as excited and as thoughtful of her well-being as she was. He began to whittle toys of a long summer evening. He talked to her tummy as if it was already a person, and the way it wiggled around inside, she guessed it really was a real person. How odd for Jim to know it before she did.

They went to town and stayed over until Sunday to go to church, and met two ladies who said they'd be pleased to come attend the birth. When her time came, Jim wouldn't have to ride far to fetch some help. They went to that church every Sunday as long as Constance was able, and when she felt she shouldn't ride anymore, those women came up to visit with her and make sure everything was progressing right. Sometimes they would bring her a special tea, sometimes a jar of preserves.

But as the winter set in and the snow began to drift, Constance worried.

"I can do it, Constance," Jim kept reassuring her, and as her ninth month waned, the strange February warmth spread again across the Cascades, the snow melted, and one springlike afternoon, Constance had Jim mount up and ride for the midwives.

She swept the cabin and put on a pot of stew. These things take time, she'd heard, and she sat down every time the baby pulled on her.

By the time Jim returned with the ladies, the stew was bubbling happily and the baby was close.

"Heat some water," someone told Jim, and it kept him busy,

while the other hung a sheet from the ceiling to make a little private room for Constance and the baby.

Little Jimmy came into the world with a sploosh and a cry, and Constance reached down and picked up her beautiful, beautiful son. She opened her dress and let him nurse, while the ladies fussed over her bedding and the swaddling. Holding him gave her such a calm feeling, it was like holding something precious and invincible.

When everything had settled down, and the baby had fallen asleep, Constance was starving. She had Jim take down the curtain partition. "Offer the ladies some stew, Jim," she said.

He got the bowls down from the shelf.

She looked down at her son, at the hairline crack that ran through the side of his nose to his lip, parting it all the way through his tender little gums.

"You can use that ladle," Constance said. "It's paid for."

Seasoned Enthusiast

Everyone shuffled away from the center of the old wooden floor, and eventually the room became as silent as death.

The basket sat calmly in the middle of the circle. No one had seen it arrive; it was as if it had always been there.

Pulses began the contagious rise to certain frenzy; the room filled with the heat and sweat of a hundred souls anticipating. The circle grew no larger. The boys ringing the inner edge felt their skin tickle, holding the circle open, gauging each other, wanting to hold it perfectly, not to crowd in, so that if they were blessed by her touch it would be absolutely accidental and not of their own doing. Not too large, the circle. Not too small. Tradition told them the exact size.

Sweat beaded and trickled.

People began to pant. Nothing else stirred the air.

Silence reigned, and within, the collective heartbeat thundered.

The basket shifted, and all eyes centered on it.

Then, like a field of wheat parting before the breeze, the crowd moved with barely a rustling sigh, and she emerged to stand in the center of the circle. Sweat darkened the edges of her tawny leather bra and breechcloth, and wisps of bronze hair stuck to her temples.

She waited until the crowd settled—until they had inspected her at rest, noting each involuntary twitch of calf muscle, each facial tic. Sweat from her lower belly deepened the color of the stained suede as she waited, hollowed eyes closed. When they murmured their satisfaction that her withdrawal was genuine, they quieted, and with barely a heroic grimace, she spread her muscled arms and took one dramatic step.

The crowd sighed.

The basket trembled.

The dance began.

Lillian paced the length of her small apartment, taking short, severe drags from her cigarette and flicking ashes nervously as she walked. I've waited long enough, she chanted in time to her steps. I've waited long enough.

The anger had begun early; even before dawn chased the stale dusk of a restless night, she'd lain awake. Angry.

Unable to concentrate, she'd left the office at noon.

And the anger had built.

She'd tried watching the soaps, but every man on the screen had Ronald's face. She tried listening to the radio, but every song was a love song they'd once listened to together. She flipped through a stack of magazines, but everything delicious, everything sensuous, everything moving, reminded her of the perfect love they had once shared.

And then he'd deserted her.

Deserted her!

And married someone else.

Stifling suddenly, Lillian tore at her clothes, pulling them off, desperate for freedom, until she stood naked in the middle of her living room. She walked to the window and pulled the draperies shut. Darkness. Quiet solitude. Time to think. Time to plan. She put the cigarette out in the green ashtray, then remembered that she and Ronald had bought that green ashtray at a garage sale one carefree Saturday morning. She scooped it up and threw it into the garbage, and put a newspaper over it, so she wouldn't have to look at it—ever again.

She lit another cigarette and used the cold dregs in her dirty coffee cup as an ashtray. She paced another length of the short apartment, flicking her ashes.

She thought of all the times she'd seen him lately, walking, laughing, running, working out. He looked happy. He looked healthy and clean and . . . and . . . in love.

How dare he be happy.

How *dare* he.

She stopped abruptly, while the tiniest of thoughts scampered across her mind.

Maybe he isn't.

She sat down, crossed her long, thin legs and began kicking her foot and tapping her thumbnail on the filter of the cigarette, while the ash burned down and fell on the rug.

Of course he was happy. He had everything. He had money, he had health, he had . . . her, that other woman, his new—

Wife.

How *dare* he.

She jumped up again and began to pace, then tried to kick the clothes out of her path. They didn't fly out of her way exactly as she wanted, and she began viciously kicking at them. A toe snagged in a buttonhole and stuck there, and she kicked at it and kicked at it furiously, then stood on one edge of the blouse and kicked and pulled until either it tore or she ripped her toe off.

Instead, she lost her balance and fell back on the couch, a cry welling up and out, her blouse absurdly attached to her toe, and for a brief moment, she wondered how that reservoir of hurt could possibly be so deep.

She cried in shallow self-pity for a short moment, then the anger returned.

She was angry because he'd abandoned her. He had left her—thrown her away like a sack of dirt on the side of the road for the whole world to see.

Now, *everyone*—everyone *she* had ever known, everyone *they* had ever known—absolutely *everyone* knew she was not worthy.

She went to the refrigerator and whipped the door open. She pulled a loaf of white bread out and and ripped the plastic.

Standing in front of the open refrigerator, feeling the chill on her naked body, she stuffed wadded handfuls of Wonder bread into her mouth and swallowed it, her eyes looking at the carton of milk, her brain seeing Ronald's happiness instead.

The dancer took long strides around the circle. Each person in the audience could now smell her as her bare feet squeaked on the worn wooden floor. Long thighs, beautiful, perfect, were the focus of every eye. With each kick as the dance began to heat, every person looked for the peek of a hair, or the evidence of a mole, a mark, a blemish.

They inspected her closely, and found nothing but smooth tawny skin moving over taut, working muscle, tight triangles of tanned leather, curly-ended strands of golden hair sticking to her neck, her back.

She began to twirl around the floor, and as she did, her face changed from gaunt and haunted, to alive and thriving.

Everyone watched, hoping to catch her glance at the basket, but she never did. She ignored it so completely that the crowd began to move in restless fascination. They wanted her to see it, wanted her to be tempted, wanted her to want it.

Musk steamed.

They knew she wanted it. They knew she needed it. Her ability to ignore it was monstrous. She would not last much longer without that basket, and her will power hurt them as her muscles contracted and she slid to the floor, pain rearranging her face, the meat of her body writhing, all of it a horrible part of the dance, and still she ignored the basket.

She left stains of sweat where her flesh touched the floor, and bits of dust stuck to the ends of her hair as she continued her dance with death, sweeping around the circle, on hands and knees and then her back, crawling, stretching, begging, but touching no one, looking not once at the basket which shifted whenever she neared.

Lillian felt something cold run down her foot and looked at the tomato seed that slid between her toes.

A half-eaten tomato in her hand was dripping onto her foot. Her other hand held a partially eaten carrot, still dirt-encrusted.

With a little gasp and scream, she threw them both into the sink, then surveyed the damage.

Empty boxes, packages and cartons littered the floor around her feet. She'd eaten her way through most of the contents of the refrigerator, including two weeks' worth of leftovers.

A little moan came up and out, and she clapped her hand over her mouth just in time and raced to the bathroom. All of it came up, in a series of gushes and heaves, and when it was over, Lillian wiped the tears from her eyes with a square of toilet tissue and tried to catch her breath.

The anger surged back at her.

He owes me, she thought, then flushed the toilet and went to stand in front of the mirror. Her face was pale, her eyelids red. Her chin was dusted with powdered sugar from eating stale donuts. She splashed cold water on her face, then dried it, rubbing hard, bringing up the pink.

He owes me, and I'm not going to take this abuse any longer.

She rinsed her mouth and went back to the living room. She kicked the refrigerator closed, then threw on the wrinkled, trodden clothes that were still in a pile on the living room floor. She grabbed her keys and went out.

Into the night.

Teeth clenched, fueled by fury, she drove hunched over the steering wheel, staring with malevolence through the windshield. She drove fast, honking at assholes, running red lights, making illegal left-hand turns, going one block the wrong way on a one-way street.

She killed the headlights two blocks from Ronald's house, and snuck down the street, barely idling.

She stopped across the street from his house and turned off the ignition.

They were home.

Her courage fled.

He owes me, she said to herself, but it didn't work.

Then, two lights went out on the lower floor and the garage door opened. Ronald's car started up, then backed out of the garage, and the automatic door closed again. Lillian could see both Ronald and his wife in the front seat. He backed out into the street, backed his car parallel to her own—he had only to turn his head and he would see her staring back at him. He looked wonderful. He looked fresh and showered and groomed and clean and ready for a date.

Lillian remembered when he used to look like that at home, when they used to be at home together.

Then he put his car in gear and drove away, smiling at something clever his wife had just said.

His wife.

He owes me, she thought, and her courage returned as Ronald's headlights flashed around the corner.

She stepped out of her car.

The circle of floor gleamed as if it, too, were perspiring. The dancer's hunger began to shame the audience, until she gracefully wrapped her feet around to the front of her, and with a burst of muscled integrity, she stood—and regarded the basket.

Muscles in her calves, thighs, back and upper arms all twitched. Her hands trembled as she held them out, seemingly in benediction, and those who could see her face wondered at the vision of intensity.

Slowly, she circled the basket.

The audience pressed in.

In the flush of her exertion, the scars showed up white; little pairs of scar dots ran the length of her neck, all across her chest, on both shoulders and down both arms. Her ragged breathing swelled small breasts up over the top of her costume, and two pairs of white dots on her left breast flashed briefly in the space of a breath.

Eyes devoured her in her deprived, sweaty glory. Fantasies ran rampant. Her entire body was memorized by those who would use that memory for years to come.

Then, with no warning, a mighty kick came and the basket top flew to one of the boys ringing the circle. He caught it with a gasp, and souls envied his blessing. Then, as his eyes grew wide at the sight in the center of the circle, the audience followed his attention to the black river that was leaking out of the overturned basket.

The snake and the dancer regarded each other as it began to coil and she began to circle it.

* * *

"He used me up," Lillian breathed to herself as she walked up the driveway. "He used up my best years. Six years I devoted to him, and he used me up."

The front door would be locked, but the back door would be open. That was one of Ronald's odd little phobias. He was terrified of being locked out of his own home. Terrified of the embarrassment. He'd rather be ripped off than to be locked out.

That was one of the quirks Lillian had always loved about Ronald, and then made fun of, and then hated, and now she grinned into the night and knew that his weakness was about to pay off.

She crossed the lawn and crashed through the hedge.

The back yard was huge, expansive, and the tiled patio had just the right amount of expensive furniture and decor.

We never lived in a place like this, Lillian thought. It took him every one of those six years to be able to make this kind of money, she thought, and went to the sliding glass doors.

They were locked.

She pulled and pulled, then pounded her fist on the glass in frustration and hate.

She paced the length of the patio. How could he lock the back door?

And then she knew. He didn't lock it, his new wife did. That meant that there was a key nearby. Lillian began to search. He would hide it in a convenient place, because he would check it every time he went out. Checking for it would be the last thing he'd do before leaving, so it would have to be hidden in a place he could check easily, without getting his hands dirty.

She looked under the mat, under the potted plants. She checked the doorframe and the drawers of the freestanding bar.

A gallon jug of scotch caught her attention. I could use a drink, she thought, and picked one of the sparkling clean glasses from the shelf and set it on the bar.

"You didn't set the ice out, Ronald," she said. "Very inconsiderate."

She picked up the bottle of scotch and poured the glass half full, then screwed the top back on. She ducked under the bar to replace it, when she saw the glint.

The key. Hidden under the scotch.

Of course. Ronald would have had a drink before going out.

She picked it up and felt its power flow through her. She gulped half of the liquor, then, drink in hand, went to the sliding glass door and fit the key in the lock, turned it and opened the door.

Gotcha, she thought, and took another swallow.

The booze warmed her belly and began to spread its warmth throughout her. She went back and filled her glass again, then parted the draperies and stepped into Ronald's dining room.

The living room was unevenly lighted. Stray rays seeped in from a dim kitchen light and a soft lamp in the den. The streetlight out in front filtered patterns on the carpeting through flimsy picture-window lace. The effect was quite dramatic: the living room and dining room looked like a picture in some photography magazine.

Her first impulse was to back out, lock the door, cover her tracks and slink back to her dark little apartment where she belonged.

Her second impulse was to trash the place.

She walked through the living room, trailing her fingertips along the back of the suede couch, turning on the lights and inspecting the artwork on the walls, pirouetting in the vastness of the white-carpeted empire, drinking down Ronald's scotch.

She walked through the tiled kitchen and the bookshelf-lined den with its leather and oak. She peered into the well-appointed bath with its color-coordinated towels and giant whirlpool tub, and walked into the master suite.

On the vanity, with the most beautiful of cut-glass bottles and jars, was a picture of them.

Ronald and his bride, cutting their wedding cake.

He was smiling at his wife with love in his eyes.

The way he used to smile at Lillian.

Her eyes left the beautiful picture and fixed on the horror in the mirror. She looked at her disheveled clothes, tasted the sour vomit in her mouth, touched her ratty hair.

Panic suddenly wrenched her gut as a momentary fragment of sanity cut through.

What the hell am I doing here?

Her knees buckled and she sat on the corner of the bed, still fascinated by her reflection. She watched herself sip the drink. I just *look* out of place, she thought, and steadying herself as she went, sat at the vanity and began to brush at her hair with the antique silver-handled brush.

The crowd began to sway to the rhythm of their own internal music as the woman and the snake played out their well-rehearsed scene.

The chant welled up from deep inside them, something primordial, no words, no meaning, except to tell the performers that the tide had turned—it was the crowd now which craved the conclusion. The performers had done justice to the paltry amount of money each voyeur had paid for the show, and now the act had gone beyond entertainment into something intensely—evil.

The woman slithered on her belly toward the snake, and the snake crawled onto her back. Then she began to dance again, at first on the floor, then upright, whirling, and the snake wound itself around her arms, her legs, her torso, their opposite movements working together in a sublimely exotic illustration of illicit greed.

Her movements became jerky as she gradually lost muscular control, and the snake reared its head back, far away from her body, and looked at her face; two lovers who had danced to the tune of death for a lifetime entwined—the snake gauged the woman's desperation, and still it withheld the drug that would save her.

The crowd began to moan as they realized she was dying for the money they had paid.

And her dancing became writhing, and she began to choke.

The hand that held a half-full glass of scotch began to tremble and amber liquid tumbled over the top and dripped onto the white plush carpet. She set the drink on the mirror-topped vanity and watched the booze sheet down the outside of the glass and puddle at the bottom. Everywhere in this house is evidence of health, Lillian thought, and I am an invading disease.

I owe him some sickness. I owe him some of what he left me with. I could slash my wrists and bleed all over this—this *white!*

She stood and began to dance around the room, shaking her hands, spraying imaginary blood on the walls, the pictures, across the bed in sweeping patterns, across the bureau—

Ronald's bureau.

Lillian ran to it, pulled open the top drawer. The scent of his cologne was as familiar to her as the scent of her own apartment. She breathed it in deeply, then began to root around.

In the back, in the left-hand corner behind his underwear, she found it. His jewelry case. He always kept it in the same place. Slowly, she brought it out and rubbed her fingertips over the lizard-skin top.

Afraid to open it, she clasped the box to her chest and returned to her seat on the corner of the bed. She held the cool black box up to her cheek and watched herself in the mirror as she rocked back and forth.

The dancer convulsed, twice, and the crowd watched in horror as the snake left her and slithered in esses back toward the basket. The dancer's eyes rolled back into her head, showing yellowed whites. The crowd felt its shame: it had paid her to do this, it had thrilled at her agony, it would speak about this night with lust in its heart, forever.

The expense, the crowd now knew, was too great.

The crowd didn't want the dancer to die.

Not on their shame.

The circle began to close in. In spite of the boys whose job it was to keep the circle open, the crowd, in its anger, crowded close.

Someone kicked the basket.

The snake coiled—wary, defensive.

The dancer shuddered, and as she did, one arm flopped.

The snake lunged, striking twice within the bat of an eyelash, and four drops of blood appeared on the inside of her forearm.

The crowd sighed and stepped back.

One of the boys replaced the basket and the snake crawled into it. Someone else threw him the top and he put it on. Tight.

Then they all looked at the dancer again.

* * *

Lillian took a deep breath and opened the box, loving the expensive sound it made when it snapped open.

There it was. The ring she had given him was carefully tucked away in his grandfather's lizard-skin jewelry case, right along with all his special treasures, all his dreams: his father's gold cuff links, the blue ringed rock he'd found on his first hunting trip, his grandmother's diamond earrings.

Lillian had forgotten about the earrings. Ronald was saving them to give to his daughter on her wedding day.

His daughter.

Her daughter.

Their daughter.

He would look so handsome, hair graying, all dressed up in a tuxedo, walking their grown-up baby girl down the aisle. The familiar fantasy came up so easily for Lillian. They had no daughter, of course, but the dream had not died at Ronald's end either—at least he had not given the earrings to his *wife*— they were still in his jewelry case.

Right alongside the ring she'd given him.

All her anger slipped away as a bittersweet tear slipped off her eyelash and down one cheek.

"Poor boy," she said.

Gently, she closed the case filled with Ronald's special dreams and kissed it, then replaced it under his socks in the back of his bureau drawer.

He still loved her; she felt guilty that she had ever doubted him. He loved her, and though that love might still be lodged in his unconscious mind, true love would win out eventually.

She left the scotch in its little pool on the glass-topped vanity, she left the imaginary blood strewn about the bedroom, she left the expensive clothes in the closets and the tidiness of the house undisturbed.

She slipped out the back door and locked it, replaced the key under the bottle of scotch, got in her car and drove away.

She would go home and wait for him.

Patiently.

* * *

The dancer's cramped muscles relaxed, and as the crowd looked on, the mysterious beauty that had been there at the beginning of the dance flowed back into the empty body. They watched as the poison which would ultimately destroy her began to revive her, and they watched as the little points of scars on her neck and chest turned from white to cherry red in the venom flush.

She lay quietly on the floor as the crowd trickled out the door, uncomfortable with their feelings. The boys who ringed the inner circle were the last to go. Within the space of the dance, each had fallen in love with her, and wished to save her, but as they watched the power of the poison return life to her exquisite body, they knew she could never be saved, except by her own destruction.

They had loved her, and that disgusted them.

They left. Affected.

· S pice

Clara wrapped her flannel-clad arms around her pudgy knees and then picked lint off the blanket as she listened to Jamison being sick in the bathroom. She felt a little tickle of guilt that she had made him sick enough to vomit—after all, it was just a little joke, and anyway he didn't have to eat it, and he certainly didn't have to eat all of it. He must have a terribly tender tummy, she thought as she heard him retch. Terribly tender tummy, she repeated again and giggled into the sleeve of her nightie.

It had been the stroganoff that had inspired her. Stroganoff was one of Jamison's favorites, and as she stirred in the sour cream, and watched the sauce turn from brown to a creamy tan, she had a wonderfully funny idea, and without much more thought, she had the white pepper down from the spice rack and had emptied almost half a jar into Jamison's huge portion.

He ate it. All of it. He complained after the first bite that it was bitter and spicy, and as Clara calmly ate bite after bite of her unspoiled portion, his face got redder and his resolve firmer, and he drank three glasses of iced water and ate the whole plateful. Clara was proud of her self-control at the table.

The toilet flushed, the water ran in the sink, then the bathroom door opened and Jamison, huge in his striped pajamas, loomed in the doorway.

"I told you that food was rotten," he said, then turned off the bathroom light. "Like to puke my guts out."

Clara reached over and flipped down the covers on his side of the bed. "You just have a terribly tender tummy, honey."

"It's tender now, I'll tell ya. Time to hire a cook." He sat down heavily on the bed, then swung his feet under the covers. "Christ," he said as he pulled the sheet and blanket up to his chin, carefully turning the sheet out so the blanket wouldn't touch his skin, "if you can't cook anymore, I'll be damned if I can think of a use for you." Having thus spoken with distressing calmness, he turned his back to her and stuffed his fists up under his pillow.

Clara lay back down, a little smile on the corner of her lips. If only Jamison had a sense of humor, she thought, she could tell him about her little jokes. But he didn't, she sighed, and she had known that when she married him.

A mosquito buzzed about her head as Clara dusted the den. Try as she might, both clapping her hands or slapping at it with her dusting cloth, the mosquito eluded her and continued to whine disconcertingly in her ear. It failed to follow her as she walked down the hall and into the utility room for the little bottle of insect repellent. One drop on each earlobe, each wrist and each ankle usually kept the mosquitos at a fair distance.

But what about poor Jamison? What would happen when he came home and found a mosquito in his den? Would he be able to kill it with a slap of his meaty hands? Would he know where to find the insect repellent? Would he know that a drop on each earlobe would keep them at bay, or at least away from his ears so he wouldn't have to listen to their infernal buzzing?

That familiar feeling of brazen naughtiness began to creep over her again. Jamison would hate to deal with the mosquito. He would just hate it. She smiled to herself as she dabbed the insect repellent on her appointed parts and decided that a good wife would take care of such an inconvenience for her husband.

She took the bottle back into the den with her and sat in

Jamison's big, loose desk chair. She pulled the felt-bottomed cherrywood pipe rack silently across the desk, and one by one, pulled each pipe from its seat and dropped two drops of the clear liquid into its bowl.

She hummed as she worked, swirling the liquid around the bottom of each pipe bowl until it soaked into the thick black carbon crust. When she finished, she snapped the little red cap back on the spout and pushed the pipe rack back to its accustomed spot in the corner of the desk. Jamison will be so pleased, she thought. Not a mosquito will bite him, for the repellent will be coming out through his pores. He will be grateful without knowing it, she thought, and began to giggle. "I hope he won't find his tobacco too spicy," she said aloud, then squeaked back in the chair, laughing, her feet leaving the floor, and for a second she lost her balance and almost went over backwards. With a surge, she righted herself, and found that even funnier yet. She laughed until the tears ran down her cheeks, until all her muscles were weak and useless. And then, as the spasms of humor began to slow down, she looked again at the pipe rack and the little white bottle with its tiny red cap and said out loud, "Oh, if only Jamison had a sense of humor." And she gave out with the last whimpers of laughter, then wiped her eyes and her cheeks, picked up the bottle and returned it to its place in the pantry.

If only Jamison had a sense of humor, she thought. But he didn't, and she had known that when she married him. Neither had Harris, and they'd had ten good years together before he died.

Jamison came home late that night, meanness on his face and a full load of booze in his bloated belly. Clara followed him into the den and took up her observation position in a straight-backed chair, carefully out of his reach and alert to anything he might throw at her. Sometimes she found him terribly unpredictable. He settled his bulk into the cheap vinyl chair and glared at her.

Let the games begin, she thought, and just a little guilt tickled up a smile at the corners of her mouth.

"Would you like some dinner?"

"I ate already."

"I made pork chops. With roasted potatoes and gravy. I kept your dinner warm in the oven. I could fetch it for you right now if you like."

"I *said,* I ate already. I don't want any of your stupid food."

"Oh. Okay."

"Bring me a drink," he said as he reached for the pipe rack.

"Yes, dear." Clara smiled sweetly and surreptitiously brushed at an imaginary mosquito as she went out of the room.

In the morning, when Clara went downstairs, Jamison was dead in his chair, the bottle of scotch empty, four of his seven pipes on the table in front of him, one still in his hand in his lap. Apparently, he just couldn't get them to taste right, she thought. Poor Jamison. She smoothed his hair, tidied the pipe rack, returned it to its customary position, and called the doctor.

"I must say I'm not surprised, Clara. He ate too much, drank too much, smoked too much, didn't exercise . . . well, I'm sure I don't need to tell you. Classic conditions for a heart attack. I'll send someone right over. Are you okay?"

"Yes, yes, I'm fine. I knew it was inevitable."

"Don't you worry, now, I'll send someone over for him."

Clara thanked him, then ran upstairs to dress and put on a fresh face for her visitors.

She pulled off her nightie and surveyed herself in the full-length mirror. Have to watch that sweet tooth, she thought, at least until she found a new husband. Maybe she'd find someone this time with a sense of humor.

"The plural of mouse is mice," she hummed to herself as she stroked a little blush into her cheeks, "and the plural of spouse is spice."

"Mrs. Jamison?" A pleasant-looking young man stood at the front door. He was dressed in a dark pinstripe suit, and his hair was slicked down tight against his head.

"Yes?"

"I'm Patrick Wilson, Hedemann's Mortuary." He handed

her his business card. "I understand your husband passed away last night."

"Yes, please come in. Would you care for some coffee?"

He seemed taken aback at her suggestion, and Clara liked that. Here's a man with no sense of humor at all, she thought, and she found him most attractive. She welcomed that little naughtiness that flirted around her attitude.

"Well, I should take a look at your husband first, ma'am, and by then, if my assistant hasn't arrived, well, then, I guess, yes, I'd welcome a cup."

She led the way to the den. One look at Jamison's blue-gray face sufficed.

"Oh, yes," Mr. Wilson said with a blush. He seemed embarrassed to be viewing her dead husband in front of her. He checked his watch. "Well, my assistant should be along presently."

"Fine," she said, and led him into the kitchen. He sat at the table, in Jamison's chair, while she poured two cups and took two cinnamon rolls from the bread box. She set the table in an exacting way, while the young man fidgeted in discomfort. Clara wished she were a few years younger, a few pounds lighter. Mr. Wilson was a very attractive man—and he would be easy to keep off balance.

"You're taking this quite well," he finally said.

"I've been expecting it, actually." She sipped the steaming liquid and took a dainty bite of her sweet roll. "Jamison— Robert, that is—was a man of excesses, as you can readily see."

"Yes." He took the other roll and tasted it, smiling his gratitude at her.

"My first husband died of *his* excesses as well."

"Oh? I'm sorry."

She waved his platitude aside. "Don't be sorry for me. They chose their fates."

"How did your first husband die?"

"Harris? Walter Harris, his name was. A nice person. A very nice person, but just a little greedy. He was an accountant. Apparently, he entered into a not-so-legal business deal that promised to pay well, and the deal went sour. His business associates had reason to believe he cheated them, but he maintained to me—after he told me the story—that he had been framed by a person or persons unknown." She sipped her coffee to suppress her naughty little giggle, and looked at her guest over the rim of her coffee cup. "The police found his body in the river."

"Good God!"

She smiled openly at his shocked face. This was fun. "Just like Jamison, though, I could see it coming. I just love ironies, don't you? I find it so ironic how people will die for their excesses." Her cinnamon roll began to unwind as she took another bite, and with a ladylike forefinger, pushed a bit too much into her mouth.

"Well, Mrs. Jamison"—he smiled at her as she chewed— "you're not young, but you're still a beautiful woman . . . vibrant, intelligent, widowed twice." She warmed at his praise. "I say you *must* have murdered them both."

Clara gasped, and a doughy wad of cinnamon roll lodged firmly in her windpipe.

"Accessory at least," he teased, flirting, smiling, then sipped his coffee.

Her eyes were open wide as she sat still, unable to breathe, unable to utter a sound. She just sat there, as still as a rabbit frozen in the path of an oncoming car.

By the time he realized she had a problem, she was writhing on the kitchen floor, choking, sputtering, her eyes bulging, little noises coming from her desperate throat, and he stood in confusion and moved the chairs out of the way of her thrashing.

In a very few moments, quicker than he could have imagined, her face turned from red to blue, her eyes rolled up into her head and she lay, quite dead, on the linoleum tile.

"My goodness, Mrs. Jamison," he said as he looked down on her body. "It was just a little joke." He reached down and touched her cheek with a finger. "I could have *sworn* you had a sense of humor."

He stood up again and looked at the remnants of sweet roll he still held in his fingers. "Never enough cinnamon," he said, and threw it back onto the plate, then went to wait at the front door for his assistant to arrive with the hearse.

• Music Ascending

I stood at the top of the crumbling steps, gagging in the foul breath of the undercity as its stench rose to dance with the early-morning street fog. Within moments, I would go below to capture one last sound, and I dwelt on this morning's strumming to quell the fear, to settle the bile, as I thought of going down there, down those slimy stone stairs into the pit, into the filth.

I cleared my mind of its fears and took a minute to think of the raw, melodic strains of the packets as they were this morning when I strummed them. I strummed them every morning for sustenance.

It was also my custom to run my thumb along the tops of the packets after each success to hear the new addition, the new harmony in their song, and each time, the sound has become clearer but still incomplete—and so I came for the final sound, came to stand at the top of the stairs. The stairs of the damned.

I am a designer of experiences. Clients seek me out to enrich their lives; they contract for a particular sensation. By use of higher mathematics and the nature of substance vibration, I collect the ingredients—sounds—which, if mixed correctly, will trigger chemicals in the human body and provide my clients with the desired event.

I have given the experience of a happy childhood to those deprived. I have given barren women babies to nurse. I have given grandchildren to young, terminally ill fathers, and I have given sight to those who are blind.

Most requests are basic, simple, and to the point. And so it seemed with this one, at first.

He had seemed such a harmless gent. This commission had come so innocently, seemingly spontaneously, on the wings of a wish during a Sunday after-church stroll through the park. He wished out loud, he saw his mortality and wished for more time. Time for what, I asked. For a life richer in experience, he replied, and when I confessed my livelihood, he challenged me—"Are you for hire, then?"

"I've retired."

"So young?"

"Young and bored. People want simple, ordinary experiences, and I'm tired of those. On my last commission, however, I published an entire circus—complete with elephants, calliope and smell of roasted peanuts, mind you—within the brain of a blind deaf-mute child. Ha!" I clapped my gloved hands together, recalling the experience. "A crowning glory to my career. After such an achievement, I could never go back to marketing the mundane."

We walked along in silence. The man was a stranger to me, a mild and gentle person, well dressed, with soft smile and manner, and I was restless in my retirement and eager for a fresh ear.

"Have you ever a bad experience? Have you ever erred, or harmed someone?"

"Harmed? No. Erred? Only in judgment," I replied. "For a short while I gave the experience of adulthood to adolescents, but then I decided that was unwise. From that point on, I refrained from administering any experience that might frighten, disappoint or depress. Bad PR, you know."

He chuckled in agreement. "How does this system of yours work?"

"Basic stuff. I design the experience, paying particular attention to detail. That's my trademark: exhaustive detail. Then with my gift of understanding substance vibrations and my propensity for mathematics, I identify the ingredients, the sounds. When the desk work is done, I search out and capture the sounds, storing them in papers. I'm very particular about each phase of my work, but the collecting is most important. One must resist the impulse to substitute an inferior sound for the sake of convenience, or expedience. The collecting can take an enormous amount of time, if it is done properly.

"After the collecting is complete comes the most crucial step, and the test of my true genius, if I may say so. I mix the sounds, delicately blending with a fine ear and a practiced hand. Then I administer the distillation, which stimulates the client's brain chemicals, and they sally forth to create the hallucination. And I sit back and observe."

"Have you ever administered one to yourself?"

"Never."

"Where do you find these *sounds*?"

"Everywhere!" I stopped, and listened, and after an extra step, he stopped too, and we both listened.

"Once I gave a bedridden old woman a bareback horse ride through the woods," I whispered.

"Yes?" I saw the intrigue on his face.

"I collected all the required sounds—every ingredient—from a farmer's market and a bakery."

"But one has nothing to do with the other!"

I smiled and began walking again.

"I wish to hire you."

"I'm sorry."

"Please. I promise this commission will challenge your creativity."

Our stroll had been pleasant, but I had had enough. "I must go now."

He named an impossible amount of money, impressive enough that it offered me pause. He interpreted the pause as weakness in my resolve and doubled the amount. I turned slowly to face him.

He seized my shoulders and fired intensity into my eyes. "I wish to experience death," he said, his gloved grip conveying the seriousness of his intent. "Experience death and live to tell of it. I will pay you whatever amount you want, if you think you can accomplish it." He pressed cash and a business card into my hand.

I started to refuse, but recognized the obsession in the man and anticipated his mindless persistence, so I took his card and departed, anticipating a few hours of research—a week, maximum—before I could, with good conscience, return his money with a regretful report. Instead, by the time I reached my doorstep, I had a glimmer of an idea as to how to proceed. That very night I worked through until sunrise—the first of many such nights.

The weeks flew by as I delved deeper into geology, astronomy, mythology. I sweat for months upon the design. Reference books cluttered my desk, my floor, the top of my refrigerator and my tables. I slept with crystals under my pillow to open my mind to new possibilities. I became completely caught up in the speculation of the myriad possibilities. I could feel my imagination stretch until it warped out of shape. When it became loose-fitting and easily maneuvered, I reveled in new-found freedom of conjecture. Boundaries were no longer identified. Indeed, such was the nature of the task that common boundaries no longer held true.

My entire life centered around this one task. It seemed that the premature experience of death must somehow be either readily available to the masses merely for the asking, or else it would be completely forbidden—yet I kept seeing progress in my design. Always, just at the edge of despair, my hope was nourished by a glimmer of progress, and the project was saved at the expense of everything normal in my life.

It was always just after those moments of encouragement that he would come to call, to assess my devotion to his commission. And he would gaze upon my desk, at my research notes, and he would look deeply into my eyes, and then depart, leaving a taint in the air.

This agony continued for years—years!—until one night I awoke and sat straight up in bed, throwing aside the book on spatial isomerism I had been reading until exhaustion had overtaken me, and I *knew* that the design was already complete.

I ran to my desk and brushed all debris from it, leaving only the musical score. I checked and rechecked my calculations. Hope rooted and began to sprout. By the time dawn etched its rude violins on my windowsill, I knew that the design was finished—I had completed it weeks before, but it was a solution so brilliant that it had almost passed me by. Even I was astonished at my own genius.

My energy reached massive proportions. I felt I could go for months without sleep—maybe I would never sleep again. Quickly, I began jotting down a list of ingredients, marveling at the symmetry, anxious to be finished with the paperwork and on with the collecting.

Eventually, I fetched hat and coat, list and score, and set out.

It was years again before I found myself at the edge—the edge of sanity, the edge of my own history. Only one ingredient had yet to be captured, and I stood at the lip of living hell, where below my feet had been cast the errors of evolution, where they have continued to exist and evolve along their own mutant designs.

One sound remained to be caught, and the stuff of it moved restlessly below my feet.

I stared down into the blackness, willing my feet to take the first step down, paper in hand and ready to catch the final sound, and I thought: of what use is the old man's cash if I must face a pit filled with the wretched excesses of an amoral humanity? What is the value of the experience of satisfaction in a job well done when the jaws of terror threaten to shred my psyche?

Yet the collecting begged for completion. The project was too important. Envelopes, precious envelopes in my hotel room contained the first whimper of a woman upon the birth of her third stillborn child. I had captured the thud of the fifth clod of dirt to fall upon the casket of a Satanist at a Christian funeral. I had the groan of an oak branch as it swung the body of a black teen. I had seen madness spit from a machine gun, and captured the sound of splintering bone. I held the final heartbeat of an abortionist and the death rattle of a drug addict.

But there was more. Beyond. I had reached into the future and into the past to fill the musical score. I had spent years extrapolating figures that led me to lie in wait to capture the pant of a rabbit whose blood will grow a deadly strain of bacteria in a petri dish. I had plucked from the air the black belch of a bus that will figure into the misinterpreted dream of an evangelist, whose political maneuvers will soon become clear. And I had sealed into my papers the stomach gurgle of a world terrorist at his first newborn suck.

If mixed in accurate proportions, all of this would delicately balance on a minute particle of tincture drawn from the sound of a virgin's lips as they brushed the pillow in smile on the eve of her wedding day.

And for a base tone, for the underlying heavy note upon which all else would rest, in order for my music to rise, I had yet to sink to the depths, descend into the fetid fields of filth below me.

My stomach churned, the trembling in my hand crinkled the delicate papers.

For what?

I stood ready, my sudden introspection daring to defy the clock. If I tarried too long, my opportunity would be lost, and all the years of work and preparation, the interminable waiting, not to mention the frustration of the design itself, would all be for naught.

But for what? For what have I worked this hard? Certainly not the money. The foolish old man who hired me could have easily paid ten times the amount—I had only to ask for it. No, it was not the money that carried me onward.

Was it to certify the genius of my design? No, my experience told me that my design was solid.

For what, then, I asked myself, as the optimum time drew nigh. My descent must begin or the opportunity would be forever lost.

I had become jealous of the experience I would create. I cared not to see the old man thrill at the result of my labor. He was a cowardly old man, selfish, wanting this experience only to better prepare himself in his few remaining years. He was a dastardly individual, Satan himself, I had come to believe, with his unfailing smile and soft words of encouragement, while I toiled night and day on his salvation. I had come to detest the senile old man.

If anyone deserved to die unprepared, it was he.

But this . . . this . . . this was the orchestration of a lifetime! When I completed my journey under the street, and had the final envelope vibrating in my pocket, when I returned to my hotel room to run my thumb across the tops of all the papers, raw collecting complete, I wanted to mix the experience for my own enjoyment. I was younger than the old man. I could mix the sensation stronger. I could take full advantage of the hallucination. The old man would need it weak, like his tea, like *him*.

I could make it last a miniature lifetime, and I would have what no man has ever had before.

It was far too important to waste on him. And besides, the Gods had given *me* the gift, had entrusted the design to *my* genius. My obligation was to *them,* not to *him.*

Dread surrounded me like a moist blanket. If I survived the depths here, if I obtained the final symphonic note, I would have to make a choice. If I did not survive, then I would compare my design with that of the Creator.

My body shifted forward; my shoes ground grit on the wet street. One step down, then another. I towered over the hole, fear grinding grit on my heart.

I would capture the final tone, and then decide.

My breath caught behind my breastbone. I had seen this place on paper, as numbers, and I had seen its result on a musical score, but the reality clogged my senses. I felt the denizens sliding about, shifting with anticipation, as they sensed my intrusion.

I descended carefully, fingertips of one hand barely grazing the mossy rock walls as I went down, one step at a time, knees trembling.

I reached my foot out—no more steps. I was at the bottom. They gathered around, pressing close, awaiting their treat, and my breath caked in my throat as I wished I had brought something to distract their attention. After a moment, I felt my aura of health radiating out from me, repelling their sickness.

To the left, as I remembered my computations. To the left.

The stench was an entity. I walked seventeen steps to the left of the stairs. The stench and its loathsome steaming cloaked me in darkness. I had to deliberately breathe.

Seventeen steps, turn to the right, face the canal and wait. I heard my heart, the blood pulsed in my veins, pressure built in my nose, in my head.

I am the maestro, I thought. The maestro in the maelstrom, and my art is enriched by my every experience.

The time drew nigh. I readied the papers. I felt the two approach.

They passed me so close I did not even need to reach out. Their twisted souls bumped together in obscurity, and I nipped the sound with my paper.

Anticlimactic. The collecting was complete, and I did not perish. My design was not forbidden after all.

Could I have erred?

No. The paper vibrated in my hand, and I felt it to be the one.

Carefully, I loaded it into my pocket, and my fingers touched the extra paper. Never before had I felt the necessity to bring an extra paper, but this time, this time . . .

I drew it out, and as I did, I heard a laugh, a wail, a wretched howl, a sound so devious that it threatened to release chemicals within my own brain—I felt on the verge of dementia. I felt—oh God—as if I had been expected here.

My delirium passed, and still within the laugh that reverberated in the humidity, I heard the song that sustained life below. I heard genius misrepresented and thrown to tragedy, come to power through sickening manipulation. I heard bitterness and revenge, and an acceptance that shamed me to my marrow.

My hand whipped out and caught the first echo of the horrible noise, and I held that sound of genius turned insane vibrating in my hand. I held it to my heart as the wretches moved on, and when I had calmed myself enough to walk, I retraced seventeen steps and mounted the stairs.

Fresh air! I bounced up the last few steps and ran from the entrance. I leaned against the alley wall, blood pulsing behind my eyes, hot breath rasping through my throat. The stench of the underworld arose like steam from my clothes. I breathed deeply and tried to calm my heart. I had descended, and survived. I had won.

I held the envelope, vibrating with wrongness, to my sweating face and it buzzed my cheek. It danced in my hand. It lived.

I could give this to the old man instead of the other. The effect would be . . .

Would be . . .

I could not be sure until I had redrawn the entire formula, but my experience told me that the basic result would be the hell of perpetual torment, not the reality of death.

Then how would the old man prepare for his eventual demise? If he thought death would bring raving insanity, how would he proceed with the rest of his life? A most entertaining thought. A most attractive experiment.

And I could mix the potion strong. And charge an extra premium.

But I would use the entire mixture, if I betrayed the old one's confidence like this, and the actual experience of death, the experience as first designed—would be forever lost.

The Gods allowed me the recipe, and I collected the ingredients. I have been chosen to administer the preview of death to the person of my choice, whether it be the old man or myself. I have been entrusted by the Gods with this grave and important task.

But like the collecting, the experience itself would surely be anticlimactic.

No. This idea was far superior.

I looked at the paper containing the echo of the laugh.

It lived.

It begged to be used.

I took the other paper from my pocket. It seemed so small in comparison. So important, yet so pale. Inconsequential, in the light of my new endeavor. I opened the seal and it escaped with barely a sigh.

Pleased with my decision, relieved of my burden, I pocketed my fortune and walked through the silent streets.

Anxious.

Eager.

A Living Legacy

Laura carefully opened the box and lifted out the old quilt. She kicked the box out of the way and unwrapped the tissue paper, then unrolled it on her bed. It was as familiar to her as her mother's face. Fresh tears stung her swollen eyes and she bunched up two fistfuls of quilt and buried her face in them.

It even smelled like her mother.

After a moment, she got up and blew her nose, rinsed off her face, then returned to the bedroom. She finished unfolding the quilt, which had been professionally boxed and shipped by someone who knew how to handle antiques and heirlooms.

The sharp little needle was still in it, midstitch.

With an ache in her soul the size of an ocean, Laura sat on the edge of the bed and quilted a few stitches. The needle glided through the perfectly matched patchwork material smoothly. She stopped for a moment and ran her hand over the fabric. She felt the lives of the women who had worked on it. The quilt top had been hand-pieced and worked by her great-grandmother, grandmother, and her mother; all three of them dead before it was finished. The last bit of quilting and the edging was up to Laura to do, and then this multigenerational thing of beauty—

this masterpiece—would be complete. She ran her hands over her bulging belly. She would complete the heirloom and give it to her daughter. The idea brought peace, a peace that replaced the pain.

"This fabric was the dress Great-grandmother—your great-great-grandmother—wore to her first day of school," Laura recited to her unborn baby. This quilt had fascinated her from her earliest recollections. Her mother and grandmother and great-grandmother all three helped her to learn which fabrics meant which things. "This fabric was a dress she wore to her first husband's funeral. This is the christening gown my grandmother—your great-grandmother—wore on the day she was christened, the day it was discovered she was deaf. These were taken from the shrouds of the twins when the measles hit. This was from the tie that Grandpa wore the day he lost his job. And here is some of the satin of his coffin lining. This was a piece of your second cousin Willie's prison shirt; this was a bit of hospital gown from Great-aunt Martha's stay up at State."

Laura stopped talking, and spread the quilt full out on her bed. It was a richly patterned kaleidoscope of colors, little squares and triangles of calicos, stripes, plaids, laces and linens. Hundreds of fabrics, thousands of fabrics, and Laura knew them all. She leaned up against the doorjamb and regarded the quilt as it lay atop the bedspread on her king-sized bed. It was too small; it had been made for Grandmother's twin bed, and Mother had added enough to cover her double bed, but it was still small. Yet it looked just fine. It looked wonderful.

She pulled it off the bed and hugged armfuls of it to her, smelling again the scent of the sisterhood, and she took it to the living room, where she sat in her rocking chair, little pillow carefully placed behind the aching small of her back. She rummaged around in her sewing basket and came up with white quilting thread, beeswax and a thimble, and she began to quilt.

As she did, she felt the sorrow of her mother's passing drain right through her fingertips into the old fabric. Laura's heart hurt for her new baby daughter, because she would never know her grandmother, the way Laura had known her mother, grandmother and even great-grandmother.

But the softness of the fabric and the needlework took away

all that sorrow. The sadness and misery leaked out of Laura and blended with the other sadnesses of the quilt and it swirled around in there, finding company, leaving Laura's soul to mend.

She expertly knotted the thread, clipped it, then rethreaded the needle and began again. Whenever there was a problem, Mother ran to the quilt, she remembered, and then she began to remember more. A quilt of many sorrows, Mother had called it. Some quilts were quilts of joy, she'd said, some were wedding quilts, some were friendship quilts, some were patriotic quilts. This was a quilt of sorrows, and nothing soothed the soul as much as working sorrow out through beautiful fabrics.

Laura stopped sewing and stroked the fabric. Little pieces of memory flickered across the screen of her mind like pieces of song across a radio dial.

Tommy . . .

Her hand stopped. She looked. There it was, a little triangle patch of her baby brother's pajamas. Tommy had been wearing them when they found him in the neighbor's pond. Next to that was a piece of the dress Laura had worn to the prom that night . . . that night she'd gotten pregnant. And sure enough, there was the lace blouse she'd worn to go to the clinic to have that problem taken care of.

Oh, Mother, how that must have hurt you.

There was more, but Laura went back to the quilting. The quilting soothed her soul. She would uncover the memories bit by bit, as the patchwork of her past matched up with the patchwork on her lap.

She worked and worked, taking tiny expert stitches as if by genetic memory. The more she worked, the more she understood the heart of womanhood. Night fell, and Laura rubbed her back and turned on the lamp and continued quilting, releasing all the bad feelings, all the harmful thoughts, all the fears and worries of the future into the serenity of the patchwork quilt.

She didn't even consider stopping when the knock came at the door. "Come in," she called without breaking rhythm, and the police came in, looking sad and official. Laura listened to their news of her husband as she tore a little square of fabric from the hem of her maternity dress and carefully pieced it into the quilt.

• The Jeweler's Thumb Is Turning Green

When Harold Hansen felt the lump in his wallet, he thought it was a bit of lint caught in the bottom corner of the pocket, and gave it no more thought than a bit of lint ought to have. Dealing with his wallet was tricky anyway, since there was always something else to do at the same time, like pick up a sack of groceries or juggle sandwiches at the deli or get money from a cash machine, and Harold only had one hand. His right. Harold had been left-handed until a train accident had relieved him of his most precious commodity, and no insurance settlement could compensate him properly for the loss of it.

Harold had been a jeweler since grade school. When other kids were drawing dirty pictures and writing their steadies' names on their notebooks, Harold was sketching rings, bracelets and necklaces. All he ever wanted to do was adorn women with beautiful stones and metals. And he had. His career was successful from the first year he opened his own shop. His unique designs were in hot demand, and soon he produced pieces that sold in all the finer shops.

And then the accident. Harold lost his left hand, and with it went his motivation to work. His mother and Karen, his sister, worried endlessly about him. They tried everything they could think of, bless their hearts, to reinstill his zest for life—they even bought him a whole set of gardening books and supplies—but he just wasn't interested. He hated to disappoint them, but he . . . well, he'd grown rather attached to a couple of soap operas.

So Harold always had a lot on his mind, and a little lump in the corner of his wallet was nothing.

Until the second time he noticed it. And this time, it was no little lump, it was a bulge.

Cursing the clumsiness of his right hand, and using the stump of his left wrist for leverage, Harold emptied the contents of his wallet onto his kitchen table. The lump was between nylon layers. He could feel it give when he squeezed it. He opened his pocketknife with his teeth and very carefully slit the stitches that held the wallet's seam and opened it up.

There was what appeared to be the tip of a finger, nail and all, growing in the seam of his wallet.

Harold folded the seams back into place and put the wallet back into his pocket.

He had no time for hallucinations.

The lump grew, but Harold had no time for it. He noticed it, but he didn't look at it again until he could no longer close his wallet. It had grown into a full-length finger, cramped and turning sideways.

It was a woman's finger, long and shapely, squeezed for room. Harold cut off the end of the fabric so the finger could poke through. It was turning sideways, though, going through some other metamorphosis, so he didn't disturb the stitching. He cut the fingernail and filed it to a pleasant shape, folded the wallet and put it back in his pocket.

Now, of course, the idea of it never left his mind. And once in the middle of the night, he woke with a thought. Something he remembered from flipping through the gardening books. Cloning. Perhaps the woman who sewed the wallet got a few of her cells caught in the seam. Perhaps the chemicals in the nylon and the thread created the perfect cloning medium, and his body heat as he carried the wallet . . . Preposterous, of course. Yet, the finger grew.

"Hello, Karen?"

"Harold?"

"Karen, I need to know something. Remember that wallet you gave me for Christmas?"

"Harold, it's two o'clock in the morning. Are you all right?"

"I'm fine. Listen, I need to know this."

"Harold, do you want me to come over? Are you, like, experiencing a flashback or something from the train wreck?"

"No, I'm fine. Really. Now about the wallet."

"Yeah?"

"Where did you get it?"

"At the swap meet."

"The Saturday one?"

"Yeah."

"Which vendor?"

"I don't know, Harold, the one who sells wallets and things."

"What things?"

"Is this necessary in the middle of the night?"

"Yes. Please."

"I don't know. Backpacks, little waist packs, wrist things, you know, that nylon and webbing stuff. All that stuff. He's short, blonde . . . Why, Harold?"

"Well, there's something in it, is all. Ought to be returned."

"You've had that wallet since Christmas and now, in July, you just discover that there's something in it?"

"Yeah, well, it's taken me a while to start using it, you know?"

"Yeah, I know. Good night, Harold."

"Karen?"

Sigh. "What, Harold?"

"I love you like a sister."

"I know that, Harold."

They hung up.

On Saturday, Harold was waiting at the doors when the market opened up. He went directly to the booth that sold the things Karen described, but there was a fat woman there, not a short blonde man.

"Hi," he said. "I, uh, got a wallet from here last Christmas, and I was wondering if you could tell me who made it?"

"Why?" She leaned against the post and lit a cigarette. Her

hair was dirty, her complexion bad, and she seemed to have quite an attitude. Karen would *never* have bought a wallet from this woman.

"There was something in it."

"Keep it."

"I'd like to know who made the wallet."

"I don't know."

"Who does?"

"Beats the shit out of me."

Harold turned away in frustration. Then he turned back. "Isn't there a blonde guy who usually runs this booth?"

"Yeah."

The woman was a veritable fount of information. "Where is he?"

"Business trip," she said, and smiled, and her teeth were bad, too.

"Will he be back?"

"Eventually."

Harold left. He drove back to his apartment, removed the wallet from his pocket and opened it up. The finger had turned sideways because another finger was coming in next to it.

It was a left hand. Harold gently felt the finger. All its bones were right, and although it didn't move, he could feel the life in it. He manicured the nail, rubbed hand cream into it and tried some of his rings on it. It was a forefinger, though, and most of his rings were created for the ring finger. He thought if he had a left hand, he could create the most beautiful rings for forefingers.

One at a time the fingers appeared, and finally, the thumb. Harold attended each new arrival with exquisite care. He cut holes in the wallet so the fingers would be more comfortable, being careful not to disturb the critical seam.

Harold marveled at the creation in his massacred wallet. The woman must have been a piano player, a violinist, an artist, with such magnificent hands. The fingers were long and thin, cool, aristocratic. But then what would that kind of a woman be doing sewing wallets? The hand never moved, but it was not limp, nor was it stiff. It simply seemed to be waiting.

Harold knew, from the moment he realized that a left hand

was growing in his wallet, that he had to have that hand. It had to be a part of him. But it wasn't until the thumb became whole that he realized that there would be a very small window of opportunity. Soon the wrist would grow, and then perhaps the forearm, until the entire woman appeared from the seam of his wallet.

He had no use for a woman, but he did have a use for a left hand. He could always wear a glove if he found that a woman's hand on the end of his arm was intimidating, but he could do no real jewelry work without it.

His nights became sleepless as the time drew near. He knew no surgeon, he knew of no way to have it done. He would have to do it himself, as clumsy as he was with his right hand.

When the wrist bone appeared, Harold knew it was time.

He assembled a sewing kit he'd bought at Woolworth's, plenty of towels, a scalpel from the feed store, his jeweler's tools and a bottle of Southern Comfort. He poured himself a healthy shot, drank it down and went to work.

In the morning, Harold awoke with a tremendous hangover. His crusty eyes cracked against the morning light, and he brought his hand up to shield them.

The screaming pain cleared his head instantly.

The hand was on. The stitching at the wrist was crude, to say the least, and it was swollen and purple, much the way his stump was for weeks after the amputation. And he had used pink thread.

But the fingers moved. Sluggishly and painfully, but he could move them.

The bottle of Southern Comfort was still on his nightstand. He took a long swallow and then poured more over the wrist. Then he went into the kitchen and made an ice pack for it. He was alive with the possibilities of a future for the first time.

Every day he worked the fingers. Every day they were better, the wrist less swollen, the fingers more agile, quicker, less stiff. There was no infection, which was a fluke, but a blessing, because he didn't know how he would explain it all to a doctor. And at night, this left hand did things for him that his other left hand never had.

Two weeks after the graft, he was talking with Karen on the

telephone, trying to explain to her that he'd been down with the flu, and dodging her questions about his interests and experiments in gardening. He'd tried growing a few things, but he didn't have any enthusiasm for it, and he had no luck at it. He told her that if he'd ever had a green thumb, it was the one the train cut off. She wasn't amused. When he hung up, he looked at the notepad, and there was a drawing of the most exquisite ring he'd ever seen. And he had seen plenty. The pen was still in his left hand, yet he had nothing to do with the drawing. Within a week, he had an entire portfolio of beautiful jewelry designs. New designs. Fabulous designs.

Her designs.

It was time. He washed his hands, manicured her nails, put on hand cream, then donned a pair of gloves and headed for his shop.

The studio was dusty and cold. He hadn't been there in over six months. He brushed off his worktable and set up his paper and pencils. Within minutes, the new left hand was creating miraculous jewelry designs, and he didn't even have to look at the page.

The phone rang.

Harold jumped at the eerie sound. Who would know he was at the studio?

It was Karen.

"You're at the studio!"

"Yeah."

"What are you doing?"

Harold looked down and watched his hand draw a necklace so intricate in goldwork it would need no stones. "Working."

"Really? Harold, that's wonderful. Wait until I tell Mom. What are you working on?"

"A necklace."

"Did you ever find out about your wallet . . . remember calling me up in the middle of the night? Or was that a dream I had?"

"No, I went there, but the guy was gone and it was some lady who didn't want to tell me anything."

"Well, I was there yesterday and he was there. I asked him and he said he buys from lots of places, and if he could see the wallet, he could tell you where he got it. He said they're all coded with who made them and where."

Harold looked over at the piece of paper. The superb necklace design had been translated into bracelet and earrings. "It's not so important anymore," he said.

"Come over for dinner tonight, okay? Mom is coming, and she's bringing her new boyfriend."

"Come on, Karen, I don't like to . . ."

"Please?"

He knew that sooner or later he would have to see both his mother and his sister. Sooner or later they would both see that he now had a hand where a month ago there hadn't been one. He took a deep breath. Might as well get it over with. "Okay," he said.

He kept his hand gloved and in his pocket the entire time. He fumbled with his eating utensils and the left hand wanted to jump out of his pocket and go to his aid, but he kept it firmly shoved deep down. No one noticed, but he didn't stop sweating.

After dinner, Roger, the new boyfriend, took Harold aside. "I understand you're a jeweler."

"Of sorts."

"Yeah. I heard about the accident. A real shame. Well, listen, I'm sure that given the right project, you could get back into it, right?"

"Well . . ." Harold wasn't all that sure that he liked this guy.

"How about a couple of wedding rings?"

"Wedding rings?"

"Yeah . . . you know." And he pointed at Harold's mother and then at himself.

"You're getting married?"

"Thinking about it."

"Well, that's . . . well, that's just *fine,*" he made himself say, and he smiled broadly and stuck his hand out for his new stepfather-to-be to shake. "Yes. Wedding rings. Let me see what I can come up with. Have you set a date?"

"Not yet. But soon. A couple of months or so."

"I'll see what I can do."

"Fine." Roger slapped him on the back and they went back to the dining room where the women were setting out dessert.

Harold watched his mother and Roger interact for the rest of the evening, and it was obvious that they were in love. If he had been paying more attention to them and less to his hand, perhaps he wouldn't have been caught so off-guard by Roger's request. Wedding rings. Sure. He could do something really nice for them. In fact, he already had an idea.

But his new left hand wouldn't draw the idea that was in his head. She drew fabulous jewelry, to be sure, but she wouldn't draw the Harold Hansen jewelry that had made his reputation and his fortune thus far.

True, he counseled himself. Everybody could understand that I've just come back from a traumatic experience with a new viewpoint, and that my jewelry is likely to be different, but yet . . . while he knew his customers could accept that, he was not too sure he could. Especially the wedding rings.

He wanted something vintage Hansen. He wanted—Hell, he knew exactly what he wanted. But every wedding ring set that she drew turned into something else. Something more. Something not Harold Hansen, and something not his mother.

He went through all his old designs, but they weren't what he wanted, either. He knew what he wanted, and somehow, he would have it.

"Harold?"

"Hi, Karen."

"They've set the date."

"They have?"

"Two weeks."

Harold felt his stomach flush.

"Did you hear me?"

"Yeah. Two weeks."

"You going to have the rings?"

"Of course."

"I can't wait to see them. I'm sure they'll be wonderful."

"Karen, would you do me a favor?"

"Sure."

"Come by, pick up this wallet, find that vendor and find out who made it, okay?"

"What's the big deal with the wallet, Harold?"

"Would you just do that little thing for me?"

"Okay. Leave it in your kitchen. I'll come by sometime today."

"Thanks."

Harold hung up feeling better. If he could just *talk* to the woman who had made the wallet, whose duplicate hand he wore, he could enlist her cooperation, and the hand would draw what he wanted it to.

Harold put his head down, cradled in the crook of his arm. That was the craziest thing he had ever thought of. Was he losing his mind as well?

His studio had turned into a battleground. Everything he tried, *she* thwarted. If he mixed his cement a certain way, she added ingredients to make it a different consistency. If he put a piece in the vice to try to work on it with his right hand, awkward though it might be, as soon as his back was turned, she had changed the setting and begun tooling it the way she wanted to.

Who is this woman? he wanted to know.

"Harold?"

"Karen."

"What did you do to the wallet?"

"That's not important, Karen."

"Jesus, Harold, that was a gift. What's the deal here?"

"Just tell me, Karen. What did the vendor say?"

"He opened up the pocket—well, actually, you'd already cut it open for him—and said he'd bought it from the mission. Someone with the initials LO made it at the mission."

"Mission?"

"Yeah. Downtown. They feed drunks, read them a little Jesus and sometimes the poor buggers help them make things to sell. It helps them get on their feet. Well, last fall they all made these wallets. The materials and sewing machines and things were donated."

"Listen, Karen, I need you to go down there with that wallet and see if you can find this LO person."

"Harold. Enough, all right?"

"Karen, do you want the FUCKING RINGS OR NOT?"

There was silence on the other end. He had never yelled at her before.

"All right, Harold. I'll go. And when I find out, I want an explanation. And an apology, do you hear me?"

"Just find her, Karen."

Harold looked at the beautiful, treacherous hand that lay so quietly in his lap. He got the manicure set and the lotions and made it even more beautiful.

And at night, as he lay in bed, that hand rewarded him with pleasures of the flesh like he'd never known before.

Day after day he fought with her about the rings. Day after day she made it clear that without her he could do nothing. The little struggle for tools and the sketching pad was nothing more than a symptom of the power struggle that threatened to reduce Harold Hansen to jelly. He would either master this hand or he would lose himself in the process.

And then Mother called.

"Harold, how are you doing on the rings?"

Harold wiped the perspiration from his face. He had just wrestled a probe from her. He thought she was going to stab him with it.

"They're very nice, Mother."

"Don't you think we should see them? Or try them on? The wedding is in just a few— Harold, are you all right? You sound out of breath."

"I'm fine, Mom. I just ran in from outside to catch the phone." He had a death grip on her thumb.

"So don't you think we should see these rings, dear? We're going to be wearing them for a long time. And sizes. You've never sized Roger."

"Plenty of time, Mom. I'll call you." Harold hung up the phone. Her hand went limp. He put it on the worktable and looked at it.

He was in deep trouble. He thought about killing himself. He thought about amputating the hand. He thought about running away.

He reached for the phone. Maybe Karen was working on it.

The hand grabbed a stylus and stabbed it right through his forearm.

Harold screamed, and looked at the thing in horror. He couldn't get it out. Her hand was in his pocket. She would not pull the rod out of his right arm, and he couldn't reach it with his other hand.

He pulled it out with his teeth.

Blood squirted when the end came free. He went into the bathroom and wrapped a towel around it.

It must have been an accident, he thought, even though he knew better.

Handcuff it to a belt loop, he thought. But where would I find handcuffs?

The phone rang.

Howard unwrapped the towel. The wound had swollen closed. One drop of blood oozed from the inner arm side.

"Harold?"

"Karen!"

"You aren't going to believe this."

"What?"

"Well."

Was that the sound of the saw? He didn't remember turning the saw on.

"You were right. It was a woman who made the wallet. Her name was Lydia Oliver, Harold, but she's not living at this mission anymore. She's—"

Harold was shoved off his stool. Then she had his other hand, and was inching it closer and closer to the saw. "No! NO!" he screamed. The phone dropped to the floor. But she had the surprise advantage, and with one push, she shoved his forearm into the whirling blade. Flesh seared, bone ground, blood swished up the wall and across the ceiling, and his right hand fell to the countertop.

But she was quick with a tourniquet, and while Karen was screaming on the telephone, she turned on the torch and seared the stump while Harold stared in horror.

When she was finished, she threw a towel over the hand, which lay twitching by the saw, calmly picked up the telephone receiver and put it to Harold's ear.

"Harold?"

"Huh."

"My God, are you all right? What the hell is going on over there?"

"Uh . . ." The studio was thick with the smell of his own burning.

"Anyway. The woman is dead, Harold. She used to be an artist, Harold, an incredibly gifted artist, or so they say."

"What happened?" Harold felt lightheaded. The sound of Karen's voice got farther and farther away.

"Well, it seems she hid out on the street for a while—that's how she got in at the mission, but then the authorities found her."

Harold tried desperately to hold on to his consciousness until he heard the whole story, but it was slipping, slipping . . . His knees buckled and he slumped against the cabinet. The phone dangled in front of him and he could barely hear what Karen was saying.

"She never really made it in the art world, it can be a struggle, I guess, starving artists and all that, so she was forced to take odd jobs. But I guess she still had the artist's temperament, and had a real problem with authority figures, because she had a habit of killing her bosses. Listen to this: Her last job was at a butcher shop. One day she cut up her boss, packaged him up and sold him. By the time they were on to her, she was gone, glassy-eyed, wandering the streets. Now they're even saying that her father died under mysterious circumstances when she was just a little girl. She cut herself in jail and died."

Harold's breath was coming a little bit easier. He felt as if he dreamed what Karen had said.

"Karen . . ." he croaked, but she took the phone and placed it back in its cradle. She slipped a pencil and pad of paper to the floor, propped it up on his knees. She sketched a pair of wedding bands that were simple, elegant, and could be made easily by the date of the wedding. "Jewelry by Lydia," she wrote at the bottom.

Harold stood up, shoved her hand deep into his pocket. Using his nose, he scooted his dismembered hand to the edge of the table. One by one, he bit off the fingers.

He planted one in his coat pocket, one in his new leather

wallet, one in the change pocket in his jeans, and two he stuck into flowerpots and put in a south-facing window.

Then he sat down and waited for his new right hand to grow, while Lydia made the rings. He hoped Lydia had a green thumb.

• Genetically Predisposed

I first walked into that tattoo parlor on my fortieth birthday. Struck dumb by the horrid, graphic visuals—the walls in the waiting room were papered with tattoo designs, typical red-and-black, violent, sadistic and macho designs—I almost backed out as quickly as I had come in.

I stilled my heart. Nobody had touched me with needle and ink yet. I clutched my purse tighter and began to look at the individual drawings. There were many skulls, knives, fists and bloody claws, for sure, but there were also beautiful flowers, birds, and mythical creatures drawn and colored with a delicate hand and fine sensitivity.

I didn't know what I wanted, I didn't even know that I was seriously considering a tattoo until I found myself walking in the door of Sailor Mike's. I just knew I was terribly unhappy with life, *terribly unhappy,* and I needed to show a little spunk, a little individuality, a little rebellion of my own, for once.

My husband had fallen in love with someone else. Our marriage was only a shadow. We continued to live together, and we kept our money in the same pot, but it was only a matter of time before that changed. Our nest was empty and so was my life.

That left a big house and just Allen and me, and we didn't have much to say to each other anymore. The tension was getting to me. I felt knots in my stomach all the time, especially those nights when I knew he was with *her*. I knew if it kept up much longer, I would run screaming from the house, tearing my hair, doing damage to myself and everyone around me. Or worse, I'd become ill. The consuming kind of ill. The *all*-consuming kind of ill.

Yet, every time I thought about taking some kind of action—moving out, kicking him out, putting the house up for sale—it didn't seem right, it didn't seem real.

But I needed to make sure I was alive. I needed to do something for myself that was a little bit risky, a little bit outlandish. And . . . secretly, I've always wanted a tattoo.

I'd finished looking at all the anchors and the panthers and the scantily clad women and was on to the second wall, starting with cartoon characters, when the inner door opened and a man looked out.

"Yes?" he said.

I felt suddenly shy. "Hi," I said.

He just stood there and I realized that he thought I was a saleswoman or something.

"I am thinking about getting a tattoo."

"Oh," he said, and he came out, coffee cup in hand. "See anything you like?"

"They're all really nice," I said, "but . . ."

"But they're not you."

"Yeah, I guess so." I wanted to leave. I felt so stupid.

"Where were you thinking of putting it? Shoulder? Back? Hip?"

"Thigh," I said, and then I couldn't believe I'd really said that.

"Inside or outside?"

"Outside. Of course." I knew I was blushing, and I hated it. This guy meant nothing to me. He was just a salesman and an artist. I was the customer. I needed to get hold of myself and get a hold on this situation. "I was thinking of something a little more . . ."

"Come inside here," he said, and opened the door to a brightly lit room.

I walked in and for a moment, I thought I'd walked into a doctor's office. One wall was curtained; there was a window on the other side into the waiting room. People could watch a tattoo in progress, if it wasn't too personal. There was an adjustable padded brown leather table, white cabinets, white countertops, an autoclave, sterile packaged instruments on a stainless-steel tray . . . and it was absolutely spotless. I watched him as he busied himself in the corner filing cabinet.

Sailor Mike was about forty-five, with a nice, full reddish beard just beginning to gray. His hair was cut short around the ears, and gray showed there, too. He wore little round glasses, which made him look curiously studious. He carried an extra ten or so pounds on his compact frame, held in by a finely tooled leather belt. When he turned around, I saw that his eyes were green and his T-shirt was clean. He handed me a drawing and I saw that his fingernails were clean, too.

"I'm Mike," he said, and held out his hand. I took it.

"Alice." His hand was warm and soft, and his grip was firm.

"I don't do women after noon," he said, and we both looked up at the clock. It was eleven-fifteen.

"Why?" And we had a moment of each other's eyes.

"Personal policy. I want to make sure they're sober, for one thing, and that they don't get hassled by a bunch of guys in the waiting room . . . you know." He looked at the floor. Suddenly *he* was shy, and that gave me a little thrill, as if I had suddenly found myself to be attractive again. For the first time in years.

I looked at the drawings he handed me, but they weren't right, either. They were too magical, too fairy. I was not a fairy type of person. I looked up to say so, and saw a queer look in his eyes. His hand came up to touch my cheek, and I moved backward.

Startled, he flushed and apologized. "I'm sorry," he said. "But your skin—" Again, he brought his hand up and I let his thumb touch my cheek. "I've never seen skin like this before." My eyes closed involuntarily as he touched me, thrills running down my back, goose pimples coming up on my arms, and I wondered when Allen had last touched my cheek. Had Allen *ever* touched my face? Then Mike had my fingertips and he was looking at my hands. He pushed the sleeves of my blouse up and looked at my forearms.

Then he reached over and locked the door. "Can I see your shoulders?"

I can't explain the lack of fear. The intensity in his eyes was more than heat, was more than desire, I was not afraid that he would touch me, I was rather afraid that he wouldn't touch me. It never occurred to me that he could hurt me.

He closed his eyes so as not to see the rejection he expected, his face showed the anticipated pain. Then he just whispered, "Please?" and I began to unbutton my blouse. He opened his eyes again and watched me. I kept telling myself I was being foolish, but I couldn't help myself.

"Skin is my business. I've been doing tats for twenty years, and I've seen all kinds of skin, but I've always dreamed of"— my blouse fell off my shoulders—"this. This skin. Oh God, *this* skin." He came away from the wall and touched my shoulder with such reverence. He pulled my blouse down in the back, and ran his fingers lightly over my shoulders, down my spine. Now it was my turn to close my eyes. This was unspeakably erotic, here in the brightly lit room of a tattoo artist's studio. "It's almost translucent. You've hardly ever been in the sun. It's almost like a baby's skin, there are no blemishes, there are no moles, no freckles, no odd colorations." He pinched some skin on my shoulder. I dared not flinch. "It's magnificent," he breathed.

Is there no fool like an old fool? I thought. The skin was forty years old. True, I never went out in the sun, never had, but I always thought I looked too thin, too pale. Allen always said I should go out and get some exercise, but I didn't. I didn't. And now this man, this tattoo man, is he taking advantage of my age, my naivete? Is he selling me a perfect con job?

Then he lifted my blouse back up over my shoulders and turned me to face him.

"Listen," he said. "I can give you a tattoo. I can give you the most incredible skin illustration you've ever seen. Know how the painters, the artists, the old masters, know how they created masterpieces that live on forever? That's because oil paints are translucent, and you can put layer after layer of paint on a canvas, and it all works to one advantage. I can do that with your skin. I can do that with *your* skin. I can make your body into the most wonderful work of art you could imagine."

"What would you do?" My mouth was dry.

"Can I see the rest of you?"

Convinced, now, that I *was* but an old fool, I shrugged off the blouse, unbuckled my pants, kicked off my shoes. Soon I stood in my underwear, hoping that would be enough. It was. He trailed his fingers over my arms, inspecting them as a jeweler might look at a new stone. He had me get up onto his table, where he looked at each leg, each foot, then I had to pull my panties down and expose all of my tummy. He was working. He wasn't going to harm me. And all the while, I gloried in his touch.

"Okay," he said, and moved to the side, where he poured himself a fresh cup of coffee.

I waited.

"A snake," he said.

I remembered the snaky pictures outside on his waiting-room walls. They were gross.

"No," he said to my frown, "not like those." He set his coffee cup down and walked over to me, took my little finger in his hand and led me down from the table. "A great snake. I would start here, with the tip of his tail coiled around your little finger. He would wrap himself here, around your hand, across your wrist." His fingers trailed his vision on my skin. "He would come across the top of this arm and lay across your chest, here, resting on your breasts. He's six, eight inches thick here. Heavy. He comes around the top of your other shoulder, down across your back, under the arm, around your belly, across your right buttock and wraps himself around your right leg. His head is here." He was kneeling on the floor, two fingers about four inches apart on my foot. "I would mix all my own inks."

I felt the weight of the snake. "I don't know."

He stood up and looked me in the face. He took off his glasses and wiped his hands over his eyes. He resettled his glasses and fixed me with a steady, serious gaze. "It would be the project of my lifetime," he said, then he turned to his coffee and I began to dress, self-consciously.

He was still facing the cabinets, his hands on the counter when I finished dressing. I didn't know what to say, so I just unlocked the door and left.

I went home to a large, empty house. I walked upstairs to what had been my son's room. I'd redecorated it for something to do and now I wished it was still his brand of colossal mess. I wished I could still smell him in this room, but it was sterile.

I went into the master bedroom and took off my clothes. I tilted the mirror forward so I could look at my entire body. It suddenly looked different to me. It had possibilities. It was not too skinny, it was not too pale. It could bear the weight of a snake.

Oh my God, what would people think?

That night, as I lay in bed, Allen a firm distance next to me, I felt the weight of the snake again on my chest. I felt Sailor Mike's fingers on my skin. I'd forgotten what it meant to be touched. I'd forgotten what it felt like to be aroused. That night, the night that everyone but me had forgotten was my fortieth birthday, I lay awake almost the whole night, and shared my birthday with the remembrance of warm, gentle fingers and the promise of a snake.

I went back to Mike's the next day.

"What would it look like?"

He didn't seem thrilled to see me. He looked intense instead, as if he dared not hope. We went back into his studio and again he rummaged in his filing cabinet. Then he came out with a tissue-covered drawing. He handed it to me.

Under the tissue was a six-inch section of snake, drawn in iridescent colors. Each scale was defined, the shadowing and shading was magnificent.

"When did you do this?"

"That, right there, is the reason I opened this shop. I knew that someday I would get to do that." He sat on a little wheeled stool. "I've been waiting. Practicing. Getting better. I can do better than that drawing on you. That's on board. On paper. On your skin, I can make that snake *live.*"

"Will it hurt?"

"Yes."

"How long will it take?"

He shrugged. "Depends upon how frequently we work, how long the sessions go, how long it takes you to recover, how thin your skin is." He looked at the floor, shrugged again. "Six months."

Six months!

I stood there, leaning against his table, while he sat on his stool, and we both looked at the floor in silence. We both knew I would do it.

"Okay," I said, and it came out like a whisper.

"There's just one thing," he said, then he stood up and came over to me. "I am a man of my word, and I believe that you are as good as your word, too."

His eyes were deeper than any I had ever seen. "I am," I said.

"Then you need to promise me that once we start, you will finish. Unless you are dead, you will finish the drawing."

I nodded, my mouth suddenly dry.

"Say it," he demanded.

"I will finish it," I said, and I felt as if I'd just sold my soul.

On the first day, I lay naked on his table while he examined me again. He looked at me from all angles, all perspectives. I lay every which way on his table, and he touched me occasionally with the point of his felt-tip pen. The second day he made dotted lines. The third day he changed the lines. The fourth day he said he was ready to begin.

Day after day I meditated to the pain, the relentless buzz of the needle and the firm way he held me as he worked. There was nothing to my life but Mike and the "work," as he called it. The routine, the pain became normal. He worked according to his own agenda, day by day I didn't know where he would be working next. But every day I went home with a fresh bandage. Somewhere I always had a bandage, a scab, and sore spots in varying degrees of healing, while he created new ones day by day.

The pain of the needle, I found, could be broken down into strings of vibrations. I lay on the table, eyes closed, and divided the pain into chords. The long sweeps of the needle had a different orchestration than the short coloring strokes, and the music went on in my head as the drawing appeared on my body. The inner thigh was the worst. Tears leaked onto the small pillow. Mike kissed my cheek periodically, handed me a fresh tissue and continued.

Sometimes, at home, when a bandage came off and I could see whole sections of what Mike had done, it appeared as if the snake was emerging from within me.

Sometimes, in bed, I would feel the weight of it pressing on me, and it grew heavier as time went on.

No one noticed.

Mike and I rarely talked; he and I were not important. There was only the work.

At three months, he was well into the color. The weight of the drawing grew, as if he breathed bulk into it as well as ink.

One night I awoke from a deep sleep with a startling revelation: *it's a male.*

It felt cold.

Mike lost weight. He greedily snatched bandages off every day and relentlessly examined and reexamined the finished portions for flaws. He worked in a rare heat, sometimes climbing right up on the table and straddling me in order to get just exactly the correct angle.

I was curiously unaffected by Mike's frenzies. I had distractions of my own. I lay on the table, day after day, feeling feminine, important, beautiful, and impatient to show my masterpiece.

And a masterpiece it was. It took my breath away. I began to understand why I never wanted to go into the sun. I now saw how the events of my life had led up to this point—I was *supposed* to wear this snake.

I began to identify with it wholeheartedly. It was my claim to fame. I couldn't wait until it was finished, and I could show the world. I could show my friends. I could show Allen.

Allen! He would die.

At night, when Allen came home smelling like her perfume, undressed and got into bed, I watched with slitted eyes. And I felt the snake twitch.

He, too, wanted this project to be finished. He waited not so patiently to be fully drawn.

When the inking was finished, there were still daily bandages to be removed, and then touch-up work when the scabs lifted. Some of the scabs went deep; the needle had a tendency to tear my fragile skin. The daily routine of going back to Mike's became a drain, not only because I was ready for it to be finished, but Mike's appearance had become seedy and unkempt. His fingernails were no longer clean, his studio no longer spotless.

The day he pronounced the drawing finished, he cried. I wanted to put my arms around him, this man who had given me back so much of myself, but I couldn't. I sat with him, but I had nothing to say. He said he was going to go on a little trip, a vacation, and I nodded my agreement that he needed a rest, and then I left. I left with my prize. After six months of meditation, anticipation, pain, and fear, all the bandages were gone, there were no more scabs, I was ready to reveal my elegance. But to whom?

I wandered the street for the rest of the afternoon, so very conscious of a snake wrapped around me. I did some window-shopping, some people-watching, wondering what to do next. I felt adrift without my daily routine of meditation to the pain and the needle at Mike's.

I passed through the alley next to a Chinese restaurant back toward the parking lot, when I felt the snake stir. I stopped, startled. It moved. My shirt bloused as the snake took its form. I felt its taut muscles as it inched its way around me, its head seeking the pavement. I felt it slide right off me. Its weight had been incredible; without it, I felt as light as air. I watched it go into the dark behind the restaurant, and I followed on tiptoe.

Four cats waited by the back door. The snake singled out the black and white one, and before the cat understood what was happening, the snake had it. It squeezed. The cat screamed. Then meowed with its last breath, then wheezed like a bellows. And then the mighty jaws disjoined and opened and the cat disappeared, inch by inch, heaved down the snake's gullet by intense, superb muscular contractions.

I watched in horrified fascination as the cat disappeared, head first. When the last of the tail had been swallowed, the snake came back to me in esses, and nosed at my pant leg. I closed my eyes. The snake came slowly, heavily up my leg—I had to help it where the cat bulged—wrapped around me, climbed into its exact position, fell asleep, and melted back into my skin.

I watched the bulge of the cat over the next week, as it diminished in size and moved from my thigh up across my butt and around my back.

I weighed myself, too. Or, rather, I weighed myself wearing the snake. He weighed sixty-five pounds.

I paid less and less attention to Allen as the weeks went by. My life was focused, instead, on the phenomenon in and on my body. The snake left me at regular intervals. I would feel him wake, and rise out of my skin at night, usually when I was in bed, and I would watch the blanket ripple as he silently left me in search of food.

Toward dawn he would return, sated, bulging and cold, and I would shiver as he took his place and soaked up my warmth. I fell in with his rhythms. They became my own.

Daytimes I would wonder at the mind of a snake, and I would sit by the window and stroke his smoothness, talking to him. Or I would undress and walk around the house naked, surprised, always, by our reflection in a mirror, a window, a glass.

A year since the inking began and still Allen hadn't noticed. He lived only for his trysts. I wondered why he didn't leave me and go to be with her. He could give two women peace with one stroke. He was a weasel, that's why. I began to hate him. I found it harder and harder to sleep next to him at night. I hugged the edge of the bed, sleepless, staring into the night, thinking empty thoughts.

Then one night, when my snake roused himself and went hunting, I went with him.

I drew on black pants and a black jacket. We went out the kitchen door and through the back yard. We cut across all the neighbor's back yards until he found the spot he'd apparently noticed before. A neighbor's dog was tied up, sleeping at his doghouse. I waited in the shadows and watched.

The dog barely yipped. And when my friend's jaws distended, I opened mine, and felt them unlock. I opened my throat to the heavens, and almost felt that dog chunking down my gullet, little hairy head first.

We were both almost too sleepy to make it back home, but just before dawn, we slithered into bed, I felt his aching coldness wrap around me and we fell asleep.

I took to curling up on the coffee table in the living room during the day when the sun shone down so brightly upon it. I'd fall into a restful nether state, neither sleeping nor awake. I was aware, yet dreaming peaceful scenes of cool caves, moist burrows and hot, flat rocks.

At night, I'd eat eggs; crack their ends and suck the goop right out of the shell. I'd eat a half dozen, and then go out. Or sometimes we'd just curl up in the bedroom easy chair and watch Allen sleep. I'd pet my friend's head and watch his beady eyes gleam in the darkness as he stared with a reptile's nonemotion at the man who had robbed me of myself.

One night I dropped by Sailor Mike's. He was there and the shop was empty, but we didn't have much to say to each other. He seemed wrung out, as if he had given me everything he owned, and I suppose he had. We hugged, and he commented on my loss of weight. I had to smile to myself. The scale said I'd gained.

Winter fell abruptly mid-October. I slept round the clock, waking only to eat at night when Allen turned on the electric blanket. I knew the signs. I knew what was happening, but while it was happening to my body, it was also happening to my mind, and it seemed the most natural thing in the world. The winter passed in a blur of half-light, half wakefulness, half restlessness.

I dreamed of Allen talking to me, I dreamed of concentrating far beyond my energy resources to understand and answer. Those periods of hard work were rare; mostly I dreamed of lounging loosely on tree branches overhanging bird nests, swimming gently in green, scum-lidded rivers, nosing out burrows of small warm rodents.

Spring dawned gently. I woke more frequently, began to wander the house in the sunshine, took regular showers. I would turn the electric blanket on and feel my friend awaken and move about my body. The smoothness of his skin delighted and energized me, and while I looked for signs of affection in his face and found none, I soon discovered that affection was no longer in my range of emotions, either.

I merely wanted him.

We played this erotic scene daily, it seemed to have no beginning and no end. I was never conscious of waking up and beginning, nor was I ever aware of finishing and drifting back to sleep. It seemed as if I merely drifted in and out of sleep, and his black, shiny skin was constantly moving, restlessly seeking, all over me, all the time.

Then one morning as the camellias were looking in the window at us, he brought my passion to a frenzy, and in the panes of sunlight on the wrecked bed, I felt him enter me, fill me, and we thrashed and rolled, tumbled and entwined with the sheets, with each other, with ecstasy and madness.

When it was over, he melted back into my skin, leaving me breathless and alone, tingling still and suspicious of my sanity.

When the eggs came, they were soft and creamy and I could feel life vibrating within them. One after another they slipped from me until the muscle fluttering stopped and I held a nest of seven of them. They were like precious fruit. I nestled them into a pillow and put it under the bed.

Allen became more of a presence, more of a mystery. He would stand in front of me and shout, but I could no longer comprehend either his emotion or his words. He gesticulated wildly, his arms flailing about; he looked cluttered, as if he had far too many appendages and couldn't control them properly. I lay curled up in my chair, trying to discern meaning, and resisted the temptation to taste his air with my tongue.

He packed boxes of things and took them away, but continued to sleep in what had been our bed. I slept in the chair.

One night he came in looking odder than usual. He was disheveled, he smelled of poisons, his hair was messed, and I thought the human species was an ungainly and ugly sort. He stood, weaving, looking down on me in the chair, then threw his coat into the corner and made his way unsteadily to the bed. He pulled off his shoes and lay back, muttering something, then began to snore.

My friend awakened, lifting his head from where it rested on my foot, his tongue tasting the close, comfortable air of our home. He disentangled himself from me and made his way across the carpeting to the nest under the bed, and suddenly I felt the activity as well. I crawled under with him and we watched as the eggs moved gently with the persistence of those within. They seemed to struggle so.

I thought perhaps they would have an easier time of it if they were warmer, so I brought the nest out and put it in the bed and turned on the electric blanket. Then we went back to the chair to watch the window, waiting for morning.

Allen began to twitch about dawn, slapping and pawing at himself. We watched with detached amusement.

Midmorning, he finally roused himself and went into the bathroom. I heard his strong stream of urine, the flush, the water in the sink begin to run. And then I heard the gasp. The shout, the faint shriek of hysteria present in his squeaky human throat.

He came out naked, and I saw my children, my wondrous children, my seven beautiful and glorious children as they were illustrated at random around his body.

One lay coiled around his right nipple.

I stroked the head of my mate and stared off into the day.

•Nightmare Flower

That spring when June and I moved into our dilapidated dream house, I licked my lips every time I carried a box past the overgrown kitchen garden. I couldn't wait to dive into the soil and turn it from hard and baked, caked and lifeless into moist and crumbly, rich with humus and earthworms. But then I'd hear June call out "Charlie!" in that musical way of hers, and I'd look at the rest of the house and sigh. A year, I thought to myself, it would be at least a year before I would have enough leisure time to devote to the garden. The garden would be a joy, and the old house had been unoccupied too long to put joyful projects very high on the priority list.

Instead, we had our hands full with cleaning, raking, painting, fencing, mowing, pruning and meeting new neighbors. All the neighbors were pleased that someone was finally taking an interest in fixing up the old eyesore. It had run down so fast after the old man died, they said. They were glad to help, and came by daily with offers of tools or trucks or snacks or manpower.

By the time the autumn leaves began to fall, the exterior had truly been transformed. The old house looked wonderful with its pristine coat of fresh white paint, and the grounds had become quite respectable indeed. There was still much work to be done on the inside, but June and I considered those items to be our winter projects, to be done at our leisure. We'd worked hard all summer, and we'd attained our goal: the house had become livable.

As my reward, I claimed one long fall weekend for the kitchen garden. I wanted to clean it up and get it ready for spring planting.

I chopped and pulled and dug and burned. I tilled and fertilized and planted a winter cover crop that barely had time to come up before the first frost, but at least the area looked cleaner and fresher, and I had a sense of pride and anticipation toward the coming spring.

There was a bad spot in the garden, though. A small spot, no more than maybe eight by twelve inches. I'd known about it from the very first. It didn't exactly smell bad, or look bad, it just *was* bad, somehow. That one spot, up against the side of the house, always seemed to be in the shade, even when no shadow fell across it. I avoided it when I worked the garden, my body automatically reacting every time my cultivating chores brought me closer to it. My feet would not step on it, they recoiled as they would if I were to deliberately step on something rotting.

I excused it. Some chemicals were poured there, I said, or something had been buried there long ago.

No weed grew there; the compost and mulch I threw on it from a safe distance disappeared overnight, so the ground was always bare in the morning.

Bare, but not empty. I never felt that space to be empty. Something always seemed to be there, hovering, lurking, protecting, defending. Something vaguely monstrous and maternal.

That corner of the garden touched the outside wall of the kitchen. June never used the cupboard that was directly on the other side of that wrong spot.

"Why is this cupboard empty?" I asked.

"I don't know," June said. "It's inconvenient." She looked at it, then looked at me, then gave a helpless shrug. "Or something."

Or something.

I tried to ignore that one weird spot in the garden, even though I would find myself standing in front of it, staring into it at times. And I tried to tell myself that I had accidentally thrown a shovelful of dirt on the wall of the house there, right above that spot in the garden, where the fresh, white paint had turned a dark, bilious yellow.

Winter arrived in early November with a wonderful snow-storm. June and I holed up with our well-stocked pantry and woodshed. We worked on our common projects like refinishing the bannister, we worked on our individual projects—I on my book; June on her quilt—and we worked on our favorite project, and by January, June was pregnant.

This was the happiest time of our lives. We stood in the doorway to the upstairs bedroom, arms around each other, and planned and replanned it as a nursery; we cozied in front of the fire and read about prenatal nutrition and child rearing. We dreamt and hoped and loved.

I'd completely forgotten about the strange spot in the garden until one bright, brisk morning in early February, when I pulled on my boots and red-plaid wool shirt and hat and set out to split some wood. I walked out the kitchen door and noticed that deep crusty snow covered the whole garden—except that one spot. The snow had melted there in a cone shape, with a black, moist center.

The soil looked fresh and fertile, dark and rich. It should be frozen, I thought, but it wasn't. It was a solid black pit against a widening yellow stain on the side of the house, snow piled up eight inches on all sides of it. And right in the center, one dark green shoot, the size of my thumb, poked through the soil into the zero-degree sunshine.

I stared at the shoot, a green penis busting through, mind-lessly thrusting its willful way into hostile territory, and revulsion curdled my breakfast.

There must be a hot-water pipe on the inside of that wall

that's turning the paint yellow, I thought, and made a mental note to check. Old houses are full of expensive surprises.

New England has some pretty bizarre plants, I also thought, and went to chop the wood.

By the end of the week, the shoot was as big as my forearm and stood about twelve inches. I would have measured it, had it not intimidated me so. I barely wanted to look at it, and *never* wanted June to have to see it. It was embarrassing, threatening, obscene. What roots must it have, I wondered, and how deep did they go? If this is a tree, and it is allowed to grow, it will probably drive the house out of square.

I wanted to nip it, but curiosity kept me from it. Curiosity and a reluctance to touch it—or go near it brandishing a blade. There was also a sinking feeling in my bowels—my testicles flinched when I thought of cutting it off. I felt that it would bleed if I cut it, bleed and thrash about.

The yellow stain on the wall had spread out in a lacy pattern, a delicate filigree. It was truly a mural of the most odd.

I successfully steered visitors, admirers of our house and well-wishers away from the garden; even June never saw this anomaly in the dead of winter. Somehow I felt responsible for this atrocity, and I was ashamed.

I was ashamed because of the dreams I had begun to have every night, and how the sprout figured into them.

At first, I began to dream of heroic encounters—of riding on quests, and rescuing damsels in distress. I, seeking the answers to the universe, was always the soft and gentle ruffian, the rogue and the rascal, and I always won the girl in the end. The girl was never June, but some lithe and simple maiden who would beg me to have my way with her. I wore a leather tunic, with a picture of the mammoth green shoot on the front—my personal symbol. In the end, I broke their hearts and rode on, searching, seeking.

It was right in the midst of one such dream that I was awakened by a noise. Outside. A noise like sweaty thighs slowly peeling from a hot vinyl car seat.

I slipped out of bed and pulled on my woolen robe. June

hadn't stirred. I went quickly down the dark and quiet stairs in my bare feet, into the kitchen, and I heard it again.

I shoved my feet into the gum boots that stood just inside the door and went outside.

The late February night was crystal clear, and a full moon shone down from straight overhead. The trees carried a thick covering of clear ice, and the whole outdoors sparkled like a winter fairyland.

And then I heard it again, and turned to the garden.

Two thick, rubbery leaves were peeling away from my shoot. They were wide, and flat, like the leaves from a corn stalk, only these were thick and meaty.

As I watched, the first leaf pulled free, and as it flopped down and fluttered gently in the moonlight, I thought I saw little muscles ripple along its length. I found myself stretching my fingers out, rubbing my hands as if they'd been bound up for too long.

Inch by inch, the second leaf struggled to come free. I urged it on, as it tugged, then rested, then tugged and rested, and finally it, too, came away and flopped down, and I felt my shoulders grow strong and I stretched my neck.

The shoot had become a stalk. The leaves were a full foot and a half long, five inches wide, and three immature leaves, each the size of my hand, now crowned the giant head. The stalk stood at least three feet high and a good four inches thick. And it was still brand new. Tender. Virile.

The stalk steadily grew through a blustery March; the winds and pelting rain wrought havoc on all other plant life, but failed to damage my plant in any way. My dreams grew more violent and sadistic as I dreamed that time was running out, and my questions must be answered. I dreamed that everyone knew the answers except me—and I didn't even yet know the questions. The symbol on the front of my tunic grew, keeping pace with the plant in the garden.

I noticed that the stain on the side of the house seemed to act as a blueprint for the plant's growth. The growth followed the yellow exactly. When the three topmost leaves unfolded, they were intricately detailed, a pattern magnificent in its complexity, and they matched, filigree for filigree, the outline stenciled for them in yellow on the clapboard. More immature leaves replaced those at the crown, and the yellow stain climbed straight up the side of the house, to just under the little bedroom window.

In April, spring brought forth a glorious day, and with it came June in her gardening clothes. I knew that sooner or later, she was bound to find it, and, of course, she did.

"Charlie? Charlie, honey, what the hell is this thing growing in the garden?"

Suddenly, I felt desperate, and stupid for allowing her to see it. "What thing?" I stalled for time.

"This one. Right out here in the garden. Next to the kitchen. What is it? A tree? I don't think I like the looks of it. And it's too close to the house. Be a dear and cut it down, okay?"

Hot blood flushed through me. Cut it down?! I could *never* cut it down. Kill it? Murder it? I would rather—I would rather— June must have seen something on my face, for she just stood there, by the kitchen door, and looked at me, and I fell back into my chair.

"Charlie, honey, are you okay?"

"Yeah, yeah," I said, and she came over and put a cool hand on my hot forehead. "I just don't want to chop down that plant."

"Okay, okay, no problem. Leave it. I just thought—you know, roots and all, that close to the house—and it's supposed to be a *vegetable* garden . . . What kind of a plant is it, anyway?"

I was getting a headache. Her nattering was more than I could stand. "I don't know what kind of plant it is. I've never seen one like it."

"Some weird hybrid, I bet. It won't win any awards, that's for sure. Listen, Charlie, do you know what happened to the paint over there? On the house. It's all yellow."

"Leave me alone," I said.

"What?" She took a step back.

"I *said,* leave . . . me . . . ALONE!" And I slammed my fist on the table for emphasis. We both jumped at the noise. I looked up into her hurt eyes and felt instantly ashamed, so I scrambled from the table, spilling my coffee, and I shut the bedroom door and fell down onto the bed.

I haven't been sleeping well, I told myself. I'm grumpy because the winter has been too long, June and I have been cooped up in here too long, and I haven't been sleeping well.

It's not easy living with a pregnant woman, I said.

I punched up the pillow behind my head and kicked off my shoes. Within moments, I was asleep. And deep into another dream.

The leather tunic felt heavy and familiar. The deep green design on the front had two lower leaves and three filigree leaves and a trio of cupped leaves at the top. The plant was long and thick, and I had shoulder-length hair and a heavy beard, wore sandals and my symbol, had muscles and girth, and I felt like a champion.

My dreams had turned disjointed, wildly violent, with much passion, and biting, tearing of flesh, breaking of bones and reveling in blood. My mother, grandmother, sisters, teachers, friends—every woman I had ever known eventually starred in one of my Technicolor dreams. In each, I was desperately trying to divine the meaning of life—the difference between male and female in the cosmic sense, and I insisted that the women knew the secrets—their bodies certainly knew the secrets of childbearing—but they were bound to silence by their membership in a secret sisterhood. I wanted that secret. I *needed* that secret. Give it to me, give it to me, *give it to me,* GIVE IT TO ME! I tried to rip and slash the information from them, and I always woke with a hot, throbbing erection.

I spent all my waking time in that little square of a garden, making a pretense of tending the little baby vegetable plants that had come up, cultivating them, pulling weeds, thinning, mulching, fertilizing, straightening rows, but all of it was a ruse to bask in the presence of the giant that had begun to dominate my life.

I meditated out there, for hours at a time, my hands thrust into the soil up to the wrists, feeling the vibrations from the master plant, and I wondered about its roots as I felt them writhe in the ground below me. Finding the answers to questions had taken on a new meaning for me; I felt that a lifetime could be devoted to that one simple premise, and I felt the earth with my hands and I listened with my heart for anything the plant might teach.

June and I avoided the topic of the plant. Several times I found her standing, staring at it with revulsion on her face, and I had to restrain myself from hitting her for her insubordination. Eventually, June and I avoided each other altogether.

I found myself spending hours just admiring the plant as it grew. I jumped out of bed first thing in the morning and went to the garden, before I went to the bathroom, before I brushed my teeth, to see what growth it had accomplished during the night. It always grew straight and tall, true to the yellow lines drawn for it to follow, straight toward the window of that little bedroom which June had just painted pale turquoise, per our nursery plans.

Every morning I would become lost in admiring its symmetry, its lines. It always seemed to be such a *male* plant, such a *masculine* thing. No wonder June didn't care for it. Women liked certain types of things, and men liked other things—like plants that bore fruit in the form of virile and passionate dreams.

One day late in July, as I was weeding the garden, June, huge and awkward in her pregnancy, slipped on a weed I'd carelessly thrown on the walk. She bent over backwards trying to regain her balance, and severely wrenched her back. The doctor put her to bed upstairs, and told me to wait on her and keep her there, or she'd have a hard time having the baby.

It was a distraction and an inconvenience, and I didn't need it. But it kept her shameless display of female fertility out of public, an increasingly embarrassing situation for me. I took food to her and she kept out of my days, and left me with uninterrupted time to worship. I slept by her side at night and dreamed of tying her up and using her parts for fertilizer.

The plant grew to the bottom of the little window and then stopped growing up and began to grow outward, its profusion of giant leaves a wonder to behold. And then, one morning in early August, I saw the bud, as big as my head, at the top of the stem, and I knew that we were to have a flower, my plant and

I, and I fell to my knees in the dirt, crushing tomatoes without a thought.

For a week, the bud grew, ballooning, barely containing itself. Every night for a week, I sat at its base and prayed and watched, falling on my face in the dirt at dawn to sleep until the sun began to burn right through my clothes. Then I'd eat something and take something to June and go back outside to wait for the night, when the plant would again awaken.

One late afternoon, I found June on the floor in the upstairs hallway. I tried to put her back to bed, but she was like a wildcat, hissing and spitting, shouting foul words. In our scuffle, she threw a table at me. I dodged, but it hit the wall, and ripped right through the new wallpaper. Sap gushed out as if she'd severed an artery. I pulled the hall phone from its outlet and tied her hands with the cord, then dragged her back to the bedroom and secured her to the bed. I thought she had gone completely insane, and then I saw her belly harden, and her eyes glass over, and I knew she was about to deliver.

I put a gag in her mouth to keep her from alerting the neighbors, and went back downstairs. On the way, I noticed the wound in the wall had swollen and closed off, sap barely trickling down to pool on the varnished floor.

I felt the expectation in the air as the night deepened and the plant came awake. I spoke to it, offering my supplications, groveling at its base, but all its leaves had an upward cant to them, as if they were paying attention to something I couldn't understand.

After the moon set, the stalk began to tremble. The filigree leaves warbled with the most magnificent of artistic motions, and I could hear the seals around the bud begin to break.

Suddenly, I felt compelled to see to June.

I ran inside the house and up the stairs.

She was there, eyes bulging, knees high in the air, as she pulled against the phone cord which I'd tied to the headboard, pulled until her wrists bled, and then I saw a vein stand out in the center of her forehead and she gave a mighty grunt and I heard the baby gasp and cry.

I whipped the covers off her, dodging her kicks, and saw the ugly, wrinkled little thing—a son!—and I pulled my penknife from my pocket and and cut the thick cord that bound the child to its mother. Then I picked him up and looked into his squalling face.

He stopped crying, and looked at me, and I knew that we were Father and Son—and of like mind.

June began twisting and choking on her gag as I carried the child out of the room, but I paid no mind. She would have another, I was sure. She would have many more. I took the child into the nursery and lay it in its crib, then opened the window.

The bulging bud waited right outside. As soon as I opened the window, I heard the seams begin to burst, and the flower began to come forth. I watched with fascination from this new vantage point, as the green sepals peeled away and the flower beneath showed through a pale, stark white in the starlight.

The child began to cry.

The blossom did not hurry.

It made crunching sounds, the sounds of a salad kitchen, as its parts separated, unfolded and unfurled. I watched the efficient process, as thin, almost transparent petals became solid and white in the night air.

The last sepal separated, and there was silence. The plant seemed to twist around a little, and I held my breath as it took a dramatic pause—and then opened.

Never in all my life had I seen anything as beautiful. The flower cup was the size of a cauldron; its insides were dark, blood-red, looking cool and clean, fresh and spiritized. The petals themselves were harsh white, fading rapidly through pink to that deep crimson, like milk-white skin next to a gaping wound.

But the scent. The scent is where heaven lay, and I filled my lungs with the fragrance of the spheres. Even the baby stopped crying as the scent wafted in. June stopped thrashing on her bed as the perfume permeated the house.

I closed my eyes and breathed in, and breathed in, and I felt as though my feet were leaving the ground. I reeled with insights—the secrets of the universe were revealed, I needed only a moment to catch my breath, to think them through, to sort out all the thoughts. Men and women, yin and yang, negative and positive—suddenly, I had a thread to tie them all together. I could taste the sweet tang of truth on the back of my tongue as everything in life made so much *sense*. It was like a thousand orgasms, this knowledge the plant had garnered through its ages of research. I saw fact and reason, and I could know all the ancient mysteries—if only I could have just a pause to put it all into perspective, it was all happening so fast, too fast—I couldn't quite manage to . . . *understand* . . .

And then it began to fade, and I cried, grasping desperately for the threads, but they turned to wisps in my mind, and all that I had gained was gone, and I opened my eyes and found myself cramped up, huddled in the corner of the nursery, and dawn was nigh.

The baby was gone, and the blossom had wilted and withered into a soft, black mass that hung from the stalk as if in shame.

I ran down the stairs to the garden, and saw one large, baby-sized lump—like an Adam's apple in slow motion—move down the center of the stalk, and as it descended, the plant above it rapidly decayed.

I looked around and saw the house deteriorating as well. The paint faded and began to flake and peel. The grass turned yellow and brittle. Weeds sprouted up and twisted, weaving, matting and crisping. A portion of the fence slowly caved in.

The trap was being reset.

If I took June and left this place, another young, fertile couple would be along right behind us.

And then I remembered the neighbors speaking of an old man who lived in the house before us; a private old man who had lived here as long as anyone could remember. He had a succession of young wives, they said, but he never had any children.

I imagined them working together; the plant and the old man. The man working in the dream state, trying to discover the thing the male plant desperately needed: the female secret of propagation.

For his efforts, the lonely, frustrated carnivore, which could flower and hypnotize but could not heed the call to reproduce, rewarded the old man with dreams of youth, vitality, virility— and the stuff of the perfume.

The old man had chosen to live out his life in the company of this house, this house and the carnivore that grew from it.

But I wouldn't. I would burn this damned place to the ground, and hack the plant to pulpy shreds.

As soon as I had one more chance at the perfume. Just one more chance. Next time, I would be prepared. And I would get it right.

•**F**ogarty & Fogarty

1

Fogarty first met his bride in a culvert under the highway one night during a full moon. He was cold and tired, and a little anxious about being caught too far from home when the cold snap bit. He wasn't happy about taking refuge out in the open, either, where who-knew-what might come along and get frisky with an old man so casually dressed.

He found some old papers and leaves piled up in the corner where the wind had swept them, and he wound his way through the culvert, shuffling his feet, scooping up more and more to add to the pile. When he'd built himself a fair little heap where it was dry and out of the wind, he stepped gently across it to the concrete corner and sat down, then fluffed the leaves up around him.

The old autumn smell of the leaves was a pleasant change from the scent of his normal home, and he breathed in their acrid mustiness. He knew they would make him sneeze, but he couldn't help himself, he was suddenly very pleased that events had taken such a turn as this. He'd forgotten about autumn leaves.

When finally the sneeze did come, it came from deep down

inside him, and his eyes opened wide as he felt it coming up, and he smiled in anticipation. Then his vision was blurred by a rush of tears, his eyes squinted up, and a blast shot through him that felt so good that he laughed out loud.

Fogarty wiped his nose on his shirtsleeve and saw that he'd sneezed almost all of the leaves off himself, so he began to gather them close again, chuckling to himself, feeling cozy in his new home.

In the midst of chuckling and gathering old crispy leaves and remembering that sneeze, he had the creepy feeling that someone was watching him. Fear jumped into his stomach and he stopped. He held perfectly still. The night was so silent, he could hear one leaf on his neck rub another in perfect rhythm with his racing pulse.

Then he heard leaves crunch. A step. And another, and finally a woman came into view, an old, frail woman, with a man's gray overcoat on, and some leather boots with good miles still in them, and socks and socks and more socks all up and down her legs. She wore a knit cap over a scarf, and she stepped gently on the leaves, warily walking around him, giving him lots of room.

Fogarty was stunned. There were indeed blessings on this night. First, autumn leaves. Then a sneeze to top all sneezes. And now, company. In the form of a lady, yet.

Look at ya, Fogarty, he thought. A lady. Where's yer manners?

He jumped up. Leaves flew from him as if he'd exploded. The woman's face reacted with horror. He realized what a sight he must make, and immediately dropped to one knee.

"My dear," he said, and stopped her, midbolt. "I dint mean to startle ya. I was just lookin' fer my manners here." Her face softened, though she took a step back. "It's a cold night, and I been caught too far from my home. Might I guess you is in the same?"

She said nothing.

"The night's full of blessings, it is," he said. "First, these leaves, ain't they glorious? And I think they're gonna be warm, too, and then a sneeze, and now some company."

She looked at him with an expression of interest, but still said nothing.

"Would you join me?" He stood up and shook out his aching knee, but held the palms of his hands out to her, so she wouldn't be afraid. "I'm Fogarty."

"Fogarty," she said.

"That's right!" He smiled, and wished he'd found a bath before now. "Fogarty. What's your name?"

She was silent.

"I bet it's a name as beautiful as yerself," he said, beginning to shiver, "but it's mighty cold here, and I'm going to get back down inside this blanket of leaves for some warmth. I would courteously invite you to join me. I can see as you're cold, too." He sat back down and began piling leaves up on his legs and his chest, moving slowly so as not to spook her.

"I don't normally live around here," he said, feeling her interest. She wanted to join him, he could tell. "I normally live way down south. Out of town. You live around here?"

She kept her silence, but took a step closer to him.

"Here," he said, and swept some leaves from the concrete. Then he sprinkled a soft bedding down. "Sit down here and I'll cover you up nice and warm."

She came over timidly, sideways, ready to run at his first false move. He held his breath—he wanted to have some company on this cold and lonely night—and gently smiled at her and encouraged her. Eventually, she sat in the spot he cleared, but as he moved to put leaves on her legs, she scooted over farther away from him.

He held up his hands. "Okay," he said. "You do it."

She picked up a handful of leaves and put them on her lap, then looked back at him. He nodded in encouragement, and scooped armfuls up around his own legs, then nodded at her. She copied his motions, and soon she was grinning and up to her chin in leaves.

They sat together in silence for a while, listening to the sporadic traffic on the highway overhead, the rumblings, mostly, of the sixteen-wheelers. Then Fogarty saw a lightening of the sky, and he shook his arm free of leaves and pointed at it.

"Moon's about to come up," he said. "Another blessing." And she smiled at him and they waited for it together.

When finally the moon, gigantic and orange, arose over the skyline, it cast a bright, colorless light on the culvert, deepening sharp-edged shadows. Fogarty smiled and sighed, and turned to the woman to speak, but the moonlight on her soft face and bright eyes caught him off guard, and the breath caught in his chest. A lady, he thought. A real lady.

Leaves crinkled as she reached up and pulled off her knit cap, and then untied the scarf from under her chin. Her hair wasn't as gray as he thought it would be; it was fairly dark, and curly. She ran her fingers through it, fluffing it up a little bit, and the moon caught the highlights, and she smiled at Fogarty, and the little wrinkles around her eyes threw nets around his heart and he fell in love.

He gazed at her and gazed at her, until the moon arose above the highway. The dark shadow sliced across the culvert and left them again in the dark.

Fogarty felt her presence as rich as if it were liquid. He was mindful of his heart pounding, his breath rasping through dry lips, and he was mindful of his clothes and his beard and he reached up a hand through the leaves and smoothed down his own thinning hair.

The feeling was vaguely familiar, this feeling of warmth and excitement that jittered his stomach and spread until he could hardly sit still. Fogarty searched his fragmented memory, but found only the unsettling feeling that there had been a woman in his life once, a woman and a child—a son—but those thoughts were uncomfortable somehow, and he didn't dwell on them. It was just this first flush of love that dredged stuff up, he thought, and he ran his hand over his face and finger-brushed his front teeth real quick and then snaked his hand back under the leaves and began to pick at a hangnail.

"Where do you mostly live?" he asked.

No answer.

He turned to look at her, and there was a sparkle in her eye that must have captured all the starlight, and the streetlights, and headlights from passing sixteen-wheelers as well as the blue neon from the diner two blocks down, and focused it into two little tiny pinpoints that beamed right into Fogarty.

He was mesmerized by those eyes—eyes he couldn't really see in the dark, he could only see the little pinpoints of light—they seemed to be looking right through him, right into his soul.

He looked for a minute into his own soul, and found it to be a good one. A worthy one. A clean one. Cleaner, at least, than the outside of him.

"I would please to know your name," Fogarty whispered, and just then the moon peeked down from between the two highway overpasses, and a swath of light fell on the concrete over her head and began sliding down. Their eyes locked and then the moon began with her hair, showing every detail, and then her eyebrows, and her eyes, those glorious eyes, were they brown? and then her nose, nice and straight, and full cheeks, then mouth with wide smile and deep laugh lines. Up to her neck in leaves, it looked to Fogarty as if a heavenly sculptor had been interrupted just as he finished the face of an angel.

The moonlight moved across the space between them, and up Fogarty's mound of leaves, and he could almost feel the light as she followed it with her eyes, up over his collar, to his loose neck, the beard stubble from his two-day trek from home, his small lips and hooked nose, deep, recessed eyes that sometimes looked green, sometimes brown, and big, bushy eyebrows that looked like they ought to be on a man with a little more meat on him. He had a shock of hair right in the front, but then it thinned out to be a pretty poor crop, but had some good growth in the back. He kept it fairly trimmed; usually he kept a pretty good toilet. It was just because he'd been caught away from home two nights in a row, now . . .

"Fogarty," she said, in a whisper as soft as a spider moving across a web.

"Fogarty," he whispered back, aching to hear his name again on her lips. No one had ever said it like that before. "Fogarty. That's me. What's yours?"

"Fogarty," she said again, and smiled, and her teeth were good and straight, and then the leaves rattled and her hand emerged from the pile, clean and as white as a lily.

"I been a good man, Lord," Fogarty said to the moon, and

he reached his spotted hand out and touched hers. Her hand was warm and soft, and he said to her, "Yes, the moon has seen to bless us tonight."

"Bless us," she whispered. "Fogarty and Fogarty."

Fogarty's mouth dropped open, and he looked deeply into her eyes, and knew that his dream had come true. A dream he hadn't even known he'd had.

He saw the shadow begin to take the moonlight from the top of the culvert over her head, moving down toward her, and he knew this was his chance. He must rise to the occasion.

"You, Moon!" he said. "You and the Lord bless us, okay? Fogarty and Fogarty." Then he laughed and she laughed and they squeezed each other's hands, and then the moon, on track to its zenith, slid right on past, leaving them in the shadows of the overpass, listening to sixteen-wheelers and the music in their own hearts.

2

The next morning, long before the sun could warm their leaves, Fogarty and his bride awakened to the sound of rush-hour traffic over their heads. They smiled at each other with a tug of embarrassment that the rational light of day often brings, and Fogarty let go of the soft hand that had held his all night long.

"Oh, such a blessing to be up before the sun," he said, and stood up, gave a mighty stretch, then shook all the leaves out of his clothes. Suddenly, he found himself shy. When the sun came up, he and his new wife would have their first real look at each other. No, he said to himself, that's not true. The moon showed our souls last night and that's enough.

"Come, Fogarty," he said, and held out his hand for her, then pulled her up. She, too, stretched and grinned, then dusted off her clothes, pulling pieces of dried leaves out of her multilayered socks. He took her hand and they climbed out of the culvert and walked into the city.

"Do you have clothes?"

She looked down at what she was wearing.

"Or belongings? Something to fetch?"

She lifted his hand to her cheek.

"Well, then," Fogarty said, with a blush and a feeling of manly protectiveness. "Let's go home."

Hand in hand, they walked through the center of the city as if it belonged to them, Fogarty and Fogarty, and for once, no one hassled them. They walked through the center of the business district, and as the secretaries and executives sped by them with their clackety high heels and brisk swinging of briefcases, Fogarty held on to his bride a little tighter, and they both walked a little taller, and when they reached the area of used-car lots and giant discount stores, both breathed a little easier.

The sun cast long afternoon shadows when they reached the far side of town. Fogarty tugged his wife's arm, guiding her down an alley. The wonderful scent of freshly cooked vegetables almost made him weak in the knees. "Come, Fogarty," he said. "Meet a friend."

Fogarty stopped at a green back door where at least a dozen cats were blinking their sleepy eyes in the dusk and waiting for a handout. He smoothed his hair back, brushed at his clothes, ran his hand over his face and finger-brushed his front teeth. Then he straightened his bride's hat and touched her cheek and knocked on the door.

After a minute, the door opened, and a little Chinese man stood with the bright light behind him.

"Fogarty!" he said, and his eyes squinted up with pleasure. "Long time. Come in, come in. You hungry?"

Fogarty looked at his wife and smiled, and she looked back at him with adoration.

"Who's this?" The man in the white coat looked the missus up and down, suspicion narrowing his face. "Fogarty, I thought . . ."

"Fogarty," she whispered, and Fogarty put his arm around her.

"Fogarty and Fogarty," he said to the Chinaman. "The moon has married us."

"Married?" The cook's expression opened up. "Married?"

Delight opened his arms wide, and the door opened wide, and he hugged and kissed them both. "Come in, come in," he said. "Marriage feast."

Fogarty led the way to the little wooden table and chairs set in the middle of the Chinese kitchen. He pulled one out, but his bride's eyes looked around wildly. "Would you like to freshen yerself?" he asked. She looked at him without understanding, so he guided her to the restroom. She went in and closed the door.

Lee returned with his wife, whose name Fogarty could never pronounce, so he called her Donna, which always made her laugh gently behind her hand. Donna was big with child, and Lee big with pride.

Fogarty stood up when his missus returned, and she picked at her hat shyly as he introduced her, and Donna touched both her shoulders and made her sit down and Donna and her husband served them more than they could eat in a week.

"I work here sometimes," Fogarty explained. "I stop here coming home, and eat and sleep, and then I clean."

"He does a good job. He's a good man," Lee said.

"Yes," Donna said. "We like Fogarty. Good man."

Fogarty blushed.

"Sleep here tonight and in the morning we'll pack up your honeymoon food and you'll go on home. You're going to live at Fogarty's?"

All eyes went to Fogarty's bride, who looked at her plate. "I must work . . ." Fogarty said.

Lee shook his head. "Wedding present," he said, and Fogarty and Fogarty spent their second night together on futons in the storeroom while a busy restaurant went on around them.

In the morning, there were two white paper sacks on the counter, each filled with little white cartons of food, and Fogarty and Fogarty each took one and started home.

Fogarty was feeling more and more comfortable in her presence, and was glad the good Lord found him fit to receive a good woman. He didn't know what he'd do if he'd gotten a bad one. This one was pretty as a picture and modest and shy, nice and gentle. She needed a bath, though, and some fresh clothes. There was time for all of that when they got home.

Outskirt buildings fell behind them as they walked the asphalt in the early morning. A few shacks came and went and they were beginning to see a few silos in the distance when Fogarty steered his bride down a rutted, packed dirt road to the right. They followed along, crossed the railroad tracks, and kept going.

"It'll be a blessing to get home early," he said.

She smiled up at him then looked back down at the road, shifting her bundle of Chinese food.

"It's not far now."

The road curved off to the left, but Fogarty led her down a footpath in the knee-high yellow weeds. Then he held the wires of a fence apart for her, and followed her through. They went to the right and followed the fence for twenty-seven fence posts, and the trail turned left again.

"Landfill," he said. "Been my home now for eight, coming on nine winters. You'll like it."

He smiled, but she failed to look up at him, and suddenly he was overcome with uncertainty. He walked a few more steps through the litter-strewn weeds on the uneven ground. His stomach was jumping around inside of his belly and it felt a lot like shame. "Hey, Fogarty," he said, and touched her arm. She stopped and looked at him, and he saw that soft face and those fabulous brown—they were brown, they were wonderfully brown—eyes. "Hey, I'm pleased to be taking you to my home." A smile flitted across her face, and she looked down again. She's nervous too, he thought.

He pointed out landmarks to her, for when she went foraging, or if she ever needed to go to town. "My house is hard to find, you see, that's why it's been here eight, going on nine winters. Just keep seein' old Mr. Boiler's pipe sticking up over there, and the three cars piled on top of each other over there. The front door's right in the middle."

They went up over hills and slid down into the valleys as the terrain of the dump became more difficult. "They dump the fresh stuff more'n a mile off," he said. "Sometimes it smells, and sometimes there's a fire. Then I *really* smell it. This part of the landfill's done, though, so they leave it alone. Ha. Eight, almost nine winters, now."

The sight of Fogarty's front yard made him happy enough to want to hoot, but he didn't want to scare the lady, so he just said, "Home we are," and walked right up to the front door that used to belong to an old blue Pontiac, and opened it.

She looked inside, which was dark, and she took a step back and shook her head. Fogarty looked inside, down the dark stairs and said, "You're right, I forget. You stay here, and I'll put in the light."

He walked away from her, around toward the old boiler, and shifted some pieces of wallboard and siding. Light shone up the stairs. Then he walked around in a big circle, moving sheets of warped plywood and roofing paper, and more and more light came up from below.

He was sweating in the late-morning heat when he came back. "Skylights," he said. "I cover 'em when I go away. Come, Fogarty," and he ducked down inside the door and went down to the bottom of the stairs, where he waited for her.

She followed, hesitantly, and when she got down, Fogarty took her hand, put his arm around her and looked into those deep, trusting brown eyes and said, "This is our home." He delighted in seeing the astonishment on her face as she looked around. "Aren't we blessed?"

Fogarty had spent eight, going on nine winters carving out a very personal space amid the debris. The ceilings were made of a patchwork of woods and old windows, propped up in crucial points by timbers that had seen better days, but never a prouder use. The walls and the floors were as colorful and kaleidoscopic as the rest of the place, a swirling interconnecting of color and form and texture. Each individual piece had been foraged from the dump, but there was no garbage, there was no junk. Everything had been used and no longer wanted by its original owner, but Fogarty had seen through stains and holes and rusts and found the nuggets of usefulness in another's trash.

The kitchen had a tiny woodburning stove, a Formica counter, and cabinets.

"Lee give me those," he said, and walked around her to touch the row of white dish towels that hung on a rod over the sink. He felt a need to break the silence, put some animation into his home. He set down his white sack of Chinese food and took hers from her. Then he took off his coat and emptied the big pockets he'd sewn into the lining. He brought out a tall bottle of lamp oil, a dozen books of matches, two handfuls of warped candles and some dented cans of meat and fruit.

He looked around at his home and was pleased that he had tidied up before leaving on this last trip. He hadn't known he would be bringing home a wife.

"Come, Fogarty," he said, and took her hand. They moved past the kitchen, past the little plastic-topped dining table with two chairs, into the living room that had a sofa, a rocking chair with footstool, a scarred coffee table with a game of solitaire laid out and ready to play, and a whole corner filled with stacks of puzzles and games. A magazine rack held some old issues of *National Geographic,* and next to it was a big kerosene lantern on an end table.

Fogarty looked at his bride's face, but her expression of astonishment hadn't changed. His pride swelled into a smile.

"Come," .he said again, and led her through a yellow gingham curtain into his bedroom. Both pillows were neatly plumped on a high double bed, an old quilt that looked handmade was folded neatly at the foot; a plain wooden dresser stood in the corner, and over it hung a mirror. A chunk of galvanized pipe hung from the ceiling, and clothes, neatly arranged on hangers, hung from it. "My apologies for that," he said. "A proper closet is next." The missus looked at him with wide eyes and a cocked head, and finally she began to smile.

"The bathroom's over here," he said, and took her gently out of the bedroom, past a blue and white striped curtain, where a plastic shower stall stood over a drain in the floor, and a stepladder was propped up next to it.

"The water heats up on the wood stove," he said, "and it goes up in that there bucket. Then"—he opened the shower curtain—"I can stop and start the water here with this hose, so's I can wet down and soap up and then rinse off." A plastic sack of little hotel-sized bars of soap hung in the corner.

A sparkling clean blue antique chamber pot had been set under a straight-backed chair that had the cane seating removed. "I use that," he said, "and empty it every day, but we can do something else, if you want."

Her eyes softened.

"There's a faucet just on the other side of that old boiler outside," Fogarty said. "It's such a blessing, it is. A picnic table used to live there too—I guess the workers used to eat there, and they put in a faucet and left it when they moved on to the north side. I been meaning to run a hose, but I don't want anybody to be finding the house, so I just go up and get water when I need it."

He got another noseful of her in his close quarters and realized that they needed some shower water right now. "I'll go get some now," he said, "and put on some tea and make us both a shower."

She just looked at him, and that jittery feeling returned to his belly. He didn't know if she understood anything he said or not.

"I only light the stove at night, usually, when nobody can see the smoke, but a hot shower and cup of tea is such a blessing when I first come home. I'll just do a little fire, just enough for baths."

He paused, anxious to get his chores done, but hardly able to move away from her. "There's clothes in that box over there, they're men's clothes, but they'll do until we can find you some fresh ones and get yours laundered."

He ran out of words and they stood together in the hallway, close, and Fogarty saw again what pretty hair she had peeking out from under that brown knitted hat, and what a soft face she had, and for some reason it didn't seem odd at all that she was here. After eight, going on nine winters living in this place all by himself, suddenly it was almost like he'd had her in mind all along as he worked every day on his little house, making it just right for her. And now here she was, and it felt normal and natural.

"So why don't you just . . . sit . . . and I'll get the water on and . . . so why don't you just sit . . . there?"

She smiled and he smiled back, and then he worked over the stove until he got a little fire going, put the pot on it, and went out with his biggest bucket. It would take at least two trips, he thought, but when he came back with the first bucketful, he found her asleep on his bed, her hat and coat still on, a warm flush on her cheeks.

"Such a blessing you are, Fogarty," he said to her, and went to take himself a shower.

3

Fogarty snapped awake, his body rigid with fear. Then he heard her soft breathing in the silent night and he relaxed. So strange to have someone else with him. In his bed. He looked at his bedside clock. Five-thirty. He looked over at her, a lump under the quilt, barely visible in the starlit darkness, and he could see shine on the little bit of curly hair that rested on the pillow.

Married you are, Fogarty, and he smiled up at the skylight. Married.

A vision of mounds and mounds of festively wrapped gifts swam up before his watery eyes.

His heart thudded. A gift! I must be giving my bride a wedding gift! He slipped out of bed and put on clothes that were clean as of the day before. He left her sleeping and walked quietly up the stairs and out into the early morning chill.

He gave a mighty stretch and a yawn, then rubbed his arms in the cold. The morning stars winked down on him as he saw the first faint glow of false dawn in the east. East. That's where he would find a present for his wife. In the east.

He walked past the old rusted boiler, and gave it a little pat, hearing the hollow sound of its deep interior. Again, as always, his mind played on it for a few moments. That big old boiler was big as a house almost. It had a big use in it, just waiting to be discovered, he knew that. Maybe he needed to spend a few hours with it, just the two of them alone, and he could feel what the old thing was about, feel what it wanted to do with the time it had left as an old boiler before the rust turned it into something else. It was real big, and good, and mostly dry inside. He would spend some time with Mr. Boiler soon.

Fogarty walked on past the boiler, toward the lightening sky. He walked up and down the hills of trash, through the areas he knew by heart. He'd picked over all this place long, long ago, and while the landscape always shifted, changing with the winds above and the decay below, the substance never really altered.

Dawn grew brighter, and the orange glow spread horizontally. Fogarty stopped for a moment to just watch as the clouds in the sky caught fire, and then he caught his breath as the surface of the debris of the dump turned yellow/orange for miles in front of him. He wheeled around and sure enough, the stars still held their ground in the west, waiting until the last minute before fading out.

Fogarty found an old, dented suitcase half buried under some plastic bags full of some rotted something, old weeds, probably, and he pulled it free and sat down on it to watch the sun make her appearance. He sat and watched, seeing the patterns in the clouds, luxuriating in the richness of the colors spread before him. Dawn was his favorite time. It meant newness to Fogarty, freshness. Dawn always tugged on something deep within him, making him think about his life, and how good it was. He always had enough of whatever he needed. He picked up cans and old bottles whenever he went foraging, and when he ran out of oil for the lantern, he went into town to the place that gave him money for his pickings. He grew his own vegetables, year after year, using seed from the previous year's harvest. He found lots of burnable things for his stove, so he was warm in the winter, and there were plenty of clothes, and he had the company of the birds and the boiler, and the sun, and now and then a meal and some work with Lee and Donna.

And now he had Fogarty, his wife. What a blessing she was.

The sky began to turn blue and shadows formed on the hills and debris in front of him, making strange patterns of light, all still with a reddish glow. He laughed aloud at the idea that he could make animals out of these shadows as easily as he made animals out of the clouds. And these changed as fast as the clouds too, turning into something different every few seconds.

Ah yes, Fogarty, he thought, plenty of blessings right here. He had everything. He had his mornings, and his quiet time, and his sunrise, and this old suitcase to sit upon as he thought about things, and he had a long life, and good teeth, and . . . he looked around. He would like to have an orange tree. He would like to grow fresh oranges.

He watched the sunrise turn to yellow and he thought of ripping deep into a rich, juicy orange, and the ache began behind his ears and his mouth began to water. Maybe I can grow an orange tree inside that boiler, he thought, and then I can just go up there and say "Hello, Mr. Boiler, I've come to thank you and your orange tree by having myself a little orange breakfast, yes, I have, thank you very much," and I'd peel myself a big, fat orange and let the juice run down my hands. Yes, he thought, that's just what I need.

He bounced up and down a little on the old dented suitcase as the sun sent glory to surround the eastern sky, and Fogarty tasted orange juice in his mind. The suitcase made a funny noise as it dented in and out, and he laughed out loud and did it some more. Then he stood up and took a look at it.

"Hey, Mr. Suitcase," he said. "You're a good old chair. You're a good old sunrise chair." And he laughed until he saw a piece of fabric sticking out the side, caught when the suitcase had been closed. It was dirty and faded, but it had flowers on it, and intrigued, Fogarty stood up and picked up the suitcase and looked closer at the fabric.

Maybe Fogarty would like that, he thought, and he snapped up the suitcase clasps. He opened the lid, and neatly folded inside was a dress, lying there pretty as you please, with a piece of its hem creased, faded and dirty where it had been out in the weather for years. Fogarty lifted the dress as if it were made of spun dreams, and held it up high to the sunrise. "Oh, you is a beauty, you is," he said, and tried to imagine the missus in it. He couldn't quite remember what she looked like, except that she had those soft brown eyes. She'd look just wonderful in this dress, he was sure.

Under the dress were little zippered bags with stockings and ladies' personal things, some makeup and bottles of soaps and lotions. There was a bright yellow sweater that smelled a little musty, but that could be washed out all right.

Oh, Fogarty, he thought. This is a wedding present fit for your bride.

He looked at the sunrise, and though the sun hadn't peeked over the horizon yet, it was full daylight out, and the shadows had softened. Fogarty would be waking up soon, he thought, so he refolded the sweater and the dress, put them back in the suitcase and began a proud walk home.

She stood in the middle of the living room as he brought the old suitcase down the stairs. She wore his old plaid bathrobe, and her hair was squished down on one side where she'd slept on it wet and fresh from a washing.

"Hey, Fogarty," he said. "Morning to ya."

She looked at the ground and picked at her fingernails. She looked small, and frail, and afraid.

"Look what I gotcha," he said, and he hefted the suitcase, then brought it over and set it on the coffee table.

Curiosity brightened her eyes and she looked at him with a question.

"It's my weddin' present to ya," he said. "Go on, open it. I think you'll like it. It was a blessing from the east."

She just looked at it, a little expression of pleasure around her mouth.

He reached over and snapped open the locks. "Go on," he said. "Open it."

She looked up at him with those doe eyes and he felt silly.

"Don'tcha like it, Fogarty? Don'tcha want to see what's inside?"

She blinked once, and his face flushed. He didn't know what she wanted. He reached down in exasperation and turned the suitcase around to face him and flipped up the clasps.

She put a hand on his arm and bent down, over the back hinges.

"What? What is it?"

She reached over, tugged on something, and Fogarty heard paper tear. Then she stood up, and in her hand she held a little, tiny piece of yellowed paper. She looked at it, and her eyes opened wide with wonder, and she handed it to him, excitement putting a flush into her cheeks.

It was a piece of a page torn out of what looked like a paperback novel, only it was so faded and water-stained that hardly anything was legible at all. Fogarty looked at it, front and back, and started to set it down, but the missus held his hand and urged it again toward him.

He took a long look at her, and she nodded in encouragement, and he looked at the scrap again, impatient for her to be done with this silliness and see his wedding present. He examined the paper again, and just where it was torn were two words, faded almost into obscurity. Almost, but not quite. The words were: Mary languished.

"Mary la lan lang ished Mary lang-ished. Mary languished," Fogarty read, and the missus nodded her head.

"Mary languished," she said. "Me," and she thumped her chest with her fingertips for emphasis.

"You?" Fogarty was astonished, surprised and delighted. He hadn't seen her with this much enthusiasm. "Mary languished?"

She took the paper and licked it, then stuck it to her cheek. Her posture took on a whole new angle.

"Well, Mary Languished," Fogarty said. "Well," he said with a big grin, "well, Mary Languished Fogarty, this suitcase must be for you. It has your name on it. And when you're done opening it, we can use it for a sunrise chair outside."

Mary Languished touched the piece of paper, smiled at him with stars in her eyes, and got on with opening her wedding present.

4

Fogarty leaned over the fender of the old red Corvair and picked little weeds out of his vegetable garden. He had vegetables growing in every engine compartment of every car in this side of the dump. His fingers touched the hairy leaves of the squash vines and stroked the smooth skins of the zucchinis and he hummed softly to them. "Beauties, you is. Beauties." He kept an ear cocked for Mary Languished, expecting to hear her footsteps. She'd taken to exploring the landfill, spending her days foraging, just as he'd done. She'd brought home some little things, some nice little things, Fogarty thought, like a pottery jar to hold the cookstove matches. It was rough on the outside and swirly blue on the inside. Very nice.

He told her about the dangers: big rats that came out at night, and about the kids, teenagers mostly, that came to shoot their guns. He showed her some hiding places he'd made, and how to find them, and she seemed happy and competent in the landfill. He tried not to worry when she went out, but he did anyway.

He left the zucchinis and went to the yellow Volkswagen, where tomatoes sprawled about. He looked out across the horizon, but could see nothing—nothing but the same landscape he'd seen every morning. No movement, no sign of life, no Mary Languished.

He spoke softly to the tomatoes, thanking them as he used his penknife to cut the ripest—four had to be cut today, that meant tomatoes for lunch and dinner and breakfast again tomorrow, but maybe he could dry some too, so they could have some hot tomato soup when the snow began to fly.

With gentle fingers, he put the four red fruits in the cut-off plastic jug he'd tied to his waist, and looked up again to see if he could see Mary Languished. She'd been gone quite a while.

The potatoes were in the bed of the old pickup truck, and he took his time going over to them. Providing food for two people was a lot more work than for just one, but most times he found it a joyful chore.

Mary Languished had turned out to be a startling and pleasant addition to Fogarty's life. He had to keep reminding her to change clothes, and he had to make sure she bathed regularly, but life took on a whole new depth with another person in the house. There was a person to talk to, instead of the clock, or the chair, even if she never answered. She was quick with certain games and puzzles, and others didn't interest her, or she didn't understand them. She kept quiet most times; she hardly ever spoke, but now and then she'd get involved in a project and begin to whistling, a sound so beautiful to Fogarty's ears that he would go all soft and wilty, listening. He'd learned to not let on, though, or she'd stop and blush and not do it again until it just came out of her automatically.

He wanted to ask her about her music, wanted to ask her about her life, her background, how she came to be in the culvert under the freeway that night, but he knew that the way to ask people things was to share with them about yourself, and Fogarty just plain couldn't remember those things about himself. Now and then, little scraps of memory, like bits of ash floating on the wind, would flutter through his mind—a child's face, a refrigerator door, an office phone number—but then they would be gone, and he would be left with just a lingering feeling of things left undone. There wasn't anything he could do about those things—he had to just let it all be.

Fogarty lifted up the black plastic that covered the heavy bunches of potatoes and cut off two nice ones for the day's eating. Then he looked off in the direction Mary Languished had gone, and worried anew. He hoped she wasn't out there in trouble. He hoped she hadn't hurt herself trying to bring something back that was too big for her to handle. He hoped nobody had seen her and given her a hard time.

He hoped she wasn't out there whistling into nobody's ears and wasting the music.

He went on to the general vegetable garden in the topless bus and checked on the seats filled with late summer meals. Between the carrots and the broccoli, he stood up and looked out the broken bus window, and saw her coming over the hill. Sure enough, she was carrying something, and she was hurrying.

His heart flew when he saw her coming toward him, and he knew he was growing to love Mary Languished, with a deep, permanent kind of love. That, too, brought a tickle from the feather of a memory, but nothing substantial enough to even stop him for a moment. He picked a sprig of parsley and pulled up one fat carrot, grabbed a handful of snap beans that were growing up over the back emergency door, put them all into his side carrier, and went down the bus stairs to meet her.

"Fogarty!" she yelled as soon as she saw him, and she began to hurry faster. He looked around quickly to make sure nobody was lurking within shouting distance, for she surely was shouting. "Fogarty!" she said again, and made straight for him. He'd never seen her so excited. Her hair was flying out from under her knitted hat, and she had on that pretty summer dress he'd found in her wedding present suitcase that fit her slender frame and made her look pretty and fresh as springtime, even though the weather was closing in on autumn and she was closing in on middle age. She wore it with her old leather boots for tramping through the trash, and a half-dozen pairs of mismatched socks, and now those unlaced old leather boots were stomping along, making a terrible racket. The dress was flying out from behind her and her eyes were as wide open as they could be, and she carried a blue bundle in front of her.

"Fogarty!" she yelled again and this time she sounded so urgent he began to run toward her.

She stopped, and bent over at the waist, he could see her taking deep breaths, trying to catch her wind, as he ran up toward her, and when he reached her, she looked at him with wild eyes and thrust the bundle into his hands.

The bundle moved, and Fogarty jumped and would have thrown it down, except for the expression on Mary Languished's face. He held it out away from him until she pulled back the blanket top and there it was. A baby. A baby looking back at him with clear blue eyes.

Fogarty just stared at the infant, astonished beyond words, beyond thoughts, even. A baby, who'd have thought a baby would be out here? Who brought him here? Nobody came out here, how'd it get here? And it was healthy—at least it looked plump and well fed—and happy—at least it wasn't crying. What was a baby doing here?

He looked at Mary Languished, whose face was still red and wet with perspiration, and she was still breathing hard from the run home with her find. She looked back at him, expressionless.

"It's Moses," she finally said, and touched the baby's forehead.

5

Fogarty carried the baby into the house, and for the rest of the day, he and Mary Languished took turns looking at him.

Fogarty could feel his shoulders relax every time he looked at Moses. The pudgy little baby with the penetrating blue eyes had the same effect on Mary Languished, Fogarty had seen it. When the baby looked up at him, he felt something move deep inside him, something big, something gentle. And all the tension went out of his neck and his shoulders, and his back, and he stood taller and felt his face get looser, and his big hands hung slack and comfortable at his sides. He could gaze into the child's remarkable eyes and let the world pass him by.

Fogarty had Mary Languished mash up some zucchini and corn and feed it to Moses, who seemed to like it all right, but Fogarty knew that the child needed milk . . . milk and other things. That night they put him down in a dresser drawer at the foot of their bed, and he stayed quiet all night.

The next morning when Fogarty got up, he found the drawer empty. Mary Languished had the baby, waltzing him around the little living room, singing.

Fogarty looked at the two of them, and he began to remember the nightmares that had flitted through his dreams. Nightmares of responsibility. How would he find milk for the child? Moses needs milk, and a crib and a high chair. And diapers, oh Lord! It was enough trying to keep Mary Languished clean . . . how could he keep the baby in clean diapers? What would he do if the water faucet were taken away? Or if something happened to him? What if the baby got sick? And whose baby is it, anyway?

Then Mary Languished laughed and twirled and handed Moses to him, and he took the child and gazed into those clear, blue eyes and the nightmares fled and his shoulders relaxed and the only thing that mattered was his son.

After breakfast, Fogarty fashioned a sling so Mary Languished could carry their boy, and they went up and out into the sunlight.

"Blue place," was all Mary Languished could say to describe to Fogarty where she'd found the baby. Fogarty had never seen a "blue place" in the dump, and couldn't imagine what she was talking about. He wanted to find this "blue place." He thought if there was a baby in the blue place, then there might be baby supplies there, too. Mary Languished gave him a queer look, then shrugged and led the way, Moses snugly tucked into the sling across her front.

They started off north, silently trudging, listening to the

crunch of their footsteps, the gurgle of the baby. They watched for people, cribs, high chairs and anything blue, and they smelled autumn on the breeze.

Fogarty hiked on, surveying his kingdom, pleased that everything seemed to be right with the dump. There was no evidence of vandals or vermin; no major disturbance around his home. The only clues that things weren't as they seemed were the baby and Mary Languished's mention of a blue place.

Suddenly, Mary Languished hugged the baby to her and began running, her unlaced boots flopping around her feet. She reached a plastic sack with handles, and lifted it high.

Fogarty caught up with her and took the bag. Inside was a nice sweater, slate-blue, Fogarty's size. He liked it. There was also a new toothbrush, still sealed in its package. "Good, Mary Languished. Good work. Thanks to you." He smiled and bowed.

"Blue here."

"Blue what?"

"Blue air."

"Blue air?"

"Blue air, blue"—she gestured widely—"trash, blue . . . Blue!"

"Where?"

"Here," she said, indicating the whole area with a sweep of her arm. "All this. Blue."

Fogarty couldn't make any sense of what she was saying. "What do you mean, blue, Mary Languished?"

"Fogarty," she said, matching the seriousness of his expression. "Blue. Everything blue."

"Where was the baby?"

She walked a little way and stopped. She stared at the ground, and then pointed. Fogarty followed her and looked where she pointed. In a little sheltered area was a wooden cradle with an odd little symbol carved in the headboard.

Fogarty squatted down and ran his finger over the symbol. It was black, as if burned into the old wood. There were three round dots like three points of a triangle inside an oval.

He straightened up. "Where's the blue?"

Mary Languished looked around. She shrugged.

They looked at each other for a long moment. Fogarty felt some deep, familiar emotion come welling up within him; he felt like running away, he felt like crying. Then Moses began to squirm inside the sling and Mary Languished pulled him free of the restrictive cloth and held him up to the early morning sunshine. She smiled at the boy and turned him so Fogarty could see his face.

The baby looked wise, somehow, and Fogarty gazed into the little face until he felt that smile come out from the inside of him, and soon they were all laughing.

Mary Languished set the baby into his cradle. "Such a blessing," he found himself saying to her. He put his arm around her and they both looked at their son, and in a few moments she picked up the baby and he picked up the cradle and they made their way back home.

6

Fogarty found it hard to go up the stairs. He was ready to go to town; he had his coat on, his lining pockets empty and ready to be filled with supplies, a few extra bags tucked away. He thought of the long walk out of the landfill, along the road and into town. He thought of finding bedding for the two days it would take for him to finish foraging in the city for the things that he and Mary Languished and Moses needed. He thought of those things, being out there in the cold, alone, while they were warm and comfortable in their little dwelling, and he was very reluctant indeed to climb up the stairs.

But Moses needed milk and meat and diapers, and Mary Languished needed some female things and Fogarty had to provide those things for his family. And he had a twenty-dollar bill that felt warm and pleasant in his pocket.

Mary Languished had gotten up to see him off, and she stood in the kitchen, wearing his bathrobe and holding Moses. Fogarty resisted the temptation to go to her, take the baby and just hold him and rock him.

He looked at her sweet face, still sleep-puffed, and wondered if she'd change his diaper even once in the two days he'd be gone. He'd already reminded her three times that he'd be gone two nights, and how she had to bathe herself and the baby each night. She never talked, so he never knew if she understood.

He wanted to leave feeling confident about her, he wanted to see a little row of white dish towels in the kitchen, too, but instead, he gave her a last smile and a wave, and went up the stairs, opened the old blue Pontiac door and his breath steamed out into the starry, dewy, early morning.

He felt naked without his customary bags of bottles and cans and selected little items he'd scrounged to sell. He felt incomplete without them, but he didn't miss them; those things never brought him more than three or four dollars anyway. He had a whole twenty-dollar bill this time, and he could buy just about anything he wanted with that.

He patted his pocket one more time, felt the money, and set off down the trail toward the fence. He wanted to be well away from the landfill by daybreak.

"Such a blessing," he said to himself, as he walked over familiar territory under familiar stars. "Such a blessing to be free and rich." He stopped for a moment and scratched his head. "And to have a family waiting at home," he said, and smiled.

Dawn began as he reached the fence; the stars had faded into blue sky by the time he reached the main road, and the full adventure of the trip before him filled his soul with excitement and his feet became lighter. He ran through the list of purchases again in his mind, and wondered if he'd have money left over to put a little wager in on one of the ponies running.

No, Fogarty, he said to himself. No more ponies. Have you forgotten the sickness?

He hadn't forgotten. No more ponies, he promised himself, and he walked along the road into town as traffic picked up, and he thought of the place where he'd found the money—the same place he'd found the cradle for Moses. The Blue Place, Mary Languished still called it.

The Blue Place.

Fogarty had gone back there a few days after finding the

cradle, and he found a high chair, right in the same place. It was a wooden high chair that looked just like the cradle; it even had the same carved symbol on the back of the seat: three dots, like the points of a triangle, inside an oval.

Mary Languished loved it. She set Moses in it, and he sat up as pretty as you please and grinned at his parents.

The few days after that kept Fogarty busy with putting down the last of the vegetables before the frost, and then he knew he was going to have to hustle to scavenge enough bottles and cans for all the things they needed to get them through the next couple of months. Usually, harvesting and laying in the last of the vegetables was a joyful chore, but this time as he worked, he worried.

He kept one eye on the sky, and the other on the last tin of meat in the cabinet, and he worked hard, and fast. The baby needed milk.

Scavenging had become harder. Fogarty wasn't as strong as he once was, and the landfill was growing. The trash shifted and changed like the ocean, with the winds constantly rearranging the top, and the rot, rust and decay rearranging below. But for eight, going on nine winters, Fogarty had scavenged the whole area, and bottles and cans and saleable goods became harder to find. The richest deposits of bankable items were closer to the fresher landfill, and that was far, far from his home and risky.

And now, the Blue Place.

The Blue Place pulled on Fogarty—pulled on him the same way that clear-eyed gaze of Moses did. Fogarty wanted to go to the Blue Place every day. He wanted to go there and wait, he wanted to be there when the things arrived, he wanted to see the magic. He wanted to see the Blue. He could hardly work for thinking about how he'd rather be at the Blue Place.

He'd rather be there or else just playing with his son. When he gazed into Moses' eyes, he felt that everything was perfect, everything was fine, everything has been, is, and would forever be just wonderful.

Both things were distractions to him—a man not used to distractions. Both were inexplicable, both were fascinating, irresistible. The Blue Place seemed to manufacture things they needed: that cradle hadn't been there, and that high chair hadn't been there, and that baby hadn't been there, and then all of a sudden they were. They just appeared, and he hadn't seen anybody coming or going or lurking around in the dump. It mystified Fogarty, and he thought about that Blue Place the whole time he worked in the garden.

As soon as he was finished putting down the vegetables, without even taking the Sabbath off to rest, he had set off to scavenge for the inevitable trip to town.

The first place he went was the Blue Place.

Fogarty got there just after sunrise. He climbed a little mound of debris and looked around, surveying the territory, looking for new things, weird things, anything blue or magic or moving. He saw nothing unusual, nothing but the normal speckled gray/white/rust landscape with its hollows and shadows, spreading out as far as he could see.

"Blue," Fogarty said. "Where are ya, Blue? And what are ya, anyway?"

The Blue didn't answer him, so Fogarty smiled, and shook his head, and stepped down off the mound, and as he did, he caught sight of something little and green, flapping in the early morning breeze.

He couldn't believe what he thought he saw, so he walked calmly over to it. It was a twenty-dollar bill, with one end caught underneath a stone, and it looked to be in exactly the same place the cradle had been. He picked it up and smelled it, then ironed it out by pulling it back and forth across his nose.

"Twenty dollars," he said. "Is that from you, Blue?" He looked up into the blue sky, and snapped off a salute. "My missus and my son thank ya, Blue." And he chuckled and pocketed the bill, then made his way back to the house, glad he didn't have to go scratching and picking for bottles and cans.

Mary Languished hadn't even seemed surprised. She just kept whistling, singing, and babbling to the baby in that silly little language she seemed to have made up, and Fogarty just smelled that twenty-dollar bill and sat in his chair, sipping tea, feeling rich and making plans to set out for town the next day.

As the heat of the sun began to penetrate the heavy coat Fogarty wore to town, sweat that cooled in the fall morning began to trickle down his face. He walked along the street, smelling city smells, morning smells, and he saw people walking, talking, driving, laughing, working, eating, and suddenly he thought that his life was blessed indeed.

Who else has some kind of invisible Blue give them money? And babies? And furniture?

Nobody, that's who, Fogarty, he thought to himself, and suddenly he had to go to the bathroom.

He found himself a Shell station and went in, locked the door and sat down. Maybe there's something wrong with me, he thought. Things like this just don't happen to regular folk. He put his chin on his hand and his elbow on his knee, and he tried to remember anybody else he'd ever heard of that had things like this happen to them.

He couldn't think of any.

When he was finished, he flushed the toilet and washed his hands, and he felt better.

Maybe it isn't wrong, Fogarty, he thought. Maybe it's *right*. Maybe we are *so* blessed . . .

A frown wrinkled his forehead. He'd never heard of anybody being *that* blessed before.

He thought of his home, and Mary Languished, and figured that right at that exact moment, she'd be feeding Moses his breakfast. He pictured them in his mind's eye, Moses sitting in his little high chair, one of Lee and Donna's used-to-be-white kitchen towels around his neck, another one around his bottom. Mary Languished would be mashing up vegetables with the last bit of meat from a dented can, and feeding him, both of them laughing, Mary Languished speaking that strange little musical language, and the baby responding as if he understood.

The home scene seemed a little weird to Fogarty, as he looked at himself in the service-station washroom mirror. Something wasn't quite right.

Yet it was all so normal when he was at home. Especially when he found himself speaking that same funny little musical language to his son.

Out here in the real world of Shell station toilets, that memory made him more than mildly uncomfortable.

He ran cold water on his hands, and splashed his face. "A

family is a blessing, Fogarty," he said to his reflection. "And
every family has its quirks. Now you go buy the things your
family needs."

"Okay!" he said back to himself, and then he got serious, and
pointed his finger at himself. "And no ponies."

He smiled and smoothed his eyebrows back and stepped back
out into the sunshine.

7

By nightfall, Fogarty had acquired almost everything he
needed. The filled pockets in the lining of his coat made it hot
and heavy, and it floated awkwardly around his legs and
banged into his calves.

He was pleased with the way the day had gone. He had
scrounged in his usual spots and come away with some good
things. He'd gotten a half-dozen dented cans of tuna and another half dozen of corned beef for a dollar. He got diapers
from the Salvation Army and Mary Languished's female things
from the loading dock of the supermarket. A new boy had cut
a carton too deeply and spoiled a couple of boxes. Fogarty was
grateful to give the lad two dollars for them. The only thing left
was cans of milk for Moses, and Fogarty worried how he would
carry cases of cans of milk all the way home.

He decided to postpone the worry; to treat himself instead,
to an extravagance—a hot dog from a stand near the library. It
cost a dollar, but he piled on the ketchup and mustard and
pickle relish and threw a few good onions on, too, just to be
sure he got his money's worth. Then he sat on the big lawn at
the library and watched the traffic and the bicycles and the birds
and the kids, and he thought about his day.

It had been a good day. He'd hardly thought of Mary Languished and Moses, except, of course, when considering the
things on his shopping list. He sat on the library lawn and ate
his hot dog and licked his lips and tried to imagine what the two

of them were doing at his home right this minute, and he couldn't even remember what they looked like. He couldn't believe there were people in his house.

But, of course, there were.

Fogarty finished the last bite of bun, licked his fingers and wiped his mouth on the sleeve of his shirt. He stood up and took off his laden coat, folded it carefully and laid it on the ground. Then he stretched out on the cool grass and put his head on the bundle.

Ahhh, the freedom. The freedom felt so cool, so nice. He was free to go wherever he wanted, to do whatever he wanted. He still had twelve dollars in his pocket, and he was almost finished with his duties. He'd thought he'd have to spend two nights out, but now he had only to spend one. He could make it back to Lee and Donna's before they closed the restaurant for the night, and have a sleep there, then get the canned milk and go home in the morning.

Canned milk.

His brow furrowed. His freedom fled. How'm I going to carry canned milk on top of all this other stuff all the way out to the landfill? He wouldn't be free until he figured out how to take the milk to Moses.

He had twelve dollars, he could take a taxi.

A taxi!

The thought made him sit up and hoot. Everyone passing by turned to look at him.

"Take a taxi, I could," he said to them, then chuckled and lay back down on the lawn. "Take a taxi. That's good."

But the problem of the milk remained.

I could buy a cow.

A cow!

This time he rolled over on his stomach and laughed, and beat the ground with his fist. "Buy a cow!" He laughed until his cheeks hurt, until his stomach was sore, until his fist was bruised, until the tears ran down his face. Slowly, control came back to him and he wiped at his face, giggling still, and he looked up at the people watching him, and he laughed some more. "Oh what a blessing it is," he said to them, although he didn't think they could understand him through his laughter, "to have a little freedom, yes it is, yes it is." And he lay back down, and tried to calm himself, but his stomach still shook in silent waves of laughter when he remembered what a great laugh he'd just had.

Then he remembered Mary Languished and Moses, and the worry over the cleanliness of his home returned. The fact that there were people in his home waiting for him, depending on him, quietly vacuumed up his freedom.

He stood up, put on his heavy coat and began to walk toward Lee and Donna's restaurant. They might have a good idea about the stupid milk.

Fogarty had to stop and rest six times—he counted them, six times—on the way home in the early morning heat. In addition to the hot, heavy coat he wore, he carried a big box of powdered milk from Lee and Donna and a case of canned milk on his shoulder. He'd told Lee and Donna that Mary Languished had a passion for drinking milk—for some reason he couldn't quite bring himself to tell them that they found a baby in the dump. They'd been very happy to send him home with a box of powdered milk, and he'd stopped and bought a case of canned milk at the last store outside the city.

He was happy to be bringing these things home to his family, but he'd never had to stop and rest before, not even after a hard morning's work at the restaurant.

He rested again as soon as he managed to put himself though the wires on the fence, and he set the box and the case down and mopped his brow.

"Almost home, Fogarty," he said to himself, and a little smile of home came to rest on his face.

Then he stood, and hefted his bundles, and with weak knees and a wobbly stride, made it down the home stretch.

"Mary Languished! I'm home! Oh, what a blessing it is to be in out of the hot, hot sunshine." Fogarty came down the stairs as quickly as he could manage, and he set the case of milk on the counter and the box of milk on the floor and shed his coat as he looked around his living room.

Mary Languished had moved all the furniture around. It

looked a little strange, but it looked all right, if only she'd put the footstool in front of the right chair, and move it all back against the walls again, like it was supposed to be.

"Mary Languished?" Fogarty set the footstool back in front of his chair, then glanced inside the bedroom and the bathroom. All was quiet, and everything was as it should be, so he went to his chair and sat down.

"A drink of water would be a blessing, Fogarty," he said, so he heaved himself out of his chair and went to the kitchen to get the water jug.

It was empty. Fogarty held it up and looked at it. That meant he had to go all the way up and around the old boiler for a drink. He was too tired. He'd do it later. He set the bottle back down under the counter and as he did, something else caught his eye.

He pulled back the other curtain, and there, under the counter, was a case of canned milk, the cardboard pried up in one corner, one can missing.

Fogarty's mouth fell open as he stared. He looked at the heavy case of canned milk he'd brought all the way from town, dark spots on the top where drops of his sweat had fallen, wet handprint stains on the sides where he'd frequently changed his grip.

He looked back and forth between the two, and then went back to the living room and sat down in his chair.

A moment later, he saw a shadow cross over one of the skylights. His heart leapt into his throat, and then the shadow passed and he heard Mary Languished's voice as she came near to the front door. He stood up as the door opened and she came down the stairs, singing.

She seemed surprised to see him. Fogarty lifted his laden coat from the floor where he had dropped it, and moved it to the sofa.

She gave him a bashful smile, and Fogarty felt somehow betrayed as he looked at her. He felt a vague uneasiness about her being in his house, moving things around, risking security by wandering around the landfill, making him go out on wild-goose chases for canned milk she never even needed.

"Fogarty," she said softly, and she brought Moses up from

where he'd been resting in his sling at her side, and she held the baby up to Fogarty.

Fogarty's hands automatically took the baby from her, and he broke his gaze from Mary Languished's face and looked at Moses.

His son.

Those clear blue eyes looked back into Fogarty's eyes and Fogarty felt rested and well. His mind cleared of all its anxiety and poisonous thoughts, and nothing mattered in the whole wide world except the nourishment and happy home life of this perfect child with the clear eyes.

Moses.

His son.

8

Fogarty awoke in the still darkness. Moonlight shone in through the skylight in the bedroom. Mary Languished breathed deeply beside him; Moses made little cooing noises in the basket at the foot of the bed. Fogarty sat up and looked down at the baby, who was gently playing with his toes and quietly amusing himself. Moses had thrown off his quilt, but he didn't seem to be feeling cold, so Fogarty let him be. He lay back down on the bed and pulled the covers up to his chin. The frost was definitely on; snow would be flying before Thanksgiving. He snuggled down and felt the warmth from Mary Languished's body beside him.

That weird feeling of things not being normal began to creep over him again, like a slow rush of goose bumps.

Mary Languished had found the case of canned milk in the landfill at the same place he'd found the money. The Blue Place.

Fogarty shook his head. He just didn't understand any of this. Somewhere in the back of his mind he had memories of a woman and a baby, and he sort of remembered, and that made him smile a lot when he was at Lee and Donna's, because they had their baby, and the baby cried a lot . . .

The baby cried a lot . . .

The baby cried a lot and the baby slept a lot.

Moses never cried. And rarely—if ever, now that Fogarty thought about it—slept.

Lee and Donna's baby cried a lot and slept a lot and Lee and Donna spent a lot of time with their arms around each other and their noses touching. They goo-gooed to their baby, and all of it made Fogarty smile as the little memories buried back there in the landfill of his mind shuffled around a little bit, not exactly springing forth to be recognized, but he remembered. Sort of.

There was no physical affection between him and Mary Languished. They never touched, or cuddled—she was too shy. And they never discussed their pride over the baby with each other, they seemed to discuss it with Moses. In his own language.

Fogarty ran his hand over his face in the dark. Something's really strange here, he thought.

Then he raised up again and looked at Moses in his cradle, and Moses stopped his playing and looked back at him, directly at him, those clear blue eyes looking deeply into Fogarty's soul.

Everything is okay, Fogarty thought, and he lay back down and went to sleep.

In the morning, Mary Languished fed Moses and rocked him, while Fogarty watched. Her eyes kept shifting around the room; she seemed restless and couldn't meet his gaze. Finally, he put on his coat and went up to forage for a while. Then he saw the hose.

A long patchwork hose made up of lots of little hoses hooked together stretched across the top of the dump from the deserted hydrant and disappeared into the trash next to his house. Fogarty was sure it went right into the kitchen, where Mary Languished could use it at will instead of having to walk up and out and over to the hydrant for water.

Anger burned up through Fogarty. That woman's going to get us discovered here, he thought, and marched right over to the hydrant. He turned it off, then disconnected the hose. He walked back toward home, disconnecting and burying pieces as he went. She didn't even try to cover it up, he thought.

"Roamin' the landfill during daylight hours, drawing a straight line toward the house, sending me out on wild-goose chases . . ." Fear of discovery turned quickly to anger and rumbled out of Fogarty's mouth in a monotone of discontent.

He reached the blue Pontiac door and pulled it open. Mary Languished stood there with Moses in his sling, Fogarty's clock under one arm and surprise on her face.

"Fogarty!" she said.

"Mary Languished," he said, and bowed his head. "Where are you about to?"

A blush came up her neck into her cheeks. "This clock's for the Blue, Fogarty," she said. "For thanks."

Fogarty was stunned. "My clock?"

Mary Languished nodded.

"Does the Blue want my clock?"

She shrugged.

Fogarty stepped aside, and Mary Languished looked down, then came out. Fogarty went inside, closing the door after him. He descended the stairs and watched her shadow cross the skylights, then he looked at the spot on the wall where his clock had hung for six, going on seven winters. He'd foraged that clock and set it to working right. He even sold pop bottles and beer cans for money to buy brand-new batteries for it.

The house didn't look right without the clock. What did the Blue want with the clock anyway? Maybe it would have been just as happy with a can of milk or a rag.

Fogarty found the hole in the wall next to the sink where the end of the hose came through. It was all wet; she'd just turned the hydrant on and let it leak inside the wall. He pushed it back up gently, then went back upstairs and pulled it out of the ground. He went to the old boiler and buried the hose up next to it.

Instead of patting the old boiler and listening to its wonderful hollow sound, Fogarty scowled at it and went to the hydrant for a drink.

* * *

When Mary Languished returned, Fogarty was sitting on the couch staring into space, waiting for her, his bowels churning. He saw her shadow pass across the skylights, and a knot tightened in his stomach. Then the door opened and closed and she stepped gingerly down the stairs.

She came into the living room, unslung Moses from her side and sat in the big chair, the baby in her lap.

"Did the Blue come, Mary Languished?"

She nodded, but did not look up at him.

"You saw it? You saw the Blue come take the clock?"

She began to pick at her fingernails.

"Did it take the clock?"

She shook her head and pulled at her hat.

"Where's the clock? Didn't you bring it home?"

This time she looked him squarely in the eyes. "Can't take back a gift," she whispered.

"If the Blue didn't want it . . ."

"Belongs to Blue," she said, and picked up the baby from where he'd been resting on her knees and brought him to her chest. She began to rock him.

"I took the hose apart, Mary Languished," Fogarty said. "You oughtn't have done that. It was like a trail, right to our house."

"Never left nothin' new, Fogarty," she said.

"What?"

"Blue never left nothing new."

"Maybe you oughtn't go there in the daytime anymore."

"Why?"

"Because we're gonna get discovered, that's why. You can't just leave a hose trail and go traipsin' about all day long, Mary Languished. Someone's going to see us and get suspicious." Fogarty felt heat come up his chest.

Mary Languished looked hurt, as if he'd insulted her.

"And they'll throw us out," he said. "Or maybe put us in a home."

Mary Languished stopped rocking and stared into her own memories.

"And take Moses away."

Mary Languished hugged the baby tighter and started rocking fast. "No, Fogarty, you don't know."

"Know what, Mary Languished?"

"Blue decides."

"Mary Languished, the Blue don't decide about the County guys!"

Mary Languished stood up and walked over to the couch. She held the baby out for Fogarty to see, but Fogarty pushed her away.

"I don't want to see the baby," he said. He knew that if he looked into Moses' eyes, everything would settle down again, everything would be fine again. No, he would only *think* everything was fine again, but nothing would be fine unless Mary Languished understood what he was saying.

Mary Languished turned again, and held Moses up in front of Fogarty, and somehow, against his will, Fogarty looked at that sweet, clean baby face, and those clear, clear blue eyes, and all his fears fled, and a sense of security and well-being settled over him.

The next day she took his footstool. The day after that she took the quilt from the bed and replaced it with an ugly, old, stained, torn blanket.

Fogarty began to mourn.

He stayed in the house because he couldn't keep Mary Languished from going out and he didn't want too many people roaming the landfill. He stayed in the house and watched her feed Moses and carry him around and talk to him in that stupid little language they had for each other. He stayed in the house and watched her loot his little home, piece by sentimental piece, and he didn't say anything. He stayed in the house and watched Moses grow healthy and strong and begin to crawl around the floor, and his emotions skidded up and down like they were on a roller coaster. He stayed in the house and stayed in the house and stayed in the house. The longer he stayed in the house, the deeper his depression grew.

Every now and then, he would look into Moses' face, and the depression would dissolve. Happiness surged through him and he felt strong and good and wise. Then Mary Languished would swoop down and pick up Moses and they would laugh and laugh together and the feelings Fogarty had only lasted for a few more moments, then they slipped away and he plunged further into the pit of desolation.

He suffered in silence for a long time, and then he couldn't stand it anymore.

When Mary Languished returned home after taking his porcelain chamber pot to the Blue Place, as soon as she started fixing dinner for Moses, Fogarty got up out of his chair, put on his coat and went outside.

The air was crisp and cold, the shadows long. He smelled snow on the air, the fresh, delicious air, and he ran in place for a moment, feeling his muscles freeing up after being inside for so many weeks.

He held his arms out and looked around his little domain, then set off to the Blue Place. He wanted to have a little talk with the Blue.

As he came over the rise, the first thing he saw was his beautiful chamber pot, atop a little pile of his possessions. Fogarty squatted down and examined each thing. It was all there, it was all intact. The quilt was a little damp, but that was no problem. He'd just pack it up and take it home.

Then he looked around and wondered if the Blue would come if he left a present for it. If the Blue came he could talk to it. He fished out the penknife he'd kept in his pocket for as long as he could remember, gave it a kiss and put it inside the chamber pot, then he sat down to wait.

He watched very carefully, because he wasn't sure how blue everything would get. Even the air came blue, Mary Languished said, so Fogarty watched very carefully for any signs of blue.

There were none.

He waited a long time. He waited until after the sun was down and the stars came out. He waited until his muscles cramped, until his joints ached from the cold. Then he stood up, shook out his limbs and retrieved his pocketknife.

"Why are ya doing this to us, Blue?" he shouted. "Why do you give us things and then make everything so confused? Here.

Take the pot. It's our thanks for the milk and the money and the baby. Take it. Take it. We want ya to."

Only silence answered him.

"How come Mary Languished wants to bring ya things ya don't want? How come you only come when she's here? How come you're doing all this to us? We're good people, and you're not doing nice things."

He stopped to catch his wind. Only the breath of an evening breeze came through.

"I'm mad, Blue," Fogarty said, then stomped off toward home.

He got madder when he saw all the lights Mary Languished had put on. She must have lit every candle and lantern in the place. Light turned the skylights into beacons.

Time to go to town for a while, Fogarty, he thought to himself. Time to go see Lee and Donna. Time to go see the City and work in the restaurant and do some normal things, live a little normal life for a while.

But he was afraid to go. Afraid of what might be waiting for him—or not waiting for him—when he got back home.

9

Fogarty awoke in the middle of the night. He got up and used the old rusted bucket that had replaced his beautiful porcelain chamber pot and then wandered though his little house. He didn't feel like getting back into bed with Mary Languished. He didn't want to listen to her breathe, and he didn't want to listen to Moses singing to himself in the cradle at the foot of the bed. Instead, he sat on the sofa and wrapped up in the soft knitted afghan that had so far escaped Mary Languished's offerings to the Blue.

The moon shone down through the skylights, and Fogarty felt his bottom lip pout out in absolute despair.

He looked across the room to his favorite sitting chair, already naked without its ottoman. "Hey, yo, Mr. Chair," he whispered in the darkness. "How long before she takes you out to the cold?"

He wrapped the afghan tighter around his thin shoulders and gripped handfuls of it in his bony fists. "And you, Missus Blanket," he said. "You're the prettiest thing I have left. Soon you'll be out there warmin' up the chamber pot while I'm in here shiverin' and peeing in an old no-account bucket."

The pout deepened. His head sunk down lower into the hollow between his shoulders. The closed-in feeling wrapped around him again, tighter than the afghan, tighter than his skin.

"Time to move on, Fogarty," he whispered to the night air, and sadness pushed behind his eyes. He thought of packing up his few precious things and carrying them out of the landfill. He saw himself, looking old and skinny, just a haggard old man, standing at the main road trying to decide which way to turn.

"I'm too old to start over again," he said, and the tightening feeling squeezed out a tear that ran down the side of his nose. He looked around the patchwork walls, and remembered how hard it was to build this little underground house all by himself. He thought of the years he spent scavenging household items—finding, fixing, replacing—until he had his home comfortable and perfect. He probably didn't have that many years left all told—he certainly wouldn't if he had to start all over again.

"What's the use?" he asked the pillow that sat next to him on the sofa, then he let go of the afghan and touched the pillow's worn velvet. "Might just as well up and die right now. There's nothing left for me."

A second tear followed the first, and Fogarty swiped at it with the pillow.

Then he got an idea that made his heart pound. He sat up straight. "I could move into the boiler, yes I could," he said. "I could move into that nice, clean old boiler, and I could move my things over and be closer to my water, and Mary Languished could live here with Moses, and she could give all her own things away. She could give it all away and I wouldn't care, because I would have all my own stuff in my own place." He smiled. "She could even give away my things and I could just go pick them up."

He sat back, shivering in anticipation of his new, good idea. "She could even give Moses away, yes she could, she could even give Moses away, and I wouldn't care. I'd just go pick up the stuff I wanted to keep. She could give Moses away and I wouldn't pick him up at all."

His smile became a grin.

And then he thought about Mary Languished traipsin' all over the landfill, carrying the baby, running water lines, and he knew that before long they'd be found out.

The smile evaporated.

They could take Mary Languished away and he wouldn't mind, but he would give up for sure if they took him away and put him someplace stupid like they sometimes did with old men.

Depression pressed him back into the couch. He bunched up the little velvet pillow and squeezed it. "I wouldn't care at all if they took Mary Languished away," he whispered, and then he got another idea, a great idea, a horrible idea, an idea that he didn't like, an idea he tried to push away.

"I could just give Mary Languished away," he whispered in the dark. "I could just give Mary Languished and Moses both away, just take them to that Blue Place and leave 'em for the Blue. And I'd make them stay there, too, I would, I would make them stay."

Thoughts of Mary Languished and her soft brown eyes and her shy manner trying to make Fogarty reconsider made him bunch up his fist.

"I would make them stay there, yes I would, yes I would."

It wouldn't go away, his idea, it was too good, but it was so awful, and it made him feel so bad, so guilty, that finally he went to bed to snuggle up next to Mary Languished's warm body to see if her sleeping sounds would make the idea go away.

It didn't go away, and it stayed with him all the rest of the night.

It was with him the next morning, too, and Fogarty couldn't look Mary Languished in the eyes. He just put his head down and went about his business, bringing in the food, foraging a little bit out toward the east, just he and his idea, alone in the world.

By the time his stomach told him it was time for dinner, Fogarty had taken control of his idea. It was a bad idea, and he felt guilty that he'd let it play so long in his mind. He stood up from his diggings and rubbed his aching back. It was time to go make a nice dinner for Mary Languished and Moses. He could never confess the thoughts he'd had about them, but he could make it up to them by fixing them a nice hot dinner. Maybe some nice vegetable soup and he'd even open a tin of meat.

He walked and walked to get home, surprised at how far away he'd gone during the day. By the time he spotted the blue Pontiac door, his heart gave a little leap. Home and hearth. "She's a good woman, Fogarty," he said to himself. "What a blessing it is to have such a fine family."

He opened the door and went down the stairs, noticing that it was bone-chilling cold inside. Mary Languished hadn't even started a fire. At the bottom of the stairs he smelled dirty diapers and noticed that the woodbox was empty.

He knew by the coldness of the house that no one was home, but he called anyway. "Mary Languished?"

There was no answer.

His favorite sittin' chair was gone. And so was the knitted afghan. It was like she heard him out there whispering in the privacy of his own nighttime. Eavesdropping on his own sleeplessness. Taking his privacy, his sleeplessness, his chair and his afghan in one slap.

Anger burned in his stomach. The bad idea returned with full force. It began to feel like a good idea.

Fogarty stomped up the stairs, hands stuffed in his pockets. He headed west, then circled around south, avoiding the Blue Place, and he just stomped and talked to himself in anger, kicking things as he went. Eventually he ended up by the old boiler and before he recognized the old crate as firewood, he gave it a kick that splintered its old slats and Fogarty grabbed it with his bare fingers and ripped it the rest of the way, driving slivers deep into the palms of his hands.

The pain brought him back to reality, and he looked at the pieces of crate, broken and twisted at his feet. He gathered them up and went home to build a fire.

By the time he got back, dusk had deepened and there was a faint light coming through the skylight.

Fogarty found one candle burning in the kitchen. Mary Languished stood in the middle of the living room, holding Moses, rocking him.

Fogarty threw the wood into the woodbox and dusted off his hands. He pulled two of the largest splinters out and left the rest for later. There was something that had to be done first.

He went to Mary Languished and took the baby from her and set him on the sofa. He put his hands on both of Mary Languished's shoulders and turned her to look him in the face.

"The chair, Mary Languished, you took the chair and the warm blanket. There's no wood and no food and too much . . . this is too much, do ya understand?"

"Never left nothing new, Fogarty," she said.

"Did it ever take the stuff you left it?"

She shook her head.

"Then let's go get it all and forget the Blue," he said.

She shook her head at him with a determination set to her jaw. "Can't," she said.

"Yes, Mary Languished," Fogarty said, and his hands burned with the slivers, "we can and we're going to. Right now."

"Blue protects us, Fogarty."

"Well, that's fine. It can do that without all my stuff in a pile out in the weather. You make a fire and some tea, all right? I'll go get the stuff."

"No," she said, and turned to the sofa to pick up Moses.

"I don't want to look at the baby."

"Here." She struggled against him to get to the sofa.

"No." He held her arms firmly.

"Here!" She lunged.

"No!" He held tight.

"Aaaaaaaaa!" Mary Languished began to scream and Moses began to sing and the whole room began to turn blue.

Fogarty let her go and he dropped to the floor. The room looked eerie, unreal, as if he were looking through a pair of blue glasses.

"I been a good man, Lord," he whispered. "I been a good man, yes I has."

A gentle calm washed over Fogarty, and he relaxed on his knees, feeling safe and warm. Then he felt a tingling in his hands and looked at his palms and noticed that the slivers, almost black in the eerie blue light, were disappearing, and the skin healed and grew smooth as he watched.

He looked up and saw Mary Languished, barely breathing, rapture on her face, eyes open but seeing nothing, standing with feet apart and arms stretched out wide.

And Moses was laughing.

10

When the blue faded away, so did Fogarty's sense of well-being. Mary Languished, still enraptured, picked up Moses and swung him around the little living room, and then she took him into the bedroom, while Fogarty pulled himself up from the floor and onto the couch, his old joints creaking like never before.

"The Blue protects them, yes it does, yes it does," he said to himself, still marveling at what had happened. He shook his head and looked around, and suddenly found it hard to believe that it really had happened.

He sat on the sofa and he thought about it, and thought about it and thought about it.

He thought about having something looking over him all the time like that—something so powerful it could melt the slivers right out of a man's palm. Something so powerful it could be summoned just by a little yell. Something so important it could change him from blood-freezing fear to calm security in the space of a heartbeat.

He thought about it and he didn't like it.

Mary Languished liked it. Mary Languished loved it. Moses liked it. Moses loved it. Moses *was* it.

Barely a slip of a moon shone down through the darkest of night when Fogarty made his decision.

Very quietly, he arose from the sofa, stretched out his legs, rubbing out the cramps from sitting motionless for hours, then put on his jacket. He went into the bedroom and saw Moses, wide awake as always, looking at him with shining eyes from the crooked arm of a sleeping Mary Languished.

"Come, Moses," Fogarty said, trying not to look directly into the child's eyes. "Come to Daddy."

Fogarty picked him up gently, and Mary Languished sighed and rolled over in her sleep. Fogarty grabbed the bedding from the cradle and took it to the living room, where he wrapped the baby up tightly, determined not to look into those eyes that would immobilize him—or at least mesmerize him into inaction.

When he had Moses snugly wrapped, Fogarty took the little bundle in his arms, mounted the stairs and opened the old blue Pontiac door into the freezing night air. His breath plumed out before him. The ground was frozen and covered with frost. Fogarty stepped gently until he was sure he was out of earshot, and then he walked quickly, even ran in places he knew were flat and without hazard.

At the Blue Place, Fogarty held the baby tightly to his chest. "I've come to give him back, Blue. It's too much, do you understand? We're grateful and all, but it's too much."

He laid the baby down in the same place where he had first appeared, and then stood back to watch.

Nothing happened.

Fogarty began to shiver, and he thought maybe he would cry. "C'mon, Blue," he said. "Please?"

But then he remembered that the Blue never came for him anyway, and he left Moses there under a slip of a moon and went back to the house.

"Mary Languished," he whispered as he shook her shoulder. "Mary Languished, you must come with me. Moses has gone back to the Blue Place."

Mary Languished's eyes snapped open and she looked around wildly for a moment, then focused on Fogarty.

"Come," he said. "Moses is out in the cold."

Mary Languished looked down into the empty bed where the child had lain moments before, threw the covers off and leaped out, fully dressed. She pushed past Fogarty, ran through the house and up the stairs without bothering for a sweater or a jacket, threw open the door and ran out without shutting it behind her.

Fogarty was cold and winded, and couldn't keep up, but he followed her beeline to the Blue Place, and when he caught up with her, she was holding the bundle that was Moses and pulling at the bedding to uncover his face.

"You have to stay here now, Mary Languished," Fogarty said. "You and Moses are *my* offering to the Blue." He began to pick up his things and pile them in the big chair . . . the afghan first, then the porcelain chamber pot and the clock. He could come back for the other things.

"Fogarty," she said, her voice as soft as a spider on a web. "Fogarty and Fogarty."

The sharp edges of broken promises carved into his belly.

He turned to look at her, and she stood in a little hollow of trash, wearing the wedding dress he'd given her, her knitted hat, and a dozen pair of old socks up and down her legs with unlaced boots open at her feet, their tongues lolling in the cold. She held the bundle to her chest, and looked at him with those soft, those wonderfully soft brown eyes, and Fogarty thought he heard the sound of sixteen-wheelers crossing over the sky.

"You'll be a blessing to the Blue, Fogarty," he said to her, then picked up the chair, an old frail man proving a point, and he staggered under its weight as he carried it with a light heart and a sweaty brow toward home.

Early the next morning he went to fetch the rest of his things, and there was no sign of Mary Languished or Moses.

He put all of his belongings back where they once were, cozying up his little home, and made a little daylight fire in celebration of his freedom. Then he went and packed up the little suitcase with Mary Languished's belongings and Moses' things and set them just outside the Pontiac door.

He took himself a shower and made himself a cup of tea and proposed himself a toast to Mary Languished Fogarty and Moses Fogarty, long may they live in peace.

The following morning he awoke while it was still dark. A sunrise for Fogarty this morning, he thought. He got dressed up in his warmest and warmed himself up by the stove, then went upstairs and into the crisp, starry early morning. He found an old suitcase by the door and carried it toward the east.

He carried the old suitcase past the old Boiler and he gave the boiler a pat on the side, loving its deep hollow ring. "Hello, Mr. Boiler, sir," he said to it. "Such a nice old boiler you are." He continued east and when he found a suitable place, he put the suitcase down and sat on it. Then he bounced up and down a couple of times. "Hey," he said. "This suitcase makes a good chair. This suitcase makes a good old sunrise chair." He admired the old suitcase for a while longer—and decided to keep it. It might fetch fifty cents or so in town, but then he'd always wanted a sunrise chair.

He sat and watched the sky lighten and expand into a blaze of glory, and was enthralled.

"Such a blessing, to have a sunrise like this, Fogarty, such a blessing on such a beautiful morning," he said to himself, his freedom feeling cool and nice, but then just a little tickle of sadness slithered in to confuse him. It felt a little like loneliness, and somewhere in the back of his mind was a memory somewhere, of a wife, and a child, but he couldn't quite place it.

• Project Stone

1

Cliff Gray sat on the hot vinyl back seat of the cab and watched the Arizona desert pass by. He felt his thighs sticking to the seat right through the fabric of his pants, despite the taxi's ragged air-conditioning. He rubbed his hands over the pebbled surface of the football he'd brought for his son and wondered, with high anxiety, about the meeting which would take place in—he checked his watch—less than fifteen minutes.

He studied the football and concentrated on his fantasy of how Miles would look. At age eleven, he should be over five feet tall. Cliff couldn't imagine an eleven-year-old Miles—the last time he'd seen his boy, Miles had only been six. At six, Miles had been quite the tousle-haired, freckle-faced, red-blooded all-American boy, with frogs in his pockets and skinned knees. Cliff's chest warmed with the memory, and he turned the football over and over, feeling the cool surface, fingering the laces.

Miles had probably changed a lot in these five years. Five years. Jesus, it seemed like only yesterday. It seemed like yesterday, but it also seemed like a lifetime since he'd seen Miles, since Marian had taken his boy to this weird place in the desert.

How could I let five years go by without visiting him? The

familiar guilt rose to the surface of his skin. He was ashamed he'd let his relationship with Miles lapse over—over what, hurt feelings? A silly issue of principle? Miles had nothing to do with the divorce, anyway. Cliff had received the papers, signed them, sent them back and the hurt had just gone on and on. Every time he thought of visiting Miles, he thought of seeing Marian, and he thought of the hurt. Suddenly, he had realized that Miles was eleven years old—and growing up without him. His hurt feelings had cheated him out of Miles's best years. And cheated Miles out of having a father.

Cliff thought of the hurt, which wasn't so bad anymore, and he thought of Marian. What had five years done to her? Had she put on weight? Gotten a little gray in her hair? Would their time together be cold and filled with barbs, or would they share a return to the good times?

Maybe Marian had a lover.

Cliff reached inside his coat pocket for a Tums. Five years had not been so kind to him. He'd lost a lot of hair in five years, put on a lot of weight. He'd ruined a lot of clothes in the washer and dryer, and spent a lot of lonely evenings in five years.

He'd gone out on a few dates, but they were nothing. He preferred his own company, and when he was alone, his mind would inevitably stray to the hurt, the hurt that came from Marian. Marian's problem with crowds and people and strangers and decisions had escalated in Chicago, and he'd been insensitive to it. Well, not exactly insensitive, it was more like he underestimated it. He never understood it. He felt confident she would be all right, eventually. He urged her to get some outside friends, go to some meetings, get involved. But he never saw her during those "attacks," as she called them, and so he never urged her to counseling.

He was too busy being the perfect provider for his little family. He was so busy building his little retail office-supplies business to make a comfortable living for his family, that his family fell totally apart, and he didn't even see it coming.

When he got home from the office, he and Marian would sit with a fresh cup of coffee, and they'd talk, and visit, and laugh, and go over the events in their day, and he knew she was getting worse, but he still didn't understand.

And then one day she just took Miles and left. She preferred to give in to her fears than to be with him.

And oh God, that hurt.

"Gettin' close," the cab driver said, and Cliff sat up and leaned forward, seeing only the desert highway ahead out of the windshield. The cab driver gunned it a little bit, and they came up over a slight rise in the road, and there it was, spread out before them. A blank, brick wall, stretched in two directions as far as he could see, topped with a spiral of barbed wire.

"Christ," he said under his breath. Looks like a prison.

They passed a big, white institutional sign. Black block letters read:

WELCOME TO THE
TONALLY OPTIMUM NEURAL ENVIRONMENT
(T.O.N.E.)
AN EXPERIMENTAL COMMUNITY.
PREPARE TO SHOW IDENTIFICATION.

How can a boy get frogs in his pocket in a prison in the middle of the goddamned desert?

Cliff fumbled for a second Tums.

Marian sat at the kitchen table, coffee cup held in both hands, watching her son finish his breakfast cereal. He rinsed his dishes, then pirouetted for her.

"How do I look, Mom?"

Tears threatened. "You look just fine, hon."

"Do these clothes look too new? I mean I don't want them to look too new, know what I mean?"

"You look just fine, Miles. Hurry, now, or you'll be late."

He kissed her on the cheek, picked up his books and slammed out of the house.

Three tears spilled over her lower lashes before she snapped the lid down again on her emotions. "Everything will be all right, Marian," she said to herself. "Clifford is a gentleman, and he wants what's best for Miles. Miles needs his father, and I mustn't be greedy." She finished her coffee and went upstairs to gaze again in her closet, even though she knew she would wear the red dress.

That feeling—that Chicago feeling—had crept right off the pages of his letter, up her arms, and settled at the back of her neck. *"Let me know if September 18 is a good time for me to visit,"* Clifford had written, and Marian had needed to close her eyes and take deep breaths. She knew that he would come, look around and pass judgment on her decision to bring Miles to The City to live. She sat quietly until the swirling fog in her mind began to subside, and she knew what had to be done. The haunting pressures she remembered from Chicago, the acrid taste of claustrophobia were suddenly too real again, too real, after lying dormant for five years.

Miles had been ecstatic at the news that his dad was coming; Marian became immobilized every time she thought of Clifford in her home. But that had been in July, and the grip on the back of her neck had eased daily, as she began to make lists. She had plenty of time, so she made a detailed plan of what to wear every day for each activity, and she made reservations for Clifford at the hotel, and made up a menu, and a list of things for them to do—something other than the three of them sitting around and talking.

Marian checked the clock. Eight-ten. He'd be here in less than half an hour. She began to put on her makeup, wondering what five years had done to their relationship, wondering if he still hated her for her decision to take Miles to Arizona, trying not to think that she wanted to wear the red dress because Clifford always liked the way she looked in red.

Cliff stepped out of the cab just as the gates opened and Marian drove through in a little white electric cart. He pulled his trousers from the backs of his legs, worried about wrinkles, then paid the driver, tipping too heavily, feeling her eyes on him. At first glance, she looked wonderful; she was slim and radiant and wearing red. Her dark hair was shorter, with casual curls glistening in the sunlight, and her lipstick matched the red of her dress. Not many women her age can pull that off, he thought. He, in turn, wore brown, a bad color for him, but one he wore to help disguise the fifty pounds he'd put on in the last few years. His heart pounded and he found himself short of breath. He desperately willed the blush from his face as he retrieved his bag and the football from the back seat of the cab.

The taxi sped off, spitting gravel and Arizona sand into a cloud as Cliff walked toward the cart, his emotions heaving and rolling inside him.

"Marian, you look beautiful."

She smiled at him, a little flighty, a little nervous, but she neglected to return the compliment. "You'll have to check in with the guard," she said, and indicated that he should put his bag in the cart.

Cliff opened the door to the guard station. It was air-conditioned. He stepped in and closed the door behind him, then heard the beep and started to apologize to the guard. It sounded as though he'd set off some sort of alarm. He quickly looked around for its source and then realized he was listening to the tone. He listened for a few seconds to the rhythmic thump, the celebrated sound and total purpose for the community where his ex-wife and son lived, and wondered why it didn't drive everyone insane. Cliff showed identification to the uniformed man and tried to concentrate on filling out a form while outside, Marian tapped her manicured nails on the steering wheel. Cliff noticed she tapped them in time to the tone, and wondered if she could hear it from out there.

Name: Clifford Gray. Address: Chicago. Purpose of visit: Visiting family. Length of stay: four days. Name of sponsor: Marian and Miles Gray. The guard took the clipboard and pen, filled out a visitor pass, and handed it to Cliff with a cartoon map of Tone Town, then saluted Cliff and thanked him. "Enjoy your stay, sir."

Marian smiled tentatively as Cliff exited from the cool air into the September desert. He climbed in the cart, felt it settle under his embarrassing weight, and with the whine of the little electric motor, Marian drove them into town.

"How's Miles?" he asked.

"Just fine. Anxious to see you. He got all dressed up for school today, because he knew you'd be here when he got home."

"School? I thought he'd be out of school."

"Kids go to school year-round here, and take vacation time, like at work. His vacation starts tomorrow."

Cliff smiled and wondered again if he'd be able to toss the football around the back yard with his son without having a heart attack. He'd wanted to take off ten pounds or so before the trip, but the anxiety of it all made him gain five instead. His weight had become a hopeless situation.

Marian pulled the cart up in front of a long, low building that looked like the standard Best Western motel and stopped. The sign in front of the office said TONE TOWN HOTEL.

"Get checked in, then we'll go over to the house."

Cliff hoped his disappointment didn't show. His fantasies had included staying with Marian and Miles.

He heard the tone again, louder this time, inside the office. After he registered and received his key, he walked out and down, past the row of doors, looking for number eight. Marian followed in the cart. He felt her eyes on him and he walked stiffly, wondering how he looked from behind, wishing he'd worn something—anything—else.

He found number eight and opened the door. The room was already hot and stuffy. He threw his bag on one of the twin beds covered with tropical-print bedspreads, and turned the air conditioner on low. As it came on, the tone came with it. Low, almost unobtrusive, like a heartbeat, the tone emanated from the air-conditioning at exactly the same speed as in the motel office, as in the guard stand. So that's it, Cliff thought. Big deal.

They drove through a tidy little community, clean, picture-perfect. The morning was clear, the sky a light, light blue with no clouds, the sun hot and penetrating. Cliff knew he'd have to buy some desert clothes, and soon. Nothing he brought from Chicago would do.

Marian kept up a running commentary as they drove, showing him around, using up time, keeping conversation light and on general, random subjects while their auras probed each other. The other residents all seemed to be courteous citizens; they all drove little white electric carts and by the way they all waved at each other, Cliff felt they all knew and liked Marian. The roads were wide and casual, the center of town was a modern-looking covered mall, with City Hall, a sophisticated, glass-sided building of government offices on one end.

"That's where I work," Marian pointed out. "City Hall. Fifth floor."

Cliff could hear the tone all through The City, as Marian liked to call it. The beat came from the stoplights, from the sidewalk cafés, from some of the other carts. Cliff began to notice that Marian had a particular cadence to her speech, and it fit right in with the rhythm of the tone. He'd noticed it before, from Miles, when talking with him on the telephone, and now he heard it from Marian.

"The tone. Is it everywhere?"

Marian smiled at him. "Everywhere," she said. "Forty beats a minute. Exactly. All the time. Forever."

Cliff recognized her humor and appreciated it. He remembered that he had once loved it. "How come your cart doesn't beep?"

"It's new, and I haven't gotten around to having it installed yet."

"Yet? You mean it's optional?"

"Yes."

"People *pay* to have the tone installed in their carts?"

Marian looked Cliff full in the face, and their eyes met and locked for the first time. "The government pays to have the tone installed. We just like to have it around, so we go to the trouble. And when we're not near the tone, we take it with us." She stopped the cart in the middle of the street and reached into her handbag. She pulled out a little black box, about one inch square, thumbed a switch and the tone beeped forth. "This is a bip box. It's portable, as you can see." She handed it to him and as her fingers touched his, she said, "We *like* the tone, Clifford. The project is important to us." She lowered her voice. "You'll find all the citizens very patriotic."

Cliff felt the blush rising again. She can still do it to me, he thought. She can still intimidate me. She says "Clifford" in that way and instantly has the upper hand.

At the other end of downtown, opposite City Hall, was a long, low, one-story, blank-faced building. TONE CULTURE YEAST, the sign outside read.

"Yeast?"

"Yes," Marian replied. "We looked for an industry that could make us and keep us self-sufficient. Yeast thrives here. I think it likes the tone."

Yeast.

They drove north past the yeast factory, into the housing area. They drove silently through the neighborhoods, past schools and parks. Cliff was amazed and impressed, but said nothing. He had a feeling that there was a lot to amaze him yet. Most amazing of all was the pleasantness of the place. It held nothing of the ominous nature predicted by the outside, with its brick wall and barbed wire. This was a nice place. Full of friendly faces and school yards with clean kids and no graffiti.

Not at all like Chicago.

2

Marian's house was one of hundreds of similar houses on a clean, sidewalked street. Some of the occupants were obviously gardeners, and they had made elaborate gardens of their grounds. Other yards lacked attention, but most were at least neat, clean and well kept. Marian's was plain, orderly, and green, with a row of red flowers bordering either side of the walk and two monolithic bushes flanking the front door.

Inside, the house looked just like Marian. Cliff could have picked her interior out of a million. Besides the knickknacks, lamps and obvious things he remembered that used to be in *their* home, he would have recognized the whole glass-and-chrome *look* that Marian had about her.

He walked through slowly, pointing out things he remembered, and she stood watching him, her arms crossed over her chest, smiling enigmatically whenever he looked at her. He couldn't read her.

The kitchen was the same. Modern, sleek, cool—Marian. She made coffee and they sat down at the little kitchen table, and groped for neutral subjects.

They talked of old friends, and Cliff's business, and insects in the desert. They skimmed lightly over old topics, comfortable topics, trying not to say "remember when . . ." but unable to help themselves now and then.

Cliff liked sitting across the table from Marian again. A lot had passed between them in five years, but she was still a friend—a good friend. And good friends are hard to come by.

Just as they'd run out of small talk and were swirling the cold dregs of coffee in their cups, they heard the front door open. Both tensed. Marian sat up straight, her mouth tight. Cliff stretched the collar of his shirt with his forefinger, then turned in his chair, ready to meet his son.

Miles came through the door, and at the sight of his father having coffee with his mother, his face beamed.

"Hi, Dad!"

Cliff stood up and held his hand out to his son, amazed at how grown-up Miles was. They shook hands, then Cliff pulled him close and hugged his boy, but could feel that hugging made Miles uncomfortable, so he let go and ruffled Miles's shiny dark hair instead. Miles hadn't really changed, he was still freckle-faced, with ice-blue eyes, dark hair and nice white teeth. Nice big teeth. Adult teeth. He stood tall and straight and eleven-year-old-thin, and he was the most beautiful sight Cliff had seen in years. Miles looked just exactly like Cliff-and-Marian.

"Nice threads," Cliff said, and Miles blushed. "How was school?"

"Okay, I guess. I'm off now, for a week."

"We're going to have a good time," Cliff said, feeling proud.

"Go change out of your school clothes, Miles," Marian said.

"Yeah, then you and I can go out back and play with the surprise I brought."

Miles left the kitchen and they heard the door to his room close.

"He looks great, Marian."

"He's a good boy."

"I'd like to take him back to Chicago with me, you know."

Marian paled. "Please don't ask me that, Clifford."

"Just for one school year, Marian. Just for one school year. Think about it. Please think about it."

"I'll think about it, Clifford, but . . . I don't think so."

Cliff felt the old anger rise. Inflexible, that was always her problem. And selfish. She grooved herself into a safe routine and would not alter it for love nor money. Minimize surprises, that was Marian's credo. He felt angry words on the tip of his tongue as she looked down at her hands on the table, but then the door opened and Miles returned, tucking his shirttail into a new pair of jeans.

"There he is. Hey, Miles, how about a little football, while your mom makes us some lunch?"

"Sure!"

Cliff nodded toward the football, which rested on the countertop next to the toaster. "Hey!" Miles picked it up and spun it in the air. "C'mon, Dad, let's go!"

Music to his ears. Cliff looked at Marian, who watched and smiled, but her brow was furrowed, as if her amusement was painful. Cliff hitched his pants as he started toward the back door.

Marian took sandwich makings from the refrigerator and stood watching Clifford and Miles out the kitchen window. Clifford hadn't changed, except for a little—well, a lot—around the waist. And maybe his sandy hair had thinned a little on top, but basically, he was still the same. He had the same soft face, the same crooked smile, the same puppy-dog way of looking at her that made her feel like a queen.

She still held great affection for him, and always would. They had shared so many important events. They were both virgins on their wedding night, had their one and only child together, and had shared eight years of bed and board. They still loved each other, Marian knew, but they couldn't live together. Little irritations—one of which had been that puppy-dog way Clifford had of looking at her, she reminded herself—like grains of sand, had eroded the protective covering of mystery in their marriage.

Marian hadn't even known she'd wanted something different until she read about the T.O.N.E. project and, with a desperation, applied for residency for her and Miles. They'd been accepted, and they went.

Clifford had been astonished more than anything else, Marian remembered. There was no blowup, or fight, or traumatic separation—there was never even much discussion, as she remembered. She would never have won an argument about it with Clifford . . . she'd never even really decided to do it. It was an automatic thing. It was just something that had happened.

But she knew what had intrigued her about The City. It was a womb. It was a retreat, it was a place to hide, it was security for herself and her son. It was a place she'd never have to think about leaving, never have to worry about Miles leaving, she'd not have to deal with most of Clifford's ambitious dreams—it erased most of the lifetime decisions the average adult and parent had to make.

The pressures in Chicago were terrible. She was afraid of everything. It was so big, and noisy, and dirty. Every time she went outside, she got lost in the enormity of all those millions of people, each living their own lives in Chicago. Each person had their own life, their own set of problems, their own joys, their own secrets. She would stand and look at a crowd and wonder how there could possibly be enough different sets of circumstances to go around.

And then one day she realized that all those lives touched each other in different ways, whether they worked together in the same office, or just lived in the same building—or in the same city, even. And she realized she had something in common—kin almost—with all those millions of millions. And she didn't want to have anything to do with any of them. She didn't want to have anything in common with giant sweltering hordes.

Then she became jealous and protective of her individuality—her opinions and ideas and possessions. It got so that she could never even concentrate on walking down to the bus stop without fear of becoming lost. Or absorbed into the great swell of humanity that Chicago sometimes seemed.

She'd tried to hide it from Clifford as much as she could, but then even the pressure of hiding it became too enormous. Marian had never been good at decisions. Anytime she made one, it never seemed as right as the decisions other people made. Her life never seemed to turn out with as many square corners as other people's lives.

Tone Town looked to Marian like an oasis. So much so, that there'd never even been a question in her mind about going.

In The City, she had fewer people to compare herself with, she had fewer places to go, fewer clothes to wear, fewer difficulties to deal with. There was a limited universe of people with whom to interact, a finite number of situations she'd be forced to face. All she had to do was keep her nose clean every day, and those nighttime monsters—those guilt beasts and the paranoia hawks—would not tear her psyche to shreds.

The acceptance letter from the Project had come almost by return mail. She had the right background—she had no family, and Miles had only Clifford—and good secretarial skills. The Project was short on secretaries, and, she suspected, on single women. She'd been given a two-bedroom house, an adequate salary, and a job in the typing pool. Administration found her to be uncommonly good at simply following orders, so she'd been promoted quickly until she reached the top. She was now personal secretary to Mayor Brad Rupert, and privy to all the sensitive issues at Tone Town. She just followed orders.

Clifford didn't know it, and even Miles didn't know it yet, but she had made a major decision—a lifetime choice for all three of them, and now it was too late. It was too late.

Miles caught a pass on the run, then tripped and rolled over and over, red-faced and laughing, and Clifford caught up with him and pulled him up and clapped his son on the back as they both laughed, the happy sound coming through the kitchen window and mixing with the tone.

A tear escaped and landed on a piece of whole-wheat bread. It soaked right in, and Marian had to laugh too, only her laugh was brittle. And bitter.

"Great sandwiches! Hey, Miles, eat another!"

Miles sighed and pushed his plate back. "I'm stuffed!"

"Growing boy like you . . . don't you want to grow up big like your father?" Cliff grabbed his waistline roll. "See that? Pure muscle. Table muscle. I exercise it three times a day."

Miles giggled and looked at his mother. Marian smiled and looked at the ceiling with mock exasperation.

"Say. Is there a theater in this town?"

"Yes, they redub the soundtrack, though, so it's probably not exactly what you might be used to," Marian said. "But we like it."

"What say you and I go to the movies, eh, boy? And then if your mother doesn't mind, you can spend the night with me over at the hotel."

Miles's eyes lit up. "Can I, Mom?"

"Sure. I guess." She looked at Cliff with suspicion.

"Go get your overnight things, Miles, and we can go sightseeing before the movie."

Miles ran from the table.

Cliff wiped his lips on the napkin, ate one last potato chip, then pushed his plate away.

"I'm going to take him for a year, Marian. I want you to get used to the idea."

"Please, Clifford . . ."

"Not today. Don't get in an uproar. He and I are just going to fool around for a week, you know, get to know each other. But you watch. You watch us, and see how good it is for an eleven-year-old to have his dad."

"Clifford, that's not . . ."

He held up his hand to silence her objections. "Shhhh. Just wait. You'll see." He smiled, then collected his son and his belongings and piled them in the cart.

"Good of you to let us use your little—beep-mobile," he said, then got in while Marian stood by, arms crossed over her chest, watching, helplessly smiling at these two male buffoons she loved so desperately. "How do you make it work?"

"Like this, Dad," and Miles reached over and put the cart in gear and it lurched backward.

"Whoa!" Cliff slammed on the brake and the little wheels left two inches of black rubber on the drive. He smiled at Marian and then waved at her. "Thanks again. We'll see you tomorrow."

She waved back as they made their way out the driveway and down the street, sadness settling in her soul, a sadness that was getting ready for a long stay.

3

"I understand your ex-husband is in town." Mayor Brad Rupert smiled at Marian, his gold-rimmed front tooth glinting in the light of his desk lamp. Mayor Rupert liked the draperies drawn; he liked to work by the soft yellowed light from the desk lamp in a darkened office.

"Yes, he is." Marian closed her steno pad.

"Have you taken precautions?"

Marian paused. She had seen the darker side of the mayor's personality, but it had never been directed toward her.

"What precautions?"

"Against pregnancy."

"I have no intentions of becoming pregnant."

"I have no intentions of having you become pregnant." He pushed a button on his intercom. "Sonja, please bring Mrs. Gray a cocktail."

Hot blood rose through Marian. She was speechless in the face of this dramatic insult.

"Relax, Marian. I know how it can be sometimes between ex-spouses. You've been single a long time now. And I'm sure your ex still finds you very attractive. It's just an ounce of prevention."

They watched each other while they waited for Sonja, wariness springing up between them. This was a test of her loyalty— blatant and without finesse. She would have preferred something more subtle, but she *was* loyal, both to the Project and to her boss.

Besides, she had little choice. She was too high up in the government here, almost second in command, actually. If she rebelled, he'd make her leave The City.

He would, too, she could see it in his eyes. She lowered hers and fingered the metal spiral on her notebook. One didn't get where she was without loyalty and discretion, but this test hurt her pride. She waited, eyes downcast, until the door opened again, and a shaft of bright fluorescent light came in.

Sonja, Marian's young, blonde, shapely assistant, came in carrying a silver tray with a small juice glass of clear, red liquid on it. "Thank you, Sonja," the mayor said, and the girl placed the tray on the highly polished desk, giving Marian a puzzled look, then retreated, her ample hips obnoxious in the tight blue dress. Marian waited while the mayor watched Sonja walk out and close the door softly after her. The harsh fluorescence disappeared, leaving Marian with her boss in the intimacy of the desk light, but somehow their real intimacy of friendship and mutual respect had flown.

"Drink up." He waved a gracious hand toward the glass, diamond pinkie ring flashing.

Marian had never tasted the contraceptive cocktail before. It was light and fruity. She drank it down, then put the glass back on the tray and looked at the mayor, hurt and defiance battling within her. "Will that be all?" Her voice was barely a whisper.

"Not exactly." The mayor squeaked back in his leather swivel chair and laced his fingers over his vest. He waited for three beats of the tone, then said, "I understand your boy spent last night with his father in his hotel room."

Marian felt her breath bunch up in her chest. It was confrontations like this that she came here to avoid. They made her feel closed in, trapped, cornered. She tasted the building panic. She remembered this horrible feeling from Chicago, whenever something came up, and something was *always* coming up there. She couldn't handle it, she had effectively escaped it for five years, and now here it was again. She took a couple of deep breaths and tried to remind herself that she had done nothing wrong, she needn't feel defensive. "Yes, that's correct." Her voice trembled.

"Your husband has no silly notion of taking the boy with him, has he?"

She shook her head.

"Speak up!"

"No, sir. Not that I'm aware of." Her knees began to shake.

"Good. I expect you'll see to it that he puts aside any such notions as they arise. Am I correct, Marian?"

"Yes, sir."

"Good girl." He sat up in his chair, putting his elbows on the desk. "Give him a pep talk on the merits of the program. See if you can enlist him in the patriotism of our little town, so he'll make his own best decision. Leaving the boy here is for the boy's own good." He got up and walked around the desk, put a hand on Marian's shoulder, and like an automaton, she rose and turned to face him. "Invite him to the Mayor's Cocktail Party tonight. I'll give him a little pep talk myself."

"I will, thank you."

The mayor leaned against his desk, and watched Marian walk toward the door. "Marian."

His voice was like a punch in the stomach.

She turned to see the expression of seriousness on his face, the shading from the dim light giving it an ominous look. "The boy will be sacrificed before the program will. You understand that, don't you?"

Marian swallowed. Nodded.

"Good girl," he said, and smiled, the gold around that front tooth glinting again.

As soon as the door closed behind her, the mayor returned to his chair. He was surprised at himself. He'd had no intention of humiliating Marian like that, but he'd always thought her cool front was about as impenetrable as a sheet of thin ice, and when this opportunity came up to find out what Marian was really made of, he just couldn't seem to help himself. He had been right, too.

He picked up the telephone, punched three buttons and waited.

"Security."

"Rupert here."

"Yes, Mr. Mayor."

"Marian Gray was just in to see me. Her ex-husband is in town, staying at the hotel. She's concerned that he might try to kidnap their son. Keep an eye on the three of them for me, okay?"

"Yes, sir."

"A close eye."

"Yes, sir."

Rupert pressed the disconnect and then dialed Washington. The line rang twice, then was answered. A long pause, then, "Seven eight."

"Rupert here, T.O.N.E."

"Yes, Rupert."

"Potential kidnapping here, of a citizen by his father, a non-resident."

"Name?"

"Gray. Clifford Gray."

"Sponsor?"

"Marian Gray."

"Your secretary?"

"Yes." Rupert's fingers tightened on the telephone.

"I'll check his file. Do you require assistance?"

"No. Not yet."

"The information has been recorded. Keep a close watch on this one. How is your population factor?"

"Down again this month, zero point one eight percent."

"Good, good, very good. Morale?"

"High. And getting higher."

"Excellent. Keep it up. Call if you need assistance. We can't afford any situations, even minor ones. The successful implementation of Project Stone is within our grasp, and your name will be mentioned as one of the key figures in its success."

Washington disconnected. Rupert waited for three beats before hanging up, then with a freshly manicured nail, he traced the wood-grain pattern on his desk. My name is mentioned as one of the key figures in Project Stone, he thought.

He reached over and turned out the desk lamp and sat in the darkness, just listening to the tone.

4

Simon Rupert, seventeen-year-old son of the mayor, and his best friend Fred Contelli threw their schoolbooks on the desk in Simon's room and collapsed, each to a twin bed, their dirty sneakers messing up the blue plaid bedspreads Simon's mother so carefully arranged after he'd gone to school. Simon was a clean, nice, average boy. He had his mother's light hair and big, square teeth, and he and his sister both shared her horse-faced profile, but Simon followed his father's height. He was shorter than his mother and his sister, and most everybody else in high school.

In contrast, Fred was tall, and had deep brown eyes and curly black hair—classically Italian.

In his first year at high school, Fred discovered he was going to have trouble with the girls. While Simon seemed to be brother, best friend or confidant to all the girls, Fred was the high school heartthrob. All the girls talked about Fred, flirted with Fred, called Fred on the phone and spied on Fred at the mall. It embarrassed him because the other guys all expected great macho feats from Fred, things that weren't like him. In his embarrassment, he shunned the girls, sticking closer to his three male friends, putting them all under suspicion. He had an eye for Mary Lou Morgan—she wasn't as silly as the others—but somehow he felt that if he took Mary Lou out, there would be even more pressure on him to score and maybe on her, too. So he didn't. He stayed closer to his parents and his sister instead.

"Where's your mom, Simon?"

"Down at the party grounds, getting tables set up. You going?"

"Oh, Jeez, I forgot all about it. Mayor's Cocktail Party tonight, right? No, my sister's supposed to have her baby, so we're just hanging around, waiting to take her to the hospital." Fred sighed. "Mom wants someone home all the time, and if *everybody's* home all the time, then she feels better. In fact I ought to go now."

"Stay. Have a Coke."

"Nah. Carla might have trouble again this time, and if she does, I ought to be there."

"Yeah."

"I don't know what for . . . moral support, I guess."

"I wish our family was as close as yours."

"No you don't. We're always in each other's way."

The boys relaxed in silence for another moment, then they heard a cart pull up out in front. Simon stood up and looked out his window. "Hey," he said, "it's Pete." He watched a tall, thin, compact man with short blonde hair, wearing faded jeans and a plaid western shirt, step from his cart, pick up a six-pack of beer from the back and then ramble up the walk. "Door's open," Simon said through the window screen, and Pete smiled, then opened the front door.

Fred and Simon shot each other a questioning glance, then Fred stood up to greet Pete as he came into the room. Pete set the beer on the desk next to the boys' books and shook hands. "How's your sister, Fred?"

"So far, so good. Baby's due anytime now."

Pete pulled the chair out from under the desk, twirled it around and straddled it, then opened a beer, took a long swig and wiped his mouth on the back of his shirt cuff. He rested his wrists on the back of the chair. "Mac's been out of his mind at work. I've been trying to tell him to take some time off to be with Carla, but he said they needed the money, and he'd rather be with her after the baby comes."

"There's nothing he can do now," Fred said.

"Yeah, I guess. I hope it goes okay this time."

"Me, too."

"Yeah," Simon said.

"Beer?"

Both boys reached with eager nonchalance.

Simon opened his beer and sat back down on the edge of his bed. He kicked off his sneakers and pulled his feet up under him. It was strange having Pete in his room. Pete used to come around now and again with Dusty when he was dating Dusty's big sister Annie, but that had been years ago. Even then, Pete had been older, and didn't quite fit in with the Famous Four: Fred, Simon, Roland and Dusty. Pete hadn't been around at all since he and Annie got married.

Simon looked at the lines in Pete's face. Pete looked more stressed out than someone twice his age, he thought. And the blue in his eyes seemed lighter. Faded. Pete was twenty-three, and worked as a foreman in the vat room at the yeast factory. For him to be here was a great mystery to Simon. A million questions jumbled around in his head, but instead of opening his mouth and asking a stupid one, he just waited. Pete would eventually get to the point. He took another swallow of his beer and tried to look cool, hoping to God his mother wouldn't come home before he could ditch the empties.

"Simon, are you going to your dad's party tonight?" Pete finally spoke.

"Sure. I always go."

"Fred?" Fred shook his head no. Pete was silent for a long time, looking at his hands. "Have either of you guys heard from Dusty? Or Roland?"

Simon and Fred looked at each other. They talked about Dusty and Roland every day, vicariously living the adventures they imagined their friends were having on the outside.

The Famous Four (so called because the local newspaper once published a picture of the local Fourth of July parade, and there they were, mugging at the camera, the four of them in red, white and blue from head to toe, looking vaguely deformed in black and white on the front page) had grown up together, inseparable, and when they turned seventeen, they all talked about joining the Army. It was a bad time for Fred—he didn't want to leave his family, especially with Carla having such problems—and wedding preparations were in full swing for Simon's sister. Dusty and Roland didn't want to wait for them, so the Famous Four decided to break up. Temporarily.

Dusty and Roland applied for exit papers at the mayor's office, but they were denied in the committee hearing. When pressured, the Mayor had the Four over for dinner one night, and he talked with them about the Project, and how important it was.

Simon would never forget that night: the four of them with his parents sitting at the dining room table. Dusty, intelligent and articulate, argued politics with Simon's dad—they talked about the good of the whole versus the good of the individual. Simon loved his father, but that one night, he felt embarrassed for him. He felt embarrassed that his dad, the mayor, had loyalties that bordered on the fanatic. His dad's arguments made less sense than Dusty's, and then the mayor resorted to the agreement that Dusty and Roland's parents had made when they joined the Tone Town experiment. That didn't work in anybody's mind—even the mayor's, Simon could tell, and he felt sorry for his dad. Dusty's parents were both dead, and there wasn't a reason in the world for Dusty to live his whole life in this little town because of one of their promises.

The next night, Dusty and Roland just packed up and went over the wall. They didn't even wait for graduation or anything. Despite oaths of loyalty and promises to write, neither Simon nor Fred had heard from them since.

"They came to the house the night they left," Pete said, and both Simon and Fred leaned forward. "Dusty wanted to say good-bye to Annie, so we had a couple of beers together, and then I took Roland outside while Dusty and Annie talked, and I made him promise to send me a postcard as soon as they got into the next town. I even gave him a dollar and a stamp."

Pete tightened his fist as his eyes stared into his memory. "I made him *fucking promise* me." Four beats from the tone in Simon's clock radio passed while the boys held their breath. Then Pete relaxed and they sighed in relief. "Annie's real upset. It's been a month now with no word, and Dusty was all the family she had left."

"Sometimes in the Army, they won't let you write letters."

"Son, in the Army, they *make* you write letters. But that's not the point. The point is, I don't think they ever made it to the Army."

"What do you mean?"

Pete drained his beer and opened another one. "I don't know, for sure. But there's something wrong. They closed the North End Grade School today."

"So?"

"So, that means there aren't enough children to fill it. There was a time when here, in Syncopated City, the population was growing so fast that there were new apartment buildings and schools all over the place. This was a fuckin' success, boys, your dad was real proud, Simon. And now they're closing schools, and Annie can't get pregnant . . . We've both been to the doctors, and nothing seems to be wrong, but we've been married four years now, and no babies."

"And your sister, Fred," Simon said.

"That's right, Fred," Pete said, his voice softening. "Carla can get pregnant all right, but her babies die."

Fred got up and began to pace. Pete drained his beer and

squished the can. "Something's wrong here, boys. Something's really wrong."

"Maybe it's the tone."

"It's not the tone. Tone Town flourished! Population boom! The experiment was a success! This place has been here what, twenty years? For ten, or fifteen, it grew and grew, and then it stopped growing. And now it's dying."

Fred sat back down, on the edge of the bed. "Why?"

"I don't know why, Fred, but I know what I think."

"What?"

"I think the Tone Town experiment is over—only they can't just put the experimental rats to death, so they're letting them die out by making sure they don't reproduce." He rubbed his hands over his face. "And they can't let their experimental subjects out to run wild, either."

"Dusty . . ."

Pete nodded.

5

Cliff let himself be led by the hand through the crowds on the football field. Miles pulled him gently onward, as Cliff tried not to bump into too many people, his eyes continually scanning for sight of shiny dark hair and a red dress.

They'd arrived late to the Mayor's Cocktail Party, and had to park way on the other side of the high school and walk to the athletic field. Miles enjoyed these parties, it was evident by the shining in his eyes. Everybody came, he said, everybody in Tone Town, and it certainly looked to Cliff as though everybody was there. Well-behaved children played and talked quietly among themselves, rows of chairs were placed here and there for the elderly to sit and visit with each other. Everybody else stood and mixed, talking and laughing and eating.

"The mayor's over by the stadium concession stand," Miles had informed him, and it was toward the concession stand that

Cliff was being relentlessly pulled. He wished for cooler clothes, he wished they didn't have to hurry, he wished there weren't so many people; he recognized that the Arizona heat was shortening his temper while it was soaking his clothes and drying out his skin.

Long tables were covered with white cloths and stacks of plastic cups surrounded giant punch bowls of a clear, red drink that floated ice rings and fruit slices. Other tables were filled with cookies and brownies, squares of homemade fudge, donuts and other goodies made by the wives of Tone Town. Cliff grabbed a brownie as they passed one table, then took a bite and pulled his son back toward him. The brownie helped his attitude.

"Hey, Miles, slow down a bit."

Miles watched him chew for a moment, then said, "I want you to meet the mayor before he starts his speech. We're late."

Cliff wiped brownie crumbs from the corner of his mouth. "These are good," he said. "Say, listen, how come everybody is looking at me?"

"Because you're new," Miles said, and Cliff understood how small The City really was. "And because you're out of step."

That's it, Cliff realized with a flash. Everyone in Tone Town moved and spoke with the same rhythm, they all walked in time to the beat of the tone, they all lived, danced the dance of life, to the driving thump of the tone.

"It's irritating when you're with someone who's not in tune. But don't worry, Dad. You'll get the hang of it. It'll only take a couple of days."

They began walking again, slowly, Miles by his side, as Cliff finished his brownie, chewing in time to the tone. He tried to follow Miles's footsteps exactly, and noticed that following the rhythm was simple. It seemed to take less energy, in fact, to fall into step, and suddenly he noticed that the subdued roar about him was the accumulated voice of thousands of happy people, talking and laughing, eating sweets and drinking the red punch, all in rhythm with the underlying thump that filled the airwaves in the pauses of speech, the space between motions.

He needed only a few moments of practice, and then he felt something large inside his chest, something heavy, and he stopped walking. It didn't feel bad, just different for a few moments, as the rhythm of the tone dragged on his heart, pulling it back, slower, slower, until it fit in with the rhythm of their surroundings. Suddenly the day seemed a bit brighter, he wasn't hurrying quite so fast, the heat lessened in intensity. He began to identify with those around him, and his self-consciousness melted away.

He resumed his walk with his boy, his spirits soaring. They were headed toward the end zone, where a stage had been set up. Red, white and blue bunting decorated the front of the lectern, as if this were a political rally. Great black speakers on both sides of the stage broadcast the tone across the entire field. A long white banner with red letters stretched behind the stage, and it read:

PROFITS HIGH—MORALE HIGHER
WE'RE AMERICA'S GREATEST SUCCESS!

"Over here, Dad," and Miles pulled on him again until he stood face to face with Marian.

She kissed her son on the cheek, then ruffled his hair. "How are you doing, cowboy?"

"Fine, Mom. I brought Dad to meet the mayor."

"Good." She turned to Cliff and held out her hand, then seemed embarrassed by her action and started to pull it back the moment he started to take it. She laughed, the flush rising in her cheeks. "I'm sorry," she said, and took his hand in both of hers. "I'm so used to shaking hands with everyone who comes by. I'm the reception line."

Cliff felt the cool perspiration rings on his shirt, and a new rush of wetness burst from him.

She wore emerald green, and Cliff thought he'd never seen emerald green look so cool and delicious.

"Been having fun?" she asked, and Cliff had to rip himself away from his fantasy of picking her up and carrying her off the field amid cheers and confetti from the crowd.

"Been having a great time," he said, then laid a hand on Miles's shoulder. "We've got quite a boy here, you know."

Marian smiled at him, an open, secure smile. "We certainly have."

"But I must admit"—Cliff leaned closer to her, conspiratorially—"the two of you live in a really weird place."

Marian laughed, her dark eyes snapping, and Cliff felt a different rush of warmth throughout his body. Maybe I can take them both home with me, he thought.

Then there was another tug on his sleeve, and he found Miles had placed him directly in front of a square little man, his dark hair thinning on top and graying at the temples, a great fleshy mole on his right cheek, wearing an expensive pin-striped suit and flashing a gold-rimmed tooth.

"Dad? This is Mayor Rupert. Mr. Mayor, this is my father, Clifford Gray."

Cliff held out his hand, and the mayor took it in a firm grasp, and held it a fraction too tight for a fraction of a second too long. "Mis-ter Gray. Welcome to Tone Town. I must say, it's a pleasure to meet you. I've heard a lot about you from Marian and Miles, both."

"Oh?" Cliff looked at Marian, standing and smiling next to her employer.

"Yes, all of it good, as I'm sure you can imagine."

Cliff's senses instantly appraised the man: Bullshit artist.

"Have you had a glass of our local elixir?"

"No. Not yet."

"Miles. Fetch your father a drink, please, that's a good boy."

The mayor and Marian traded looks. She backed down. "Excuse me," she said, and left.

"What do you think so far, Mr. Gray?"

"Please. Call me Cliff."

"All right, then, Cliff. I'm Brad."

"Well, it's an interesting place, Brad, and, I guess, a nice place to visit, but I don't think I'd want to live here."

"Twenty thousand people do."

"That's wonderful for you."

"We have no crime, no punks. We have no rock radio stations, we have no unemployment, we have peace and harmony."

"That's nice. It's a clean town, I noticed that."

"Has Marian told you about Tone Town? What makes it—excuse the expression—tick?"

"No, not really."

"The experiment was originally stress-related. Laboratory scientists found that rats living in overcrowded cages died from stress, but when a tone was beeped into their environment that was slower than their normal resting heartbeat, stress-related deaths slowed down."

"Very interesting."

"Isn't it? Their hearts beat to it, their breathing became regulated by it, their breeding cycles became extraordinarily punctual. Nothing upset them, their bodily functions, especially their involuntary processes, became quite impossible to disrupt."

Miles arrived with a plastic cup full of punch. "Drink up, Cliff," the mayor said. "It's filled with vitamins and minerals." He winked. "They say it does great things for your virility."

Cliff busied himself with sipping the drink, to cover his embarrassment. Had the mayor been reading his mind?

The mayor put his hand on Cliff's shoulder and began guiding him through the crowd, his head bent to give the impression of earnest conversation as they moved past well-wishers. "We got a grant to start Tone Town to see if we could reduce ulcers and mental illness, and you know what else we found out? Sort of a convenient by-product, you might say."

"What?"

"People lived longer. We have more active, golf-playing, happy, *virile"*—there was that word again—"old folks than you've ever seen in one place before. All that *in addition* to healthy, happy people with no ulcers and no attitude problems. Pretty nice, wouldn't you say?"

"I would. Very nice."

They stopped walking, and Cliff noticed they were at the steps to the stage.

"Think about it some more, Cliff. The City is really a nice place to be. We'd love to have you here as a resident." The mayor put a foot on the first step. "It's show time," he said. "Finish your drink!" He smiled and the gold glinted.

Cliff backed up and turned around to see both his wife and his son watching him.

The audience settled into silence as the mayor took his place on the podium. He stood smiling, calmly waiting, as the thousands finished their business with each other, settled down, and turned to wait for his words.

With no motion on his part, the beep stopped from the big speakers on the stage, and without missing a beat, the tone emanated from speakers hidden beneath refreshment tables all over the field. The transition from a loud tone broadcast over the heads of the crowd to the low, underfoot thump was dramatic and effective. It sounded like the earth's heartbeat. Goose bumps crawled over Cliff's skin.

The mayor raised his hands in the air as if in benediction. "Hi!" he said, with a big smile, his voice booming out through the black speakers on stage.

The crowd roared back "Hi!" and then everybody laughed.

"Good to see you. Good to see you. Well, we've got nothing but good news up here this month."

He went on to talk about the yeast industry and give information on the basic prosperity of the town, sliding over the statistics comparing Tone Town with other municipalities, and Tone Culture Yeast with other industries around the nation.

Cliff was listening halfheartedly as he watched the crowd, words drifting in and out of his consciousness as he surveyed the smiling faces of all the people. It was a mystery, how this man could get all these people to stand in the heat of a fading afternoon and listen to him over the low, dull beep of a tone. It wasn't just mysterious, it was downright eerie. He could see the heat waves coming up from the field, and damn if they didn't seem to fluctuate in time to the tone, too.

The only pleasant thing about it was Marian beside him and Miles in front. Both were concentrating on the mayor's words.

". . . isn't that *wonderful?* There's only one place in the world—in the *world,* my friends—where people enjoy the kind of health and prosperity that we do . . ."

Snake oil was the only thing Cliff could think of. Snake Oil Evangelism.

The mayor's speech was shorter than Cliff had anticipated. It contained a financial report, a little message on who needed help and/or prayers in the community, and a bulletin on new books in the library. The mayor ended it with a real razzamatazz pep talk, "The Name of Success is Tone Town," and left the stage. Cheers, whistles, applause and shouts filled the air, all in time to the tone, all adding a surreal effect to the clear day, the otherwise typical, patriotic gathering.

Big deal, Cliff thought.

A crush of people met the mayor at the bottom of the steps, and Cliff found an opportunity to put his hand on the small of Marian's back, his other on Miles's neck, and he guided them away from the pack and toward the main stream of people leaving the field.

Miles was enthusiastic—the crowd in general seemed jubilant and pumped up—and he started talking about all the things they'd see during the next few days, while Marian walked quietly along. Cliff sensed something amiss with her, and his heart ached to be let in on her secrets once again.

What the hell happened between us that was so bad, he wondered, but even as he thought about it, he knew. He remembered. They disagreed about everything basic, everything important.

Miles took off running cross current to the stream of people, and Cliff reached for him, but missed. He looked at Marian, who shrugged her shoulders, and they cut across to follow him.

"Dad, Dad, c'mere. I want you to meet some guys."

They approached two young men and a woman. The older man was teasing Miles, and Cliff could tell they were very fond of each other.

"Dad, this is Pete, and his wife Annie, and this is Simon Rupert. The mayor is his dad."

Cliff shook hands all around, smelled beer on the breath of all three of them. Pete looked like a misplaced cowboy, his wife, a pear-shaped plump little cutie with chin-length wavy blonde hair and bangs. The mayor's son—Simon, was it?—was a surprise to Cliff; the mayor was probably quite handsome in his youth, but his son was not.

"These're my good friends," Miles said.

"Nice to meet you folks." Didn't Miles have any friends his own age?

"In town for long?" Pete asked.

"A week."

"Hey, Pete, Dad brought me a football."

"Yeah? Well, you'll have to bring both your folks over for a barbecue, Miles," Pete said, then ruffled the boy's hair, turned him around and played like kicking him.

"Okay, okay," Miles said, giggling.

"That would be nice," Cliff said, then looked at Marian. She looked surprised, as if put on the spot.

"Sure. Of course. Anytime, Annie." And the two women smiled at each other.

As they continued around the high school, Miles found more friends and more reason to run ahead, leaving his parents to stroll along behind at their leisure.

"Pete's been a real good friend to Miles," she said. "Kind of like a big brother."

Cliff felt a tightening in his chest. No beer-drinking kid should have to be a father to his son, he thought. He put his hand firmly on Marian's back and quickened the pace.

He wanted to be home with his family.

6

Pete nodded to Miles's dad and watched the three of them walk away. Miles was proud of his dad, Pete could tell. It made him happy for Miles, and he put his arm around Annie. Happy-family scenes always made her melancholy. Annie wanted a baby so bad she cried herself to sleep every month when her period came.

Miles and his folks disappeared into the crowd streaming from the football field, and he and Annie and Simon stood off to the side, apart, watching.

Pete's uneasiness had been growing for almost two years. He'd kept his ear tuned to the gossip at the plant. The yeast factory itself was experimental. All the loud packaging machinery (designed, of course, to operate in rhythm with the tone) was kept in one area, the labs in another, and the vat room where the yeast grew was in its own silent warehouse with muted colors and soft lighting. Pete wore disposable whites and a face mask, and it was requested that it be a silent room, except, of course, for the tone. Everyone who spoke, spoke in whispers. Most people didn't speak. They just tended the yeast in the silence. Pete liked his job. It gave him time to think.

But the silence of the vat room made the cafeteria that much noisier. There were no restrictions on speaking in the other areas, and those who worked with the machinery were used to speaking loudly in order to be heard. The cafeteria was bright and hard, with tile walls and floor, fluorescent lights in the ceiling, and shockingly noisy with all the noise from plates, trays, silverware, shoes and loud voices.

Pete, and usually the other guys in whites, kept to themselves at their own little quiet table in the southwest corner of the cafeteria. They ate in comfortable silent camaraderie, and listened to the others talk. It was this talk he'd been listening to over the past two years that made him nervous—suspicious.

It had caused him to read up on the T.O.N.E. experiment—its charter and all the publicity and opinion attending its opening—and to philosophize about it. He and Annie would lie in bed at night, face to face, and speak quietly and gently to each other about their ideas of the Universe. Those discussions prompted other research, and theories, and speculation about the tone. They shared with each other what they learned, and talked about the primordial surf as it beat upon the shores of a brand-new, unoccupied world—the "rhythm of the universe" to the first sparks of life. They talked about the beating of the heart. They talked about music through the ages; though they'd heard only that which kept time with the tone, they knew there was other music on the outside. They talked about primitive tribal drums—threatening, primal, sensual.

They came to no conclusions, just more questions.

He also read up on mob psychology and patriotism. He

researched Maslow's hierarchy and social theories behind cultism. It surprised him. It fascinated him. It scared him. He thought of it again as he waved to a few people he knew as they passed by him on their way home from the Mayor's Cocktail Party.

"I've been coming here every month for years," Pete said, "and it never ceases to amaze me that everybody else does, too."

"I know," Simon said. "It amazes my mom, too."

Pete brought Annie close to him and gave her a little squeeze.

"Hey, Simon," she said. "Come have dinner with us tonight."

"Okay, yeah, thanks, I'll just go tell my folks."

"We're parked over by the flagpole." Pete pointed and they all looked, and what they saw, instead of the flagpole, was Fred, running at them, his face white and distorted in pain, his lips red and sobs of breath choking out of him. He pushed people aside as he ran toward his three friends, and when he reached them, he put his hands on Pete's shoulders, but didn't meet his eyes. Fred took two steps back, his fists tight, the cords standing out in his neck. He stomped his foot and twirled around in frustration. Then the breath seemed to leave him and he just slowly sank to the sidewalk and began to cry.

Pete and Simon looked at each other in confusion, but Annie sat down on the sidewalk next to Fred and cradled his head on her shoulder. His arms went around her and he wailed in pain, and then they understood.

Another of Carla's babies had been stillborn.

"She wants to die," Fred choked out, "and she won't let Mac in to see her."

Annie stroked Fred's arm, and his back, and finally the desperate helplessness began to subside, and he broke away from her. She pulled a wad of Kleenex from her purse and he wiped his face and blew his nose, then sat there for another moment to catch his breath, then he looked up at his friends.

Pete thought it looked like a plea for mercy. "Come on," he said. "Let's go to the house."

* * *

Pete and Annie had spent a lot of time fixing up their house to make it unique, distinguishable from the tracts of sameness. Pete had bricked in a patio out back, and his barbecue outfit was set up and ready to work on a moment's notice. Annie had hand-made a lot of the things inside the house, giving it a homey atmosphere. A quilt hung on one wall, another over the back of the couch, needlepoint pillows were scattered about, and she had scavenged a lot of furniture and refinished it. The house looked very cozy, very warm, very human.

When the four friends entered, the house adopted Fred's sorrow, and it darkened.

Simon and Fred sat in the two chairs facing the couch, Pete set a six-pack of beer on the coffee table, threw a can to each of the boys and fizzed open his own. Annie stood slightly behind him, to the side, leaning against the wall, her favorite place to stand and watch when Pete had friends over.

"Okay," Pete said, after he drained his beer. "This is what I think we should do. Simon?"

Simon's head snapped up. He put his hand over his mouth to mask a series of burps.

"Simon, if you don't feel right about this, or if you feel like, you know, you're betraying your dad or anything, you just say so, okay?"

Simon swallowed, then cleared his throat. "You don't think my dad's, uh . . . you don't think my dad's doing something wrong, do you?"

"I don't know what to think, Simon. There's something really wrong here, and I'm tired of feeling guilty for not doing something about it. I think we should do something about it. Tonight." He paused and looked around. Annie looked at her feet. Fred was looking into the hole on top of his beer can. Simon looked at the vase of flowers on the coffee table. "So whatever we do here tonight, I want it to be a secret among the four of us. I don't want anyone else to know what we've done here."

"Why?" Fred looked up.

"Because we're either really wrong and it would be embarrassing, or else we're really right and it could be dangerous."

Fred gave a humorless grunt. He was becoming surly.

"Are we agreed? Annie?" Annie nodded. "Simon?" Simon's eyes looked haunted. He nodded. Fred nodded.

"Hey, I know," Simon said. "Let's write a letter to Carl Bernstein and Bob Woodward at the *Washington Post.*"

"And say what?" Fred opened another beer and sat back against the couch.

"Say that there's something fishy going on at Tone Town and they should come investigate it."

"Sure." Fred's sarcasm bit and Simon sat back, defeated.

"That's not a bad idea, Simon," Pete said, shooting a look at Fred. Simon brightened at praise from his elder.

"Or 'Sixty Minutes,' " Simon said, the beer giving his face a flush.

"What's 'Sixty Minutes'?"

"I'm not sure. It's a television show. Crusaders for justice, I think I read."

"I wish we got television," Fred said.

"Annie, could you whip up a little something to eat?" Pete nodded his head toward the two tipsy teenagers, then removed the unopened beer from the table. "Let's write a letter, and Annie will type it and copy it and we'll send it to all those places. Including the FBI and the police in Phoenix."

"And Tucson."

"And Tucson." Pete went into the bedroom and returned with a yellow legal pad and a pen. He detoured to the kitchen for a bag of chips and kissed Annie on the back of the neck.

Simon wondered what it would be like to have a wife and a nice, clean house of his own. No parents, regular sex. Get drunk, get laid, nobody would even know. Sounded great.

Pete tore open the bag and stuffed a handful into his mouth, then clapped the salt off his hands and began with the letter.

"Dear Sirs," he said, then looked at them for inspiration. Fred was tapping his hand on the armrest to the time of the tone, his thoughts probably with his sister. Simon was sitting slumped in his chair, a silly grin on his flushed face.

Pete looked at the two of them and for a moment was almost overcome with affection for his friends and his family. His fear of something happening to his home jerked on his insides.

"You idiots," Pete said, and threw a pillow at each of them.

* * *

By the time they had finished eating Annie's tuna casserole, the boys were sober and the letter was done to their satisfaction. "Okay. This is it," Pete said. "One last run-through. 'Dear Sirs: We are writing to you as concerned citizens from the experimental government community in Arizona known as T.O.N.E. (Tone Town). There seems to be something going wrong with the experiment here, the community seems unable to produce enough new infants to support the local grade schools, and occasionally, people vanish from the community without a trace. Please investigate this matter as soon as possible, as all of us here at Tone Town are concerned about our families. Sincerely,' and then the four of us can sign it, okay?"

"It sounds stupid," Fred said.

Pete threw the tablet on the table, sending potato-chip crumbs flying. "What the fuck do *you* want us to do, Fred? Kee-rist, it's your *sister* we're talking about!"

"Pete, sit down." Annie took hold of her husband's wrist and brought him back to the couch.

"I think it sounds good," Simon said.

"Me, too," Annie said. "I think we should send it."

"Yeah, okay, me too. I'm sorry, Pete. I'm kind of . . ."

"I know. It's okay. Well, let's go do it."

"Now?"

"Of course, now. When did you think? God, what a bunch of numbskulls."

"Ease up, Pete," Annie said. "We're all pretty wound up here."

Pete laid his hands atop his knees, closed his eyes and took a deep breath. "All right," he said. "Let's go."

Four silent people in Pete's quiet little electric cart whirred through the darkened town; a scene each of them had been through countless thousands of times. This time, though, it was new, it was different, it was ominous, it was adventurous. There was a secret here, a pact, a mission. Maybe—only Pete dared to think it—the seeds of a rebellion. Four hearts in that little cart beat in time and a half to the tone, and the cart that whined its way down the main street toward Annie's bookstore was highly charged.

"Won't we look suspicious?" Annie whispered.

"Nah. If anyone asks, just tell them you forgot and left something here, so we just stopped by to get it. We can't *look* suspicious, or someone will stop us. Just act normal." Easier said than done, Pete thought. His hometown had never been a threat to him before, and now danger and Gestapo or something lurked in every shadow.

Pete parked on the empty street right in front of the bookstore. Annie unlocked the front door and all four crowded inside. The tiniest tone emanated quietly from the red glowing exit sign over the door. Their breathing sounded moist and close. "Should I turn on the lights?"

"I don't think so. C'mon, let's all just go into the back."

Annie in the lead, they threaded their way around the gondolas filled with books and magazines to the office in the back. She turned on the desk light and with it came the tone. Pete closed the door behind them. Bundles of twine-tied magazines were stacked all over the floor, odd copies of books and boxes of books covered every other available surface in the tiny office.

"Warm up the copy machine," she ordered, and Simon punched the "ON" button. The "warm up" light came on and the tone began to emanate from it, too. Annie rolled a sheet of blank paper into the typewriter and waited for Pete to hand her the folded sheet of yellow paper he'd stuck in his pocket. She smoothed it out and began to type.

"C'mon, Fred," Pete said. "Let's go get some addresses." They slipped out the office door, closing it quietly behind them. Pete led the way to the magazine racks, and the two of them began canvassing the newsmagazines and newspapers for appropriate addresses.

When they had thirty, Pete and Fred returned to the back office, breathing heavily, perspiration standing out on their foreheads. Each carried an armful of periodicals. Annie had finished the letter; Simon was making copies.

Annie rummaged in the back of a file cabinet and when she came up, she had a handful of plain white envelopes. She sat back down at the typewriter, fed one in and waited for Pete to read the name and address he wanted her to type. Each letter bore four signatures before it was sealed into its envelope.

Less than an hour later, feeling even sneakier, guiltier and more desperate than before, they emerged from the bookstore. Pete resisted the temptation to look both ways before stepping out into the fresh night air. Simon carried the stack of envelopes. Annie locked the door, and the four of them got into the cart. Pete drove straight to the post office; they all felt the presence of the envelopes as if they were living creatures. Fred jumped out of the cart before it had completely stopped, ran in and dumped the lot of them into the mail slot.

Mission accomplished, they breathed a collective sigh of relief, and Pete began to drive again, headed first to drop Fred at his house.

It wasn't until he was home, in bed, his wife snuggled firmly up against him, under cover of darkness, surrounded by the nighttime paranoia that insomnia sometimes brings, that Pete really began to worry about what they'd done. He worried about mailing all of the letters in one pile, all to major media, all with no return addresses. They looked too suspicious, Pete thought, and he wished they'd spaced mailing the letters out over a week or so.

Annie lay next to her husband feeling a pressure within the walls of The City, a pressure she'd never known before. She thought of all the residents asleep in their beds, innocent, naive by choice. She thought of what the four of them had done that night, and knew that the letters would have little effect in the long run. The kind of pressure she felt building in her town was going to result in some sort of explosion, and their silly little letters would have no real effect on it—except maybe to bust it open a little earlier.

Simon lay in bed, guilt gnawing behind his breastbone. He felt he'd done something wrong. This was the same feeling he'd had when he told his parents that he saw his sister Alexandria smoking cigarettes. They'd punished her, of course, and since he was the only one who knew, she'd instantly known it was he who had told on her.

He lay in bed and felt that he'd told on his parents—betrayed them in a way they trusted him not to. He wished he hadn't signed his name to the stupid letter.

Fred sat propped up in his bed all night listening to his mother cry alone in her room. His father and Mac had gone off to get drunk and he could see Carla aching all by herself in her hospital bed. Last time she'd wanted to kill herself. This time, Fred was afraid she might. He could just picture her deciding that suicide was the only fair thing a barren wife could do for her husband. He clenched his fists again under the covers as his mother wailed into her pillow, and he hoped to God that Pete was right. He hoped that there would be somebody to blame for this.

7

Marian watched Clifford regard his last forkful of steak. He shook his head and with a sigh, set it down on the edge of his plate.

"Wonderful meal, Marian," he said. He pushed his plate away and sat back in his chair, patting the sides of his stomach. "You're still a great cook."

Marian smiled and fingered her napkin. She'd forgotten how good it was to cook for a man, a man who could eat and eat and enjoy food the way Clifford did. She rarely cooked anymore; cooking for two was less satisfying—Miles preferred convenience foods, anyway.

"Finished, Dad? C'mon, I want to show you some of my stuff." Miles hadn't slowed down since the Mayor's Cocktail Party. Marian couldn't remember ever seeing him so wound up. He and Clifford had played catch with the football while Marian fixed dinner, then they came in and Miles set the table while a winded Clifford made the salad. Marian enjoyed working silently next to Clifford in the kitchen while Miles yakked nonstop about school. At dinner, Miles said nothing, just shoveled the food into his mouth, and when it was gone, he waited not very patiently for his father to finish eating.

"Slow down, cowboy," Marian said. "Let your father have a cup of coffee and digest his meal."

"You go on ahead, Miles," Cliff said. "I'll just have one cup, then while your mom is cleaning up—" he turned to her and said, "it *is* your turn to do the dishes, you know—I'll come wrestle with you some more." He rolled his eyes at Marian and his expression told her that he was filled to the gills and would never wrestle again.

"Okay." Miles stood there and grinned at his mom, waiting for her reaction to his father's clowning.

"Shoo," she said, and he grinned even wider, then cleaned his plate at the sink and disappeared down the hall.

"You cooked, so I'll do the dishes," Cliff said.

"Okay."

"What do you mean 'Okay'? You're not supposed to say 'Okay.' "

"Oh? What am I supposed to say?"

"Listen to you, Miss Innocence. You're supposed to say, 'Oh, no, that's all right, it will only take me a minute. Besides, you don't know where everything goes.' "

"Oh."

"Oh, what?"

"Oh, is that what I supposed to say?"

"Yes."

"Well, instead, I think I'll sip my coffee and watch you do the dishes."

"Bet you don't have an apron that will fit me."

Marian wanted to write this down. She wanted to remember what it felt like to have this big man in her kitchen, toying with her, flirting with her. It had been so long. It had been *so* long. She smiled at the love she saw in his face, and she wanted nothing more than for him to bunch up her hair in his meaty fists and kiss her tenderly all over her face.

Clifford cleared his throat and scraped his chair back, breaking the silence. "I'm a man of my word," he said, and picked up her plate.

Marian watched him clear the dishes and load the dishwasher. In only two days, his movements and speech had become synchronized to the tone, and he was quite pleasant to watch. In another couple of days the tone would start to wear off a little of that extra yardage he carried around his middle—his eating would become as automatically regulated as the rest of his functions. He could stand to lose a few, that was for sure.

She was surprised at her emtions and how receptive she was to him. Perhaps time *had* healed all the old wounds. Perhaps things *were* different now, perhaps they had both grown through their stages and had reached a level of individual stability, where once again—dare she think it—they could offer Miles a happy home.

She felt her cheeks burn and tried to push the thought away. It would be good to have a man around again. It would be good to have someone in her bed, it would be good for Miles to have someone to play football with. She and Clifford had both changed a lot—grown, she liked to think—in the past five years, but Clifford was still the man with whom she had fallen in love, married and had a child. He was the only one who had talked to her unborn son from the moment they had decided to have one—a full six months before she conceived—joked around and did things just for the joy of hearing her laugh.

Oh, Clifford, she thought. Oh, Cliff.

They were both still single.

That doesn't mean anything, Marian thought. There are no men in Tone Town, at least no eligible men, no eligible, available men—of an appropriate age . . .

Yes there are. There are plenty, plenty who are interested, yet when you think of their hands on you, you can only think of one who was so gentle, just one man. The only man you've ever had . . .

Marian jumped up from her seat, almost upsetting her coffee. "I'm going to check on Miles," she said, and rushed through the kitchen and down the hall. She detoured into the bathroom, closed the door, turned on the light and stared at her flushed face in the mirror.

"Get a grip, Marian," she told herself with a firm jaw, and a smile returned to the corners of her mouth. "You refused to look at this part of his visit, and now it's here. What are you going to do?" She watched the dark pupils of her eyes for a long time while the thoughts tumbled about inside her head, bits and pieces of scenarios, all pleasant, each one better than the last. She knew what she would do. She had always known. That's why she had bathed and powdered so carefully before the party.

She ran a comb through her hair and dabbed at the eye shadow in the corners of her eyes, took a deep breath and opened the bathroom door. Clifford stood outside, and he held a finger to his lips. "Shhh," he said, and pointed.

Miles was stretched out sound asleep on his bed, a model airplane on his chest.

She felt Clifford's body heat in the hall, felt the tone thump through their bodies like their two heartbeats had become one. She heard his breathing, and his arm came up behind her and he laid a hand gently on her shoulder. She trembled slightly when he touched her; her skin burst into thrills of goose pimples. He moved his face closer to hers and whispered, "Look at our son."

She nodded. It was a familiar scene to her, and yet somehow Clifford's wonder at the sight of his son passed through the space between them and she felt the emotional wallop. Miles's breathing was deep and regular, exactly five beats to the breath, his dark lashes quiet over his pink and freckled cheeks. Miles was a powerhouse of energy when he was awake, and an absolutely beautiful child when asleep.

Clifford pulled her close, turned her head and kissed her. Her nostrils filled with the familiar scent of him, and for the second time in less than a minute, her emotions threatened to overflow. Her skin was starved for a caress . . .

Marian pulled back from the kiss and searched Clifford's eyes for a moment. There was love there, and desire, but she also read concern. He wanted what she wanted, and neither of them wanted more hurt. She touched his cheek with a finger, turned out the light in Miles's room, then opened the door to her bedroom, and invited him in.

They undressed each other slowly, savoring the moment, flashes of memory keeping both of them silent. They had done this—undressed each other—the first time they had made love, thirteen or so years before. Then, Marian had been shy and self-conscious about her body; now, Clifford was. With tender fingers and soft kisses, the familiarity of their lovemaking took over and they came together with practiced knowledge of each other's bodies.

They moved quietly, not wanting to awaken Miles, and their lovemaking became intense, almost violent. Marian's sobs of orgasm turned to sobs of grief, and she tried to turn away from Clifford, but he wouldn't let her. He held her and stroked her, and she thought maybe a few of his tears had mixed in with hers. They slept the night through, wrapped up in each other's arms.

"Hey. Take the day off." Cliff, propped up on pillows, sipped his coffee as he watched Marian get ready for work.

"I can't."

"Please? C'mon, I only have a couple more days. Let's the three of us spend them together. Let's have a picnic today."

"I have so much work."

"Potato salad," Cliff said, and put his hand over his heart. "Please?"

She watched his clowning out of the corner of her eye with an expression of affectionate exasperation.

"Besides, the mayor won't mind," Cliff said with a twinkle. "Tell him you've about got me convinced to stay."

Marian, wearing only her bra and half-slip, stopped rummaging in her drawer. "What do you mean?"

"Mayor Rupert gave me quite a sales pitch on this place, and wanted me to stay."

"Really?" She came over to the bed and sat on the edge.

"You could tell him I'm on the verge of deciding."

"Are you?"

Their eyes met amid a flurry of unspoken emotion. Like magnets, they attracted and held. Cliff saw the flush in her face, shame, maybe, at the bold question. Cliff wasn't sure of the answer, wasn't sure of his footing. There was no way to win.

He set his coffee cup on the nightstand. "Just take the day off, will you?" He tugged at her slip. "Please?"

Marian picked up the telephone. "I'll see." She dialed, then watched him while it rang.

We're like two sharks in heat, Cliff thought. Wary of being hurt too deeply to recover, yet not willing to pass up some opportunities. Risking. Always risking. He smiled at the thought, proud of his analogy. He'd have to share that with her sometime, she'd appreciate it. He watched her watch him, and wondered if sharks went into heat.

"Marian Gray here," she said into the telephone. "Is the mayor in yet?"

She listened, and raised an eyebrow at Cliff. "He is," she whispered over the receiver.

"Good morning, sir. This is Marian . . . Fine, yes . . . It was an excellent turnout, as always. Yes, thank you . . . Well, that's why I'm calling. Clifford must return to Chicago soon, and I thought I might take today off, if you didn't need . . . Oh? Well, that's fine. Thank you, sir. Okay."

She replaced the receiver and smiled. "No problem."

Cliff grabbed her in a bear hug and pulled her across him, her giggles suddenly stifled as she remembered Miles, but they were giggles nevertheless, music to his ears, the touch of her skin electric on his fingertips. He remembered the rhythm of the tone in their lovemaking the night before and wanted to try it just one more time.

Mayor Rupert hung up the telephone and then pressed the intercom. "Sonja, Marian won't be in today. Bring me last night's security report." Within minutes, the report was on his desk, and he flipped quickly to the back, to the last page where his requests of special patrols were always listed.

Aha. Marian's ex had spent the night with her. Good. The more involved they became with each other, the less potential trouble for the Project.

The mayor gave himself a mental pat on the back for his foresight. It was a damned good thing he'd given each of them a cocktail.

8

Pete hid in the silence of the vat room at work. Etiquette in the vat room precluded idle chatter. He was not required to speak, even when spoken to, and there was no reason to explain or apologize. It was no slight. The aura of the vat room was quiet, it seemed almost irreverent to break it. Sometimes vat room workers took the silence too seriously, and had to be transferred for their own good.

Pete blessed the silence this day. His bowels growled and his nerves were on edge. There would be repercussions from those letters. He'd be able to deal with that all right, but the waiting was a bitch.

At noon, he took his lunch and sat in the back of the cafeteria, the other voices loud and obnoxious. He kept his silence to himself, trying to listen to the tone, only the tone, a stress-reduction technique. He tried to block out all conversation, block out all lunchroom noise, hear only the tone. Concentrate. Hear only the tone.

And then, the boy sitting next to him spoke to the man across the table. "My grandfather died last night," he said, and Pete began to think about his own grandfather—both grandfathers, in fact—who'd died before Pete was born. Pete had no family other than Annie. Both his parents had died here in The City—his father in a construction accident, his mother from lung cancer. Annie had no family, either. Her father had come here with the kids when Dusty was just a baby, then he died of a ruptured blood vessel just after Pete and Annie were married.

Simon's whole family was here, so was Fred's. So was Miles's, except for Clifford.

Suddenly light came into Pete's brain. He turned to the boy next to him. "Where was your grandfather?"

"In a nursing home."

"Do you have any family outside The City?"

"Not anymore. Just Grandfather."

"What about you?" Pete began to sweat as he pointed at the man across the table.

"Nope. Just me and my brother and our families. We're all here."

"You and your brother. Did you both come at the same time?"

"No, I applied first, and then they contacted my brother and made him a hell of an offer."

Pete turned to the man sitting on the other side of him. "What about you? Any family outside The City?"

"Nope."

He pointed his fork at the woman sitting across.

"No," she said. "Well, some cousins somewhere, I think."

Pete's lunch turned cold and hard in his belly. There was a standing joke in The City about Tone Town being not only the end of the line, but a whole collection of end-of-the-lines. It was one of those things he'd grown up knowing but never understanding. It was the truth, though, and everybody else knew it. No one in Tone Town had family on the outside.

Good God! Why hadn't he ever noticed that before? That smacked of something essential to the experiment. Something ominous. They must have a good reason for it, and whatever it was, it smelled. It reeked.

He stood up and trashed his dishes, then went back to the vat room. He needed some silence to think this thing through, but he knew he was in trouble. Big trouble. And so was Annie. And so were the boys. Those letters just might've let loose something none of them were prepared to deal with.

Marian lay back on the checkered tablecloth they'd spread on the grass at the park and looked up at the cloudless September day. The tone quietly beeped at them from the bip box in the picnic basket and over that, she heard Clifford finishing the fried chicken with finger licks. This is probably as close to heaven as I'll ever get, she thought.

"Doesn't this place have a zoo?"

"No."

"No!? All that barbed wire"—Clifford made a sweeping gesture at the wall with his napkin—"and no animals? Why not?"

"The barbed wire is to keep out the bad element, Clifford.

Everyone in The City is open and trusting with each other and that makes us vulnerable. The wall is our security. And we don't have pets because animals don't get the rhythm of the tone, and so they become a detraction. It's like radio and television. We only have one local radio station, and a jamming device keeps all the rest out. The tone is supposed to soothe, and that's the purpose of the experiment. If the tone becomes irritating, or conflicting, then the purpose is lost. Understand?"

"Yes, but you mean there aren't any dogs or cats?"

"Nope."

"A boy should have a dog, Marian."

"Not our boy, Clifford."

Marian felt him stiffen, and he wiped his hands and face on his napkin, then lay down next to her. They both watched Miles fly his kite high in the blue Arizona sky. Every time he ran close by them, they could hear the bip box he kept in his pocket.

"Where does the tone come from?"

"A machine. In the basement of City Hall." There was tense silence between them. "Look," Marian said after a while. "This is a great place for Miles to grow up. He's got some good friends, he has good schools, it's clean, healthy, it's a nice place to be. He can be a junior security guard when he turns thirteen. He's looking forward to that. In fact, he wants to be mayor here someday."

"That's good, that's good. I've got no argument with any of that, Marian. This is a fine place. But life is about *experiences,* Marian, experiences. He should go snow skiing and meet different colors of people. He should take a train ride and go to Germany. He should see the Statue of Liberty, and . . ."

"And?"

"And Lake Michigan. I want to take him home with me. Tomorrow."

Marian felt the breath whoosh out of her. Here it came, this was it—the confrontation. Her fingers moved while the rest of her went numb.

"Just for a year, Marian. Just for a while."

She thought desperately of something to say, of something to do, of something that would distract her from the terrible thought. She would do anything, *anything* to keep this from happening. She groped, then an idea popped into her head and she spoke without thinking. "What about the idea of you staying here?" It worked. It broke through that terrible immobilization. She sat up and began throwing things back into the picnic basket. Clifford was silent. A fresh rush of adrenaline flushed through her and she scooted across the tablecloth toward him. She took his face in her hands and held it very, very tightly.

"Don't take him, Clifford. Please don't even *think* about it. Please. I know you don't understand, I know you probably *can't* understand, but you have to trust me, just this once, on just this one thing. Please don't ask me if you can take Miles with you."

He gently removed her hands from his face, held them in his lap. "Trust you on this one thing? Marian, I trust you with my son's life! I trust you completely, and I *can* understand. I understand that you're too attached to him. He has to grow up and see new and different . . ."

"No!" She began to sob. "You don't understand, you don't *know!*" Tears erupted and she covered her mouth with her hands, then moved, trembling and crying, to a far corner of the cloth.

Tell him, she thought. Tell him. She saw him waving at Miles, and she jerked around, fingers in her mouth, and saw her son just standing, looking at them, his kite flying on the end of the string he held. At his father's wave, Miles went back to directing the kite, but Marian thought she was going to throw up. Visions of Brad Rupert came up before her mind's eye. Brad Rupert filled with wrath, Brad Rupert's cutting sarcasm, Brad Rupert's low, ominous warning. This was the only home Marian had, she thought, and she looked around wildly, and knew she had to preserve everything just as it was. Everything must remain the same. The park. She touched the ground, pulled up a blade of grass. The basket. She touched the lacquered wicker. The sunshine. She squinted and looked up. In a moment, her heart was back to normal, she felt better. She finally looked at Clifford and saw him staring at her, worry and concern on his face. He would never take Miles away, she thought. Don't be silly. She smiled at him, then finished repacking the food.

Clifford stood up and shook the wrinkles out of his pants and stomped some blood back into his legs. He held out his hand for her, and she took it and he pulled her up to him, and held her close. He held her quietly and she smelled Arizona fresh air, and Clifford and the scent of their sex, all in his shirt. "Come with us," he said.

For a second she couldn't breathe, and then she pictured it, the three of them, and she began to shake, and he cooed in her ear, thinking she was crying again, but she wasn't, she was laughing. He pulled away to look into her face, and she saw her own red, hysterical eyes, mirrored in his sunglasses. "That would be just great, if I went with you. The three of us." And she laughed again, nervously, tears pouring down her cheeks, and Clifford just held her again until she settled down.

When the cart pulled into the driveway, Marian was quiet, her large sunglasses disguising her thoughts. Miles caught the mood of his parents, and he sat in the back, quietly inspecting his football.

"Run inside and get a change of underwear, boy," Cliff said, "and you can come spend the night with me again at the hotel."

Miles ran inside.

"Get a good night's rest, Marian," Cliff said. "We'll talk again in the morning."

"Clifford." She lay a well-manicured hand on his forearm. "Clifford, listen to me. Just this once." She took off her sunglasses and he looked into red-rimmed, puffy eyes with smeared mascara. "Clifford, if you take Miles with you, he'll die."

She really believes that, Cliff thought. "I think we all need a good night's sleep, Marian. Miles and I will come by to pick you up for breakfast in the morning. At eight."

Marian got out of the cart and walked up toward the house. Miles, underwear in hand, met her on the walk, and Marian grabbed him in a bear hug and squeezed him until he began to complain. She let him go, kissed his cheek and without a backward glance, entered the house.

"Your mother going to any kind of therapy, Miles?" Cliff asked as they pulled out of the driveway and the little cart began to whine down the street.

"No, she quit. Why?"

"Just wondering. No Tarot cards, none of that spiritualism stuff?"

"No, not for a long time."

"Okay. What would you say to a nap before dinner?"

"Yeah, I think that's a good idea." Miles sounded tired, and Clifford felt such affection for his boy, he understood how Marian would hate to lose him for a year. It was going to be hard to bring Miles back.

The message light was on the telephone when they got back to the hotel. It blinked exactly in time with the tone. That machine must power the whole bloody city, Cliff thought, and he called the front desk.

"A message from Mayor Rupert," the clerk told him. "Shall I ring him for you?"

"Please."

The desk clerk put him on hold, and Cliff watched Miles throw his football into the air and catch it while he lay on the second twin bed. The football was a good idea, he thought again, and again he congratulated himself.

"Mr. Gray." It was the mayor's voice.

"Yes. Call me Cliff, please. How are you?"

"I'm fine. Listen, Cliff, Marian just called me, and she tells me you're wanting to take Miles to Chicago with you."

"Yeah, don't you think it's time the boy went sailing on Lake Michigan?"

"I do, I do, Cliff, but there are a few problems with that."

"Oh?" Cliff listened to the highly polished voice that reso-nated with the tone until the two seemed to be indistinguishable from each other.

"Well, the first is Marian's agreement to have Miles stay here until he reached the age of majority."

"Oh?"

"Yes, and this is a federally funded community, and those agreements are very important to the success of our little town."

"Agreements can be changed. Or broken."

"Yes, Cliff, indeed they can. We don't want anyone to stay here that really feels they need to leave, but there are certain channels, forms, you know, that have to be filled out, and then there's a board meeting and a hearing. I strongly recommend you go through the proper channels, Cliff. If you just take the boy, it's grand larceny of federal property."

"Federal property?"

"Until Miles is twenty-one, he is a part of this federal experiment," Mayor Rupert's voice glided on, smooth and unruffled.

"How do I fill out the forms?"

"They're available at our office."

"Fine. I'll come pick them up."

"Excellent, Cliff. Doing things the proper way is the best for all of us, don't you agree?"

"I do."

"It's been a pleasure having you as a guest of ours, Cliff. Please come back again."

The mayor rang off without waiting for a reply.

Cliff hung up the phone and turned to his son. Miles threw him the football, and they passed it back and forth between them for a few moments.

"Want to live with me in Chicago, Miles?"

Disbelief, surprise and delight all crossed Miles's face. "Really?" Then it passed and he threw the football back to his dad. "Nah. I can't."

"Why not?"

"Because I'm here until I'm twenty-one."

"We could fill out papers and get permission for you to leave."

"It's never approved."

"What do you mean?"

"They never let anybody go."

"If you want to go, Miles, they'll let you."

"What about Mom?"

"I invited her to go with us."

"You did?" Miles smiled. And then his smile widened. "You really did? What did she say?"

"I think she'll think about it. I don't think she's ready for us just yet. We'll give her time."

Miles's smile faded a bit.

"Anyway, you come with me and I'll take you to see the Cubs

play baseball and the Bears play football. We'll go sailing on the lake, and see the museums and go to movies. What do you say?"

"Yeah!" Miles came across the bed and into his father's arms, knocking him over backwards. They rolled over once and Cliff pinned Miles down and started tickling him. "Uncle!" Miles screamed in laughter, and Cliff kissed his son and let him go.

9

Suddenly too antsy for an afternoon nap, Cliff and Miles jumped into the cart and headed for the mall. Miles held the door to City Hall open for his dad and together they walked up to the reception desk in the lobby.

"Excuse me," Cliff said to the gray-haired woman at the desk. "Is this where I pick up the forms to fill out so I can take my boy out of here?"

"Request for Special Dispensation. Right here." She swiveled to a large metal cabinet and opened the door. She collated three copies of four pages and handed them to Cliff. "Fill these out and bring them back here. There is a waiting period of ten days, and then a hearing. You'll be the boy's guardian?" Cliff nodded. "You'll have to come back for the hearing."

"When will the hearing be?"

"You'll have to schedule it after the ten-day waiting period."

"I won't be here."

"You have to do all of this in person. File the papers, make the hearing appointment, go to the hearing."

"What about the boy's mother? She lives here."

"Sorry. You're the petitioner."

"She can't just bring these papers in here and make an appointment for me?"

The woman shook her head. It looked to Cliff as though she had been through this before.

Cliff felt his frustration grow, but he was determined to play by their rules so Miles could be free in Chicago. He drummed his fingertips on the backs of the papers, thought for a minute about his obligations back home. He'd work it out somehow. "I'll have to extend my stay."

"I can do that for you," the clerk said. "May I have your pass?"

Cliff fished the pass from his wallet and handed it to her.

"Oh," she said. "You've already been here three days. Maximum stay is seven days. You'll have to come back."

"I can't stay more than seven days?"

"No, sir."

"I see." The situation was crystal clear. Cliff was no stranger to bureaucratic nonsense. "Okay, thank you. Here." He gently lay the forms back on her desk. "Keep 'em."

Cliff put a hand on his son's back and guided them out of the building. He slammed the cart into gear and drove back to the hotel.

Miles sat in the cheap swivel chair at the little round table while Cliff lay on the bed, head resting on the hard headboard. He watched Miles turn his football over and over in his hands. Cliff laced his fingers across his belly. I should just kidnap him, he thought, then he thought of all those missing-children reports, and the whole parental kidnapping thing. Miles shouldn't have to go through that. Besides, it was criminal.

"Hey, Dad," Miles said. "It's okay, you know. I like it here."

"It's *not* okay, Miles." Cliff sat up. "Do you study American history in school?"

"Sure."

"Then you know about freedoms. Well, this is not freedom."

"I know, but it's voluntary. It's an experiment. We agreed to it."

"I didn't agree."

"You don't live here."

"Miles." Clifford got up and sat in the chair across the table from his son. "Kids have adult parents because adults are supposed to have longer vision than the kids. Kids have two parents, because adults don't always agree. Your mother and I disagree here. I think you ought to be able to go out and see things, new things. I want to take you places, and if you want to go with me, you should be able to. You can *always* come back!"

"I know, Dad, but if everybody did that, it wouldn't be an experiment."

"I'm not talking about everybody, Miles. I'm talking about you and me being together."

"You could live here."

"Not me, kid. I'm a Cubs fan."

Miles began to pick at the cracked edging on the table.

"Come with me, Miles."

"What about Mom?"

"She understands. I already told her you were coming with me."

"You did? What did she say?"

"She didn't like it. But it's not forever, Miles. Just a year, or a season. We'll have a lot of fun, and you'll be back in time for your junior security job. I would never do anything to hurt you, son. Please. Miles. Come with me for just a while."

Miles went back to picking at the table.

"Baseball games with hot dogs. Football games wrapped up in red plaid blankets while it snows."

Miles looked up, smiled, and went back to his picking.

"Snow skiing in Wisconsin, Miles. Making a snowman. Christmas lights all over the city, fireplace fires. Eggnog."

"Girls?"

Clifford almost laughed at Miles's deadpan expression.

"Snow bunnies. So many beautiful girls in pretty sweaters you won't be able to stand it."

"Okay." He gave his dad a tentative smile.

"Are you sure, Miles? I want you to be absolutely sure."

"I'm sure."

Cliff didn't want to push it. "Okay," he said, and gave his son a smile. "Okay!" He came out of his chair and put both his hands on his son's shoulders and gave a squeeze. "Great! I promise you, boy, your old dad's going to show you the time of your life."

The decision made, Miles began to show signs of enthusiasm. "Well, let's see . . ." Cliff looked around the room. "Let's go." "Now?"

"Now."

Miles frowned. "What about Mom?"

"We'll call her from Phoenix, Miles. If we tell her, she'll have the police, or whoever, stop you."

Miles was silent. Cliff could see he didn't like the idea, but it would all work out. It wasn't kidnapping if Miles went voluntarily. He fished in his wallet for the business card the cab driver had given him for the return trip and made the call from the room phone.

"It'll be an hour before the cab gets here, Miles," Cliff said. "We should work out our strategy."

Fifty minutes later, Clifford checked out of the hotel, put his suitcase in Marian's cart and drove, with his son, to the gate. He surrendered his pass to the guard, and explained to him that a cab was on its way and that his son would wait with him outside the gate until Marian arrived to pick him up. Then, without waiting for an answer, he left the guard shack and stood next to Miles in front of the gate. The guard put the tone on an outside speaker, then—just as Cliff expected—the gate opened and they walked through, leaving the cart inside.

As if on cue, the taxi pulled up, and Clifford made a show of hugging his son, keeping one eye on the guard, who was watching the scene from his window. He didn't seem at all suspicious. Cliff went into his little routine of looking toward town, then shrugging and pointing toward the guard, all charade to throw the guard off balance. Then he opened the taxi door, got in, and reached his arms out for a final hug. At the last moment, he pulled Miles in beside him, slammed the door, and said, "Take off!"

The driver stepped on it, and Arizona sand spit from the wheels as he turned on the highway toward Phoenix.

Cliff squeezed his son's hand and leaned back as the acceleration pushed him into the upholstery, and he had a triumphant moment. He'd beaten the system for once, he thought, and it felt great. Marian would never press charges. It was only going to be for a year. A good year.

Exhilaration subsided quickly, though, and uneasiness crept in. Cliff reached for the handle to roll the window down—it was stuffy in the cab—there wasn't enough air. Perspiration began to flow down his face, and he felt a tightening in his chest. Then he realized.

The music.

Rock music blared from the driver's radio and it was suffocating him.

"The radio," he gasped. "Turn off the radio!" He gripped the back of the driver's seat, and his eyes rolled toward Miles, whose face showed desperation as he fumbled in his pocket.

The cabbie clicked off the radio. "You having a problem, mister?" He looked at Cliff in the rearview mirror, then glanced briefly over his shoulder. "You want I should stop the cab?"

"No," Cliff gasped, the grip in his chest easing a bit with the silence. But there was something really wrong with the driver's speech; Cliff could barely understand him.

Then his whole body relaxed, and with a flood of relief, Cliff sat back in the seat before he realized that the tone was back. His body responded before his mind did. Miles still had the miniature box in his pocket, the bip box Marian had given him when he ran into the park to fly his kite. The tone thumped through the cab and both Miles and Clifford felt their systems return to automatic.

"It's okay now," Cliff said, and patted the driver on the shoulder. The cab sped on toward Phoenix.

In less than five minutes, they outdistanced the range of the tone transmission. The tone faded, and the box in Miles's lap died.

And so did Miles.

10

Brad Rupert threw his pencil across the room, then swiveled angrily in his chair. "Wait a minute," he said into the phone, then laid the receiver in his lap and pushed on his temples with his fingertips. "Sonofabitch," he whispered.

He waited six beats, trying to squeeze out the terror that was seeping in, trying to pound a little calm into his voice, trying to clear his head. He picked up the phone again and his mind whirred into action. "Dispatch the ambulance and call the hospital in Phoenix. Make sure they get Dr. Burgess. Got that? Dr. *Burgess.* Write that down, you idiot. God *damn,* I can't believe you let that kid get away."

Rupert slammed down the receiver and clicked off the desk lamp. Soft light crept in around the drawn draperies. He lay both his hands palm down on the smooth desktop and spread his fingers.

"Sonofabitch," he whispered. He closed his eyes and counted the beats. At ten, he opened his eyes and looked at the two stacks of white envelopes that rested on the corner of his desk. The ends of four were neatly sliced off, and identical photocopies of a letter protruded from each.

Brad had looked at the first letter and opened the second in disbelief. And the third, and the fourth. Then he resisted the temptation to rip through the rest of the pile in a rage of denial.

But there was no denial to be made. It was Simon's signature, there was no doubt. And it was original on each letter, not just some forger's photocopy trick.

Oh, Simon, what have you done?

Mayor Brad Rupert looked at the envelopes, and he looked at the telephone, then he looked at his hands. His mouth tasted sour.

Simon and the traitors would have to wait. Clifford Gray was first on his list.

He picked up the phone and ordered a murder.

Marian's oven was hardly dirty, but it was one thing she could do that took some energy, one thing she could do that was productive, and took no concentration. She worked quietly and listened to the tone, trying to relax.

The phone rang, jangling her nerves. She thought for a moment about not answering it, but by the second ring she had a rubber glove off. She picked up the receiver.

The mayor's voice broke in before she even said hello. "Marian? Brad."

Marian's heart skipped a beat, her breathing slowed. "Yes, Brad?"

"Miles is gone."

"Gone?" As her mind grappled with the concept, wrestled with the questions, conjured up possibilities to defer the reality, her body knew the truth and her knees weakened. She slipped into a kitchen chair, both hands gripping the telephone so tightly her knuckles were white. Oven cleaner smeared on her chin.

"You didn't do a very good job, Marian."

"What?" Her breath had gone, the phone slipped from her ear. Vaguely, through a noise in her head that sounded like escaping steam, she heard Brad's voice continue through the telephone. Miles is gone. How could she deal with this? How could she face this? Miles is gone. How could this be? Two hours ago he was flying his kite in the park. How could Miles be gone? They were going to have breakfast together in the morning. There must have been some mistake. There must have been some mistake. She had to tell Brad that he was wrong. She lifted the phone back to her ear. Brad was still talking.

". . . about Clifford now, Marian. You know I have no choice."

Marian's muscles weakened anew. "Clifford?"

"The Project is too important, Marian. I'm sorry."

The mayor hung up and Marian sat and stared out the window at the beautiful Arizona afternoon, while swirls of darkness and incomprehensible phrases floated through her brain. She sat until the fire in her middle turned into soggy cement, and then she knew the mayor had spoken the truth. In her desperation to make no choices, she'd made the big one, the bad one, probably the only really wrong choice one woman could ever make in a lifetime.

Finally, coldness settled in, and she knew her life had ended with the lives of her men.

11

Cliff shook his son, desperately willing life into the boy, as he yelled at the cab driver. "Get on the fucking radio and get an ambulance!"

The driver pulled over, bumping along the shoulder, shouting into the microphone, but the cab's radio was past its transmission limit. He finally threw the microphone down, lurched the cab to a halt, and came over the top of the seat into the back.

"Here," he said. "I learned CPR. Is he breathing?"

"No." Cliff began to sob.

"Get out of my way." The driver shoved Cliff out the door and began to breathe into the boy's mouth.

"Oh, Jesus, sweet Jesus," Cliff said, and then pounded on the roof of the cab in impotent frustration. "Jesus," he said again, then spun around, trying not to look in the back seat, trying not to look at his beautiful son's darkening face, and the maniac that was pounding on his little chest.

The cab driver came out, dragging Miles's body with him. "Here," he said. "I gotta have more room."

Miles's head hit the roadway with a hollow thunk that rifled through Cliff, and he looked away, down the stretch of highway that went endlessly toward Phoenix, with no traffic on it at all. No help.

He looked the other way, back toward Tone Town, and a vehicle appeared in the distance. Heat waves from the concrete blurred it, and Cliff actually rubbed his eyes in disbelief. It was an ambulance. He giggled, nervously, hysterically.

"Hey!" he shouted. "Hey, look! An ambulance!"

The cab driver didn't even look up. Cliff stepped into the center of the road and waved his hands over his head. The ambulance pulled over, poofing dust and grit into Cliff's eyes, and two men in white jumped out and ran to Miles and the cabbie.

"What happened here?"

"I don't know," Cliff said, and with practiced speed, one of the attendants in white had Miles on a stretcher and the other had an IV going and they were still working on his heart and breathing for him. In another moment, they were loading him into the ambulance. "Coming?" the driver asked, and Cliff handed the cabbie a wad of money and jumped into the back with the attendant.

They sped toward Phoenix with lights flashing and siren blaring at the desert sand. Cliff watched the expert attendant work on his boy, and he saw futility in the attendant's attitude, in his posture, and knew he was going to give up. Eventually he did. He sighed, and sat back, looked at Cliff and shook his head.

Cliff's boy was dead. Cliff's sweet-faced son that looked just like Clifford-and-Marian, would never grow older, would never learn to ski and flirt with the ski bunnies. With one hand, he kept the attendant from pulling the sheet up over Miles's face.

In the strange, peaceful moment between panic and grief, Cliff could find nobody to blame but himself. When the driver turned the siren off, the pain devoured him, and Cliff buried his face in his hands, buried his soul in guilt, and tried to remember how to pray.

The ambulance pulled quietly up to the loading dock at the emergency room entrance. Cliff walked alongside the gurney as the attendants brought it in, and a nurse whipped a long white curtain around them to give a grieving man and his dead son some privacy.

Cliff stared at Miles's face, and scenes of the past few days flashed past. Miles flying a kite, running, laughing. Miles introducing him to the mayor, hero-worship written all over his face. Miles talking about his future, concern on his face for his mother, looking forward to seeing girls in sweaters. Miles running out for a forward pass.

Where's the football?

His suitcase and Miles's football were still in the cab. The cab company would save them, the cab company would remember them. How many people, do you think, drive all the way out to the middle of the desert to pick up a fare and then have the kid die during the getaway? They'd remember him, all right.

Cliff didn't want to think about the football or the cab company or the suitcase. He touched his boy's cool cheek and closed his eyes, wanting the yammer-yammer inside his mind to just stop. Stop, please, he thought. Just give me a moment's rest here with my boy.

For an instant, all the sounds of the emergency room in a busy hospital subsided, and Cliff reached inside himself for something to sustain him.

Then the shape of a nurse bumped into the curtain rattling it in its track, and the emergency room was alive again. "Dr. Burgess! Dr. Burgess, over here!"

On the curtain, Cliff could see the silhouette of a man join the nurse, and their heads dipped together.

"This the kid from Tone Town?"

The nurse nodded.

"He had a heart attack."

The nurse began writing, and Cliff could tell she held a clipboard. "Do you want to see him?"

"No. What's his name, so I'll know when the certificate comes around."

"Gray. Miles Gray."

Stunned at what he was hearing, Cliff listened until the shape that was the doctor's white coat began to walk away. Then he ripped the curtain open. "Hey, wait! Wait a minute. You're not going to look at my boy?"

The doctor, young-looking for his closely cropped gray hair, stared at Cliff in surprise, then, eyebrows together in anger, looked at the nurse. "He was in there?"

The nurse nodded.

"He was in there and you didn't tell me?"

"How do you know my boy had a heart attack?" Cliff had touched that place of sustenance within him, and it emerged as anger. "He was running and playing football today, and he was fine. How do you know it was a heart attack? Why a heart attack? He was eleven years old. What do you mean a heart attack? What do you know about him? You don't know a fucking thing about my son, yet you just say that he had a heart attack?"

The doctor looked at the nurse with dark anger. "Excuse me," he said, then began walking briskly down the hall.

Cliff started to follow him, but the nurse held up her hands, running interference, fending him off, "I'm sorry, sir, sir, please, sir, please, *Mis-ter Gray!*"

That last got Cliff's attention, and he looked at the little woman who held him back with surprising strength as the white-coated physician retreated down the hall.

"Mr. Gray, now it's understandable that you're upset . . ."

The nurse's voice droned on and Cliff let himself be led toward the emergency-room waiting area, as hammers of understanding rained blows upon his head. Tone Town? Heart attack. Tone Town, heart attack. Tone Town heart attack. It became the accustomed beat.

Marian had said, "If you take him, he'll die."

He sat down as the nurse guided him into a chair, suddenly grateful that he needn't concentrate on keeping his balance when he was so busy thinking about the conspiracy. It *was* a conspiracy, and this wimpy little doctor was just a pawn. And so was the nurse.

He looked up into her face, his eyes focusing on the tired wrinkles around her eyes. "Pawn," he said.

"I'll get you a drink of water. You wait right there."

The newest shock began to wear off, and the anger came sliding in, riding on injustice.

Tone Town. A successful experiment. Everyone in the whole damned community danced the dance of life to the tone, and when the tone stopped, so did life. That's why they used red tape to keep people from leaving. They didn't want *anyone* to leave. They didn't want anyone to know that when people left Tone Town, they died. That's why he could only stay seven days; at three and a half days he'd almost had a heart attack himself. At five years, Miles's system was so addicted to the tone that it commanded his heart to beat, commanded his lungs to breathe, and when it failed, his parts failed to perform on their own.

Clifford slumped in the chair. The experiment was a success, all right.

Marian. Marian knew. Marian knew that Miles would die, and yet she let him take the boy. She killed our son, he thought, the anger burning furiously inside his belly, fueled by his earlier feeling of impotence in the face of Brad Rupert, burning with the desire for revenge. Marian had known Miles would die and did nothing, *nothing* to prevent it.

If you take him, Clifford, he'll die.

Christ, she could have said it like she meant it. She could have shaken him and slapped him and said "No! Clifford! If you take Miles, he'll *die!* Really die! He'll gasp and turn blue and have a heart attack and our boy—our *son* will DIE! *Do you understand me?*"

But she hadn't. And he knew why she hadn't. Mayor Rupert. Mayor Sleaze-Bucket. Mister Mayor Snake Oil. Mayor Rally-for-the-Good-of-the-Project Rupert. Brad We-Are-America's-Greatest-Success Rupert.

How *dare* they.

Clifford stood up and walked back into the emergency room, slipped behind the curtain where his son still lay. "Miles," he whispered. "I'm sorry, boy. God *damn* I'm sorry."

The tears began to come down his cheeks, loosening the wad in his chest. "They'll pay, son, I promise you. They'll pay." He leaned over and saw a tear drop onto the sheet that covered Miles to the neck. He kissed the boy's cold cheek, recoiling inwardly at the sensation, but calmly kissing him nevertheless. Kissing the cold, blue cheek of his dead son sealed his commitment to revenge.

He looked down and wiped his face on the sleeves of his shirt. Then he raised the sheet to cover Miles's face and whipped open the curtain. He strode out of the emergency room door, right past the nurse who held a styrofoam cup of water, and out into the Phoenix twilight.

The nurse ran to find Dr. Burgess.

Cliff fished the cab-service business card from his pocket and walked across the street into the Happy Hour Lounge for a scotch and a phone call. As soon as he entered the dark bar, he felt off balance again. It reeked of stale beer and cigarette smoke. The rhythms were all wrong. The talking, moving, walking, dancing, the music in the background—it was all wrong. He hitched up onto a bar stool and held on to the padded edge as he waited to adjust, sweat pouring from his forehead.

"Scotch, straight up," he ordered from the bartender, and after he knocked it back and had another in front of him, the room seemed a little less intimidating.

Nick Nystrom and John Charles found Dr. Burgess in his office.

"I don't know anything about it," the doctor said, and refused to say any more. John tended to get a little nasty with the regular folks, so Nick talked to the scared doctor, tried to calm him down.

"Mayor Rupert sent us," he said, and the doctor visibly relaxed. "We don't want anybody getting into trouble here. He's got a little problem, is all. The mayor's had a little accident, you might say. And now, Dr. Burgess, he needs your help."

Suddenly, Burgess came alive. "I'll help you this once, and that's the end of you and Brad Rupert and the whole stinking mess. You're all . . ."

Nick felt John stiffen beside him, and the doctor must have seen the expression on John's face, because he stopped what he was saying and just sidled around them and opened the door. The three of them walked down the hall together, getting stares from the other medical personnel—it must have looked like Dr. Burgess was being arrested by two plainclothes bluesuits.

They found Nurse Butler and Nick began to question her.

"He walked right out that door," the nurse said, and pointed to the glass doors with EMERGENCY ROOM printed across them in red letters.

"When?"

"Couldn't have been more than maybe five minutes ago," she said.

God, Nick thought. I hope I never end up in this emergency room. What a stupid nurse. "Thank you very much." Nick turned to the doctor. The doctor wasn't much better. "We'll be in touch," he said.

"Don't," the doctor said as he turned and walked away.

"Where to, Nick?" John said, as they stepped outside and

scanned the street. Lights were coming on in windows, the few cars that drove by had parking lights on. It was dusk in the hot city, and the two bluesuits had nothing to go on.

"Hell, I don't know. Walk two blocks that way and look around. I'll go this way and meet you back here." Nick saw that John patted his side before he took off down the street alone. Then he noted the bar across the street. *That's where we'll call Rupert from if we don't find the fat man. That's where we'll both probably lose our jobs via long distance if we don't locate one escaped asshole.*

12

"Annie?" Annie's office door opened and the bookstore sales clerk poked her head in. "Annie, someone's here to see you."

"Who?"

"I don't know."

Annie sighed and got up from the desk. Tired. Still tired. She maneuvered around boxes of books and checked her hair in the mirror next to her office door before opening it and going out into the shop.

A little blonde in a bright orange dress waited, foot tapping, at the front counter. Annie held out her hand. "Hello," she said.

The little blonde laid a plain white envelope in her hand, and Annie recognized it with a flush. "The mayor asked me to return this to you. He said you dropped it the other night. By accident." The blonde stood there, and Annie didn't know what to say to her. It was as if she were expecting a tip or something.

The envelope jiggled as Annie's hand trembled. She looked at it and noticed that the end had been sliced off and the letter she and Pete and the boys had written stuck out a half inch. "Thanks," Annie said, and turned her back on the girl. By the time she got to her office door, she heard the front door open and close. Annie closed her office door and sank into her desk chair, exhausted, sick to her stomach, numb with fear.

I should call Pete, she thought, then realized she couldn't. This was a little message from The Big Boss Mayor that he had a tight fist around this town, and that meant her telephone and maybe her throat. She sat, holding the envelope in her own tiny vise grip, wondering about jail, about death, about moving, maybe, to San Francisco.

She'd heard a lot about San Francisco.

Maybe Dusty was there.

"Hi, Mom, I'm home!" Fred threw his school books on the table in the foyer and went directly to the refrigerator.

"Freddie? Please come into the living room."

Uh-oh, Fred thought. His mother had *that* tone in her voice. He thought over his day and couldn't think of anything the school could have called about, so he finished pouring his milk, grabbed a handful of cookies and took his snack with him into the living room.

His mother, her eyes red and swollen, was sitting on the davenport, and in his father's chair sat a little blonde woman wearing a bright orange dress.

"This is Sonja Peterson," his mother said. "Sonja, this is my son, Freddie."

The lady held out her hand and Fred shook it, embarrassed by the hand-shaking routine and not at all sure how it was to be done. He was also embarrassed by the woman's look—it was a familiar way some older women looked at him—and he hoped his mother didn't see it.

"Sit down, Freddie," his mother said, then held a handkerchief to her face. She took a deep breath, then handed him a plain white envelope, stamped and addressed to the *San Francisco Chronicle.* One end was cut off and a letter protruded. Guilt charged up his throat and almost choked him. He set his snack on the coffee table and forgot it.

"Aren't you going to look at it?"

"No."

"You know what it is?"

Fred nodded, tears pushing behind his eyes at the shame he'd brought to his family.

"Maybe I better go," Sonja said. She got up and let herself out.

"Oh, Alfredo! How could you do this in the midst of our grief?" And she continued to boo-hoo and blow her nose into her sodden handkerchief.

Kee-rist, it's your daughter we're talking about here, he wanted to say to her. It's exactly *about* Carla and Mac and their babies and the family grief—but Fred saw that his mother wasn't listening, and wouldn't understand.

Fred's mind clicked onward. Simon's father would have something to say to his son, that's for sure, and Simon's father was the mayor.

"Something is wrong here, Mama," he said, then lay the envelope in her lap and left. He needed to get to Simon before his dad did.

Pete emerged into the sunshine, taking a deep breath of fresh air, as he always did after a day inside tending the yeast. He joked with the guys as they walked to the parking lot, but the smile left his face when he saw a blonde girl leaning up against his cart. "Catch you later, guys," he said, and they all fell quiet, too, as they saw her.

"Go easy, Pete," one of the fellows said.

He saw a smirk on her face as he approached. A challenge, almost.

"Are you Pete Mallory?"

"Who wants to know?"

She rolled her eyes with an air of superiority, and handed him the white envelope. "The mayor, that's who. He asked me to return this to you." Pete took the envelope. "Said you dropped it *by accident* the other night." She moved her body so her tight orange dress showed it to its best advantage. She lowered her lids and raised an eyebrow. "Did you?"

Pete saw a blonde child acting like a fool. He brushed her away from his cart. "Excuse me," he said, then got in and put it in gear. He saw her face flush as he calmly stepped on the accelerator and drove away, leaving her standing there.

He drove directly to Annie's bookstore, but the "CLOSED"

sign was up. She'd closed up early. He made a U-turn in the middle of the street and headed back toward home.

Her cart was in the driveway and as he pulled up, she came out to meet him, fear on her face. They hugged outside, and Pete cursed himself for putting his wife in political danger.

It was stupid, what they did, and he was responsible.

He was responsible for Fred, too. And Simon.

Oh God. Simon.

"I'm sorry, Fred," Mrs. Rupert said, fending him off at the front door. "Simon's doing his homework."

"Please, Mrs. Rupert. I just need to talk to him for a moment."

"Tomorrow, Fred." Her stern look told Fred that she was not to be persuaded.

"Oh, okay. Just tell him I came by, okay? And maybe he could call me when he's . . . when he's finished."

"I'll tell him."

Fred turned and walked down the steps, looking toward Simon's window. He wanted to just plant one foot squarely in Mrs. Rupert's flowers and step over to the window and look in. But he didn't. He got on his bicycle, and with one look back, sped out of the driveway and over toward Pete and Annie's.

The mayor held the last white envelope in his hands. The others had been either destroyed or delivered to the traitors, and he had one last task to pursue. His son. His pride and joy. He tapped the envelope against his thumbnail. What would he do about Simon?

The boy was home now, waiting for him.

How dare he treason against his father? How *dare* he? Even as Rupert asked himself, he knew. He'd been a teenager once; he remembered the power of peer pressure. Simon was just a boy, a child, easily persuaded, prone to get carried away. The others, though, were older. They should have known better.

Mercy would be hard, Rupert thought. Mercy would be very difficult indeed. For now, however, they could stew in their own juices. He'd deal with them eventually.

He punched the button on his desk intercom. "Sonja."

"Yes?"

"Have any calls come through to Marian Gray yet?"

"Just a moment."

Rupert turned off his desk lamp and tapped the white envelope, letting the darkness soothe his psyche. In a moment, his intercom buzzed.

"Yes?"

"Security says no phone calls to Mrs. Gray, sir."

"Thank you, Sonja."

He whipped the envelope against the edge of the desk, pleased at the loud crack it made. Why the hell hasn't Clifford Gray called to tell his wife about Miles's death?

Why the hell?

Then he relaxed. Nick and John, of course. They got him. Nick and John. Weird little guys they were, but very efficient.

Fred dropped his bicycle on Pete and Annie's lawn and ran up to the door. Annie opened it wide before Fred had time to knock, and Fred walked right in. They stood together, the three of them in the front room, with no words to say to each other.

"Simon?" Pete asked.

"His mom won't let me see him," Fred said.

"I'm worried sick about him." Annie looked to Pete for a suggestion.

"Come on," Fred said. "What is his father going to do to him? Simon's his son, after all. And besides that . . ." he began to relax. "What we did wasn't so awful, was it?"

Pete sat down on the edge of the couch. "It was only awful if the mayor has something awful to hide. The worse his crimes, the worse our crime in his eyes."

"How do you suppose he got those letters back from the post office?"

"Spies," Pete said. "Rupert's a powerful guy."

They stood in silence for a long moment. "I wish I'd get a letter from Dusty," Annie said.

Pete put an arm around her. "Yeah."

* * *

Marian's headache disappeared in a flash of wisdom. She sat up in bed, astonished at herself, blew her nose one last time, wiped at her swollen eyes, and said aloud, "This insanity has to stop."

Filled with a new energy, she went to the bathroom to wash her face, all the time wondering how she could have allowed herself to be led along like that for such a long time, with such terrible knowledge. Innocents were killed while she held the knowledge of the power of the tone, and did nothing.

Dusty and Roland, and now Miles and Clifford. And there were others. And all the babies. *Three* of Carla and Mac's babies.

She was astonished at her behavior. It seemed like it had been another woman working in that office.

But it hadn't been another woman. It had been her. She deserved to lose her son, and her husband.

Now I have nothing left to lose, she thought. The time for inaction is over.

She started putting makeup on her face, drawing strength from the normal, everyday activity in the face of the strangest of all possible situations. Maybe she'd been protecting the program this whole time because she wanted Miles to grow up. But now that everything she had lived for was gone, she would blow the whistle on the whole terrible, terrible thing.

What about other boys who still have a chance to grow up and marry if the project goes on?

Barren marriages, barren lives. No children. They will just die out until there are only one or two left, and then they will shut the Project down.

Ha! They will shut the Project down long before that.

Maybe the residents can be weaned off the tone. That's what she'd been told, and had believed. Maybe it was true. Maybe something can be done to reintroduce the residents here to normal society.

No way.

Mayor Rupert was a monster and she had worked with him, for him, for a lot of years. She was an accessory, and just as guilty.

A new shame stabbed below her breastbone, but she carried on with getting her face ready for the showdown.

"Dinner, Simon!"

Simon closed his books and turned off the radio. He wondered if whatever it was in the house that felt so weird would come out at dinner. He changed his shirt for a nicer one, and brushed his hair.

His parents were already seated at the dinner table when he slipped into the dining room. His father had a dark expression on his face, and his mother looked between them like a nervous little bird. The back of his tongue tasted like guilt, and he sat in his chair and folded his hands for the grace.

His plate crinkled as he touched it.

He looked down and almost choked.

The white envelope, addressed to the *Washington Post,* lay there, quietly, its end cut off and the letter—one of the letters they'd all signed—protruded.

He looked up to find his father staring at him.

13

"Pull over here," Clifford said, and the cab driver obeyed. "Wait. I'll just be a moment." He jumped out and went into the hardware store with "OPEN 'TIL 9" plastered across the window. The tone came from a machine in the basement of City Hall, Marian had said. A machine. Quickly, he gathered up a small socket set, a series of screwdrivers, a pair of wire cutters and a hammer. He paid cash and ran back to the cab.

"Now Tone Town. Let's go."

Clifford sat in the back seat, feeling his anger pump through his veins. He took the hammer from the paper bag and hefted it, then squeezed the rubber covering on the handle. He liked the way his hand felt when he squeezed the hammer. He squeezed it again. And again.

He squeezed it in time to the tone. That rhythm was in him, through him, *of* him, and probably would be for the rest of his life.

The cab sped into the desert.

Brad Rupert watched his son's face as he recognized the envelope on his plate. Simon flushed, then paled, and he slipped the envelope from his plate to his lap. Brad wasn't sure how he was going to proceed with this act of treason in his own family, in fact until just this moment he couldn't believe that Simon was really involved.

Simon sat, hands in his lap, head lowered. Brad looked at his wife, whose eyes were wide with tension. He could see that she felt the electricity passing between father and son.

Then the phone rang. Joanna jumped to answer it.

"Sit!" Brad commanded his wife, who jerked back to her seat in response to his command, and he slowly rose, his eyes on his son. He refolded his napkin and placed it beside his plate. This would be a good opportunity for Simon to stew, he thought, then went to the den to answer the telephone.

"Hello?"

"Rupert?" It was Nick.

"Yes?"

"We lost him."

Brad's head began to thump, a driving ache that began at the base of his skull and pulsed upward. When next he spoke, his voice was low, controlled. "How?"

"I'm not sure. He slipped out of the hospital just before we got there. He just disappeared."

"Do you two idiots have a fucking idea between you? What are you going to do now?"

"Well, he must have either gone to the airport, or . . . Hell, Phoenix is a big place."

Incompetents. Everywhere, incompetents. "Where are you now?"

"In a bar, across the street from the hospital."

"What's the number?" Rupert wrote it down. "I'll get back to you. Stay put!"

He put his finger on the disconnect button and closed his

eyes. Damn. Washington would not be happy. He dialed, 1-202-. Shit. He didn't know the number, and didn't have it at home. He'd have to go to the office.

He slipped the paper with the bar's phone number on it into his shirt pocket, took his keys from the desk drawer and walked through the dining room. His wife and son sat exactly as they had when he had gone into the den to answer the phone. "I'm going to the office. An emergency. You." He pointed at Simon. "Don't leave."

Marian brushed blusher on her cheeks and stroked on a little mascara. It didn't help her blotchy appearance or her swollen eyes. She slipped on a comfortable pair of slacks and a shirt, brushed her hair and left the house. She felt the chill evening air on her skin as she rehearsed her speech to the mayor all the way to his home.

She pulled up to the curb, strengthened her resolve and stepped out. Feeling small and inadequate, she marched to the door, tears blurring her vision. She knocked.

His wife opened the door, and her face mirrored Marian's own.

"Is Brad home?"

Joanna just shook her head, unable, it appeared, to answer. She clutched a sheet of white paper in her hand.

"Joanna, what's the matter?"

Joanna stood back to allow Marian to enter, then closed the door. She handed Marian the paper.

Marian read it quickly. "Simon? Simon signed this?"

Joanna nodded.

"Is Simon home?"

Simon appeared in the doorway. "Hello, Mrs. Gray."

"Simon." Marian held up the paper. "Is this why your father isn't home?"

"No." Simon looked at his feet. "He got a phone call just as he was ready to rip into me."

"A phone call." Marian sat on the edge of a chair. Joanna sat down, too, her eyes on her hands in her lap. A phone call to say that Clifford had been killed, per his instructions. But would that send him to his office? "What phone call?"

"I don't know," Joanna said. "He just said it was an emergency."

"An emergency." Maybe they hadn't killed Clifford. But that was no emergency. But if Clifford was alive, he would have called to let her know about Miles, wouldn't he?

He'd call, wouldn't he, even though she'd told him that Miles would die?

Unless Clifford knew *why* Miles died.

That would be an emergency to Brad. She looked at the paper in her hand. That's an emergency, all right. Clifford would see it as her fault and he would come for her. After he went to the police.

To clear her mind, she slowly read the letter again. "Who'd you send this to?"

"Newspapers and stuff."

"How many?"

Simon shrugged. "About thirty."

"Why?"

"Dusty," he said. "And Carla's babies. Pete said they closed down the North End grade school. He said that this experiment has run its course, so they're shutting it down by letting us all die off. And if anybody leaves, he kills them."

"Who?" Joanna suddenly came to life. "Who kills them?"

Simon looked at the floor.

"Who kills them?"

"Come with me, Simon," Marian said. "Let's go talk to Pete."

Joanna was suddenly right in front of Marian's face. "Who, Marian? Who kills them?"

Marian looked into the woman's eyes. Joanna, long-suffering, obedient wife of the mayor. She took his abuse all these years, her unflagging loyalty both a mystery and an inspiration to the whole community. How could Marian tell this woman the truth about her husband?

"No one, Joanna," she said, then put her arms around Joanna's slender shoulders. "They just die by themselves."

"Seven eight."

"Brad Rupert here, T.O.N.E. I've got bad news."

"Go."

"The kidnapping we anticipated took place. The kid's dead and the father is on the loose."

"Details."

Brad gave him all the details he could, up to and including his dinnertime phone call. He ended up giving Washington the phone number of the bar where the two goons waited.

"Tap on the mother's phone?"

"Yes. He hasn't called her."

"Taking it out of your hands, Rupert. Project Stone is on the line here; you may have just queered it. Think about that."

Washington rang off.

Rupert thought about it, and it made him very sad.

14

"We must be getting close, eh?" Cliff leaned up close behind the driver's shoulder, watching out the windshield.

"Just on the other side of this rise."

"Let me out here."

"Here?"

"Yeah." Cliff dropped some bills onto the seat next to the driver, and the cab pulled off onto the shoulder.

Cliff got out with his bag of tools, and handed the man a twenty through his window. "You never saw me, okay?"

"Hey," the man said. "Don't get me involved in nothing here."

"You're not involved," Cliff said.

"You look pretty suspicious."

"You want the twenty?"

The driver thought for a moment. "Okay," he said and pocketed the bill. He made a U-turn and drove off down the highway, back toward Phoenix.

Cliff watched the taillights disappear down the road that

looked silver in the desert night. Phoenix was just a faint glow in the sky. When the car was out of sight, Clifford listened to the silence. He was alone in the dark on a lonesome desert highway. Just he and his mission.

Feeling naked and conspicuous, he began walking, and hoped to hell the cab driver was right about The City being right on the other side of the rise.

Before long, the backs of his thighs began to ache. The pleasant cool of the early evening had faded under the oppression of unaccustomed exercise. He twisted the sweaty neck of the paper bag where it wrapped around the handle of the hammer, then changed it to his other hand. Perspiration stung his eyes, and he wished he had seriously dieted before coming out here. He could do without thirty pounds. Or forty.

He turned and walked backwards, hoping to stretch out the muscles a bit, and saw that he'd been walking up a slight rise. Very slight. He kept walking backwards, then turned around and watched his feet, kicking pebbles out in front of him. No traffic at all.

He paused and leaned over, elbows on his knees, panting for breath, his leg muscles screaming. Slow down, he said to himself.

Then he started again, and he noticed he could almost see over the top of the rise.

Aching disregarded, he picked up his pace and paused at the top. Disappointment almost tripped him.

A quarter of a mile farther, the wall stood sentry around The City. Tall and brick, with a blank, unscalable, unreadable face, the wall was topped with reels and reels of wicked barbed wire that shone with bizarre beauty in the moonlight. The wall stretched as far as he could see in both directions.

He hitched up his little bundle of tools. They clanked in the desert silence. How in the hell was he going to fight *that* with *these?*

Then he saw the tiny spot of light that shone on the highway in front of what must be the guard station, and he remembered his mission.

He heard a car coming up behind him, and he took off

running across the desert, into the darkness, into the wilderness, ready to come face to face with the mocking wall, to try to find some way to penetrate the evil fortress.

Two dark-suited men in their classic black sedan sped down the long highway.

"Hey, what was that?" John grabbed Nick's arm.

"What?" Nick stepped on the brake.

"Pull over. I saw something."

"Rabbit," Nick said, impatient with John's lack of intelligence. He was still smarting from the verbal abuse he'd taken on the phone from Rupert and that other guy, and John was a convenient outlet. He stomped on the accelerator and the car shot up over the rise. He whistled, long and low. "Jesus Christ, would you look at this place?"

They both forgot the activity in the brush as they approached the wall, and the light, and the guard, and their problem.

When Pete opened his front door and saw Marian Gray standing with Simon, he found himself speechless. He loved Marian and he loved Miles. But Marian worked for Rupert, she had worked as Rupert's assistant, she was that twit Sonja's boss. Now Rupert and Sonja were the enemy, and that meant Marian must be the enemy, too.

His eyes locked with hers, but he read something different in her face. He read something he didn't understand.

Then he looked at Simon. "Simon, buddy, you okay?"

"Yeah," Simon said. "Sort of. My dad—"

"May we come in?" Marian asked.

Pete opened the door and stepped out of the way to allow them in. Simon crossed the living room and sat next to Fred on the couch. Marian followed him and sat on a chair. Annie came out of the kitchen, wooden spoon in hand, and raised an eyebrow at Pete. Pete shrugged.

"Seen your dad, Simon?" Pete asked.

Free of parental constraints, and amongst his friends, Simon lightened up. "Yeah. He's not very happy with us."

"What did he say?"

"Nothing. He was just getting ready to let me have it, when the phone rang and he had to leave. What about you guys?"

"Sonja delivered one of the envelopes to each of us," Pete said.

The room settled into silence. Pete's gaze rested on Marian. "Excuse me for being blunt, Marian, but why are you here?"

Marian's eyes went wild for a moment, casting about for something to say. "I read Simon's letter. I want to help you."

Pete scoffed. "Deserting the enemy camp? Turncoat?" He felt a little ashamed of his sarcasm, but couldn't help himself. "*Spy,* Marian? How much is Rupert paying you to infiltrate?"

"Stop it, Pete," Simon said. "My dad's not a bad guy."

"Your father, Simon," Marian said, "has become involved in a terrible, a terrible situation . . ."

"Spare us, Marian," Pete said.

Annie poked him with the wooden spoon. "Let her finish."

"No. I'm not interested in anything she has to say. There's no excuse for what Rupert is doing, and if she's here . . ."

"Stop it, Pete!" Simon jumped to his feet, his face red, his fists clenched.

"Hey, hey, okay." Pete backed down, crossed his arms over his chest and leaned up against the wall. "Okay, Marian. Shoot your wad."

She looked at the floor, and six beats passed. "Miles is dead," she said.

Astonishment silenced the room as tears leaked out of Marian's eyes.

Shock thunked in Pete's belly. Then something enormous began as goose bumps on his legs, and rose up through him, and with a grunt, he punched his fist right through the wall. Everybody jumped. The pain in his hand helped the hurt in his gut. While his hand hurt, he didn't have to think about Miles. Then he couldn't help thinking about Miles. He began to pace, rubbing his knuckles.

"He left, didn't he?"

Marian nodded.

"He left with his dad, because you didn't tell Cliff that Miles would die if he took him out."

Marian sat watching the dark spots appear on her slacks as tears of guilt fell from her eyes.

"You should be crucified," Pete said.

"I did tell him," Marian whispered.

"Well, you didn't tell him *enough!*" Pete clenched his fists, pumping his anger in time to the tone. His face reddened, and he bounced on the balls of his feet. He spun around, took aim again at the wall, caught himself, and instead rubbed his sore knuckles again.

"I want to help you." Her voice was weakening.

"Don't you bring your fucking guilty conscience to my house. Don't you murder your son and then come here to fix it." Pete was shouting now. "Get out of here! Get out of here!" He crossed the room in two strides, gripped Marian by her wrists and pulled her up from the chair.

"Pete!" The other three moved as one body to restrain Pete, to keep him from hurting Marian. Pete had loved Miles. Loved him as a father would love a son. The hurt in his soul was overpowering.

"She can help us, Pete," Annie said. "She knows everything. She can help us get Rupert." That stopped him.

Pete let go and Marian dropped back into the chair, wailing. Annie fetched a paper towel from the kitchen and dropped it into Marian's lap. Then she backed Pete up to the other side of the room. As the tension eased, both Simon and Fred sat back down on the couch. The only sound was that of Marian whimpering and blowing her nose.

"What's happening here?" Simon asked, his face blank, worried.

Marian told him.

Brad Rupert sat at his desk, in the dark. In a circular motion, his thumb worked the big, fleshy mole on his cheek. He was having a serious moment of introspection.

Project Stone was lost to him now, and new thoughts were sprouting in the void it had left in his consciousness.

Thoughts of Simon. And Alexandria. Miles. Joanna and Marian. Sonja. And the future of The City.

He'd never exactly known what Project Stone was, only that

Tone Town's success was an integral part of it. The decision to bring Joanna here, to make this experimental community their home, the place in which they would rear their children, was based totally on the twenty-year plan.

After twenty years, if he, as mayor, performed with loyalty, patriotism and diligence, then the recognition of Project Stone would be his. And Tone Town was just a tiny, minute part of the whole project.

He had given his life to this project. He had sacrificed his whole being for it. He had denigrated his will, had put his family on the back burner, had done everything humanly possible for Tone Town to work.

And it had. The experiment was successful beyond anyone's wildest expectations. And this was the end of the nineteenth year.

He didn't like the forced population reduction, but it was part of the program, and he had seen the design at the outset, and understood why it was important. He had agreed at the time, and even now, when the reality was harsh, he knew it was the best thing. Hell, he had toasted to his daughter's fertility at her wedding while Alexandria and her groom and all the guests drank down his sterility cocktail. Now, that was dedication!

He knew the whole project had a master plan, one that must not be changed, especially at the whim of an aging man's changing heart.

He could be proud of the community, he told himself. It was a clean, pleasant place, with a nice mix of people. Thousands of happy families lived here. Was what he did—what he had to do in secrecy—so wrong?

Pete and Annie and Simon and Fred thought so.

But they didn't know the whole story. They didn't understand the motivation, they didn't understand the whole scope of the experiment. The population was declining, true, by design, and when it was time to turn off the tone, the remaining residents would have a portable appliance to help them reenter society. Alexandria would still be young enough to have children out in the world, and so would Simon. Everything would have been fine. Everything would have turned out all right.

But now, because of meddling incompetents, nineteen years of dedicated hard work was evaporating before his eyes. Experiments have downside risks, everybody knows that. Everybody who signed up to live in Tone Town knew it, was prepared to take the risk. Rupert was prepared for his. Almost. He'd not been quite prepared to have the whole project jerked out from underneath him at the eleventh hour. But now that it had been, he and Joanna would have no reason to leave. The day they turned off the tone, he and his wife would probably just sit down on the couch together and wait for silence.

Silence. Wonder what silence sounds like? No tone, no heartbeat, no blood rushing through the veins. No sound at all.

Well, now he'd find out. His dream bubble had burst, and all because of Clifford Gray. Clifford Gray and an inept guard at the front gate.

He stopped playing with his mole and thought for a moment about killing himself.

And then he thought again about his life ambition. How can one abstract incident negate an entire lifetime of work? There had to be something he could do. There had to be *something.*

He picked up the phone and dialed.

It rang once.

"Seven eight."

"Brad Rupert again."

Silence. Suddenly he was ashamed that he had called, and he didn't know what to say. "Any word?"

"Computer consensus is that he's on his way back to you. My suggestion is to get him."

"Is there a chance . . ." Brad knew he was begging, and he hated himself for it.

"Project Stone has mobilized. If it's premature, it'll die. Stifle this situation, Rupert. Stifle it. Now."

Washington rang off.

Brad hung up and knew there was still a chance for his life. He grinned into the darkness and thought about getting Gray.

15

Cliff leaned against the hard, gray face of the wall and concentrated on catching his breath. The muscles in his legs were cramped and the dry air rasped the insides of his lungs. He must have been crazy to run all that way. The bag of tools slipped from his lax fist and dropped to the ground with a clink. He scratched his forehead against the pebbly surface of the wall. He wanted to surrender to it, admit that it had won, and with that admission, suddenly, magically, he wanted his wife and his son alive, healthy, happy, and all this to be a terrible, terrible dream.

His breath slowed, and he felt the coldness of the masonry, and then he felt the tone. He could feel the tone in the wall. The drumbeat so permeated the town that it throbbed in the wall that surrounded the town. The wall *is* the town, Cliff thought. The cold, gray, rough-surfaced wall *is* the bloody town.

And then he remembered the sensation of his lips touching the cold, gray, angel-soft cheek of his son, and the blood roared in his head. His mind cleared of sentimentality, and rage took its place, clearing a path to his goal.

This wall was his first obstacle. He had to get inside.

Maybe there was a back door.

He peered into the darkness and tried to remember the cartoon map the guard at the gate had given him on the first day. Was there a service entrance or something? He couldn't remember, but he knew from being inside that the wall was almost two miles long each way, and in his present condition, he would never make it all the way around. And there probably wasn't a back door anyway. Or if there was, it would be as impenetrable as the chunk of wall right in front of him.

He sat for a minute, catching his breath, massaging the calves of his legs, trying to think. All he could think about were the jelly donuts and double Whoppers with cheese that had gotten him into this condition.

Finally, the last of the tingling left his legs, and he stood up and faced his adversary.

First things first, he thought, and removed his belt.

The moon suddenly shone its face over the hills illuminating the desert, casting his shadow against the wall. He walked back a dozen paces and stood on his tiptoes to look along the top of the wall. It was about ten feet high. Posts of reinforcing rod jutted out the top of the wall about every five to six feet. The rounds of razor-ribbon barbed wire were affixed to those posts. He returned to the wall and threw his belt buckle up at the wire.

On the second try, the buckle sailed beautifully through a loop of wire, and for the first time in his life, Cliff was grateful for his forty-two-inch waist. He reached up and slipped the end of the belt through the buckle and pulled steadily, until the spring of wire came down off the top of the wall, toward him. He reached up with the wire cutters and snipped it as close to the top as he could reach.

Then he did the same thing at the next post and let fall a chunk of wire covered with evil-looking triangles that begged to slash his flesh. He kicked it aside, carefully, then loosed his belt from the cut end of the wire at the top of the wall.

A five-foot area of the wall was clear.

Now what?

Cliff reached up, but his hand fell way short of the top. If he were thinner, maybe, and/or younger, he could take a running leap and get a hand over the top. But he was not thinner, and he was not younger, and that meant he had to use whatever wisdom, common sense or creativity he had learned in those years while munching pretzels and eating ice cream.

He gauged the wall again, then put the loop back in his belt and threw it at the post. It was a good, strong leather belt; maybe if he could anchor it at the top—slip it over one of those rebar posts—he could climb up the wall like a mountain climber.

He couldn't get it. The buckle tinked against the remaining barbed wire, and the sound in the stillness of the desert night rang out like an alarm to him, but then it seemed as though the little sound was lost in the immensity of the universe. He tried again and again, but he was just not quite tall enough, the belt was not quite long enough, the wall just too high, the angle too sharp. The loop in the makeshift lasso closed up too much before it reached the pole. He needed a step up.

He dumped the tools from the paper bag into the dirt and poked at them with a finger. Then he looked again at the wall. He picked the heaviest screwdriver, the straight-edged one, and dug a little mortar out from between the blocks. It scraped away like gray powder in the moonlight. He picked up the hammer, then lay his ear against the wall and waited until he got the rhythm of the tone. Then, in perfect time, or so he hoped, he began to slowly and steadily hammer the screwdriver into the wall.

The sound seemed to fill the night, and he felt the familiar tug in his chest as the tone called to his heart to slow down, relax, surrender to its control. Cliff ignored it all; he just concentrated on hammering the screwdriver in straight. It disappeared into the wall a bit at a time, and then the yellow plastic hilt hit the wall with a different thud, and he stopped.

Now the silence was deafening. He wiped perspiration from his face, and sat down for a minute to quell the shaking.

After a moment, he looked back at the little yellow handle sticking out of the wall. It, too, looked gray in the moonlight. He would stand on the screwdriver and then heft the belt buckle over the post.

He looked again at the tools. There was a Phillips screwdriver, the same sturdy size as the straight edge he'd used. He wiped his forehead again, then stood up and planned a second step. He didn't even need to listen to the wall to know the tone rhythm by then. It was inside him. The calm for which the tone had become known had descended upon Cliff and turned his anger, his panic, into steady, methodical revenge.

He hammered the second screwdriver in, above and to the right, just as he had the first, and when he was finished, he had one handle-step about knee high and another one at waist height.

He stored the hammer by putting it through a belt loop in his pants, slipped the wire cutters into his shirt pocket, selected two medium-sized screwdrivers from the pile in the dirt and put them in his pants pocket, slid the socket set in its little red case inside his shirt, and wrapped the end of his belt around his right fist.

Okay, he thought as he readied himself. Quickly, now. Step

on one, step on two, throw the belt over the post, and then up and over, while the momentum is going. He mentally rehearsed a couple of times, talking to his stressed-out muscles, getting them ready for a serious undertaking.

He felt his heart gear up, leaving that steady forty beats per minute, and he knew it would slip into time and a half to the tone, and if he didn't act soon, his adrenaline would push it to double time, and then he might not live to land on the other side.

Land on the other side. Jesus Christ, he was going to fall ten feet. All two hundred and twenty-five pounds of him.

The screwdrivers in his pocket would probably castrate him.

Too bad. Too late. He tightened his grasp on the leather once again and thought himself light. He stepped his left foot up on the first screwdriver and felt the plastic crack. The metal began to bend, and he pulled his pants leg up and stretched his right to the other screwdriver, his knees out to both sides. His foot was slipping off the first, and his fingernails grabbed at the little bitty ledges where the mason had troweled off the excess mortar. He put his weight on the upper foot and the fingertips of his left hand grabbed hold of the top of the wall. He threw his belt at the pole and missed.

The second screwdriver bent and the edge of leather sole on his shoe pushing on the edge of the plastic began easing it out of the wall. He held on tighter to the top of the wall with his left fingers while he readied the belt again, then threw it.

Son of a bitch! It stuck on the barbed wire, and he pulled it back to him, but it wouldn't come. It was firmly snagged.

His fingers were giving up, his screwdriver was slipping out, and his hope was deserting him.

No, goddammit! He jerked hard on the belt and the fickle barbed wire sprang around and caught on itself behind the post.

Cliff yanked on it, tested it. It was stuck there, solid. He eased his weight onto the leather strap, taking the pressure off his poor fingers.

What's the difference if I fall on this side or that side, he thought, then let go of the wall in order to get a better grip.

The belt held, stuck only to one arrowhead-shaped shard of steel. He gripped the belt with his aching left hand, and swung out, knuckles rasping on the wall. He managed to pull his right hand above the left, and then, feet running up the wall as if it were a sheet of vertical ice, three panic paces to ascend six inches, he grabbed the top of the wall with his whole forearm, and he rested there for a moment until he knew his heart would not burst.

Kicking both legs, he managed to get his chest up on the wall, shredding the fabric of his shirt where it scraped against the metal of the socket kit. The wall was wider than he thought; it was at least twelve inches, and he looked out into the park where he and his son had flown the kite, and then he looked straight down ten feet into bushes that helped to disguise the wall. A good morale-building strategy, he thought. Good work, Rupert. Plant bushes in front of the wall so the residents will ignore the barbed wire on top of it. Well, maybe the bushes will help break my fall.

I'll be lucky if I don't break my neck.

He wiggled around on the top of the wall until he could sit up, holding on to both sides, then he swung his legs over. Humpty Dumpty, he thought, then realized what a target he made, backlighted by the moon to any resident, security man or strolling mayor who happened to look his way. Without thinking, he held his breath and slipped off.

He hit and rolled, but he hit too hard, and rolled the wrong way, catching the little metal case between his elbow and his ribs. He felt something crack—his whole side felt on fire.

He rolled over, trying desperately to draw some air into his lungs, his face in dirt, mulch and shrubbery fertilizer. The pain was ferocious, but he had made it.

He was inside.

When Marian finished speaking, the small apartment rang with the silent echo of her words. Just the tone, suddenly a monster—a life-threatening, yet life-sustaining monster—sang to all those in Pete and Annie's living room.

Marian rubbed her thumbs over the tops of her hands, something she'd been doing since she began talking. Her hands looked red and sore. No one offered her anything—a drink, a snack, a tissue—to ease her pain. Everyone empathized with her loss, but felt a singular lack of pity for her plight. The sogging, shredded paper towel lay in a clump on her lap, and her eyes stared at the crease in her pants.

"I don't believe it," Simon said.

No one looked at him.

Pete began to thump his knuckles on the wall in double time to the tone.

Fred spoke next. "You mean Carla's babies all died because of . . . because of what?"

Pete knocked hard, twice, on the wallboard. "That's the question, Marian. I understand the closing down of the facility, and I understand the secrecy, and I understand that we're now addicted to the tone and can't live without it. But there's a missing piece here—two, actually."

He began to pace back and forth in the little living room. Fred watched him, Simon and Annie stared into nothingness, complete within themselves and their own thoughts about family. Simon was mentally with his father, Annie with Dusty. Marian seemed void.

"Number one. Marian, pay attention." Marian's head snapped up, and her eyes came into focus on Pete. "They will close down this facility long before the last person dies here. What are they going to do with all the people left?"

"Rehabilitation. Most everybody will be able to reenter society."

"*Most* everybody?"

"Those born here will have a harder time of it. They're working on some sort of portable thing they can carry with them, or an implant, sort of like a pacemaker."

"What's the experiment been for? What's the purpose? What use have we all been, that we can be disposed of so conveniently?"

"I don't know." Marian mumbled.

Pete stopped and stared at her.

"Come on, Marian. The truth."

"Something . . . I'm really not sure."

"Somebody was gathering statistics here. Rupert must have been talking to—*reporting* to—somebody, at some time, about something. He must have talked with someone, reported to someone, continually. Who was it?"

"Seven eight," Marian said. "Seven eight. That's all I know."

"What . . ."

"He answered the phone, 'Seven eight.' "

"Do you know the telephone number?"

Marian shook her head.

"Was there a seven eight in the number?"

"No. No, I remember, the first time I called it for Brad, and the man answered, I thought I'd called the wrong number, so I checked, and he said it was the right number and what did I want. I was embarrassed, and didn't call it anymore after that, but Brad called it all the time. It was on his phone log."

"What was the area code?"

"Two-oh-two."

"Washington, D.C."

"That tells us *nothing!*" Annie came to life, jumped up from her chair and stomped into the kitchen. A moment later she began slamming cabinet doors and pounding things on the counter.

Everyone stirred, as if awakening from a drugged sleep. Annie, the gentle heart, was tearing the kitchen apart.

"Pete . . ." Fear showed in Simon's face.

"Hey," Pete said, spreading his hands and shrugging his shoulders. "She's been having some pretty weird exams and doing fertility drugs for three years. Now she's just been told that your father puts contraceptives in the punch. Leave her alone."

In a few moments, a wild crash came from the kitchen, and then it was silent.

Pete walked into the kitchen and touched his wife's back as she sobbed into her hands. Her rage was spent; sadness had taken over. He pulled a strand of hair away from her ear and stroked a finger down her cheek. She didn't respond, so he kissed her shoulder and pulled a beer from the refrigerator and went back to the living room.

"Okay. Washington. That tells us nothing, simply because

we're a federally funded project. What else can you think of, Marian? What's the purpose of this experiment?"

"Well, the longevity, and the reduction of stress, and the environmental things. They want to put tones in major factories, now, to reduce the stress . . .

"Except the tone has one major drawback," Pete began to fill in for her. "People become addicted to it and die during withdrawal. Now that sounds like it's right up the old Department of Defense alley, doesn't it? Only to them, it's not a drawback, it's a side effect."

"I think I'd better go home," Marian said, and stood, looking thin and unsteady. No one helped her, as the mound of shredded paper towel fell from her lap to the coffee table, and as she walked, taking small steps, from the house. She stopped at the kitchen door, but said nothing to Annie. She just continued out the door, closing it gently behind her.

He's on his way back here, Rupert thought. Of course he is. He's coming back for Marian.

He punched buttons on his phone.

"Security."

"Rupert here. We're expecting an intrusion tonight. Put a double guard at the gate and patrol the perimeter."

"Yes, sir."

"Double patrol. *Triple* patrol."

"Yes, sir."

Rupert hung up. That sonofabitch Gray has got my balls in his grip, and I will not let him have them. He thrummed his fingers on the desktop.

Then the first button on his phone lit up. An incoming call.

Blood rushed to his face. They got him! He picked up the phone and punched the button.

"Sir?"

"What?"

"There's been a breach. A section of wire has been cut and removed from the south wall."

"Where?"

"At the park, sir."

Rupert slammed the phone down. Gray may have gotten inside, but he would not get back out.

He left the office and got into his cart. Then he got back out. Gray was on foot—Rupert would catch him on foot.

He left the cart in the parking lot and began walking briskly toward Marian's.

16

When in doubt, take a walk, Pete thought. That's what he and Annie had done to iron out their difficulties ever since they'd known each other. The fresh night air always revived them, and walking past all the houses, knowing all their friends were inside their homes dealing with their own difficulties, always gave them a sense of security. It didn't usually take more than two or three blocks before they began finding solutions to their problems instead of wallowing in the argument.

"C'mon, Annie. A walk will be good."

Reluctantly, Annie took the jacket Pete handed her and stuffed a handful of Kleenex into the pocket. Head down, she went out the door into the cool Arizona night. Simon and Fred followed her; Pete followed them.

The four of them, Annie and Simon in front, turned left at the sidewalk and walked leisurely toward Simon's house. Pete felt the living bond of friendship tighten among them. Together they had conspired and been found out. Together they had discovered the terrible truth, and they would live the rest of their lives dealing with the things they did in the next twenty-four hours. Now, though, they were breaking apart—if even for the night—and committing Simon to the home of his father, and Fred to his family. Then Pete and Annie would deal with their own misery and hate and anger in their own way in their own home.

"Mur-der. Mur-der. Mur-der." Annie chanted in time to the tone that emanated from the base of the streetlights.

"Annie, stop."

"Mur-der. Mur-der. Mur-der."

"Annie!"

She stopped, but the chant continued in everybody's mind.

"I don't believe it," Simon said.

"Believe it," Annie whispered with ferocity. "Believe it. Dusty"—her breath caught in her throat—"and Roland, and Miles. And Carla's babies. That's the worst, you know. They must have just *killed* Carla's babies." She reached her hands into the air, and an expression of helpless pleading crossed her face. "Why? Please, God, tell me *why?*"

Pete stopped, and grabbed Annie's jacket.

"What the hell are we doing? We must be insane to be out here like this. We can't send Simon home." He saw understanding flow into Annie's eyes. "We can't go home, either."

The momentary panic passed from Annie's face. "What are we going to do, Pete, hide? Where?" Sarcasm thickened. "Want to leave?"

"I don't want to go home," Simon said.

"Me neither."

"Me neither."

"Unanimous. We can't hide, we can't run. Let's just walk."

It was something to do. They continued down the sidewalk, their steps, their heartbeats, their breathing, all in perfect, uncontrollable time to the tone. Their feelings swirled about them, almost visible. They felt wronged, trapped, doomed.

Annie stopped when they reached the edge of the park. "Look," she said. "A nice, big park. We could run out there and play, chase each other around, except that we can't go there without our bip boxes. Wouldn't you think someone would have noticed that before?"

"I didn't," Simon said. "I just was never comfortable in the park without mine. Mom said it was because I'd start to get stressed-out without the tone, and I believed her. I just never went out there without it."

"Yeah, my mom said it was contrary to the experiment."

"I could just walk right out there and commit suicide," Annie said.

Pete put his arm around her. "Come on. Let's keep walking."

They continued to walk past the park, eyes inadvertently straying to the darkened interior, each mind wondering what it would be like, to just hear the silence, to just feel the—heart—quit—beating. Just to hear silence and nothing else. Absolute silence rested within the center of the park, and it was suddenly *so* attractive . . .

"Listen!" Fred stopped so suddenly that the others ran into him. "I heard something," he said.

Cliff crouched with his agony in the narrow triangular space made by three bushes on the street side of the park and watched the four young people walk toward him. He recognized them immediately. The tall, skinny one was the one Miles had loved. Pete, his name was. All these people had loved Miles. God, he hoped they'd help him now.

Five minutes ago, the park had been full of rent-a-cops in blue uniforms. It hadn't taken them long to discover his handiwork at the wall, he'd barely had time to find this place to hide. Now the park was empty—or so it seemed. As soon as the kids came closer, Cliff would step out of his hiding place.

They approached. He realized he could not step out of his hiding place, he'd have to crawl out the same way he'd crawled in. He whispered "psst" at them, while pulling at a branch with his good arm, trying not to jangle the tools or bump his throbbing elbow or touch his bruised and possibly broken ribs.

Then a security guard came up, not fifteen feet away, and a flood of perspiration ran down Cliff's face. His strength drained out at the close call.

The security man stopped to talk with the four on the sidewalk. Cliff could hear the tone coming from him; he must carry one of those things—a bip box, Miles had called it. Pete seemed agitated at something, but his soft little wife calmed him down. Then the security guard turned and walked away from them. The four friends stood there and talked for a moment, then began walking again, past him.

"Psst," he said again, and rustled the branches of his bush.

"There!" The tall dark-headed kid pointed right at him. Pete punched down the kid's pointing finger, and looked around for the security guard.

He whispered something to the others, then the three huddled together on the sidewalk while Pete came over to the bush.

"Pete."

"Who is it?"

"Clifford Gray. Miles's dad."

"What?!" Pete looked around. "Jesus, man, are you nuts?"

"You're all in danger here."

"Hey, you don't know the half of it."

"Will you help me, then?"

"I'll help you get out of this bush. I don't know what else I'll help you with."

Slowly, painfully, with great humiliation, Cliff crawled out of his hiding place.

"Listen," he said. "We've got to talk."

Annie, Simon and Fred all looked to Pete, who regarded Cliff and his heaving bulk with suspicion.

"We know Miles is dead," he said.

A calm settled over Cliff. These people really cared about my boy, he thought. "That's why I'm here. Is there someplace we can go and talk? I've got an idea."

Pete turned to Annie. "Our place?"

She shrugged, and the five of them walked with forced nonchalance back to Pete and Annie's little house.

As soon as the door closed behind them, Cliff felt everyone lighten up. This was on familiar ground. Pete and Annie's house was a safe house, a clubhouse, no enemies allowed. How often had Miles come here, Cliff wondered, and where did he sit when he did?

Fred and Simon took the two chairs across from the couch, Annie leaned up against the wall next to the kitchen, and Pete indicated the far chair to Cliff. It looked like the hot seat to him, but he didn't mind. He emptied his shirt of the red socket set, took the tools from his pockets and put all the paraphernalia on the coffee table, next to a wet, shredded paper towel with red lipstick on it. He probed his tender side. It was sore all right, but seemed intact. The same with his elbow. Bruised and mad, but still usable.

Pete sat on the corner of the couch, watching him.

When he finished, he adjusted his clothes, brushed some dirt from his hands and face, closed his eyes and took a deep breath, sinking deeper into the chair. He listened to the tone, and realized it had sucked away his anger, it had intonated him into lethargy again, and he would have to pump himself back up— and these people, too, if they were to help him accomplish what he came back to do. But . . . where to begin? How much did they know? Annie didn't wear lipstick, but Marian did; she wore the same color that was on the shredded paper towel. Had she been here? Why? Who was the enemy here?

"Let's start with those tools," Pete said.

His voice jarred Clifford back to action. Lay it on the line, Cliff, he thought to himself, you've got nothing to lose. "I'm going to turn off the tone," he said.

The four stared at him in stunned silence.

"With your help, of course," he added.

"Good!" Annie shook her fist at the ceiling.

"Yeah," Fred said. "I'm for that."

"Whoa," Pete said. "Hold on a minute here."

"Yeah, wait," said Simon. "You're talking about killing everybody in The City."

"We're all going to die anyway," Annie said. "They're just going to turn off the tone whenever the fuck they feel like it anyway. Why don't we catch them at their own number?"

"What about rehabilitation?" Simon asked. "Marian said that we'd be rehabilitated."

"That's a joke, Simon," Annie replied. "They're not going to rehabilitate me. They *can't!* After what they've done . . ." The tears began to choke her. "After what they've *done!*"

"Me neither," Fred said. "They can't rehabilitate anybody, Simon. You know why? Because none of us would ever be able to forgive them. They can't rehabilitate you out of . . . of . . ."

"Injustice," Annie said. "I'm on your side, Cliff. Let's go blow up the machine."

"Wait a minute. Wait." Pete held up his hands. "We're not going to do anything tonight. Annie, can you fix Cliff here a snack, and then we're all going to get some sleep, and then we'll talk about it again in the morning."

"We can't wait," Cliff said. "I'd love a sandwich or something"—he touched his tender ribs—"and some ice, maybe—

but we can't wait until tomorrow. Rupert"—he looked apologetically at Simon—"he isn't going to waste any time. I'm a threat."

"We're all threats," Pete said, and told Cliff about the letters and what they'd done.

By the time he was finished, Cliff had two sandwiches and a glass of milk in front of him. He wolfed down half a sandwich and gulped half the milk. "All the more reason we can't wait until morning," he said.

"Well, we're not doing anything for a while."

"Why, Pete?" Fred said. "Let's go now. It's the perfect time."

"First, I'm not sure I want to have anything to do with it. Second"—he stood up and put his arm around Annie—"if we're all going to die tomorrow, I want to make love to my wife tonight."

She smiled up at him, and the situation suddenly became very real and very scary to Cliff. He felt like he was back in the sixties, a revolutionary visiting a camp, organizing a march, or getting ready for some not-too-peaceful demonstrating.

"Get some sleep, you guys," Annie said. "I'll set the alarm." Then she and Pete went around the corner into the bedroom.

Cliff watched them go, and thought about Marian, about her dark hair and her red dress. He thought about how she tasted that night, and how she looked the next morning when she called in at work. He wanted to be with her tonight, too, but then he remembered that it was Marian's fault that their son was dead, and he lost warmth in his loins and the food turned to sawdust in his mouth.

"You take the couch, Mr. Gray," Fred said. "Simon and I will sleep on the floor here."

Cliff thanked the boys, then turned off the table lamp and eased his aching body onto the couch. He kicked off his shoes, pulled an afghan off the back of the sofa and threw it over himself, punched up a little needlepoint pillow, adjusted the ice bag between his ribs and his elbow, and finally, tried to relax. He listened to the boys getting themselves settled, then whispering to each other on the floor, and the next thing he knew, he and Marian were announcing to Miles that they were going to be one big happy family again. It was the most pleasant dream Cliff had had in a long time.

17

Marian had no idea where the notion came from, but once it struck her, she moved like a woman possessed. She rummaged through Miles's dresser drawers, throwing aside all his clothes, ignoring his scent, ignoring the fact that he would never return to this room, to all his special things. She was intent on her mission, wired up tight, and nothing would distract her.

She found his tape recorder in the bottom drawer. She tugged, then jerked, then pulled on the tangled cord until it came free from the junk, then took the recorder and a new cassette tape into the kitchen. She plugged the recorder into an outlet, found side one, rewound it to the beginning, set it next to the tone speaker in the refrigerator and pressed "record." She counted off twenty beats of the tone, then stopped the tape, rewound it and listened. Adequate.

She opened the battery compartment and looked inside. Four C batteries. Miles had extras, she'd seen them. She put the cover back on, rewound the tape, set it up and began recording the tone. She found more batteries in Miles's bottom drawer, and an unopened package in his desk. She put all the batteries into her purse, and waited, listening to the tone, while it recorded.

As soon as she had said the word "rehabilitation" at Pete and Annie's, she had known it was a lie, and at that moment, she knew that she had always known it was a lie. It was a lie that everyone in the mayor's office grasped and held because there was nothing else to be done. There were things that were beyond one person's control, and the tone was one of them.

Side one finished recording. She flipped over the cassette and recorded side two, while sitting in the dark, thinking about all the people—all her friends—who would just cease to be when the tone was finally shut off.

Then, not because she was sleepy, but because she was exhausted, she unplugged the recorder, wound the cord around it, then set it on the dining room table. She put her purse there, too. She took off her clothes and slid between the sheets, naked, without bothering to remove her makeup or brush her teeth. She lay there gripping fistfuls of sheet, and stared at the ceiling.

Her shame possessed her. Speaking of the terrible, terrible things she did—or failed to do—in that living room to those four people had shamed her beyond tolerance. By the time she'd arrived back home, she could barely breathe, wondering what on earth she would do now to survive.

If she *should* survive.

How could she face the others? How could she face the mirror?

She couldn't.

And then her shame had turned to desperation. She found she had a terrible need to leave this wicked place and do something *good* before she died—to make amends somehow for her unforgivable behavior.

She stared at the same ceiling she'd looked at just twenty-four hours before, wrapped in bliss and the arms of her man, and she worried about dying before she had a chance to redeem herself. She didn't know how she would leave; she didn't know how she would get through the desert without a car; she didn't know how she would survive without the tone; she didn't know how to rehabilitate herself to live in a normal world. The enormity of her plan threatened to immobilize her. She tried not to think about it. She just knew that she had to do something—she had to make good for the deaths of her men—and she would, as soon as she got some rest. She needed real energy, not nervous energy.

It was a long time before she slept, but when she did, she dreamed it was her birthday, and Miles and Clifford woke her up, fluffed her pillows, then brought her eggs benedict, on a white tray, with a red rose in a vase. They hugged and kissed, and somehow, she had presents for them too, and they all opened their gifts amid laughter and love.

In her sleep, Marian cried with happiness.

Brad Rupert stood, feet apart, hands in pockets, in front of Marian Gray's house, and he looked at the darkened windows and tried to talk himself into walking up to the front door and ringing the bell. He wasn't successful.

He paced for a moment, wondering what was so bloody intimidating, and he couldn't put his finger on any one thing—it seemed the whole of the situation was . . . was . . . well, he'd gotten in over his head. It wasn't just that the house was dark, that Marian was undoubtedly sleeping. It was also that it was Marian inside—mysterious, beautiful, gentle, unapproachable Marian. Brad had always been intrigued by the curious mix of characteristics in Marian—her unassuming beauty and dislike of social events; her unwavering, direct, eye-to-eye contact and her meek manner; the way she draped clothes over her exquisite body and lived a chaste life-style.

Marian herself intimidated him. He'd overstepped his bounds the other day in his office, and he knew it, but he couldn't seem to help himself. It was the first opportunity he had ever had to see Marian squirm, and once he began, he just couldn't stop.

And then he'd told her that Miles would be sacrificed before the project would; a terrible thing to say to the boy's mother.

And then Miles *had* been sacrificed.

And now Marian slept, alone in this darkened house, wrapped in grief—a grief Brad couldn't even imagine.

It was unlikely that Clifford Gray was inside this silent house, Brad thought. Those boobs he called security guards had let him in and for now he was free and running wild, but they'd eventually catch him. They'd eventually catch him, and when they did . . .

Suddenly, Brad thought of Simon, his own traitorous son, and his shoulders sagged as exhaustion weighed him down. He looked again at Marian's dark house and wished her restful sleep, then turned and walked home.

*   *   *

Nick tried every tactic his streetwise training had taught him, trying to reason with the guard at the gate of this weird place. It was exasperating. The man would not listen to reason. And he wouldn't let them bring the car inside.

John stood outside, watching, and Nick felt like bringing him in to pound a little sense into the stupid guard, but that wouldn't be the right thing to do, so he finally agreed. He left his beautiful black sedan outside the gates, and went to wait outside the guard shack with John while the sentry called for a cart to be delivered.

When it came, the two got in and drove away, feeling foolish and disgusted. They felt like spies playing golfers in a Bob Hope movie, especially when they had to consult the cartoon map of The City to find out where they were.

The man in Washington who answered the telephone by saying "seven eight" began coordinating the mobilization of Project Stone. Sixteen warehouses in New Jersey were emptied of boxes and cartons that had been stacked to the ceiling; those cartons contained specially outfitted, custom-built appliances. Seven hundred and forty pretrained people across the country had received their calls and were packing their suitcases, excitement thumping in their chests.

The opportunity to serve their country had finally come.

18

Cliff felt a small hand on his shoulder, and he smiled in his sleep. Marian, he thought. Then the hand pressed harder and began to shake him. Cliff's head slid off the little needlepoint pillow and the pain in his side flared. He came instantly awake and alert in the darkened living room.

"Clifford, wake up." It was Annie, wrapped up in her bathrobe. The tone pulsed in the darkness. "It's two o'clock."

"Coffee," Cliff said, and rubbed his face.

Annie sat on the edge of the couch. "Do you really want to go through with this? I mean, do you want to wake up those boys there on the floor, and go turn off the tone? Do you know what will happen if you do? We'll all die, Clifford. We'll all die, and you will be the only one left alive."

Cliff couldn't see her face in the darkness, but what she said reverberated inside his chest.

"I'm going to make a pot of coffee now," Annie said. "And then we can go. I'm behind you all the way. It's only a matter of time before we all die anyway, and this way you'll get some major attention about what's happened here, rather than all of us just dying out the way they have planned. But I want to make sure that you know what you're getting into, and that you can live with it for the rest of your life."

She got up, and Cliff slowly swung his feet to the floor. That woman sure knows how to wake a man up, he thought, and got up to go to the bathroom. He emptied his bladder, and as he did, he heard the others up and moving around. He pulled up his shirt and checked his side. A tool-kit-size purple bruise branded the spot. He winced as he touched it, then checked his elbow. No serious damage. He looked at his face in the mirror. He was pale, his eyes bloodshot, and he needed a shave.

In light of what he intended to do in the next few hours, shaving seemed a ludicrous notion. On the other hand, what could be more ludicrous than Clifford Gray, Cubs fan, plotting to murder a whole townful of people? Unable to answer his own rhetorical question, he turned off the light and opened the door.

Annie had turned the range-hood light on, and everyone stood around her as the coffee burbled in the percolator. Pete stood behind her with his arms around her, and Simon and Fred looked like cranky little kids with puffy faces who had gotten too little sleep. Cliff smelled the brewing coffee and remembered fishing trips with early-morning starts and everyone standing in the kitchen, waiting for the strong black coffee to awaken their enthusiasm. Miles would never know that enthusiasm. Miles would never even know the taste of coffee.

"So?" Annie asked. "Are we still going to do it?"

"I think so," Cliff said. "I guess I won't know for sure until I have my hand on the switch."

"Think it's a switch? I kinda always thought of it as a plug." Fred laughed nervously. No one joined in.

Simon scowled and went to sit in the living room, alone, in the dark. The others waited in the kitchen, avoiding each other's eyes, shuffling their feet, listening to the tone and the percolator battle it out.

Annie poured cups full before it finished perking, and they all drank it down; Pete, Annie and Cliff with ice cubes to cool it quickly; Simon and Fred with plenty of milk and sugar. They drank quickly, but once the cups were rinsed and in the sink, they all stood around again, avoiding each other's eyes while they waited for Annie. She was checking the house to make sure it was the way she wanted it when the authorities found it.

It would be too easy, Cliff thought, to sink back into the tone, to just quit fighting it, to forget it all and just relax, slow down, reduce stress and live a long time.

Too soon, Cliff felt, Annie was ready, and as much as he wanted to continue with the delay, he pocketed his tools instead and led the pack out of the house and down the street. They walked silently, each with their own thoughts, and again, Cliff realized that these four were headed for their deaths—*willingly* —and at his hand.

Marian's eyes snapped open and her fingers took a fresh hold on the wadded-up sheet. She felt the tension throughout her body, and looked around the darkened bedroom for a moment before the horrible, gut-wrenching memories flushed through her. She got out of bed and used the toilet, then put on a pair of jeans and a light cotton blouse with a bulky sweater over it. She slipped tennis shoes on her bare feet, brushed her teeth and ran a comb through her hair. She rummaged in the kitchen junk drawer until she found a bip box and turned it on. It worked. The tone came through loud and clear. She turned it off and slipped it into her purse, then grabbed it up with the tape recorder and tapes, and went out the door, not bothering to lock it behind her.

Outside, for a moment, confusion jarred her. Her cart was

gone. Clifford and Miles had taken it and left it at the gate. She would have to walk. She didn't want to walk, because walking would give her time to think, and if she thought, she might change her mind.

The Parkers' cart was in their driveway and Marian considered it for less than a second before heading toward it. She threw her purse and the recorder in, unplugged the cart from its recharging umbilical and backed down the Parkers' drive. Eyes straight ahead, she drove with a single-minded purpose: get to the gate.

As she approached it, her pulse made the leap from time-and-a-half to the tone to double time. She saw the guard in his lighted stand, reading a paperback. Just outside the gate—she blinked her eyes—was a big, black automobile. Parked. Empty. Marian gathered herself together and pulled up in front of the gate. She stepped out of the cart and up to the door. She took a deep breath before speaking, so her breathlessness wouldn't show.

"Mrs. Gray!" The guard knew her, as did most of the mayor's security personnel.

"Byron. I need to get something from that car."

"That car?" Byron's eyebrows came together.

Marian thought her heart would burst. "Yes, Byron, that's the only car here, isn't it? Please open the gate."

"Yes, ma'am," Byron said, and pulled the lever back. Marian stepped out of the way, and then slipped through the gate. Byron, bless his heart, turned the tone on the outside speaker.

The car was unlocked. Marian slid into the driver's seat. The keys were there. Unbelievable. She reached into her purse and got the bip box, activated it. The tone reverberated in the small space. She turned the motor over, flipped on the headlights, made a tentative U-turn and then stepped on it, squealing the tires, and headed down the highway toward Phoenix.

Byron's mouth hung open as he watched her go. Then, with shaking hands, he dialed the emergency number posted next to the telephone.

When City Hall came into sight, the group of five began to walk faster, then to trot, and then they all ran. Cliff felt exhilarated—he hadn't felt like this since . . . since . . . since he and Miles were throwing the football around Marian's back yard. Suddenly his wind gave out and his flesh was bouncing and his side flamed up and he had to stop. The others slowed, reluctantly, it seemed, but they were close now, very close.

"Come around back," Simon whispered, and took the lead. He led them across the street, through the back parking lot, eerie in its emptiness, then down to a stairwell with a metal door at the bottom. "When I was in Junior Security, this was my beat," he said. "I can get inside the building, but that's all."

"That's enough," Annie said, and Simon punched a series of numbers into the combination lock and the door clicked open.

With reverence, they entered.

"The elevators are closed down at night," Simon whispered. "Dad uses a special key when he works late."

"What about stairs?"

"Over there," Simon said, "but I think the door's locked."

It wasn't. They opened the door and ran down the cement stairs, their footsteps echoing in the chamber. The big metal fire door to the basement wasn't locked, either. They opened it and entered a long, carpeted hall, lighted only by the green exit sign over the fire door. Pete tried one door. Locked. Another. Locked. Fred ran down the length of the hall, trying each knob. They were all locked.

"Which door is it?" Cliff looked at Simon.

"I'm not sure. I only saw it once . . . a long time ago . . ."

Fred came up and grabbed Simon's shoulder. His face showed fierce intensity. "Remember, goddammit! Which door?"

Simon shrank back from his friend and looked down the hall. "It was on the right side, I think—somewhere in the middle."

Fred grabbed the hammer from Cliff's hand and ran down to the middle door and began banging on the knob. He made a terrible racket, pounding like a madman, and the other four huddled together in amazed silence as they watched this strange thing come over Fred. After a dozen ringing blows, Fred stood back and lashed out with his foot, giving the door a mighty kick right alongside the smashed-up knob. The doorjamb splintered.

A second kick busted the door loose, it slammed open, and without looking back at them, Fred stepped inside.

Mayor Brad Rupert came home a defeated man. Standing in front of Marian Gray's house had changed him. He sat in his favorite leather chair and reviewed his life. His wife lay sleeping upstairs, dreaming peacefully, he hoped, while he contemplated suicide in his study directly below her bedroom. Simon's bed was empty.

Simon's bed was empty. Simon's bed was empty and Simon's signature was on that letter to the media.

Have I been *that* wrong? Has my entire life's work been dedicated to something so terrible . . .

"He's old enough to have his own politics," Joanna had said that night that Dusty and Roland and Fred came over for dinner, *"and you must allow that. The boy must begin to think for himself, Brad,"* she had said, and now Brad wondered if *he* had ever thought for *himself.*

Loyalty, he'd heard when he was young. Loyalty, son, is everything. And loyalty had gotten him this job. Blind loyalty. He didn't even know what Project Stone was, but he was loyal to it. Loyal to the death.

It seemed now, as he sat in his leather chair, as if a major portion of his personality was missing. The portion that had original thoughts and ideas. Convictions to beliefs instead of causes.

It seemed as though Joanna, Alexandria and Simon would carry on better without him. If his loyalties had been appropriately placed here at Tone Town, then they could be posthumously proud of him. If his loyalties were wrong, or bad, then the stigma of his actions would not touch them. They could believe he'd seen the error of his ways and killed himself to avoid shaming them.

They would be right.

Yes, they would be better off without him.

The phone rang. He snatched it up before the end of the first ring; he would hate it if Joanna awoke and came downstairs.

"Mayor Rupert?"

"Yes! Do you know what time it is? What is it?"

"Byron Hadley, sir. Front Gate."

"What?"

"Marian Gray just came through, sir, stole a black sedan that had been left just outside the gate and took off, sir. She was headed toward Phoenix, sir."

Rupert was speechless.

"Damn," he finally said, and hung up the phone.

19

Cliff glanced over at Pete, whose thin face had hardened. Annie's eyes, wide open with fear, met Cliff's, and Cliff knew he wasn't alone with his heart pounding double-time to the tone. He felt Simon press close behind him, so he took the lead again, and followed Fred through the doorway.

A metal desk with two boxes of computer paper on it, and a supply cabinet against the wall were the only adornments to an otherwise barren, carpetless room. A door in the back stood ajar. Cliff pushed it open and walked through.

A gray metal cube, about four feet to the side, stood bolted to the center of the concrete floor. Digital numbers and lighted meters shed a faint glow into the darkened room.

The machine hummed, a low, throaty, breathless growl.

The tone thumped from baseboard speakers ringing the transmitter.

Fred stood on the far side and looked at Cliff over the top of it as he entered. "This is it," Fred said. "This is the source of the evil."

Evil.

It *was* evil, it reeked of evil, it looked dark, hunched, misshapen. It was squatty, menacing and inhuman, and Cliff felt his frustration and rage growing along with a subtle relief that he could take his revenge on an electronic monster rather than confront the flesh and blood that conceived, built and maintained such a beast for the past twenty years.

Cliff felt Annie standing on his left, Pete next to her, and Simon crowded in on his right. He liked their closeness, there was power in friends huddling together, joining forces, combining strengths to combat this—this evil.

He began to examine the machine; he looked for a switch or a cord or something to move, flip, turn or press. Nothing. Nothing but meters, digital readouts and riveted seams. As Cliff moved around the machine, running his hands over its smooth metal surface, the others began to take an interest in the electronic beast that imprisoned them. They, too, moved their hands over the face of the machine. For a brief, horrible moment, Cliff saw, as if from afar, five people with their hands upon an idol, their faces lighted only by yellow and greenish glows. Cliff returned to reality with a jolt. It *did* look as though everyone was touching it with reverence and worship.

Reverence, maybe, but not worship.

He stood back. When he spoke, his voice was hushed in deference to the inhuman entity in the room with them. "We'll have to smash it," he said.

Fred brought the hammer over and gave it to him.

Cliff hefted the hammer and walked around the machine again, looking for the likeliest place to begin his strike. When on the opposite side of the machine, he saw the other four, his new friends, standing together. Pete had his arm around his wife, and Simon and Fred both stood close to them. They all looked at him with serious expectation.

A flash of memory—Miles gasping for breath in the back seat of the taxi—passed through him.

He stared at the four people, and they stared back at him. No one had any delusions at this point; there was no reason to talk. This was it. Life or death, right here, right now, for those four, along with every single relative, friend and acquaintance of theirs.

Annie looked eager, excited; Fred looked intently back at Cliff, as if his every nerve fiber was tuned to Cliff's next movement. Simon looked like he wanted his mother, and Pete . . . Pete looked as scared as Cliff suddenly felt.

Cliff lowered his eyes, then squatted down so they couldn't see him.

Miles had clutched his chest and gasped desperately for air. Cliff had held his boy, hugged him tight, whispered in his ear, and then Miles convulsed in his arms. He remembered the choking and gurgling; he remembered the hollow thunk of Miles's head hitting the pavement when the driver pulled him out of the cab; he remembered the awful thudding sounds of the driver pounding on his son's chest trying to start his heart up again. He remembered the siren, and the silence when the siren was turned off, and he felt the aching maw that had opened in his soul when he realized his boy was dead.

Cliff listened to the tone and his heartbeat slowed. He remembered the hospital and the nurse and the doctor who was in on their little scam; he remembered kissing Miles's cold cheek, and he felt weak, all of a sudden, as if all his strength had just run out his fingertips. He set the hammer on the floor. If he smashed this machine, he would have to watch these four people die. He would have to watch them—his *friends*—twist and writhe, gurgle and gasp on the floor in this room, and as he did, he would know that everyone else in The City was doing exactly the same.

He would live with that memory every waking—and sleeping—moment of every day for the rest of his life.

That memory would destroy him.

He stood up and faced them. "I can't," he said, then walked toward the door. He saw Pete relax in relief.

Annie met him at the door, her face flushed with fury. "You chickenshit sonofabitch," she said, then slapped him hard across the face. Cliff fell back in astonishment. "You bring us here, at peace with ourselves and ready to face our deaths, and then you rob us of that dignity. You *bastard*!" She hit out at him again, but Cliff parried, held her tiny wrist, then pushed her back against her husband, slipped out the door and closed it firmly behind him.

He heard her screaming at him all the way down the hall. He ran up the steps, feeling lighter than ever, his side hardly hurt at all, and he opened the door to the outside. He breathed in the fresh air and the black sky with its million stars. He was glad, somehow, to be alive. Alive. Alive, even if he was without a wife, without a son.

A wife.

Marian.

He *had* a wife.

He looked around, got his bearings, then headed toward her house.

Fred walked around the machine and picked up the hammer. He tested its weight in time to the tone and began to examine the machine. "No," Annie said to him, and tried pulling away from Pete, but he held her shoulders with firm fingers. She fought him, and finally pulled free of his grasp, her anger and hurt desperate for an outlet. She walked around to Fred and put her cheek against his shoulder for a moment. Then she took the hammer from his hand. "Let me," she said.

Simon covered his face with his hands and began to cry.

"Can't you bloody read a stupid frigging map? You idiot!" Nick stopped the cart under a streetlight and jerked the map out of John's hands. It ripped in half.

"Don't call me an idiot," John said calmly, and Nick ripped the rest of the map out of his hand, getting all of it but a thumb-sized chunk that John still held between his fingers.

Nick looked around him at the neighborhood, at the night. "Let's try to get a logical fix here."

"He's only going to go to Rupert's house or his kid's house. Those are the only two people he knows."

"He's gotta eat. He eats a lot."

"Don't remind me. I'm starving."

Nick rolled his eyes at his partner. "Try to concentrate. Where would he eat?"

"Probably at his kid's house. Or Rupert's."

Nick tried to fit the map halves together and smooth them out against his thigh. The guard at the gate had circled the locations of the Rupert house and the Gray house in red. But the map had cartoons all over it and the dimensions were out of whack, and it was more cute than it was practical. "Okay. Here are the houses. Now, where the hell are we?"

"I think—" John prepared to shove a fat finger into the map, but Nick moved it.

"There's a street sign." He put the cart in gear and idled up to the corner. Movement down the street caught his eye. He jerked back.

"Didja see something?"

"Yeah. We're in luck."

"What was it?"

"The fat man. Keep quiet." They turned right and crept down the street, silent except for the stupid, irritating beep that came from somewhere in the cart.

Marian's bip box gave out long before she thought it would. She pulled over onto the shoulder of the highway and sang the tone to herself, "beep, beep, beep, beep," out loud and in perfect rhythm, as she fumbled around putting the cassette into the recorder. Finally, she got it, and pushed "play," then slowly brought the volume up. No problem.

She spun gravel from the back tires and got back on the road, trying not to think about where she was headed, trying not to think that she had nowhere to go—no one to go to. She just drove, listening to the tone, feeling snug in the little atmosphere of the car, not looking at the desert that stretched on either side of her, not looking out the upper part of the windshield that showed a vast universe filled with stars and anticipation. Instead, she watched the highway in front of her and noticed the glow in the early morning sky that turned out not to be dawn, but the night lights of Phoenix.

The car turned almost automatically into the driveway of the Rancho Diego Motel. She clutched her recorder to her chest and went in, awakened the manager and rented a room. She took the key from him, walked to number 104, and let herself in. It was a dingy little room, but it was close, personal, and maybe only fifteen minutes from The City. She put her purse and the recorder on the nightstand, closed the curtains, then lay down on the bed. She felt cold, and wrapped her arms around herself and brought her knees to her chest. She was safe here for the moment, she didn't have to decide where to go in Phoenix, or what to do—in fact, there were no decisions to be made at all. She felt her muscles relax, and she just watched the recorder and listened to the tone.

* * *

"The shit has hit the fan," Rupert whispered to himself. The news about Marian gave his adrenaline a little pump; he no longer felt lethargic. Before the phone call, suicide seemed convenient; now it seened imperative.

He sat for a moment longer with his melancholy, and he thought about Marian. Then his pulse quickened as he thought of her in that car, headed for Phoenix. How far would she get? All the way to the police? Seven eight had a handle on the police. What could Marian accomplish?

Maybe nothing.

He'd gotten all the letters Simon and his friends had sent out—stopped that rebellion dead cold. Maybe he could still get Clifford Gray—nip that situation in the bud, too. Maybe his suicide thoughts were just a little premature.

He sat up straight, feeling a new strength. He could still have the courage of his convictions.

No one can condemn a man for his convictions.

Then I must have enough conviction to die in action, defending my cause. I can't die like a coward in my own den when the going gets a little rough.

Save the Project. That's my conviction. Save the Project at any cost.

Adrenaline rushed through him again. If I die, it will be on the battlefield, he thought, and the picture in his mind made him smile.

Save the Project at *any* cost, he thought, and left the house.

Seven hundred and forty people made contact at their respective international airports and were met and briefed. They boarded planes and took off, heading for their new locations, riding high on patriotism.

20

Annie held the hammer high and circled the machine. It looked the same from all sides—mysterious, unapproachable, invincible, impregnable. Its blind efficiency enraged her. This machine had stolen her future, stolen her soul. She thought of her four years of wasted dreams. Four years, dreaming of a little towheaded girl named Angelica with pale blue eyes like Pete's. If it was a boy, they'd name him Dustin, and she hoped he would look either exactly like Pete or exactly like Dusty. She'd written letters to her unborn children, she'd assembled her scrapbooks with them in mind, she read everything she could find on childbearing and child rearing.

Annie wanted to have babies that Pete could bounce on his knee, babies they could teach about love and caring. She looked at this gray metal monster and thought of how she had yearned and yearned for children, holding her breath every month for years, and how it had robbed her of her life, of her dreams. Every month she felt like a failure as a woman. Every month when the blood came on her panties, she felt guilty. Every month her spirits stepped down a notch. Every month she was less and less a wife to Pete. Every month.

Every month!

With a mighty shout, she swung the hammer, and it smashed a dial, denting in the side a little bit. Nothing more. With a sob, she brought the hammer back, and a tear flicked off her cheek and landed in the tangles of her hair as she brought it down a second time.

It landed with a hollow sound.

"Look!" Fred shouted from Annie's left.

A control panel had opened in the side of the machine. Buttons, switches and dials were laid out in futuristic proficiency, but that wasn't what Fred was looking at, and not where he pointed. When Pete, Simon and Annie had gathered to look over Fred's shoulder, he pointed to a little, round black button, way at the top, in the back. In white letters, it said FUSE.

Fred reached up and began to unscrew it.

* * *

"I can save this project," Rupert said, over and over in time to the tone as he rushed to his office. He knew what he'd have to do. Deal very harshly indeed—maybe even evict Fred, Pete, Annie and Simon (oh God, Simon!) from The City. He'd have to call and get someone on Marian right away and make sure those goons nailed that sonofabitching husband of hers.

He unlocked the front door of the City building, and walked through the dark and silent lobby. He put his key in the elevator lock.

As he did, the tone stopped.

Everyone in Tone Town awoke.

Marian sat up, alone, in her Phoenix motel.

Hearts froze, breathing stopped.
A second beat went by. No tone.
A third.
The elderly began to gasp.
Then it came again, strong, loud, and hearts kicked back in to a normal routine, breathing returned.
Everyone went back to sleep; most wouldn't remember the incident in the morning.

Marian slowly lay back down, uneasy and unsure of what had awakened her. She pulled the edge of the bedspread up over herself and shivered, alone in the dark.

Brad Rupert entered the elevator and pressed "Basement."

Marian's house was in sight when the tone failed. Cliff almost tripped. He was walking in time to the tone, and when it didn't come, his body jerked and twitched in discomfort. He looked toward Marian's, so close, so reachable.

"Not yet!" He screamed at the emptiness and then began to run.

Then the tone began again, and with relief, he strode up the walk to the front door. Somehow he had known they wouldn't succeed in silencing the tone. Somehow the whole Tone Town experiment seemed too despicable to be foiled so easily.

He pushed the button on the doorbell again and again, insistently, hearing it ring inside, then he stepped into the shadows behind a monolithic shrub Marian had planted next to the front door. Impatiently, he waited long enough for Marian to don a robe and answer the door, but the house felt cold and empty to him, and there was not a sound from within. He began to panic.

He ran around the side of the house, to the back, to the window of her bedroom. It was open, and he quickly removed the screen and parted the curtains. Her bed had been slept in, but was now empty.

"Marian!" His whisper came through loudly in the silent darkness, and he knew she was gone.

Gone.

He turned from the window, and the loss of his family hit him the same time John's silenced bullet did. Cliff felt the thud squarely in his chest, and fell backward against a chair. "Marian," he whispered, and he knew his heart was truly broken.

He died on the patio where once he had hugged his son.

A sharp pain shot through Marian's chest. She sat up, and it subsided to a slow ache. A soul ache, she thought. She took a couple of deep breaths and then lay down, staring at the darkened ceiling, as tears rolled into her ears and down along her hairline.

When the mayor entered the basement transmitter room, Pete felt Annie's knees weaken. He put his arm around her and willed his strength into her exhausted body. He looked at Simon, who was still crying, face red and splotchy. Fred's face was filled with hate as he glared at the little man. Annie just looked at the floor. Pete had to take control, and quick, or else Rupert would.

He tightened his arm around Annie's shoulders and looked Rupert full in the face. Their eyes met, and Pete showed no shame, would back down not one inch. It was the mayor who looked away first.

"Go home," Rupert said, and Pete guided Annie toward the door and held it open while Annie went first, then Simon, and then Fred. He was going to take his wife home and they would wait, like the responsible adults they were, for whatever would happen as a result of their insubordination.

He saw Fred drop the fuse into Rupert's hand as he passed. It looked like a dramatic gesture, but then he caught Fred's eye, and both of them almost burst out laughing. Comic relief, Pete thought.

In the hall, he put one arm around Annie, the other around Fred, and Annie put her arm around Simon.

"Let's get some fresh air," Pete said, and the four walked up and out into the dusk of early morning.

The emergency crew burst into the transmitter room. Mayor Rupert took the foreman aside and handed him the fuse. "The auxiliary kicked in too slow, Richard," he said. "See to that, will you?" The foreman nodded, took the fuse and joined his crew that had swarmed around the machine.

Rupert went upstairs to his office. He had to make arrangements—some kind of arrangements—for the four traitors and Marian Gray. He felt somehow victorious—he had saved the Project, hadn't he?—and it felt somehow shallow.

Marian heard the tone slow, and she knew the batteries were wearing down. All she needed to do was plug the stupid recorder into the wall, but instead, she pulled the bedspread tighter around her thin shoulders and tried to imagine the enormity of her life without the tone, without Miles, without Clifford. She couldn't. Her idea of the future seemed an immense, shapeless amoeba, with her lost somewhere in the middle, powerless, wrong, at the mercy of everything unimportant.

Even as she lay there, she was at the mercy of everything unimportant: the tone, and those who designed it, and those who would need scapegoats when the whole mess came out in the open.

She lay there, quietly listening, feeling the slowing tone tug at her heart, drawing it down.

The tone deepened, and finally stopped.

"Seven eight."

"Rupert here, T.O.N.E."

"Yes?"

"We got Gray, and—"

"You're out of it, Rupert."

"But—"

"Carry on. Business as usual."

"Yes, sir."

Seven eight hung up, then pushed the button on his desk that drew the heavy curtains away from the new wall in his office. It pleased him, the dramatic sweep and swish of electric curtain.

Seven hundred and forty little lights blinked on and off across the wall-sized world map. They blinked in rhythm, exactly forty beats to the minute. Each light signified the location of a discrete tonal device. Each location was central to a strategic foreign national capital or military installation.

The tone was about to become the medical find of the century.

Seven hundred and forty. Soon technology, greed and political one-upsmanship would turn seven hundred and forty into fourteen hundred and eighty, and then more, and more. Everyone would insist on having one.

Persuading a guilty government to cut costs by providing autonomy was abnormally easy, and now he—and only he—held the switch that would eventually silence the tone—and every world leader who danced to its music.

But. First things first.

He looked at the sole light in the United States, the one that blinked in Arizona, and his heart ached to exercise his power.

Be patient, he told himself. If he turned that tone off too soon, he would blow his own project.

He would wait.

He sat back in his chair and thumped his thumb in time to the tone.

Let Rupert stew awhile, he thought.